THE
PALADIN
PROPHECY

www.randomhousechildrens.co.uk

THE PALADIN PROPHECY

BOOK I

MARK FROST

CORGI BOOKS

THE PALADIN PROPHECY
A CORGI BOOK 978 0 552 56531 8

First published in Great Britain by Doubleday,
an imprint of Random House Children's Publishers UK
A Random House Group Company

Doubleday edition published 2012
Corgi edition published 2013

1 3 5 7 9 10 8 6 4 2

The Random House Group Limited supports the Forest Stewardship Council® (FSC®),
the leading international forest-certification organisation. Our books carrying the FSC
label are printed on FSC®-certified paper. FSC is the only forest-certification scheme
supported by the leading environmental organisations, including Greenpeace. Our
paper procurement policy can be found at www.randomhouse.co.uk/environment

Set in Minion

RANDOM HOUSE CHILDREN'S PUBLISHERS UK
61–63 Uxbridge Road, London W5 5SA

www.**randomhousechildrens**.co.uk
www.**totallyrandombooks**.co.uk
www.**randomhouse**.co.uk

Addresses for companies within The Random House Group Limited can be found at:
www.randomhouse.co.uk/offices.htm

THE RANDOM HOUSE GROUP Limited Reg. No. 954009

A CIP catalogue record for this book is available from the British Library.

Printed and bound in the CPI Group (UK) Ltd, Croydon, CR0 4YY

For the lost and lonely ones . . .

Every crime is punished,
Every virtue rewarded,
Every wrong redressed,
In silence and certainty.

—Ralph Waldo Emerson

THE
PALADIN
PROPHECY

I couldn't see his face.

He was running along a mountain trail. Running desperately. Pursued by black grasping shadows that were little more than holes in the air, but there was no mistaking their intention. The boy was in unspeakable danger and he needed my help.

I opened my eyes.

Curtains fluttered at the dark window. Freezing air whispered through a crack in the frame, but I was drenched in sweat, my heart pounding.

Just a dream? No. I had no idea who this boy was. He appeared to be about my age. But I knew this much with iron certainty:

He was real, *and he was headed my way.*

JUST ANOTHER TUESDAY

The Importance of an Orderly Mind

Will West began each day with that thought even before he opened his eyes. When he did open them, the same words greeted him on a banner across his bedroom wall:

#1: THE IMPORTANCE OF AN ORDERLY MIND.

In capital letters a foot high. Rule #1 on Dad's List of Rules to Live By. That's how crucial his father considered this piece of advice. Remembering it was one thing. *Following* Rule #1, with a mind as hot-wired as Will's, wasn't nearly as easy. But wasn't that why Dad had put it on top of his list, and on Will's wall, in the first place?

Will rolled out of bed and stretched. Flicked on his iPhone: 7:01. He punched up the calendar and scanned his schedule. Tuesday, November 7:

- Morning roadwork with the cross-country team
- Day forty-seven of sophomore year
- Afternoon roadwork with the cross-country team

Nice. Two runs sandwiching seven hours of Novocain for the brain. Will took a greedy breath and scratched his fingers vigorously through his unruly bed head. Tuesday, November 7, shaped up as a vanilla, cookie-cutter day. Not one major stress clouding the horizon.

So why do I feel like I'm about to face a firing squad?

He triple-racked his brain but couldn't find a reason. As he threw on his sweats, the room lit up with a bright, cheerful sunrise. Southern California's most tangible asset: the best weather in the world. Will opened the curtains and looked out at the Topa Topa Mountains rising beyond the backyard.

Wow. The mountains were cloaked with snow from the early winter storm that had blown through the night before. Backlit by the early-morning sun, they were sharper and cleaner than high-def. He heard familiar birdsong and saw the little white-breasted blackbird touch down on a branch outside his window. Tilting its head, curious and fearless, it peered in at him as it had every morning for the last few days. Even the birds were feeling it.

So I'm fine. It's all good.

But if that was how he *really* felt, then what had stirred up this queasy cocktail of impending doom? The hangover from a forgotten nightmare?

An unruly thought elbowed its way into his mind: *This storm brought more than snow.*

What? No idea what that meant—wait, had he dreamt about snow? Something about running? The silvery dream fragment faded before Will could grab it.

Whatever. Enough of this noise. Time to stonewall this funk-u-phoria. Will drove through the rest of his morning routine and skipped downstairs.

Mom was in the kitchen working on her second coffee. With reading glasses on a lanyard around her thick black hair, she was tapping her phone, organizing her day.

Will grabbed a power shake from the fridge. "Our bird's back," he said.

"Hmm. People-watching again," she said. She put down her phone and wrapped her arms around him. Mom never passed up a good hug. One of those committed huggers for whom, in the moment, nothing else mattered. Not even Will's mortification when she clinch-locked him in public.

"Busy day?" he asked.

"Crazy. Like stupid crazy. You?"

"The usual. Have a good one. Later, Moms."

"Later, Will-bear. Love you." She jangled her silver bracelets and got back to her phone as Will headed for the door. "Always and forever."

"Love you, too."

Later, and not much later, how he would wish that he'd stopped, gone back, held on to her, and never let go.

Will reached the base of their front steps and shook out his legs. Sucked in that first bracing hit of clean, cold morning air and exhaled a frosty billow, ready to run. It was his favorite part of the day . . . and then that droopy dreadful gloom crept all over him again.

#17: START EACH DAY BY SAYING IT'S GOOD TO BE ALIVE. EVEN IF YOU DON'T FEEL IT, *SAYING* IT—OUT LOUD—MAKES IT MORE LIKELY THAT YOU WILL.

"Good to be alive," he said, without much conviction.

Damn. Right now #17 felt like the lamest rule on Dad's list. He could blame some obvious physical gripes. It was forty-eight degrees and damp. His muscles creaked from yesterday's weight training. A night of slippery dreams had left him short on sleep. *I'm just out of whack. That's all. I always feel better once I hit the road.*

#18: IF #17 DOESN'T WORK, COUNT YOUR BLESSINGS.

Will hit the stopwatch app on his phone and sprang into a trot. His Asics Hypers lightly slapped the pavement . . . 1.4 miles to the coffee shop: target time, seven minutes.

He gave #18 a try.

Starting with Mom and Dad. All the kids he knew ripped their parents 24/7, but Will never piled on. For good reason: Will West had won the parent lottery. They were smart, fair, and honest, not like the phonies who preached values, then slummed like delinquents when their kids weren't around. They cared about his feelings, always considered his point of view, but never rolled over when he tested the limits. Their rules were clear and balanced between lenient and protective, leaving him enough space to push for independence while always feeling safe.

Yeah, they have their strong points.

On the other hand: They were odd and secretive and perpetually broke and moved around like Bedouins every eighteen months. Which made it impossible for him to make friends or feel connected to any place they ever lived. But, hey, what do you need a peer group for when your parents are your only friends? So what if that messed him up massively for the rest of his life? He might get over it, someday. After decades of therapy and a barge full of antidepressants.

There. Blessings counted. Always works like a charm, thought Will dryly.

Will had shaken off the morning chill by the end of the second block. Blood pumping, his endorphins perked up his nervous system as the Valley stirred to life around him. He quieted his mind and opened his senses, the way his parents had taught him. Took in the smoky tang of wild sage and the oxygen-rich air of the orchards lining the East End roads, wet and shiny from the rain. A dog barked; a car started. Miles to the west, through the gap in the hills, he glimpsed a cobalt-blue strip of the Pacific catching the first beams of sunrise.

Good to be alive. He could almost believe it now.

Will cruised toward town, down lanes of rambling ranch houses, grouped closer together as he moved along. After only five months here, he liked Ojai more than anywhere they'd ever lived. The small-town atmosphere and country lifestyle felt comfortable and easy, a refuge from the hassles of big-city life. The town was nestled in a high, lush valley sheltered by coastal mountains, with narrow passes the only way in on either end. The original inhabitants, the Chumash people, had named it Ojai: the Valley of the Moon. After hundreds of years of calling

Ojai home, the Chumash had been driven out by "civilization" in less than a decade. Tell the Chumash about "refuge."

Will knew that his family would move on from this nearly perfect place, too. They always did. As much as he liked the Ojai Valley, he'd learned the hard way not to get attached to places or people—

A black sedan glided across the intersection a block ahead. Tinted glass on the side windows. He couldn't see the driver.

They're looking for an address they can't find, Will thought. Then he wondered how he knew that.

A faint marimba ring sounded. He slipped the phone from his pocket and saw Dad's first text of the day: HOW'S YOUR TIME?

Will smiled. Dad with his Caps Lock on again. Will had tried to explain texting etiquette to him about fifty times: "It's like you're SHOUTING!"

"But I am shouting," Dad had said. "I'M WAY OVER HERE!"

Will texted back: how's the conference? how's San Fran? He could text while running. He could text while riding down a circular staircase on a unicycle—

Will pulled up short even before he heard the rasp of rubber on wet pavement. A dark mass slid into his peripheral vision.

The black sedan. Shrouded by exhaust, throttle rumbling in idle, dead ahead of him. A late-model four-door, some plain domestic brand he didn't recognize. Odd: no logos, trim, or identifying marks. Anywhere. A front license plate—generic, not California issue—with a small US flag tucked in one corner. But that was no civil service car pool engine under the hood. It sounded like a hillbilly NASCAR rocket.

He couldn't see anyone behind the black glass—and remembered: tinting windshields this dark was illegal—but he knew someone inside was looking at him. Will's focus narrowed, sounds faded. Time stopped.

Then a marimba broke the silence. Another text from Dad: RUN, WILL.

Without looking up, Will slipped his hoodie over his head and waved a faint apology at the windshield. He held up the phone, shaking it slightly as if to say, *My bad. Clueless teenager here.*

Will thumbed on the camera and casually snapped a picture of the back of the sedan. He slipped the phone into his pocket and eased back into his stride.

Make it look like you're just running, not running away, Will thought. *And don't look back.*

He trotted on, listening for the throaty engine. The car tached up and peeled off behind him, turning left and heading away.

Then Will heard someone say, "Fits the description. Possible visual contact."

Okay, how did *that* voice get in his head? And whose voice was it?

The driver, came the answer. *He's talking on a radio. He's talking about* you.

Will's heart thumped hard. With his conditioning, he had a resting pulse of fifty-two. It never hit triple digits until he was into his second mile. Right now it was north of a hundred.

First question: *Did Dad just tell me to RUN (from San Francisco?!) because he wants me to stay on pace for my target time, or because somehow he knows that car is bad news—*

Then he heard the sedan a block away, stomping through its

gearbox, accelerating rapidly. Tires screamed: They were coming back.

Will cut into an unpaved alley. Behind him the sedan burst back onto the street he'd just left. Before the car reached the alley, Will veered right, hopped a fence, and jammed through a backyard littered with the wreckage of Halloween decorations. He vaulted over a chain-link fence into a narrow concrete run along the side of the house—

—and then, *damn,* a vicious blunt head burst out of a dog door to his right; a square snarling muzzle shot after him. He leaped onto the gate at the end of the run and scrambled over, just as the beast hurled its body into the fence, jaws snapping.

Half a block away, he heard the twin-hemi yowl as the car raced to the next corner. Will paused at the edge of the yard behind a towering hedge and gulped in air. He peeked around the hedge—all clear—then sprinted across the street, over a lawn, and past another house. A wooden fence bounded the rear yard, six feet high. He altered his steps to time his jump, grabbed the top, and leaped over, landing lightly in another alley—three feet from a weary young woman juggling a briefcase, a coffee flask, and her keys near a Volvo. She jolted as if she'd just been Tasered. Her flask hit the ground and rolled, leaking latte.

"Sorry," said Will.

He crossed the alley and raced through two more yards, the sedan rumbling somewhere nearby all the while. He stopped at the next side street and leaned back against a garage. As his adrenaline powered down, he felt faintly ridiculous. Thoughts and instincts argued in his head, tumbling like sneakers in an empty dryer:

You're perfectly safe. NO, YOU'RE IN DANGER. *It's just a random car.* YOU HEARD WHAT THEY SAID. PAY ATTENTION, FOOL!

Another text from Dad hit the screen: DON'T STOP, WILL.

Will motored down open streets through the outskirts of the business district. The team should be waiting at the diner by now. He'd duck inside and call Dad so he could hear his voice. But he realized he could hear it RIGHT NOW. Reminding him of a rule that Dad repeated like a fire drill:

#23: WHEN THERE'S TROUBLE, THINK FAST AND
ACT DECISIVELY.

Will pulled up behind a church and peeked around. Two blocks away he saw the team, six guys in sweats outside the diner, RANGERS stitched across their backs. They were gathered around something at the curb he couldn't see.

He checked the time, and his jaw dropped. No way that could be right: He'd just covered the 1.4 miles from home, steeplechasing through backyards and fences . . . *in five minutes?*

Behind him, the snarling engine roared to life. He turned and saw the black car charging straight at him down the alley. Will broke for the diner. The sedan cornered hard behind him, swung around, and skidded to a halt.

Will was already two blocks away. He flipped up his hood, stuck his hands in his sweatshirt, and casually jogged up to the team.

"Whaddup," he mumbled, trying to keep panic out of his voice.

11

The team mostly ignored him, as usual. He blended in, keeping his back to the street. They parted enough for him to see what they were looking at.

"Check it out, dude," said Rick Schaeffer.

A badass tricked-out hot rod sat at the curb. It was like nothing Will had ever seen before, a matte black Prowler slung long and low on a custom chassis, with a slanted front grille and wheels gleaming with chrome. Bumpers jammed out in front like Popeye's forearms. The manifolds of a monster V-8 burst out of the hood, oozing latent power. Baroque, steam-punk lines, crafted with sharp, finely etched venting, lined the body. The car looked both vintage and pristine, weirdly ageless, as if there were countless miles on this clean machine. A stranger's ride for sure: No local could have kept these hellacious wheels under wraps. It might have come from anywhere. It might have come from the nineteenth century by way of the future.

Will felt eyes find him from behind the diner window. They landed hard, like somebody poking him in the chest with two stiff fingers. He looked up but couldn't see inside; the sun had just crested the hills behind him, glaring off the glass.

"Don't touch my ride."

Will heard the voice in his head and knew it came from whoever was watching. Low, gravelly, spiked with a sharp accent, bristling with menace.

"Don't touch it!" snapped Will.

Startled, Schaeffer jerked his hand away.

The bald man driving the sedan didn't see the Prowler until the kids shifted away. He thought he might be hallucinating. He clicked the necro-wave filter onto the lens of their onboard scanner. The pictures of the family on-screen—father, mother, teenage boy—shrank to thumbnails. He focused on the hot rod until it filled the screen, pulsating with blinding white light.

No doubt about it: This was a Wayfarer's "flier." The first field sighting in decades.

Hands shaking, the bald man lifted his wrist mic and tabbed in. He tried to contain his excitement as he described what they'd found. Contact immediately approved a revised action.

No one had ever tagged a Wayfarer. It was a historic opportunity. The boy could wait.

The bald man ejected a black carbon-fiber canister the size of a large thermos from the nitrogen chamber. His partner picked it up and eased his window down. He raised the canister, chambered the Ride Along into the tracker bug's payload slot, then broke the vacuum seal. The open window helped dissipate the sulfurous smell as he prepared to fire, but it couldn't eliminate it.

Nothing could.

Will watched the black sedan ease forward, drawing even with them. He chanced a sidelong glance as it slid past. He saw a man holding a black canister up to the passenger window. Something skipped out of the canister, bounced onto the pavement, and came to rest. A wad of gum?

Will waited until the sedan moved out of sight. He reached for his phone, ready to fire off an urgent text to Dad. Then the coffee shop door swung open. A massive pair of buckled, battered black military boots etched with faded licks of flame stepped into view below the door.

That settles that. I don't want any part of this guy, either. Will took off toward school in an all-out breakaway. Barking about his head start, the rest of the team scrambled after him as Will turned the corner.

Behind them, the "wad of gum" in the street flipped over and sprouted twelve spidery legs supporting a needle-shaped head and liver-colored trunk. It skittered to the curb, sprang into the air, and attached to the Prowler's left rear fender with an elastic *thwap*, just as the engine rumbled to life.

As the hot rod drove off, the tracker bug crawled up and around the fender, then snickered forward along the Prowler's side, heading toward the driver. Before he reached the corner, the driver extended his left arm to signal a turn. The bug sprouted an inch-long spike from its snout and launched into the air toward the back of the driver's neck, ready to deliver its invisible payload.

The driver swung the Prowler around in a controlled skid, and what looked like a small derringer appeared in his left hand. He tracked the airborne bug into his sights and pulled the trigger, and a silent beam of white light pulsed from the barrel. The tracker bug—and the invisible Ride Along it carried—puckered, fried, and dropped to the ground, a burnt black cinder on the road.

The derringer disappeared back up the driver's sleeve as he completed his turn—a full, smooth 360-degree spin—and kept going.

DR. ROBBINS

Anxiety gnawed at Will like termites as he ran. He never let up, glancing over his shoulder only once. No black car, no Prowler, no more texts from Dad. And no other runners: Will arrived at school alone. He hit his stopwatch and was shocked to see that he'd covered the 1.2 miles from the diner to school in 3:47.

His best times shattered, twice, in less than an hour, and he'd hardly broken a sweat. He'd always known he was fast. He'd found out he could run like a deer at ten, when a dog chased him and he discovered he had another gear. But when he told his parents about it, they'd been dead-set against letting anyone see him run. They wouldn't even let him try out for cross-country until this year, and only after he promised to hold back in practice and meets. Will still didn't know how fast he really was, but based on this morning, he could have crushed every record in sight.

Will was already halfway dressed for class when the Rangers staggered into the locker room almost two minutes later. Gasping, a few threw strange looks his way.

"What the hell, West," whispered Schaeffer.

"Sorry," mumbled Will. "Don't know what got into me."

Will hurried out before anyone could ask more questions. If nobody else on the team had kept time, maybe by this afternoon they'd forget how fast he'd run. He would hang back in practice, in line with his mediocre standards, and they wouldn't give the torching he'd just laid down another thought.

But he still couldn't explain it to himself.

Will hustled through the halls and slipped into his seat a minute before the start of history class. He checked his messages one last time. Nothing. Dad had either gone into a breakfast meeting or headed out for his morning run.

Will switched the ringer to vibrate as the bell sounded. Classmates trudged in looking cranky and sleep deprived, fumbling with their phones as they digitally wrangled their frantic social lives. No one paid any attention to him. They never did. Will made sure of that. The perpetual "new kid," Will had long ago learned how to cork his emotions deep inside, showing nothing but a bland mask to his peers.

#46: IF STRANGERS KNOW WHAT YOU'RE FEELING, YOU GIVE THEM THE ADVANTAGE.

Will was the tall rangy kid who always sat near the back, slumping to minimize his height, never making waves. The way he dressed, the way he spoke, the way he moved through life: quiet, contained, invisible. Exactly the way his parents had taught him.

#3: DON'T DRAW ATTENTION TO YOURSELF.

But a pounding bass line of worry still pulsed in his chest: RUN, WILL. DON'T STOP. Could the timing of Dad's texts—at the moment the black car spotted him—be a coincidence?

#27: THERE IS NO SUCH THING AS COINCIDENCE.

Mrs. Filopovich launched into her daily drone. Today's subject: the Napoleonic Wars. The annoying buzz that leaked from the intercom on the wall above her desk sounded more interesting. Half the class struggled to stay conscious; he saw two wake-up jolts as chins slipped off propped-up hands. The air in the room curdled, like even the oxygen had given up hope.

Will's mind drifted to the last thing Dad had said before leaving two days ago: *"Pay attention to your dreams."* Suddenly he flashed onto the dream that had eluded him earlier. He closed his eyes to reel it back in and caught a single, fleeting image:

Snow falling. Stillness in an immense forest, large trees laden white.

For all their moving around, he'd never once seen snow in real life until that frosting on the mountains this morning. But this felt more real than a dream. Like a place he'd actually been before.

The door opened. The school psychologist slipped in, making an exaggerated effort to not be noticed, like a mime overacting a burglary. Will knew the man vaguely. He'd conducted Will's new-student orientation tour three months ago, in August. Mr. Rasche. Midthirties. Pear-shaped in corduroy and loud plaid, a prickly academic's beard fringing a cascade of chins.

Rasche whispered to Mrs. Filopovich. The class stirred to life, grateful for anything that spared them from Death by Bonaparte. The adults scanned the class.

Mr. Rasche's eyes settled on Will. "Will West?" he asked with a weird lopsided smile. "Would you come with me, please?"

Alarms tripped through Will's nervous system. He stood up, wishing he could disappear, as a gossipy ripple of intrigue ran through the class.

"Bring your things," said Mr. Rasche, as bland as milk.

Rasche waited at the door and then led the way, springing up on his toes with every step.

"What kind of trouble is this?" asked Will.

"Trouble? Oh, no, no, no," said Rasche, forcing a canine grin. "It's 'all good.'" Rasche hooked his fingers around his words with air quotes.

Yikes.

"But I feel you, dawg," said Rasche. He offered a fist bump to show he was on Will's side. "It's all pret-ty awesome and amazing. As you will see."

As they walked past the long counter outside the principal's office, the staff behind the counter beamed at Will. One even gave him a thumbs-up.

Something's totally messed up.

Principal Ed Barton bounded out of his office. The hearty, pie-faced man pumped Will's hand, as breathless and buoyant as if Will had just won the state science fair.

"Mr. West, come in, come in. Good to see you again. How are you today?"

Even weirder. On any other day, armed with Will's class photo and a bloodhound, Barton wouldn't have been able to pick him out of a three-kid lineup that included Siamese twins.

But then Will always made a point of missing school photo day.

"To be honest, I'm kind of worried," said Will as he and Mr. Rasche followed Barton into his office.

"About what, Will?"

"That everyone's being so nice because you're about to lay some tragic news on me."

Barton chuckled and steered him inside. "Oh, no. Not at all."

Rasche closed the door behind them. A woman stood up from a chair in front of Barton's desk and extended her hand. She was as tall as Will, athletic and lithe, wearing a dark tailored suit. Her straight blond hair was pulled back in a crisp ponytail. A pricey leather briefcase rested at her flashy spiked heels.

"Will, this is Dr. Robbins," said Barton.

"Really nice to meet you, Will," she said. Her grip was strong, and her violet eyes sharp.

Whoever she is, Will thought, *the doctor is smoking hot.*

"Dr. Robbins is here with some incredibly exciting news," said Barton.

"You're a hard-core facts and numbers guy, aren't you, Will?" asked Robbins.

"As opposed to . . ."

"A sucker for marketing slogans and subliminal advertising designed to paralyze your conscious mind and shut down rational impulse control by stimulating your lower brain?"

Will hesitated. "That depends on what you're trying to sell me."

Dr. Robbins smiled. She leaned down, picked up her briefcase, and slipped out a sleek black metallic laptop. She set it on Barton's desk and opened it. The screen lit up with a waterfall of data that arranged artfully into animated graphs.

Principal Barton sat down behind his desk. "Will, do you remember the standardized test you and your classmates took in September?" he asked.

"Yes," said Will.

Dr. Robbins said, "That test is conducted by the National Scholastic Evaluation Agency. On every tenth grader at every public school in the country." She pointed to a large cluster of squiggling lines in the middle of the chart on her laptop's screen. "These are the nationwide average scores they've collected over the last five years."

Robbins punched a key; the image zoomed in on the top of the chart, which blossomed into a smaller group of what looked like dancing sixteenth notes. "These are the scores of National Merit Scholars," she said. "The top two percent of the database."

Dr. Robbins punched another key, and the image moved again, zooming in on a single red dot above the highest cluster. Alone.

Tendrils of fear wrapped around Will's gut. *Uh-oh*, he thought.

"This," she said, "is you. One in, to be precise, 2.3567 million." She cocked her head to the side and smiled again, dazzling and sympathetic.

Will's heart skipped a beat. He tried to hide his shock as a single thought raced through his mind: *How did this happen?*

"Attaboy, Will," said Barton, rubbing his hands with glee. "What do you think about that?"

Will had attended the man's stunningly average high school for less than two weeks when he took that test, but Barton clearly intended to grab whatever credit he could for his results.

"Will?" asked Dr. Robbins.

"Sorry. I'm kind of . . . speechless."

"Perfectly understandable," she said. "We can go over specifics if you like—"

A buzzer on Barton's console sounded. Barton snapped his fingers at Rasche, who turned and opened the door. Will's mother walked in wearing a scarf around her neck, her eyes hidden behind her big sunglasses.

Will looked for some indication of her disappointment—he had screwed up big-time and blown his anonymity—but his mother just smiled at him. "Isn't it exciting?" she said, rushing to give him a hug. "I came as soon as Dr. Robbins called."

Will pulled back and caught his reflection in his mother's mirrored sunglasses. That was odd. She never wore sunglasses indoors. Was she wearing them now so he couldn't see her eyes? She was acting all excited for the benefit of the other adults in the room, but Will knew she had to be really angry with him.

As Belinda stepped back, Will caught a faint trace of cigarettes. *Odd. She must have been around some smokers at her office. Could workers in California legally light up anymore?*

Will's phone buzzed. It was a text from Dad: CONGRATU-LATIONS, SON! Mom must have called him with the news.

21

Will's mom shook hands and exchanged pleasantries with everyone in the room. Then Dr. Robbins took charge again. "If you'd indulge me, Will," she said, "and if everyone will excuse us, I'd like you to take one other quick, simple test."

"What for?"

"Curiosity," she said simply. "When somebody shatters the existing statistical model, scientific minds crave confirmation. What do you say? Are you up for it?"

"If I say no, what's the worst that could happen?" asked Will.

"You go back to class, finish your day, and forget we ever had this conversation," she said.

Talk about a convincing argument. "Let's do it," said Will.

THE TEST

Will trailed Dr. Robbins down the hall to an empty office with a small table and two chairs. A black tablet computer the size of a small square chalkboard rested on the table. Robbins sat on one side and silently offered Will the opposite chair.

Dr. Robbins tapped the tablet and it powered up with a faintly audible *whoosh*. Using her fingers, she stretched out the dimensions of the borderless black square the way a sculptor might manipulate wet clay. Except the tablet was made of metal. When she was done, the tablet had grown in size until it nearly covered the entire table.

"What the heck is this thing?" asked Will.

"Ah. That would be telling," she said playfully. "Put your hands here, please."

The glowing outlines of a pair of hands appeared on the screen. The blackness beneath the lines glistened, as if there were unseen depths below. Will felt like he was staring into the still water of a moonlit lake.

Will set his hands down just inside the lines. The instant

he made contact, the screen thrummed with energy. The lines glowed brighter, then faded, leaving his hands floating on top of a bottomless liquid void.

"I'm going to ask you some questions," Dr. Robbins said. "Feel free to respond any way you like. There are no wrong answers."

"What if you ask the wrong questions?"

"What's your name?"

"Will Melendez West."

"Melendez. That's your mother's maiden name?"

"Yes."

A pleasant wave of heat rose from the screen, washing over his hands like soft seawater before subsiding.

"And Will's not short for William?"

"It's not short for anything. They wanted a cooperative kid, so they named me the opposite of *won't*."

She didn't smile. "How old are you, Will?"

"Fifteen."

"When's your birthday?"

"August fifteenth. Every year, like clockwork."

A swirling riot of colors erupted from the depths below, then disappeared. Will had the disturbing thought that if he pushed his hands through the surface, he would fall right into the screen.

"Is this some kind of lie detector?" he asked.

She narrowed her eyes. "Would it make you more comfortable if it were?"

"Is that a question from the test, or are you really asking?"

"Does it make a difference to you?"

"Are you going to answer all of my questions with questions?"

"Why, yes, I am, Will," she said, smiling pleasantly. "I'm trying to distract you."

Will's defenses ratcheted up a notch. "Keep up the good work."

"What's your favorite color?"

"Cerulean blue. I had a little zinc tube of that paint once in art class. Real dark blue, like the sky on a cold, clear day—"

"It's not an essay question. Where were you born?"

"Albuquerque," he said. "We only lived there a few months. I can spell that for you, if you like."

Subtle tones sounded from deep beneath his hands, like muted woodwinds. Corresponding shapes—obscure mathematical symbols, or some archaic language he couldn't decipher—swam around below him in complex patterns.

"It's not a spelling bee, either. What's your father's name?"

"Jordan West."

"What does he do for a living?"

"He's a freelance rodeo clown."

"Hmm," she said, chewing on her lip. "That might have been a lie."

"Wow. You *are* good."

"Oh, it's not me," she said, then leaned forward, pointed to the screen, and whispered, "You can't fool the machine."

"Okay, busted. He's an academic researcher."

Robbins smiled. "That sounds slightly more plausible. In what field?"

"Neurobiology, at UC Santa Barbara."

"What is your mom's full name?"

"Belinda Melendez West."

"What does she do?"

"She works as a paralegal."

"Where is her family from?" asked Robbins.

Will raised an eyebrow. "The Melendezes? Barcelona. Her parents came here in the 1960s."

"Are your grandparents still living?"

"No."

"Did you know any of them?"

"Not that I remember."

"Would you classify yourself as Caucasian or Hispanic?"

"Neither. I'm American."

Dr. Robbins seemed to like that answer. "Where else has your family lived besides Albuquerque?"

"Tucson, Las Cruces, Phoenix, Flagstaff, La Jolla, last year Temecula, and then here in Ojai—"

"Why do your parents move around so much?"

Good question, Will thought. Out loud, he said, "That's the price Dad pays for working in the exciting and highly competitive field of neurobiology."

"This part's going to hurt a little," she said.

He felt something sharp and prickly—like a steel brush—scrape his palms as the surface of the tablet crackled with a hot flash of light that filled the room, then just as quickly went dark.

Will yanked his hands away in alarm. The surface of the screen glowed like a pool lit underwater. Dust and debris floating in the air above rushed down into the black square as if caught in the pull of a magnetic field. Then the light went out, the surface stabilized, and the black tablet shrank back to its original chalkboard size.

Okay, Will thought. *That is truly deeply weird.*

Will looked at his hands. Both palms were red, and they pulsed as if he'd set them on a hot stove. Robbins took his hands in hers and examined them.

"I warned you it was going to hurt," she said softly.

"What's all this really about?"

"Sorry for the mumbo jumbo, Will. You'll understand eventually. Or you won't." She gave him back his hands. His palms already looked less inflamed.

"Thanks for clearing that up. How'd I do on your test?"

"I don't know," she said, smiling like she had a secret. "Why don't you ask the Mystic Eight Ball?" Robbins held up the black tablet in front of him. A photo-real 3-D image of an eight ball appeared on-screen. "Go ahead."

Will lowered his voice in a parody of concentration. "Did I pass the test?"

Robbins gave the tablet a shake. The "Eight Ball" revolved and revealed a small window on its opposite side. A miniature white tile floated into view: *Looking good!*

"There you go. So sayeth the oracle," she said, sliding the tablet back into her bag. "I have one last question of my own, Will. Nothing to do with the test."

"Shoot."

"Aren't you absolutely bored to the edge of living death with high school?"

"Yes, ma'am."

She smiled. "Let's go talk to Mom."

"I represent the most academically accomplished college preparatory academy in the country," said Robbins as she typed commands into her laptop. "That you've never heard of."

"Why haven't we heard of you?" asked Belinda West.

"I'll address that in a moment, Mrs. West. I think you'll appreciate the answer."

Dr. Robbins opened her laptop until it lay flat on Barton's desk. A multidimensional image of thick cloud cover projected into the air about three feet above the screen, like an impossibly detailed children's pop-up book. Barton and Rasche stood back in amazement.

As they all watched, the point of view circled above the clouds and then descended into them. As the clouds thinned, a stately array of buildings on vast green lawns surrounded by thick woods appeared. They floated down toward this astonishingly conjured world, swooped suddenly lower, and leveled off. They flew toward the campus above a long, straight entrance road lined with towering trees. As they passed over a gate and guardhouse, Will caught the glow of illuminated letters engraved on an impressive stone facade:

THE CENTER FOR INTEGRATED LEARNING

"We're offering Will a full scholarship," said Robbins. "Completely on the merits. We'll include travel, living expenses, textbooks, and supplies. This won't cost your family a dime."

"Where's the school?" asked Will.

"Wisconsin," said Robbins.

The simulated flyby continued. They glided over classic ivy-covered stone halls connected by wide symmetrical walkways. Beyond the central campus, they passed over a huge retro-style field house. An outdoor all-purpose stadium. Stables and riding rings. Fields for a variety of sports, including a golf course.

"What's the catch?" asked Will.

"There's only one," she said. "You have to want this, Will. The Center opened its doors in 1915. You haven't heard of us because we value privacy. We never look for or encourage publicity. That's one of the ways in which we protect our students and our reputation. But I assure you all the best colleges and universities in the world know who we are. Our graduate placement into those institutions has no equal. Among our distinguished alumni, you'll find fourteen senators, a vice president, two members of the Supreme Court, nine Cabinet members, seven Nobel Prize winners, dozens of leaders in business and industry, and several foreign heads of state. To name just a few."

The tour continued over a large meandering lake tucked back in the nearby woods. The trees were ablaze with spectacular fall colors. A big rustic boathouse sat on the shore. A tall, twisting Gothic-looking structure—almost a castle— occupied a craggy island in the center of the lake. Then the "camera" withdrew up into the virtual clouds and the image faded from view.

"That was . . . like . . . *magic*," said Rasche, his mouth agape.

"Bear in mind, *magic* is the name we've always applied to tomorrow's technology," said Robbins, "when we see it today."

Dr. Robbins turned to Will and his mother. "No one applies to the Center. You have to be invited." She pulled an oversized packet from her briefcase and handed it to Belinda. "We think you'll find everything your family needs to make an informed decision in here. Take your time. We know you have a lot to think about."

Barton chimed in. "And you can certainly be excused from class for the rest of the day to get started if you like, Will."

"I *do* like," said Will.

Everyone chuckled politely.

"All of my contact information is there," said Robbins, packing up her notebook. "As you go through your process, please don't hesitate to call with any questions or concerns you might have."

She shook Will's hand again and headed out.

"Dr. Robbins?" asked Will.

She stopped at the door. "Yes, Will?"

"What's your first name?"

"Lillian," she said, amused. Lillian Robbins knew how to leave a room, and now she did, briskly.

After a few minutes of predictable fawning from Barton and Rasche, Will left the office with Belinda. An intuitive flash went through his mind as they walked down the empty halls:

I won't be seeing this place again.

Dr. Robbins was right: He had an avalanche of things to think about, hundreds of questions piling up in his mind. But none were more troubling than the one that had snared his soul the moment his mom had walked through Barton's door that morning. He'd initially tried to dismiss it as an insane distraction. An off-kilter headtrip cooked up by the compounding weirdness of the day.

But now that they were alone, it was worse. Much worse. And it wasn't going away.

He glanced at his mother. Still wearing an insipid smile and those damn dark glasses. She saw him look at her and gave his hand an excited little squeeze.

Wrong. Completely wrong.

As he left for home with someone who looked and sounded *exactly* like Belinda Melendez West, the question was, Why did he have the feeling this wasn't the same person he'd said good-bye to two hours ago?

NO PLACE LIKE HOME

This was her, but at the same time it wasn't.

What about her makes me feel this way? Will couldn't put his finger on it. It was a subtle feeling, but it gripped him like a python.

This was his mom's *car,* no doubt about that. The old beater Ford Focus she called the Green Machine, down to her macramé back support and the floating compass on the dash. He felt below his seat and found the plastic In-N-Out cup he'd stashed there two days earlier.

"Well, I just don't know what to say, Will," she said, hands fluttering on the steering wheel. "I mean, if this isn't the most amazing thing ever."

Looked like her and sounded like her . . . but that wasn't the right thing for her to *say.* She should be worried about how this test result came about. Asking him why he'd gone against their instructions and drawn attention to himself this way. *That* would have been the first thing she said.

Will kept his eyes forward, afraid she'd see the creeping terror on his face if he looked directly at her.

#14: ASK ALL QUESTIONS IN THE ORDER OF THEIR IMPORTANCE.

"Are you all right?" he asked.

"Yes, I'm fine. I'm just so excited," she said, jangling the bracelets on her wrist. "The principal called when I got to work, and put Dr. Robbins on the line. I called Dad as soon as we hung up. He's ditching the rest of the conference and coming home tonight. He sounded pretty jazzed."

Dad would have a lot of reactions to this, but "jazzed" wouldn't be one of them, Will thought.

Will worked to keep his breathing under control, the way his dad had taught him. It got harder to stay calm when they passed a black sedan parked on a side street a block from their house. It looked like the same car from this morning.

"I guess we have a whole lot to talk about," he said, trying to sound calm.

"Indeed. But I have to say, Will-bear, *you* don't sound all that excited."

"I want to look over what's in here," said Will, gripping Robbins's packet in his hands. "One step at a time."

#20: THERE MUST ALWAYS BE A RELATIONSHIP BETWEEN EVIDENCE AND CONCLUSION.

"You know, you're absolutely right," she said as she pulled into their driveway. "We shouldn't get ahead of ourselves. One step at a time."

She parked and gathered her things. Will hurried in ahead of her. He ran upstairs, threw on some sweats, grabbed his

MacBook, and brought it down to the kitchen. Fighting to stay calm, he clung to what he knew he had to do: Open his senses, clear his mind, notice every detail.

#9: WATCH, LOOK, AND LISTEN, OR YOU WON'T KNOW WHAT YOU'RE MISSING.

"You get started, then," said Belinda, grabbing a Diet Coke from the fridge. "I've got to head back to work. We'll go over everything later with Dad."

She hugged him from behind as he sat at the table. Her touch felt tense, fraught with twisted anxiety, *wrong*. Her dark glasses slipped down, and for the first time Will saw her eyes: they were Belinda's, but chillingly glassy and vacant.

"We are both so proud of you," she said, and then she was gone.

He heard the front door close, then hurried to the living room and watched her drive off. The Green Machine slowed as she turned the corner where he'd seen the black sedan. Her window slid down as she edged out of sight. Will ran to the next window, where he could see both cars. Stopped beside each other, driver to driver.

She's talking to them.

Will locked the doors. He tried his dad's cell—*please, Dad, please answer*—but got voice mail. Will hung up, then tapped a text: NEED TO TALK. CALL ME.

Caps. SHOUTING. Anything to grab Dad's attention. Will set his phone beside his laptop and picked up Dr. Robbins's packet. His hands were shaking. It took every ounce of self-control to keep his terror from breaking loose. . . .

His phone marimbaed. Will jumped out of his skin and picked up before the second ring: *Dad calling.*

"Dad? . . . *Dad?*" Will heard a hollow metallic whistling, like water echoing through a storm drain. "Dad, are you there?"

There was a burst of static, then silence. Will hit CALL BACK and heard the same swampy interference. Dad must be out of range or driving through a dead zone. Will killed the call and set the phone down where he could see it. He needed to stay focused, ground himself in facts. Analyze, manage, arrange: *The Importance of an Orderly Mind.*

He opened Robbins's packet and paged through some forms, including an admission application for his parents to sign. A magazine-sized blank rectangle, made of strong, flexible material, slid out. The words TOUCH HERE appeared, and he did. More words appeared, in a simple, elegant font:

THE CENTER FOR INTEGRATED LEARNING

Below that, the school's crest took shape. It was a coat of arms, an ornate shield in navy blue and dark silver, divided into three horizontal sections, each with an image. On top, a winged angel held a book and a sword. In the middle, a majestic black horse reared, its hooves rimmed with flames. On the bottom, a knight in armor pointed his sword at a vanquished foe lying on the ground. A scroll unfurled below the crest with a date, 1915, and a motto: *Knowledge Is the Path, Wisdom Is the Purpose.*

Photographs of the campus filled the screen. An audio track with quotes about the school's credentials and distinguished faculty began to play. One of the photos stopped him cold: a shot of a still forest in winter, shrouded in thick mist, hardwoods and evergreens buried in thick snow. The female voice on the audio said, "You'll feel as if you're in a dream."

It was the image he'd remembered from his dream the night before.

The image dissolved into video of students in classrooms listening to lectures and working in labs. Hanging out in a coffee shop and a bowling alley. Performing plays and concerts, riding horses, playing a dozen different sports. Bright, eager faces of kids Will's age or older. All wore clothes in variations of the Center's colors—navy blue and gray. The voices on the audio track were saying, "Life-changing opportunities around every corner . . . I made friends I knew instantly would be mine forever . . . I gained a feeling of confidence and belonging that's stayed with me my whole life."

Will knew this was advertising, designed to arouse specific feelings: *The Center makes students smarter, stronger, and more popular. My best qualities will be recognized and rewarded and all my dreams will come true.*

The screen shifted to video of the school choir singing in a candlelit jewel-box chapel. The beauty of the song gripped him, a slow, celestial melody that continued over heartwarming images of a graduation. Proud parents embracing their beaming cap-and-gowned kids. This was the part of the deal known as *closing the sale.* But knowing he was being manipulated didn't prevent it from working. The Center made the life he'd spent stumbling through overcrowded, underfunded public schools seem futile.

Could a place this perfect really exist?

Will Google Earthed the school's mailing address: New Brighton Township, Wisconsin. A rural community, seventy miles northeast of the corner where Iowa, Illinois, and Wisconsin came together. He zoomed in on the town, then scrolled out until he found the Center. It appeared exactly as he'd seen it in Robbins's 3-D preview: the grand old buildings, the playing fields, the nearby lake.

It's real. It's all there.

Will's parents didn't have money or connections, and they'd trained him to leave no tracks, so he'd reined himself in. Posing as a B+ student, flying under the radar. Following Rule #3: DON'T DRAW ATTENTION TO YOURSELF meant he had no chance of earning academic or athletic scholarships and the life that went with them. But now, without asking for it, a door to this astonishingly better world had opened.

What if the Center was a place where he could finally be *himself*?

Will's phone dinged. It was a text from Dad: IN THE CAR. BAD RECEPTION. HOME BY SIX. TALK THEN.

Will glanced at the time and was shocked to see it was the middle of the afternoon. He'd been grinding this for hours. "Belinda" would be home from work soon, and he didn't want to be in the same room with her again until Dad returned.

I need to see what Dad thinks. Then we'll decide what to do about it together.

Will made a PB and J and wolfed it down as he prowled the house. He looked at the meager possessions they'd dragged around to six cities in fourteen years. They owned a small TV but seldom watched anything but news. All they did with their free time was read. Shelves lined every wall in the house—scientific, medical, legal texts.

#82: WITHOUT A LIFE OF THE MIND, YOU'LL LIVE A MINDLESS LIFE.

His eye landed on a shelf of family photos. He picked up a picture of his parents on their wedding day, playfully feeding each other cake. Belinda wore a gathered velvet gown, her long black hair woven with lace. Dad sported a burgundy velvet tux and a doofus grad-school haircut and scruffy beard.

Happy, laughing, carefree. He'd always felt a special connection to this picture, because he could glimpse the start of his own life in this moment, as if his spirit were right there, hovering, unseen: the *spark* in his parents' eyes.

He thought of the glimpse of "Belinda's" eyes he'd gotten when her sunglasses had slipped down—empty, vacant—and compared it to the vibrant woman in this picture. *That's* what was different. Her *soul* was missing.

What had they done to her? Would they try to do the same thing to him?

He heard a car door shut and peeked out the window. *Three* black sedans had stopped in front. Men in black caps and jackets were headed for the house. One of them, a bald man, was pointing and giving orders.

Will's chest tightened, and the air in the room clamped down: RUN, WILL. He fled out the back door, hopped the fence, and headed north. With a startled flap of wings, the little blackbird lifted off the fence and settled in a nearby tree. Two hours and change until Dad got home.

Dad will know what to do.

* * *

The bald man in the black cap jogged around the side of the house. Raising binoculars, he caught a glimpse of Will as he disappeared over a rise, sprinting toward the hills. He ordered the others to hold back and spoke into his wrist mic. "He's on the fire road, headed north."

"Is he Awake?"

"Hard to say," said the bald man. "But we can't take any chances. Bring me the Carver."

PROWLER

Will reached the trail beyond the last house at the end of the street and followed it up a slope to a locked gate at the base of the fire road. Slipping through a gap between posts, he headed straight up the fire road. The sun dipped low in the west, painting the slopes above him in vibrant crystalline light.

Air pumped through Will's lungs as he followed a series of severe switchbacks carved into the canyon. The road leveled off and ran flat along a ridge before grading up again. Deep thickets of chaparral and dried bramble lined both sides of the road. Sharp sunlight around him faded to dusk. He stopped to look behind him and noticed a strange circle of light farther down the hill, as if the sun's last rays had shot through a huge magnifying glass. The light looked so intensely bright, he thought the brush might burst into flame.

The weirdest day of my life, he thought. *Dr. Robbins shows up right after the black sedan, the Prowler, and just before the fake Belinda. But if there's a connection—and according to Rule #27 there* has *to be—what is it?*

The test. That had to be it. What if his score had raised a red flag that caught someone *else's* eye? Someone whose interest in him wasn't nearly as positive or benign as the Center's?

What if that test had set in motion whatever happened to his mom?

Will heard an odd noise, faint and scratchy. Something was moving through the underbrush near where he'd noticed that peculiar circle of light, which had now faded. He heard branches cracking; it was a deer, most likely. These hills were full of whitetails. Then there was more rustling off to the other side of the road. Louder.

Will stopped. The crackling in the brush stopped as well. When he ran forward again, the sounds picked back up, paralleling his progress forward.

What kind of animal reacts that way?

Will stopped again, but this time the movement continued, on both sides, edging closer to the road. Mountain lions? Not likely. They were native to the area but almost no one ever saw them. And they always hunted alone.

He heard a low, guttural snarl.

Coyotes. Had to be. Will saw more movement in the thickets. Branches were shaking on both sides as the pack closed in.

The wind shifted and he caught a nauseating smell: burned rubber or hair, a heavy dose of rotting eggs. Was it coming off these animals? Will picked up a sturdy dead branch from the side of the path. Down the slope, he noticed a clearing where a mudslide had piled against the edge of the brush line.

As he watched, astonished, impressions appeared in the mud. They were blank and round, like bony knobs. And they appeared in a pattern: two, then one; two, then one, with big gaps in between. Like a tripod working its way toward him up the slope. An *invisible* tripod.

The snarling began again, all around him on both sides of the road. He heard a low gibbering embedded in the growls, dotted with glottal pulses and a guttering wheezy percussion. It sounded like some sort of *language*—

Cold terror burst in the pit of his stomach. *There's only one way down from here,* Will thought, *and if whatever these things are cut off the road . . .*

Will spun around and sprinted down the hill. An instant later he heard them crash after him with a wild whooping yowl. As he neared the end of the ridge, a shadowy mass leaped over him from behind and landed directly in his path. Without breaking stride, Will swung the branch with both hands as hard as he could. The branch shattered as it smacked something he couldn't see, and whatever he'd hit snarled in pain.

The impact threw Will off stride. He nearly fell, but pivoted, pushed off the ground, and kept his legs churning. Whatever invisible nightmare he'd just smashed with the branch wheeled after him. The air rippled. Something sharp sliced through Will's sweatshirt and raked across his back. A fiery spike of pain spurred him to run even faster down the winding road.

It was getting hard to see. He could hear the things behind him, but he'd opened up some space. Desperate to extend his lead, Will headed into a sharp turn without slowing. As he planted his left foot to veer right, he hit a patch of mud and skidded. He lost his balance, turned as he fell, and—

Wham. He landed on his left side, rolled, then stuck out his hands as brakes, skidding along the road. He stopped on the outside edge of the curve, just short of plunging over a twenty-foot drop into blackness.

Will dragged himself to his feet and limped on. He heard nauseating yawping sounds, the snorting and snuffling of something wet and fleshy; the things weren't more than thirty yards behind him now and closing fast. With at least a quarter mile to the end of the fire road, he'd never make it before they caught him.

Farther down the road, a blinding light sliced through the night. A deafening throttle roared and a pair of white-hot headlights hurtled toward him, torque screaming. Was it the black sedan? He couldn't tell.

Will threw himself to the side of the road as the car passed, the heat of a massive engine warping the air. He caught the acrid smell of burning rubber as it spun sideways and curled behind him. But it *wasn't* the sedan. Eyes blinded by the headlights, Will could only make out the black outline of the Prowler he'd seen outside the diner and its hulking driver behind the wheel.

Flames erupted from the Prowler's twin exhausts with a deafening *whoosh*. A wall of fire shot into the road behind it, and the creatures chasing Will ran straight into it. Their howls changed to revolting high-pitched squeals. Will saw writhing misshapen masses thrashing around, outlined in fire.

The car skidded beside Will. "Get in," growled the driver. It was the same voice he'd heard—but in his *head*—outside the diner that morning.

Will threw himself onto the backseat as the driver gunned the Prowler down the road. Will looked back and saw the burning creatures flail off the edge of the cliff, pinwheeling fiery spirals falling away into a void.

The car roared through the open gate at the base of the road and reached the flats in moments. Will crouched down as they weaved through sharp turns at what seemed like impossible speeds. With the driver hunched over the wheel, in the light of passing streetlamps, Will noticed a large round patch on the back of the man's leather jacket. Inside it were three images and words he couldn't make out.

Then, in a strip of darkness, the Prowler skidded to a stop.

"Out," said the driver.

Will leaped out of the car and backed away. The driver remained in shadow, motionless, staring at him from behind black aviator shades. The man's taut presence and unsettling stillness held a promise of violence.

"What were those things?" asked Will.

"You don't want to know," the driver said.

"But—"

"Stow it. You may think you're dux, mate, but unless you want to kark it early days, next time don't be such a nong."

Will couldn't place the driver's accent, which was harsh as a blade. "I'm sorry," Will said. "I have no idea what you just said."

The driver leaned forward into the light and lowered his shades. He had fierce black brows above a raptor's piercing eyes. And scars. *Lots* of scars.

He held up his right index finger. "That's *one*," said the man. Then he stomped on the gas. The Prowler sped off around a corner, the sound of its engine fading quickly into the night.

Will looked around. He was standing fifty feet from the back door of his house. Music drifted through an open window, a woman's voice backed by a big band with old-fashioned orchestration:

> *"If you go out in the woods tonight*
> *You're in for a big surprise . . .*
> *If you go out in the woods tonight*
> *You'd better go in disguise . . ."*

DAD'S HOME

Will peered around the side of his house: The black cars were gone.

He hurried to the back door and entered silently. Someone was in their kitchen. He caught a whiff of his mom's perfume and cookies baking. Will edged down the hallway and peeked into the kitchen.

"Belinda" was pacing back and forth, holding a cell phone to her ear. As he watched, she raised a hand to the back of her neck and flinched, as if in pain.

Then she spoke into the phone in a monotone voice he hardly recognized: "He's not back . . . I don't know where he went . . . yes, I'll let you know if he . . ."

Will backed away down the hall. He landed on a creaky floorboard, then bumped into the wall trying to avoid it.

"Will-bear?" she called. "Is that you? Are you home?"

Damn.

"Hi," he said, reopening the back door as if he'd just come inside.

"Come in the kitchen! I made cookies!"

"One sec. I've got mud on my shoes." He wanted to run again, but Dad would be home soon. But he couldn't face her yet, either, and with that loopy song blaring away, he couldn't think straight. Will closed the door loudly and followed the music to the living room.

The antique turntable sat next to Dad's precious vinyl collection: LPs and stacks of old 45s, still in their paper sleeves. The soundtrack of his parents' lives. Will knew this music better than his own generation's.

#78: THERE'S A REASON THE CLASSICS ARE CLASSICS: THEY'RE *CLASSIC*.

> "At six o'clock their mommies and daddies
> Will take them home to bed
> Because they're tired little teddy bears—"

Will jerked the needle off the record. A scratch popped in the speakers. "Belinda" came in behind him.

"You always *loved* that song," she said.

"I haven't heard it for a hundred years," he said. "It's kind of creepy."

"You played it all the time when you were little—"

"I'm not really in the mood right now."

"But you *loved* it—"

"Yes, I did," said Will. "And when I played it over and over again, it used to drive *you* crazy."

Her smile never wavered. She didn't even blink. She held out a plate of cookies and a glass of milk. "Oatmeal raisin," she said.

Will stared at the milk. Were his eyes playing tricks on him, or did it have a faint greenish glow?

She kept the plate in front of him. He finally took the milk and a cookie, hoping she wouldn't wait for him to eat it. "Where'd you go?" she asked.

"For a run."

"It looks like you fell. Did you hurt yourself?"

"I'm fine."

"Come help with dinner."

He followed her to the kitchen, trying not to limp. He broke off half the cookie, dumped it into the umbrella stand in the hall with half the milk, then pretended to chew as he walked in after her. She stood over the stove tending pots, one of them pouring steam into the air. Dr. Robbins's packet sat on the table where he'd left it, next to his laptop.

"How's the cookie?" she asked.

He held up the remaining half. "Good."

"Did you look through all the stuff from the school?"

She'd emptied the packet onto the table: the electronic brochure, a small pamphlet about the school's history, and a stack of official forms and paperwork.

"Most of it," said Will.

"So what do you think?"

His iPhone dinged. He fumbled it from his pocket and switched it on. An unfamiliar app popped up on his greeting screen: a feathered quill pen poised over an old-fashioned parchment. The title below read UNIVERSAL TRANSLATOR.

Where did this come from?

"Seems pretty interesting," he said.

"I have to say, I'm having trouble with the *boarding school* thing. It's halfway across the country. When would we ever see you? Know what I mean, jelly bean?"

She stepped past him and reached to an upper shelf for the pasta. Her hair parted for a moment, and Will caught a glimpse of a gnarled knob of flesh on the side of her neck, just behind her left ear. A more vivid pink than her skin tone, it looked like recent scar tissue, or an inflamed insect bite. And it was *twitching*.

What the hell?

As she turned back, Will looked away, trying to mask his fright. He gathered up the laptop and the contents of the packet from the table.

"I have time for a quick shower?"

"Twelve minutes," she said, looking at her wristwatch.

With the same hand, she poured the whole box of spaghetti into the pot of boiling water. Then shoved the tops into the water with a spoon.

Mom always breaks the spaghetti in half before she drops it in the water.

"I'll be quick."

Will walked out of the room and up the stairs, fighting the urge to break out of the house at a dead sprint.

#5: TRUST NO ONE.

He tossed the cookie out the back window and closed his door quietly. It had no lock, so he tilted his desk chair and wedged the top rail under the knob. He started his phone's stopwatch app and set it on the bed. *Eleven minutes.*

He stepped to the bathroom and turned on the shower

so she'd hear water in the pipes. He peeled off his shirt and sweatpants and checked the road rash on his hip. It was red and raw but he'd had worse. He cleaned it with a washcloth, then splashed on hydrogen peroxide. The scratch on his back looked nasty and inflamed. He poured peroxide on it, then gripped the sink and grimaced through the burn. Moving back to the bedroom, he glanced out one of the windows at the street in front. Empty.

Will dressed in fresh sweats. He picked up his iPhone and tapped the new application. A moment later the "Universal Translator" opened into a blank gray page. No menu or on-screen instructions about how to use it.

He logged onto his laptop and opened his email. A new message was waiting from Dad. The time tag read 8:18 that morning, but it had only just arrived. He double-clicked it. A blank message opened. No text. But it carried an attachment. He clicked on the attachment and it transferred onto his hard drive. It was a video file. He clicked on it repeatedly but couldn't open it. *Six minutes.*

He tried every program on his drive that could play video. Nothing worked. Then he noticed the subject tag on the email: *Translated.* He transferred the Universal Translator app from his phone to the laptop. This time a pull-down menu appeared. On the menu were two options: *Translate* and *Delete.* He clicked *Translate.* A video player's graphic interface came up on-screen. A triangular PLAY arrow floated into view. Will clicked on the arrow. The video file began to play.

A generic hotel room faded in, shown through the wide-angle lens of a laptop's on-board camera. There was a framed generic still life on the wall and a fragment of window on the left side of the screen. Pale morning light.

"Will."

Dad's voice. A moment later, Jordan West sat down in front of the camera. Will felt a flood of relief just seeing his father. But it didn't last. Dad's face and sweats were drenched, as if he'd come back from a hard run. His wire-rimmed glasses were fogged up; he took them off to clean them. Will realized it wasn't just fatigue or urgency in his eyes: Dad looked terrified.

"Pay attention now, Will," his dad said. "I'm in room twelve-oh-nine at the Hyatt Regency."

He held the front page of a San Francisco newspaper close to the lens. He pointed to its upper right-hand corner. His hands were shaking.

He's showing me today's date. Tuesday, November 7. Then Dad held his phone in front of the laptop's camera: 8:17 a.m. *So I'll know exactly when he recorded this.*

Jordan leaned in close and spoke in low, controlled tones. "Son, I'm making a big bet that only you will be able to open this: I've always bet on you. From what I've just seen, I don't have much time, and by the time you see this, neither will you.

"I know how strange and how frightening this sounds, Will. The first thing you have to know is that none of what's happened, or might happen, is your fault. Not one bit of it. We're responsible for this. And the idea that something we did would bring pain or sorrow into your life is the worst feeling your mom and I have ever known."

Will felt panic spread from his gut.

"We always hoped this day would never come. We've done

everything in our power to prevent it. We've tried as best we could, the only way we could, to prepare you if it ever did. Someday I hope you'll understand and forgive us for never saying why—"

A startling *bang* rocked the screen. Will recoiled along with his dad. The camera shook as Jordan West looked to his left: Something powerful had crashed into the door. He turned back to the lens, his eyes frantic.

"My dear boy," he said, his voice breaking. "We love you more than anything in life. Always and forever. Tell no one about this or about our family, no matter who they say they are. Believe me, these people will stop at nothing. Be the person I know you can be. Use the rules and everything we've taught you. Instincts, training, discipline, hold nothing back. Run as far and as fast as you can. Do whatever you need to do to stay alive. I'll come for you. I don't know when, but I swear I'll tear down the gates of hell to find you—"

Another explosion blew out the laptop's equalizer into white noise. The hotel room filled instantly with a cloud of dust and debris. The image spun around as the laptop flew through the air and landed on the floor at a crazy angle. Will was looking at the window he'd seen earlier but the camera had turned sideways. In the near distance, a tall, singular skyscraper jutted horizontally across the window: the Transamerica Pyramid. San Francisco. The video signal fractured into static lines. Dark figures rushed into view. A curtain closed across the window, and then a hand reached into the keyboard. Dad's hand: He hit the key that attached the video and sent the email—

The screen went dead.

"Dad. Oh my God. Oh my God." *Please don't hurt him, please don't hurt him, please let him be okay.*

Too stunned to move, Will gazed at the poster on his wall. THE IMPORTANCE OF AN ORDERLY MIND.

Listen. No matter what's happened, you have to do exactly what he's telling you. The way he taught you: rationally, systematically, ferociously. Now.

Start by asking the right questions: *When did this happen?*

Tuesday, November 7, 8:17 a.m. *While I was in history class. Dad sent his last real texts before I got to school:* RUN, WILL. DON'T STOP. *Every text after 8:17 was either coerced or sent by the men I saw in Dad's hotel room. They're working with the ones who've chased me all day. The ones who've done something to my mother.*

But why? What do they want from us?

Out of the corner of his eye, Will saw movement in the back window. He grabbed a rock paperweight from his desk, a birthday gift engraved with a single word: VERITAS. He whirled and pegged it at the window. It punched a hole through the glass and clipped something that spun and fluttered to the roof.

Will hurried to the window. Lying on the shingles outside, in a sharp rectangle of light, was the little white-breasted blackbird. It twitched once or twice, then lay still. The sight of the small pathetic creature pierced Will's soul. He opened the broken window, gathered the still-warm bird in his hands, and brought it inside.

A puff of smoke rose from the center of the bird's chest; it smelled acrid, almost electrical. Looking closely, Will noticed an irregular line under the bird's chest feathers, a seam where smoke continued to leak.

Will grabbed his Swiss Army knife from the desk, opened a blade, and pressed it against the seam until he felt it give. Something small, black, and insubstantial—like a shadow—flew out of the widening crack. Startled, Will leaned away; the shadow veered out the back window and vanished.

Will pried the crack apart. Inside he found no flesh or blood, sinew or bone. Only wires and circuits. The bird was some kind of complex machine. And its cold blank eye looked a lot like a camera lens—

There was a sharp knock at his door. The doorknob turned. "Will, honey, are you all right?" asked Belinda just outside. "I heard something break."

"I dropped a glass," he said. He stood motionless, waiting for the door to open against the chair and give away that he'd blocked it. "I'm just cleaning up."

She paused. "As long as you're all right. Be careful. Dinner's ready."

He listened as she moved down the stairs, then grabbed a hand towel from the bathroom and folded it around the bird. As he came back into his bedroom, he heard a car outside. Through the window that looked toward the front of the house, he saw a familiar set of headlights coming slowly down the street.

It was Dad's car, but after viewing that video, Will had no idea who would be behind the wheel.

That decided it. They'd rehearsed the drill as a family countless times: two minutes to drop everything and run. Will threw first-aid supplies into his kit bag, then hurried to the bedroom and pulled out his cross-country duffel. He dropped the kit bag in with some clothes: jeans, T-shirts, his best sweater, a bomber jacket, underwear, and socks. His iPhone, iPod, MacBook, power cords, sunglasses, and the bird in the towel went in as well. He set the wedding photo of his parents on top. He grabbed a hundred and forty-three bucks—emergency savings—from a hidden slot in his desk and tossed in the Swiss Army knife.

#77: THE SWISS ARMY DOESN'T AMOUNT TO MUCH, BUT NEVER LEAVE HOME WITHOUT THEIR KNIFE.

He added the worn notebook with the black marbled cover; over the years, he'd collected Dad's rules in it. He pulled Lillian Robbins's business card from the school packet, memorized her number, then stuck it into his wallet. He stuffed the packet into the bag with his wallet and passport, and zipped it shut.

Will crouched by the front window as Dad's battered Volvo station wagon rolled to a stop in front of their house. The passenger and back doors opened, and three men wearing black caps exited. The driver's side door opened, and Jordan West stepped out. The Black Caps surrounded him as he looked up at the house.

Is that really Dad, Will thought, *or does he have a scar on his neck like Mom?*

As Will watched, one of the men brought out a steel carbon-fiber canister the size of a thermos, just like the one Will had seen that morning in the window of the black sedan. Another shoved Jordan toward the house. Jordan turned and pushed the man away, and that's when Will knew in his heart that the man he was looking at was still his father: *He's only cooperating because they told him I'm here. Whatever they did to Mom, they haven't done it to him yet.*

Will took five seconds to look around his room. At every possession he'd cherished enough to keep through fifteen years of life with his parents.

Remember what Dad said: "I'll come for you."

Will had to believe that now. He stepped silently to the broken window. As he heard the front door open below, Will slung the duffel over his shoulder and climbed onto the roof.

"Do whatever you need to do to stay alive."

Will swung over the edge of the roof and lowered himself, hanging on to a downspout. Keeping away from the windows, he dropped silently to the ground. He figured he had three minutes, at most, before the strangers made their way upstairs and forced open his bedroom door.

LEAVING SHANGRI-LA

Out the back gate and onto the road, Will ran into the welcome cover of darkness. He started his stopwatch and then booked it toward town for the second time that day. No limits. Even faster than this morning. Faster than ever. Running for your life is a hell of a motivator.

Three minutes to get a head start.

#2: STAY FOCUSED ON THE TASK AT HAND.

They'd get into their cars and spread out to look for him. If they missed him, Belinda could notify the cops: Post an Amber Alert about a missing kid and you can roll out the army, navy, air force, and marines, as well as local police. They might even set up roadblocks at both roads leading out of Ojai Valley. How long before that happened?

Half an hour at most. He might reach the western exit on foot by then, although if he stayed in the open, they'd eventually find him. But these people didn't really know him and that was his advantage. They had no idea—and maybe he didn't yet, either—just how resourceful and determined Will West could actually be.

Trust your instincts and training. Hold nothing back.

He swung the duffel off his shoulder, pulled out his iPhone as he ran, and punched in the number that he'd memorized. She answered on the third ring.

"Lillian Robbins."

"Dr. Robbins, it's Will West."

"Hello, Will. You sound a little out of breath."

"I'm out on a run at the moment."

"Always helps to clear your head, doesn't it?"

"Sometimes more than others," said Will.

"How was the rest of your day?" she asked.

"You were right—I've had a lot to think about."

"So how can I help? Do you have any questions?"

"As a matter of fact, I do. Where are you now?"

"In my car, driving back to the Center. I flew out this afternoon and landed here about an hour ago."

So much for hitching a ride out of Dodge with the doctor.

"How quickly do you think I could start?" asked Will.

"At the Center? Does that mean you're accepting?"

"Yes."

Will reached the end of the road where it dead-ended into the hills. He turned left and flew down the slope toward town, picking up speed, even faster than he'd run that morning.

Where's Spooky Hot Rod Dude now that I really need a lift?

"First let me say, Will, that I am really pleased," Dr. Robbins said. "And to properly answer your question, our next semester begins in January. We'd encourage you to transfer then."

"This is going to sound a little strange."

"Try me."

"I'd like to start tomorrow." All he heard was his own breathing as he sprinted down the hill. He lowered the phone, powered around a corner, then brought it back up: "I told you it would sound strange."

"I've heard stranger," she said. "But not many. So you'd like to transfer in effective immediately."

"Is that possible?"

"Well, we have your transcripts. I assume your parents are on board; this is a family decision?"

"One hundred percent."

"They've signed the consent forms, filled out all your paperwork?"

Note to self: Next free moment, forge their signatures. "I have them with me."

In the distance, Will heard the deep bass purr of an approaching helicopter. Then sirens. He looked at the stopwatch: *Four minutes. That was fast.* Cops would be all over Ojai soon, then the Ventura sheriff and CHP. *Unless I stay ahead of them.*

"You also mentioned that you'd pay my travel expenses," he said.

"That I did."

"So if it's not too much trouble, I'd like to catch a flight tonight."

She hesitated. "Will, is everything all right on your end?"

Will hesitated, too. "That needs to be part of the longer conversation you wanted us to have."

He had reached the edge of town in record time, skirting the north end of the business district, all the shops closed for the evening. He stopped a moment and leaned back against a wall on a dark side street and took a deep breath. By her silence, he sensed she needed more convincing.

"You helped me today," he said quietly. "Helped me realize that I need a . . . really, really big change in my life."

Another pause.

"I didn't ask for this," Will continued. "This morning I didn't even know the Center existed. You came looking for *me*. So what difference does it make if I start tomorrow or seven weeks from now?"

"It doesn't make any difference, Will. It's just . . ." She trailed off.

Time to play his last card.

"By the way, about that test in September? They gave us three hours to finish, and I spent at *most* twenty minutes on it. The truth is, I wasn't even trying."

Will heard the helicopter droning closer, making a sweep toward town.

"And what's up with the fingerprints and DNA sample you took this morning with your magic chalkboard? You want to tell me why a school needs *that*?"

"Is that what you think it was?"

"I'm saying I don't *care* what it was. You want me there, and my answer is yes. I wouldn't be asking if I didn't really need this."

"Tell me what you need . . . exactly."

"A plane ticket. From the closest airport that'll get me there. Right now."

She paused, then said, "I want to help, Will, but I need to talk to the headmaster's office. Can I call you back in five?"

"Yes."

She clicked off. More sirens wailed in the distance, drawing in from three directions. He had stopped across from the local taxi office, a small company that serviced the Valley and ran shuttles to southland airports. Their storefront was lit up inside, but empty. A yellow minivan with the company's logo sat at the curb.

The white-hot beam of the helicopter's eye-in-the-sky flicked over buildings and the tops of trees a block away. Will broke from cover and crossed the street to the taxi company. An old-fashioned bell jingled as he entered.

A stocky Latin guy with a billy-goat beard walked out of a back room. Elaborate tattoos peeked out from his sleeves and neckline: barbed wire, the edge of what looked like feathered wings, the tip of a spear. The embroidered name tag on his company polo shirt read NANDO.

"That's a sound you don't forget," said Nando. "You don't want to be tracked by one o' those bogeys."

Will unglued himself from the wall and stepped to the counter, smiling harmlessly, trying to channel his best inner chess club nerd.

"Boy. Yeah. Really," said Will. "What's up with that? Hi."

Nando looked him up and down. "How's it goin'?"

"Good, good. So, uh, how much is it for a ride to the airport?"

"LAX is forty dollars; Santa Barbara, twenty. Which one you need?"

Will held up his phone. "I'm waiting to find out. Would it be okay if we left now and I told you which one on the way?"

"No, man. That's totally uncool."

"How come?"

Nando crossed his arms and pointed to either side: "Different directions, dude."

"But I'll know before we have to decide which way to turn."

"If it's LAX, I just quoted you the four-passenger price. But we're not supposed to launch that ride without a full cabin."

"Is anyone else going to LAX?"

"Not right now."

Nando stood his ground, expressionless and unyielding as an Easter Island rock head. He even looked like one. The sirens were getting louder.

"What's the one-passenger price?" asked Will.

"You take math? What's four times forty, bro?"

"I get your point. I could give you sixty-five." Almost half his entire reserve.

"Wouldn't hardly pay for the gas, my friend."

"See, the thing is, I just found out my dad was in a really bad accident, so I got to get a flight out tonight and I'm just waiting for Mom to figure out which airport and call me back."

Nando paused, skeptical. "So where is he now? Your dad."

"Intensive care. In San Francisco. That's where it happened."

Nando frowned. "Sorry, little dude. That totally sucks."

A police car—siren howling, lights flashing—zipped by outside. Will pretended to bury his face in his sleeve and hide a tear, turning away from the window. His iPhone rang. He looked at the screen: DAD.

"That your moms?" asked Nando.

"No. Wrong number." He put the phone in his pocket and kept a hand on it.

"I just work here, a'ight? The boss man's in Palm Springs tonight."

"So?"

"So screw company policy, holmes. We gotta get you to an airport."

Nando grabbed keys from under the counter and led the way to the door. Will followed him outside, scanning the street for pursuers. Nando pressed a key fob and the minivan's side door slid open. Will hopped in back and sank down in the nearest seat. Nando climbed behind the wheel and fired up the engine.

"What's your name?" asked Nando.

"Will. Will West."

"Will. Trying to help your pops while he's lying there all messed up in some distant city? That's awesome."

"Thanks, Nando."

"I love my pops, too, man. And if I knew he was like shot or stabbed or taken down on some kind of bogus weapons charge, I would do whatever it took, just like you, to be by his side."

Nando steered away from the curb. As they turned onto the highway leading west out of town, two more patrol cars raced by, sirens wailing.

"Man, what is up with the po-po in our sleepy town tonight? We brought our baby girls up here from Oxnard to get away from junk like this, know what I mean?"

Will noticed a photo of a sturdy young woman holding two chubby babies in a glittered frame on the dash. A jiggly plastic hula dancer and a pair of fuzzy black dice hung from the rearview mirror, which glowed in the dark.

"Yes, I do," said Will.

"I got some Chumash in me, from my momma's side. You know, the Indians? This used to be our hang, so no wonder, right? Love this town, man. It's paradise. They shot this movie up here, long time ago, 'cause they said it looked like that place, what's it called . . . that old group did the song 'bout that biker dude and his old lady."

"Shangri-la," said Will.

Nando snapped his fingers. "The Shangri-Las! *My boy-friend's back and there's gonna be trouble—*"

"Hey-na, hey-na—"

"And in the *movie,* Shangri-la is this mystical valley with this tribe of blissed-out ancient dudes who all look thirty-five. Except you find out they're all like five hundred 'cause they don't ever stress or freak out about nothin'."

"It's from a book called *Lost Horizon,*" Will said. "My dad told me about it when we moved here. That's the name of the movie, too."

"I gotta check that out. You think it's on DVD?"

Will's phone rang. He looked at the incoming number: Dr. Robbins's cell.

"That your moms?" asked Nando.

"Yes," said Will, and answered, "I'm here."

"There's a flight from Santa Barbara to Denver at eight forty-five," said Robbins. "That's the only way I can get you out tonight. Can you make that one?"

"Yes."

"We'll have a ticket in your name waiting at the counter."

"Thank you, really. You have no idea—"

"It gets in at eleven. We're still working on a red-eye from Denver to Chicago, but I'll have that by the time you reach the airport. A car and driver will meet you in baggage claim at O'Hare in the morning . . . and, Will?"

"Yes?"

"The headmaster and I both want to discuss this, in detail, when you arrive."

"Of course. I'll see you then."

"Have a safe trip," she said.

Robbins ended the call, but before he hung up, Will added, for Nando's benefit, "Love you, Mom. Always and forever."

"Which way we headed?" asked Nando.

"Santa Barbara. Eight-forty-five flight."

"Got you covered, bro. And don't worry about your old man, okay? He's gonna pull through fast once he knows you're there for him."

Will leaned back and took some deep breaths. He was starved, shaking with exhaustion and stress. As they drove out of town, he watched the lights of Ojai fade behind them, wondering if he'd ever see them again.

What would the Mystic 8 Ball say about that? *Outlook not so good.*

A ping from his iPhone: a new voice mail. Will plugged in his earbuds and hit PLAY. Dad's voice. Low and controlled.

"We're really worried about you, son. It's not like you to run off like this. But I want you to know we're not upset with you. If it has to do with this new school, we would never force you to do something like that. Your uncle Bill went away to school and he had a great experience, but it has to be up to you. Just let us know you're okay. That's the only thing that matters. Before you do anything, or go anywhere, please talk to us first."

The message ended. Will didn't have an uncle Bill. Will felt a huge wave of relief: Dad was still Dad. And he was telling him, *It's not safe here. Keep running.*

"Will, you want to listen to the radio, man?"

"I'm good for now, Nando."

"You hungry? I got water and trail mix in the console."

"That'd be great."

Nando handed back a bag of trail mix and a cold bottle of water. The trail mix had berries and flecks of yogurt mixed in. Will scarfed it down and chased it with the water. Just then, brake lights lit up ahead of them and traffic began to slow.

"Yo, Will, Highway Patrol's setting up a checkpoint before the turn to Santa Barbara. In case that means anything to you."

Will leaned forward to look. Traffic had come to a stop. They were ten cars away from three CHP cruisers turned sideways, blocking both lanes headed south.

"What should we do?" asked Will.

"If you're gonna make your flight, we can't get caught up in a situation here. Between the seats, on the floor behind you, see a black strap?"

"I see it."

"Pull on it. Yank it up. Hard."

Will undid his seat belt and grabbed the strap. On his second pull, the floor lifted, revealing a storage well big enough for two suitcases. Or a medium-sized person.

"Hop in," said Nando.

"What?"

Nando turned and looked at him calmly. "If I'm crazy and the cops aren't looking for you, then stay in your seat. I'm cool either way."

Will took in Nando's steady, untroubled gaze and thought, *Can I trust you?*

"Yes," said Nando.

"What?"

"Yes, you'll fit. Should be room for your bag, too. What's your cell number?"

Will told him. He pressed his duffel down into the well on a patch of carpet covering the floor, then curled his body around it. A tight fit, but he just squeezed in.

"Pull down the strap and hang on to it," said Nando. "Mute your phone and put your earbuds in. Gonna hit'chu on the cell."

Will pulled the hatch closed and disappeared in darkness. He thumbed on his phone, filling the well with faint white light. Black molded metal boxed him in all around. He heard the van inch forward, tires crunching on pavement just below him. Will's phone buzzed. He answered, then heard Nando's voice in his ears.

"Four cars to go. Chill now, we got this. Gonna put this on speaker."

He heard Nando set the phone on the console and switch on a Lakers game. Every twenty seconds, the van rolled forward a few more feet. Will slowed his breathing, closed his eyes, and focused on what he could hear: a power window opening, traffic moving north toward Ojai. They rolled forward and stopped one more time. He heard footsteps, then an authoritative male voice.

"Where you headed tonight?"

"Got a pickup at LAX, Officer."

"Would you lower your rear windows, please?"

"Of course, sir."

Will heard Nando power the windows down and the scrape of the patrolman's boots as he stepped toward the rear of the van.

"The roads closed up ahead or anything?" asked Nando.

"No," said the patrolman.

Will heard a second set of footsteps. Something rolled beneath the van. He pictured a wheeled security inspection device with angled mirrors. It stopped directly under the well where he was lying.

"Are you carrying a spare tonight?"

"Always, sir," said Nando.

"I'm going to need you to step out of the car, sir."

Will coiled tensely, expecting a hand to bang on the well and order him out. But the silence was shattered instead by a sound that set his heart pounding—a raucous, unmuffled V-8 roaring up behind them on the highway. It accelerated wildly as it raced at them. There was an eerie pause, followed by a massive shattering crash; then the engine growled away. On the far side of the checkpoint.

"Whoa," said Nando.

The Highway Patrol officers yanked their mirror from under the van and ran, shouting into their radios. Moments later, their cruisers peeled out, sirens screaming as they gave chase to the south.

"Hang tight," said Nando into the phone. "We're back on the move." The van edged forward, slowly picking up speed. "You should've seen it. That was crazy."

"A hot rod doing about ninety that jumped the roadblock?"

"Dude went Evil Knievel on 'em. Airborne, baby! Over three

cruisers, sticks a landing on the *roof* of a fourth one, rides down the hood onto the highway, and takes off like a rocket, and the whole time I'm like, *Are my eyes seeing what I'm seeing?*"

Will heard the turn indicator. The van eased to the right, and he knew they'd branched off onto the road that would take them northwest to Santa Barbara.

"Come on out, Will. All clear."

Will pushed open the hatch, stretched out a cramp, and settled back in his seat. They were alone on the road now, moving through the dark.

"So you seen that Prowler before?" asked Nando, glancing at him in the mirror.

"Earlier today. In town."

Will heard a ding in his earpiece. He looked at the phone. Words appeared:

GET AWAY. FAST. I'LL FIND YOU.

Not a text. Just big block letters, by themselves. From Prowler Man?

"Who is that guy?"

"I have no idea," said Will. "Think they'll look for me at the airport?"

"They're gonna be chasing that Prowler for a while. Dude's probably in downtown Oxnard already. Waiting at the drive-through for In-N-Out."

They both laughed a little. As the words on Will's phone faded, it hit him: *Prowler Man's Australian. That was the accent I couldn't place.* Then another question: *Do I want him to find me?*

"Turn off your phone, right now," said Nando. "No more calls."

"Why?"

"There's a GPS in there, my friend. You call or text while you're hooked into the network, they'll ping your IP address off the closest relay tower. Track you down to the inch."

"I didn't know that."

"Nobody's supposed to know that. Heavy-duty Big Brother stuff. They can tag any conversation, trace texts, find you anytime they like. You can use the camera or calendar and stuff, long as you're not on the network. But no calls."

Will turned off his phone, feeling a lot more vulnerable.

"You tell anybody else where you're going tonight?"

"No," said Will. "Think we're okay?"

"Think we got us a clean getaway," said Nando.

He kept them at the speed limit as they twisted and turned through the hills around Lake Casitas. Will fought a powerful urge to close his eyes, then remembered:

#41: SLEEP WHEN YOU'RE SLEEPY. CATS
TAKE NAPS SO THEY'RE ALWAYS READY
FOR ANYTHING.

Will woke thirty minutes later fully alert and surprisingly refreshed. They'd merged onto the interstate, heading north along the coast near Santa Barbara. He saw foamy whitecaps to their left, moonlight glinting off the open sea, and distant offshore oil platforms lit up like Christmas trees.

"When you get to the airport," said Nando, "buy a plain black bag and switch your stuff into it. The one you're carrying now's got your school name on it. Lose the team sweatshirt, too. Pick up something touristy at the gift shop and grab a new lid. Yank the brim down low so it's harder to see your face on security cameras."

"Okay."

"You'll still need photo ID to get on the plane. Too late to trick out a fake, but as long as your name's not in the TSA system yet, you're good to go. If it is . . . that's where the rubber meets the road."

They turned off the freeway, following signs to the airport. Nando took a no-frills Nokia cell phone and charger from the console and tossed them back to him.

"Use that one to make any calls for now," he said.

"Are you sure? I don't want to take your phone—"

"Don't worry. It's not exactly mine, know what I'm saying? It's got a camera and you can text using the number pad."

When they turned into the airport, Will took out his wallet.

"Put that away," said Nando. "Your money's no good with me."

"But I got to pay you, Nando. What are you going to tell your boss?"

"How's he ever gonna know? I got you covered, *esse*. Gonna find me a fare heading back the other way and charge 'em double."

They laughed again. Nando slid to the curb in front of the Spanish-style terminal a few minutes before eight. The side door slid open.

Will hesitated. "Why'd you help me, Nando?" he asked. "You didn't have to do any of this."

Nando turned to face him, his big brown eyes wide and solemn. "Glad you asked me that," he said. "When I was out back, right when that chopper flew over? I heard this voice in my head. Like I went into some kind of trance and this voice mixed in with the sound of the blades. It told me the next person who walked through my door was going to be this really important person. Like in human history. That they needed my help and I better step up big-time. Or it could mean the end of the world."

Will gulped. "Really?"

"No, I'm just messing with you, holmes!" said Nando. "Who you think you are, LeBron James or something? Ain't you heard? *He's* the Chosen One. I got'chu good, though, right?"

"Yeah, you got me."

Nando's smile vanished instantly. "I am totally serious, *cabrón*. I heard a voice."

"Okay, you're freaking me out now."

"But I wouldn't have listened to it if I didn't like you, man. You got an honest face." They shook hands and Nando gave him a business card: NANDO GUTIERREZ, OJAI TAXI COMPANY. "You call me when you get there. Lemme know you and your pops got hooked up, 'kay? Promise me now. I wanna hear from you."

"You will."

"*Vaya con Dios,* my friend," said Nando.

"And you tell Lucia and Angelita for me that they should be very proud of their dad," said Will as he climbed out.

"Thank you," said Nando. "Wait, I don't think— I never told you my daughters' names, man."

"No?" said Will as he waved and walked away.

"Okay, that's a little strange, man. How'd you know that? Hey, how'd you know that?"

Will just shrugged. He actually *didn't* know how he knew, but he did. He shouldered his duffel and headed for the terminal.

#28: LET PEOPLE UNDERESTIMATE YOU. THAT WAY THEY'LL NEVER KNOW FOR SURE WHAT YOU'RE CAPABLE OF.

Two minutes after Will went inside and Nando drove away, a black sedan pulled up to the curb.

DAVE

As Dr. Robbins had promised, Will's reservation to Denver was in the system at the ticket counter. She'd also booked a connecting flight to Chicago, on another airline, that left Denver about midnight. Will showed the agent his passport. She handed over his boarding passes without any questions.

He stopped at a gift shop before security and bought a cheap black carry-on, a gray sweatshirt, and a blank baseball cap. In the men's room, he changed into the sweatshirt, took everything out of his duffel, and packed it into the new bag. He had just enough room left to stuff the duffel inside before zipping the new bag shut. He pulled on the cap, checked himself in the mirror, and walked back out.

The terminal was nearly deserted; he was booked on one of the last flights out. Will showed his pass and ID to a weary female TSA guard at the security entrance. She glanced at him, stamped his pass, and waved him between a set of ropes that led around a corner. Will had only been on a plane twice and not since before 9/11, when he was a little kid. Whenever his family moved, they always traveled by car.

A stack of plastic trays waited beside a long stainless-steel table that fed a conveyor belt through the X-ray machine. The businessman ahead of him slipped off his loafers, watch, and belt, dumped them in a tray, and laid his coat on top. He set his carry-on, cell phone, and laptop in a second tray and nudged them onto the conveyor. The tag on his carry-on read JONATHAN LEVIN.

Will stepped to the table and copied the man's moves. Levin waited behind a white line in front of a metal detector. He handed his pass to the TSA guard manning that post, a scrawny redneck straight out of a country-western song, with squinty eyes and tattooed ropy forearms. He looked from the pass to the man a few times, taking his job way too seriously, then handed back the pass and waved Levin through.

Will looked behind him. Two men in black caps and jackets were walking toward security, looking around. They hadn't spotted him yet.

Will tugged down his cap and stepped to the white line.

Maybe it's a random check and they don't know I'm here. Maybe they can't follow me once I get through security.

As his trays entered the X-ray machine, he remembered he'd left his Swiss Army knife and the metallic bird in his bag. Both would start a conversation he couldn't afford to have. He looked at the young female attendant watching the X-ray monitor.

Trust your training.

When Will was little, younger than five, his parents discovered that he had an unusual and startling ability—he could "push pictures" at people from his mind straight into theirs. His mom first realized it when images began popping into her mind—a toy, a drink, a cookie. Ultimately, she realized Will was trying to tell her what he wanted.

Since then, his parents had worked with him to develop the skill, as a game at first, then more seriously. They had also taught him never to use his power on anyone, because it was ethically wrong and because it violated Rule #3: DON'T DRAW ATTENTION TO YOURSELF.

Unless he was in extreme danger. Like right now.

Will felt like his heart was going to beat right out of his chest as he stared hard at the girl behind the monitor. He'd never tried to push an image into anyone's head other than his parents'. The girl stopped the belt with Will's bags in the heart of the machine and leaned in for a closer look.

A toothbrush. An alarm clock.

Will concentrated, silent and trembling, and pushed those pictures at her. He *felt* them land. *Toothbrush* and *alarm clock* replaced knife and bird.

A moment later, the attendant leaned back and advanced the belt. Will's trays appeared at the far end. Relieved, he turned and came face to face with the redneck TSA guard, who was eyeing him coldly. He asked for Will's pass. Will gave it to him. The man examined it, then looked at him sharply. The hairs on Will's neck bristled.

The guard walked to the other side of the detector and waved Will forward. He stepped through without setting off any alarms. The guard pointed him to the right, toward an area screened and divided by portable partitions.

"Wait over there," said the guard.

Will had just been kicked up to another level of scrutiny. Between the time that he had checked in and now, the people chasing him must have gotten his name onto a watch list. The guard held Will's boarding pass as if it were a live grenade and walked into the maze of partitions. He showed it to a heavyset African American woman in a blue blazer. She glanced briefly at Will, her sharp eyes veiled with practiced indifference, then nodded the redneck toward a nearby computer.

He's about to confirm that my name is on a watch list.

Will looked back and saw the men in black caps outside security. Looking at passengers. He turned away. The guard leaned over the computer, his face turned ghostly white by the flickering screen.

Will focused his eyes on a single spot in the middle of the guard's scraggly unibrow. Will's pulse slowed. He "saw" his target. Felt a wave of heat shoot up his spine, flow around his throat, and rush up to create the image he wanted to push:

A picture of the computer screen with Will West *erased.*

It landed. The guard scrunched his eyes and blinked a few times. Will pushed another image at him, adding a name where his had been: *Jonathan Levin.*

The guard leaned in, like he couldn't believe what he was seeing.

Then, for the first time ever, Will tried to push words: *That's right. The guy who just cleared the checkpoint.*

The redneck's head jerked above the partitions, his neck swiveling like a prairie dog sentry. His eyes shot past Will to the businessman, dragging his carry-on toward the gates. The guard spoke to his supervisor. She lifted a walkie-talkie and issued orders. The redneck and other guards started after the businessman. Will held out his hand. The redneck gave back Will's boarding pass as he hurried past. Behind Will, police officers stepped in to close off the line to the metal detector.

Will put on his shoes and slipped his laptop into the bag. He glanced back. The Black Caps were gone. Maybe they hadn't even seen him. Will picked up his bag and walked away. Twenty steps later, he passed the petrified businessman being manhandled back to the checkpoint by the TSA posse, the sideburned redneck leading the way.

Will rounded a corner. Exhaustion buckled his knees. His vision faded to spots and dots. The room spun like he was about to black out. He stumbled into the men's room, dropped his bag, and grabbed a sink, holding on with both hands. He splashed water on his face and neck, which were hot to the touch.

So the mind pictures still work—stronger than ever—but using them kicks my ass. It took him five minutes to recover. Unsteady on his feet, he walked back into the terminal and bought two sandwiches from a snack stand. His flight had already begun boarding; a line formed at the Jetway.

He stepped onto the plane and found his seat two-thirds of the way back: window, right side, looking over the wing. He unzipped his carry-on and took out his iPod and earbuds. He considered checking his iPhone for messages, then remembered Nando's warning and thought better of it.

Boarding didn't take long; the flight was less than half full. Olds mostly, business drones in dull suits, zombied out and preoccupied. Will leaned back, closed his eyes, and tried to turn off the loop running through his head: *Who are these men, and what do they want with me and my family?*

#49: WHEN ALL ELSE FAILS, JUST BREATHE.

He turned on the iPod and clicked a mash-up Mom had given him to use for studying or meditation. Ocean surf and soothing nature sounds were mixed into low ambient musical phrases with pan flute, acoustic guitar, and light percussion.

The music helped. Will's hands relaxed their death grip on the arms of his seat. He needed to let go of the entire nightmarish day. Needed a quiet, uneventful flight to restore something like sanity so he could face tomorrow.

He barely noticed the voice at first, a deep baritone humming in tune to the music. It grew steadily louder but blended so seamlessly with the melody, he assumed it had always been in the mix and he'd never noticed it before.

Until it spoke to him. "Just breathe, nice and slow. Oldest trick in the book. That's the ticket, Will."

Low, gravelly, that same piquant accent. But the guy was in a decidedly better humor than earlier that evening, when he'd dropped Will off behind the house. "Stay in your seat, mate. Eyes closed. Don't give the game away."

Will's eyes flew open. The seat next to him was empty. So were the two across the aisle. He leaned over and looked up the aisle. Ten rows ahead, from an aisle seat, a man's hand signaled a thumbs-up. He wore a weathered leather flight jacket. A heavy black boot, laced with faded red flames, rested in the aisle.

Will shot back into his seat. *So much for an uneventful flight.*

"Steady on, now," said the voice. "Keep your cool and we'll be aces."

"Who are you?" whispered Will. "Why are you following me?"

"Can't hear you, mate. Doesn't work that way. Sit tight. Be back in a tick."

Will looked down the aisle again. The Prowler Man's seat was empty. *What was the* deal *with this whack job?*

One last passenger, a grotesquely overweight woman, wobbled down the aisle. She was bulging out of purple velour warm-ups and dragging a small floral-print carry-on. Thin greasy hair fell sloppily around a full-moon face that made her features look tiny. Darting, beady eyes located her seat, four rows in front of Will, across the aisle. She plopped down, panting with exertion.

A flight attendant's voice came over the speakers, saying they were ready for departure and that all electronic devices should be turned off.

Will yanked out his earbuds and switched off his iPod. The plane rocked back from the gate and cabin lights dimmed as they rolled away. Will looked again; Prowler dude still hadn't returned to his seat.

Maybe he's not real. I'm just imagining him. Some kind of holographic side effect of creeping insanity.

Will closed his eyes and pictured what he'd glimpsed earlier on the back of the man's jacket. A few images shifted in front of his eyes. One of them was the silhouette of an animal, but he couldn't nail it down.

The plane lurched forward, accelerating for takeoff, shoving Will back against his seat. The flaps pivoted down and the plane lifted sharply into the air. The city of Santa Barbara quickly receded, the coastline a necklace of lights. The plane banked out over the ocean, then turned back to the east. He wondered if their flight path would take them over Ojai.

Welcome but unexpected relief flooded through him. He'd escaped his pursuers, whoever they were, for the moment. He tried to quiet his mind and ride the euphoric high for as long as it lasted.

The plane leveled. A bell tone sounded. The attendant came back on the PA, saying it was safe to use electronics. Will popped the buds in and played the same song again. No voice this time. He raised the iPod to his mouth.

"Are you still there? Hellooo?"

"You look a bit daft talking into your iPod, mate. Folks'll think you've got loose kangaroos in the top paddock." Will still heard the man in his earbuds.

"Do you have any idea what I've been through today?" Will asked out loud.

"A good deal more than you know."

"I am *this* close—*this close*—to a complete, totally justified meltdown."

"Don't chuck a wobbly, mate. Slide your seat back. All the way—that's it, nice and easy."

Will eased back into his reclined seat. The man leaned forward; he was sitting one seat to the left behind him. Will saw his rugged profile less than two feet away, draped in shadow. His eyes were shielded by his aviator shades but the scars were there, a raised and livid road map crisscrossing the left side of his face.

"You're from Australia, right?" Will said.

"No, mate, I'm a Kiwi. *New Zealand.* Maybe you've heard of it."

"Of course I've heard of it."

"Bully for you. If you've shaken them, maybe this will be an 'uneventful' flight. There's some crooked weather ahead. Could give us a few bumps."

"So you do weather reports, too."

"A full-service operation."

"So who are you?"

"Name's Dave. From here on out, keep one eye peeled at all times. Expect the worst, hope for the best. Once they've got you in their sights, they never let up."

"Are you referring to the men in the caps, or those 'things' that tried to eat me earlier?"

Dave kept completely still as he talked. "Both."

"Can you at least tell me what those things were?"

"A species of three-legged lasher. I'd say either gulvorgs or burbelangs."

"Those New Zealand animals?" Will asked sarcastically.

"Don't carry on like a bloody pork chop, kid. I'm saying that's what they *looked* like. An opinion supported by the fact that I could actually *see* 'em." Dave tapped his dark glasses.

"And why would whatever they are be chasing *me*?"

"We obviously shouldn't open that particular can of worms at the moment—"

"Obviously in what way?"

"Obviously for reasons upon which it would currently be unwise for me to elaborate. Let me ask you this: Did you smell sulfur or smoke before they attacked? Did you see a round window in midair or a ring of fire—"

"A ring of fire. In the hills. I thought it was the sunset."

"No, mate. That was a High-Altitude Drop. Some of their heaviest nasties from the Never-Was. Dropped in from a great height like daisy cutters. Serious spagbog."

Will paused. "Do you speak a different language in New Zealand?"

"They have ships—airships. Not like ours. You can't see 'em, or only rarely—" Dave caught himself and sighed. "More than you need to know. The truth is, I just drew the mission this morning. Last minute, no proper briefing. Haven't even had time to review your file."

"My file?"

Dave took from his jacket pocket a small transparent glass cube. Inside floated a pair of gleaming black cubes. They looked like dice without dots, suspended in air, revolving at different angles and speeds from one another.

"That's my *file*?" asked Will.

Lights beamed from the black cubes, and three-dimensional images appeared above the large cube: two groups of hideous, slathering trilegged beasts.

"Those are burbelangs," said Dave, pointing at one group. "And those are gulvorgs."

"Good God."

"From here on out, Will, you'd better believe I've got your best interests at heart, or the mission could go south faster than a bucket of prawns in the sun—"

"If you think you're helping me by not telling me the *truth*, then you've got a lot to learn about me."

Dave stared at him hard for a moment. "Agreed."

"Can I see that?" asked Will, pointing at the cube.

"Not in this lifetime," said Dave.

The images vanished. Dave stuck the cube back into his pocket, leaned forward between the seats, and gave Will a longer, appraising look.

"Given the resources they've committed," said Dave, "we have to assume that you're their target. That's why I led them away. Took hours to shake 'em."

"So what kind of mission are you on?"

"Escort and protect. Just be grateful they didn't tag you with a Ride Along. Don't get me started on those beauties."

"What's a Ride Along?"

"That's what they turned your mum with, kid."

Will felt his stomach turn over. "What does that mean? Is she all right?"

"No way of knowing right now," said Dave with surprising gentleness. "I could delve deeper, into a great many things, but the last thing you need now is a lot of Level Twelve intel that could make your head explode."

"Then just tell me this . . . is my dad okay?"

"I'll try to find out. I need more information, and *you* need rest. Get some grub in your belly. Catch a few winks. If things turn 'eventful,' the only gear you'll need's in that pouch in front of you. Next to the in-flight magazine. Keep an eye out."

Will fished around in the seat-back pocket and retrieved a small, rectangular gray pouch. Inside he found a pair of medium-sized sunglasses with plain black retro frames. The lenses had a grayish blue tint like the ones Dave wore.

"How do these work?" asked Will, leaning back. "Is it like three-D?"

The seat behind him was empty again.

Will turned the iPod back up and heard only music: No Dave. He examined the glasses, then put them on. Everything looked exactly the same, only dimmer.

"It is totally possible that I've completely lost my mind," he muttered.

But he followed Dave's advice. He put the glasses away and ate both sandwiches, which were about as moist and flavorful as a drawing of a sandwich. When attendants rolled the beverage cart by, he took two bottles of water and drained them. He pulled the unfinished paperwork for the Center from his bag and filled it out. Then he carefully forged his parents' signatures on the appropriate lines.

Will closed his eyes and saw fractured images of his dad's ruined hotel room. Dad's last words kept circling back:

"We're responsible for this. And the idea that something we did would bring pain or sorrow into your life is the worst feeling your mom and I have ever known."

Responsible for *what*? What had they done? What kind of terrible price had they now paid for it?

About forty-five minutes into the flight—as they passed over the garish glow of Las Vegas—he managed to drift into a shallow, fitful sleep.

I spent the whole day dreading going to sleep again . . . or maybe because I couldn't wait. Then it felt like I tossed and turned for hours before I could let go. But once I finally dropped off, I was ready.

I found myself high in the night air, soaring through storm clouds, lit up by bolts of lightning cracking in the distance. I had no more of an idea where I was, but this time I seemed to know exactly where to find him.

I saw something small and dark sailing far ahead of me against the clouds.

An airplane.

SABOTAGE

A jolt of turbulence woke him. Will felt a presence to his left and turned, expecting to find Dave. Instead he found the obese woman in purple standing in the aisle, motionless, staring at him. Her face was in shadow; her eyes were pinpricks of dark, gleaming light.

"Can I help you?" Will blurted.

The woman blinked, inert, as blank as a stone. The smell coming off her, as if she hadn't showered in weeks, made Will's eyes water. Another jolt rocked the plane, harder this time, and they rode it as if cresting a wave. The woman's lips chewed around but no words came out. She turned and shuffled down the aisle with a peculiar waddling gait.

Will glanced around. There was no sign of Dave. Acting on instinct, he fished the sunglasses from his pocket, slipped them on, and leaned into the aisle.

Will saw a glowing nimbus of light around the fat woman, sickly and green, like flickering fluorescence. The outline of her body wiggled and squirmed like a bagful of angry cats, bulging out at nauseating angles.

Will lifted the glasses. The woman looked normal again. Or as close as five four and three hundred pounds stuffed into purple velour five sizes too small could get to normal. She walked past her seat to the lavatory, opened the door, and squeezed her bulk inside. Her hand shot out and yanked the door shut.

"Dave?" whispered Will. "Dave!"

No answer. Will grabbed the arms of his seat as lightning flashed in the distance, flaring a jagged skyline of ominous clouds. He looked at his watch: They were less than an hour from their scheduled arrival in Denver, flying over the Rockies now, closer to the storm.

A bell toned. A flight attendant announced that the captain had turned on the seat belt sign and everyone should return to their seats. Will fastened his belt and yanked it tight. Then he leaned over and looked down the aisle again.

Water or some kind of fluid was seeping out from under the lavatory door.

Will threw off his belt, stood, and moved forward. The floor rolled under him like a fun-house barrel. He reached the door and planted his feet on the soaked carpet. The status panel by the handle read OPEN. Will gripped the knob and quickly pulled the door open. Lights flickered beside the mirror.

Lying in a deflated pile, crumpled on the floor, were the woman's purple warm-ups. Fluids leaked from the arms, legs, and neck. The right arm of the suit extended into the toilet. A loud sucking sound filled the room from the bottom of the bowl, stuck open in the flushing position. That same nauseating smell he'd noticed before hung in the air.

He saw motion inside the suit. A shape the size of a football slithered from the torso, down the arm, and out the open commode. The purple suit collapsed and lay flat. Then, in a single move, something yanked the suit down into the hole and out of sight. Something fleshy and loose slithered with it; it looked like the discarded skin of an enormous snake, studded with tangled hanks of hair.

The disk in the toilet snapped shut. The sucking sound cut off. A flight attendant appeared behind Will, pulling the door from his hands.

"Sir, you need to go back to your seat," she said.

"I saw water coming out under the door," he said.

The attendant glanced at the wet carpet underfoot. The plane jolted. "We'll take care of it," she said. "Please go back to your seat. Right *now*."

Will saw no point in arguing. Using seat backs to steady himself, he worked his way down the aisle as the plane bucked and swayed.

"I might need to throw up now," he mumbled.

Will glanced back and saw the attendant shut the door and head toward her station. He passed the fat woman's row and saw her floral carry-on under the seat. He grabbed the handle and brought it with him to his own row as the plane dipped into a hard pocket of air. The cheap bag felt weightless. A price tag hung on the flimsy handle. He zipped the bag open. Empty. The roll-on was a prop. Had that pathetic creature even been a *person*?

"What did you see?" asked Dave.

The man was suddenly standing beside him. Will described what he'd seen.

"A Carrier," said Dave. "Bugger's luck, they snuck a Carrier on board."

Another flash of lightning—closer, brighter—drew Will's attention to the window. Sparks spit out from the rear of the engine below the right wing. He turned back to Dave, but he was gone. Will reached for the glasses in his pocket, put them on, and turned to the window.

After his shock wore off, he counted six of them. They looked like crazed animated sacks of cement or stunted life-forms dredged from the depths of the sea.

A Carrier: And these *are what she was carrying?*

Squat, repulsive, rubbery plugs of flesh. Bushel-basket mouths tangled with razor-sharp fangs. A sturdy curved horn shot from the center of each pale forehead between wide, pebbled white eyes. Four stout limbs sprouted from the ribbed, sec-tioned torsos, equipped with curved talons. Nightmarish crea-tures designed—or customized—for the purpose of wreaking mindless destruction.

Exactly what they were trying to do right now to the plane's right engine.

Will lifted his glasses. He saw nothing but the sparking en-gine and empty wing. Dropping the glasses back over his eyes, Will saw the awful writhing swarm again. He took off the glasses and turned them over in his hands.

Got to be some sort of projection system inside the frame that throws a moving image onto the lenses, Will thought. *I can't be seeing this. It's a trick, a special effect.*

But the frames looked solid and seamless, incapable of hiding technology sophisticated enough to manufacture what he was seeing. He was considering taking them apart with his Swiss Army knife when he heard an alarming, sputtering choke outside. A burst of sparks spewed from the engine, then a stream of dark smoke.

He fumbled the glasses back on. In a flash of lightning, he saw all six creatures attacking the engine housing in a frenzy, hammering away at it with tooth, horn, and claw. The plane dropped into another pocket of turbulence that lifted Will out of his seat. He refastened and tightened his seat belt. The creatures remained glued to the engine through every buck and tilt. Will realized their hideous torsos were studded with suction cups that clamped to the metal.

They were moments away from tearing the engine to pieces.

Will pushed the glasses up on his head, struggling to make sense out of madness. Somehow, somewhere, he found a string of logic:

They're related to the things that chased me in the hills. Monsters somehow set loose from the same twisted nightmare realm— what did Dave call it? The Never-Was.

Then Will remembered where he'd seen creatures like these. Devilish monsters attacking airplanes in flight. It didn't make any more sense than the rest of it but there it was, from an old cartoon set in World War II:

Gremlins.

Will turned to the window and saw his reflection in the glass. And something else. *Someone* else—*inside* his reflection— staring back at him.

A girl. Somehow she was out there; he *felt* her presence. Trying to *say* something to him.

The plane jolted, and the dark glasses dropped down over Will's eyes again.

A gremlin was pressed against the other side of the glass, staring at him with its blank white eyes. It pointed a talon at him, opened its mouth in an evil grin, and drew a finger along its throat. Then the thing gripped either side of the window and reared back, ready to thrust its horn straight through the glass. Will recoiled.

Something grabbed the loathsome beast from behind before it could strike. A hand closed around the creature's horn and yanked it away from the window. Dave was outside, standing on the wing. As the creature bucked furiously, Dave flung the thing out into space and out of sight, its limbs flailing.

Dave tossed a salute at Will, then drew a long-barreled sidearm from a holster under his jacket, some kind of hybrid handgun/rifle. He walked farther out on the wing, working to keep his balance but eerily unaffected by altitude, temperature, air speed, and every other principle of physical science that should destroy anyone in these circumstances.

Anyone human.

Dave stopped halfway to the engine, raised the gun, and opened fire on the hideous swarm. Bursts of light shot out the barrel, ripping holes clean through the creatures. One after another, they fell away into darkness.

Will watched through the window, his jaw hanging open.

The last two gremlins whipped around and launched themselves at Dave like missiles. He fanned the hammer, blasting one in midair, and it tumbled into the void. The survivor landed on Dave's right shoulder. Pincers snapping, it scrabbled around to the back of Dave's neck. He twisted after it but couldn't grab hold as it worked itself into position to stab its horn into the base of Dave's skull.

Dave holstered his weapon. He staggered to the front edge of the wing, dropped to his knees, and lay flat. Grabbing the wing, with one powerful thrust he drew up his knees and planted his boots on the wing's tapered rim. Struggling against ferocious g-forces, Dave slowly straightened his legs until he stood pointed straight ahead, parallel to the wing, leaning into the wind like a ski jumper. The creature on Dave's neck hung on desperately, unable to strike, pinned by the crushing wind.

Finding his balance, Dave turned 180 degrees until he faced skyward. The gremlin clung to him, fighting the pull from the engine's intake draft directly below. Then with a silent scream the gremlin was sucked down into the whirling grill of the jet's turbine. The engine stuttered and the whole wing flapped like a startled bird.

Will's stomach flipped over. He ripped the glasses off and held his head in his heads, gripped by feverish vertigo.

This can't be happening. This can't be happening!

He wiped sickly sweat off his forehead and forced himself to look outside. Dave was standing on the wing. He walked over to Will's window. Will watched through spread fingers, unwilling to let go of his head, afraid it might splinter into pieces.

Dave peered in at Will. He looked tired and annoyed. He held up two fingers in front of the glass and said something Will couldn't hear. He didn't have to: "That's *two*."

Dave shook his head, and then shot straight up into the clouds, out of sight, like he'd been launched from a cannon. Will yanked the shade down over the window, closed his eyes, and tried to imagine he was someone else, somewhere else.

Anyone, anywhere.

He'd had a good look at the round patch on the back of

Dave's jacket and tried to settle his mind by thinking about that. Three things inside it: The outline of that animal he'd seen was a red kangaroo. Beside it was a drawing of the helmeted head of a knight. The third was a silhouette of a helicopter. Printed above it was the word *ANZAC*.

And although he couldn't see her, that girl was still looking at him. From *inside* his mind. Her haunting eyes asking him a silent question:

Are you Awake?

DAN MCBRIDE

They landed in Denver forty minutes later without further incident. No one said a word as they shuffled off, grateful to be back on earth. Will's next flight was delayed an hour by the storm. That gave him time to cover his tracks.

He found another airline with a nearly empty midnight flight to Phoenix. He handed the tired ticket agent his boarding pass to Chicago and pushed a mind picture at her—of a pass for the Phoenix flight. Then another of his name on her computer's passenger list. She checked him in. He wandered away.

He did the same thing in reverse before boarding his flight to Chicago: the agent *voided* his name from the manifest. "Pushing pictures" was getting easier; this time he felt tired, but not drained. Once in his seat, Will put on the dark glasses and scanned the plane. All clear. With any luck, whoever was tracking him would think he'd taken the flight to Phoenix.

Within minutes, beyond exhausted, Will surrendered to a thick, dreamless sleep. He didn't stir for hours, until he felt the landing gear drop as they descended into Chicago.

Central standard time: 5:45 a.m. Will entered an empty O'Hare terminal. At baggage claim, an older white-haired man held up a message board: MR. WEST spelled in moveable type. He spotted Will, gave a wave, and started forward.

"Is that you, Will?" he asked.

"Yes, sir."

"Dan McBride, from the Center. I'm a colleague of Dr. Robbins. A genuine pleasure to meet you."

McBride locked eyes in a friendly, benevolent way. He stood six feet tall, upright and spry. His ruddy face looked as weathered and lined as that of a man in his seventies, but he moved with the energy of someone half that age. His handshake crushed Will's hand; he squeezed back defensively to avoid wincing.

"May I take your bag? And are you expecting any others?"

"No, sir, that's it," said Will, handing over his bag.

"We can move right along, then. The car's just outside."

McBride gestured to the doors and took the lead. He walked with a noticeable limp—a knee or hip problem—but powered through it as if he considered physical pain a minor inconvenience. Will heard the tart, astringent flavors of New England in his clipped and proper phrasing.

"How are you feeling?" asked McBride, as if he really wanted to know. "Rough night?"

"Does it show?"

"I'll wager most of your fellow passengers were business travelers, rushing to another meeting. At the risk of sounding like an academic fuddy-duddy, Will, the red-eye has always symbolized for me how worship of money makes us behave with utter contempt for our own humanity."

Will stared at him.

"That may have sounded a bit obtuse after a sleepless night on a plane."

"I understood you," said Will. "I just don't hear people talk like that much."

"Now, Will, plenty of folks on the West Coast speak perfectly good English."

"Yeah, but it'd be more like, 'The red-eye, dude—that blows chunks.'"

McBride laughed agreeably. It was still dark outside as they exited. A wall of cold walloped Will, bypassing his thin cotton sweats as if they weren't there. He inhaled sharply and his nostrils froze.

"We're in the grip of an early cold snap," said McBride. "You're not used to this sort of thing in California either."

"Is it always like this?"

"No, no, no. For the next five months it's usually much worse."

"What's the temperature?"

"As we drove in this morning, a balmy twelve degrees."

Will couldn't believe it: *"Twelve?"*

"Walk quickly; it'll get the blood flowing."

Will felt paralyzed. He'd never been in temperatures below thirty-six degrees before. He had trouble making his lips move. "I'm sorry, people actually *live* in weather like this?"

"I will now be the first, and far from the last, to recite one of my favorite canards about midwestern winters: They build character. Fiddlesticks. But, adaptable creatures that we are, you'll acclimate with a speed that will amaze you."

A blue Ford Flex stood at the curb, the Center's coat of arms on its side. An immense man in a fur coat and matching hat popped open the rear gate and came toward them like a building on wheels. He wore a big, irresistible smile. His wide, flat nose seemed to cover half his face. He took Will's bag and swung it into the back.

"Say hello to Eloni, Will," said McBride.

"Nice to meet you," said Will.

Eloni smiled broadly and cradled Will's hand in both of his, which felt like the world's largest catcher's mitt. Thankfully, he didn't squeeze. Will's bones would have been crushed to pulp.

"Brother, your hand's an ice cube. I got the heater running. Get in before you freeze. Never been in cold like this, huh?"

"Not even close."

Eloni chuckled, a rumble deep in his chest. Moving nimbly for such a huge man, he opened the rear door and gestured Will inside. "I know how you feel, Mr. West," said Eloni.

"Eloni is from American Samoa," said McBride.

"Closest to snow I'd ever seen was a snow *cone*," said Eloni.

Will hopped into the SUV's toasty interior. The seat felt plush and heated. Will pressed himself into its embrace and tried to stop shivering. Eloni moved to the driver's seat, while McBride climbed in beside Will.

"It's just coming up on six-fifteen, Will. We have a two-and-a-half-hour drive ahead. I thought we'd have breakfast on the way. Eloni, a stop at Popski's is in order."

McBride had a nice habit of rubbing his hands together when he spoke, then clapping them once to punctuate things, as if in constant prospect of improved circumstances.

"Popski's it is, sir."

Eloni guided them into the flow of early-morning traffic. The cabin felt as snug, safe, and still as a bank vault. As the heated seat returned feeling to his body, Will felt his troubles melt away. McBride's gracious hospitality gave him the same comfort of unqualified support he'd felt from Dr. Robbins.

Which boded well, Will thought, for where he was headed. No regrets, so far, about his decision.

#19: WHEN EVERYTHING GOES WRONG, TREAT DISASTER AS A WAY TO WAKE UP.

* * *

Half an hour later, they were huddled in a red leather window booth in a stainless-steel railroad-car diner called Popski's. It sat on a frontage road, a stone's throw from the interstate, surrounded by 18-wheelers. A feast crowded the table in front of them: stacks of pancakes as thick as paperback novels and laden with melting butter and hot syrup; a platter of perfectly fried eggs and fat, pungent sausages; waffles so big a toddler could have used them as snowshoes, smothered with plump blueberries; a pile of crisp, sizzling bacon; pitchers of fresh-squeezed orange juice; and pots of strong black coffee.

Will ate with a desperate craving. Every bite tasted better than any version of these foods he'd ever eaten, as if Popski's was the place where they'd invented breakfast and no one had improved on it.

"This place is unbelievable," said Will finally.

"The legend of Popski's is known far and wide," said McBride, "to every wayfarer who travels these lonesome roads."

"We say that a meal at Popski's," said Eloni, "can revive the dead."

Eloni gave out an astonishing belch that made them laugh.

Will tried to match it, and they laughed even harder. When he pushed his empty plate away, stuffed and satisfied, Will felt indeed as if he'd come halfway back to life.

Eloni paid the bill and McBride led the way back to the car. Properly fortified, Will felt less assaulted by the cold as they stepped outside, just as the sun peeked over the horizon to the east. He stopped to take in the austere beauty of the unfamiliar landscape, a flat, featureless gray-brown plain stretching to the horizon in every direction. It made Ojai seem like the Garden of Eden.

It had been only twenty-four hours since the last sunrise. In his own room, in his parents' little house, in a distant region of the country, in what now seemed an entirely different life. Will couldn't keep the loss and sorrow from his eyes.

"Not the easiest day for you in recent memory, I imagine," said McBride. "Is there anything else we can do for you?"

"What state are we in?" Will asked, changing the subject.

"Northern Illinois," said McBride. "We'll be in Wisconsin shortly. It's always wise to know what state you're in, isn't it?"

Will thought that over. "It's good to be alive," he said under his breath.

Within minutes they were back on the highway, heading north by northwest.

"Do you teach at the Center, Mr. McBride?" asked Will.

"Thirty years now. American history, nineteenth-century. My particular subject is Ralph Waldo Emerson. You're an athlete, aren't you?"

"Cross-country."

"Terrific. That'll give you the stamina for any sport. We encourage students to play as many sports as possible."

"I don't really know what to expect. This all happened pretty suddenly."

"So I'm given to understand. Whatever the circumstances, if you'll forgive me for dispensing advice, here you are: a new day. And you must make the most of it."

"That sounds like something my dad would say."

"I assume we should regard that as a good thing," said McBride.

Will didn't try to mask the sadness in his eyes before he looked away. McBride kept his gaze on Will, steady and kind.

"I know how hard leaving home can be," said McBride. "I was fourteen when I first boarded. Filled me with uncertainty, fear of the unknown. This may sound odd, but if you're able, Will, don't push these feelings away. Embrace them. They're yours, and part of you. They're here to teach you some of what you've come to learn."

"What would that be?"

"That's a question only you can answer. And probably not for some time."

They rode in silence. The landscape changed when they left the interstate for a smaller, two-lane highway. The road began to ramble through gently rolling hills covered with hardwood forests. Will's mind wandered back to the events on the airplane, landing again on the image he'd seen on the back of Dave's jacket.

"What does ANZAC mean?" asked Will.

"ANZAC?" asked McBride, puzzled. "What made you think of that?"

"Something I read on the plane," said Will.

"ANZAC is an acronym for Australian and New Zealand

Army Corps. An expeditionary task force from both countries. Formed in World War One."

"Does it still exist?"

"Absolutely."

Will saw McBride and Eloni exchange a look.

"Not even sure why I thought of it, to be honest," said Will.

At quarter past nine, they left the highway for local roads. Eloni executed a bewildering number of turns. Will caught a glimpse of the small town he'd seen online—New Brighton Township—and his senses sharpened. From there, the road threaded through hills dotted with distant barns and farm-houses. When they turned onto a long straightaway, Will rec-ognized the wooded lane leading to the school that he'd seen in Robbins's tour.

"Have a look, Will," said McBride.

McBride slid open a moonroof overhead. The trees were all stripped of leaves, but even their bare branches formed a thick canopy over the road.

"American elms and red oaks. Legend has it they were planted by the region's first people, the Lakota Sioux, to mark their sacred ground. Most are between three and four hundred years old, roughly the same age as our country. They were sap-lings when Washington and his men camped at Valley Forge."

At the end of the tree-lined drive, they stopped in front of a traffic gate beside a stone guardhouse. A large man in a tan uniform stepped out. Slightly shorter and less stout, the guard might otherwise have been Eloni's twin brother. The two spoke in low tones, in a language Will didn't understand—Samoan, he assumed.

"Say hello to my cousin Natano," said Eloni.

"Hey, how's it going, Mr. West?" said Natano. "Welcome to the Center."

Will returned his wave and saw that Natano wore a holstered automatic on his belt. Natano raised the gate, and Eloni drove through.

After cresting a short rise, they eased down toward a broad, bowl-shaped valley. Through the bare trees, Will got his first glimpse of the Center for Integrated Learning. The photographs he'd seen had not exaggerated its beauty; if anything, the campus looked even more perfect to the naked eye. Bright sun, clear blue skies, and glistening ivy gave the buildings of the main quadrangle a glossy glow. In the clipped hedges and pristine landscaping, not one blade of grass looked out of place. Through the commons between buildings, dozens of students moved along the graceful walkways. A flagpole stood in its center, flying an outsized Stars and Stripes that flapped taut in a steady breeze.

Will felt the same eerie sensation he'd experienced while looking at the website: He *belonged* here.

"Straight to Stone House, please, Eloni," said McBride.

They followed the road as it curved away from campus, past a broad gravel parking lot filled with cars, a fleet of SUVs, and school buses in silver and navy blue. Around the parking lot stood an assortment of smaller buildings bustling with activity, a vibrant, self-supporting community.

"These house our infrastructure," said McBride. "Laundry, kitchens, communications, transportation, power plants, and so forth."

They turned onto an unpaved lane that climbed through thick woods, until they passed through a notch between converging ridges into an open clearing. Directly before them, connected to one of the ridgelines, an immense, broad granite pillar rose sixty feet in the air. It looked as if giants had stacked colossal children's blocks.

Spanning the top of the column was a jaw-dropping structure. Crafted from soaring lines of wood, stone, and steel, the building looked as if it had grown naturally out of the ageless geological formation below. The house seemed ultramodern and at the same time stark and primitive. Defying an identifiable style, its elements conspired to form a unique, inspiring, and powerful creation.

"Stone House," said Will.

"No mystery about where it gets its name," said McBride. "Connected to the earth. Reaching for the sky. Fair description of a headmaster's job, isn't it . . . and this is where he lives."

STONE HOUSE

Will followed Dan McBride to the rock, past a steel staircase that curved around the column to the house above. They went under an arch carved in the rock and into a small foyer with an elevator. McBride pressed a button and the doors opened.

"This goes straight up through the boulders?" asked Will.

"Indeed. Our founder, Dr. Thomas Greenwood, was a great admirer of an architect named Frank Lloyd Wright. Have you heard that name before, Will?"

"I think so."

McBride followed Will inside and the doors whispered shut. Dark wood and mirrored glass paneled the interior. A phrase was engraved above the door:

NO STREAM RISES HIGHER THAN ITS SOURCE

"That's his saying. Wright opened a study center not far from here about a hundred years ago, called Taliesin. When Dr. Greenwood decided on this location, he consulted with Wright about Stone House. Nothing like it had ever been built in this country before. Like the Center itself."

Will caught the scent of damp concrete as they rose through the heart of the rock. He could feel the solidity of the granite around them—protective, somehow, rather than claustrophobic. The doors opened and they stepped into a reception area with concrete walls. A friendly white-haired woman waited to welcome them. Her name tag read MRS. GILCHREST. McBride called her Hildy.

She led them into an adjoining great room. The dimensions of the space overpowered Will's senses. Enormous rectangular windows rose up to an arched cathedral ceiling. Breathtaking views of the surrounding countryside—hills, valleys, a distant river—filled the windows on either side of the room. Clusters of solid, simple furniture hugged light hardwood floors. Vast tapestries hung on the walls, woven with what looked like Native American symbols and hieroglyphs. A stacked rock fireplace that climbed to the ceiling dominated the far wall, and a roaring fire blazed.

Lillian Robbins walked forward to greet them. She wore a black skirt and crisp white blouse, black leggings, and knee-high black boots. Her hair was down on her shoulders, longer and fuller than Will would have guessed. She gripped Will's shoulders with both hands and gave him a searching look.

"Are you all right?" she asked.

"Yes."

"I'm glad you're here."

"Me too."

Another man entered from a door near the fireplace. He was

tall and angular, with big hands and long, rangy arms. He wore brown corduroys, a battered shearling coat over a pale plaid shirt, and riding boots, weathered and muddied, like he'd just climbed off a horse.

"This is our headmaster, Dr. Rourke," said Robbins.

He had an outdoorsman's face, broad and tanned, and piercing blue eyes framed by a full head of tousled graying hair. Will guessed he was somewhere around fifty.

"Mr. West. Stephen Rourke." His voice was deep and agreeable.

#16: ALWAYS LOOK PEOPLE IN THE EYE. GIVE THEM A HANDSHAKE THEY'LL REMEMBER.

They shook hands: Stephen Rourke's were rough and strong, like a rancher's. Will saw nothing remotely "academic" about the headmaster. He looked like he could pick his teeth with a bowie knife and seemed as confident as a four-star general.

Rourke smiled at him. "You've had an interesting journey," he said.

"That I have, sir."

Dan McBride headed for the door. "All the best now, Will. See you soon."

"Thanks for your help, Mr. McBride."

McBride gave Will a crisp two-finger salute as he left. Robbins invited Will to sit on a sofa near the fire. A tray of fresh-cut fruit and rolls sat on a nearby table. Rourke poured coffee and sat down across from him.

"Did you finish the paperwork I gave you?" asked Robbins.

Will fished the papers from his bag and handed them over. She paged through them, while Will tried not to watch. Rourke casually studied him.

"In many cultures, including our local Oglala Lakota," said Rourke, "to *wish* anyone an 'interesting journey' is considered something of a curse."

"I'd have to say my last twenty-four hours have been . . . interesting," said Will.

Robbins looked up from the papers and gave Rourke a nod: *Everything in order.*

"What would you like to share with us about it, Will?" asked Rourke.

TELL NO ONE.

Will wanted to honor Dad's warning, but he also felt he owed them an explanation. He was here and, for all he knew, still alive because of their timely help and interest in him. But the *whole* truth—Dave, doppelgänger parents, gremlins, and special sunglasses—wouldn't buy him anything but a room at the Laughing Academy with no handle on his side of the door.

#63: THE BEST WAY TO LIE IS TO INCLUDE PART
OF THE TRUTH.

"My parents wanted me to come here right away. As soon as I could. Today. Because they thought I was in danger."

Rourke and Robbins exchanged a look of concern. Rourke leaned forward. "What sort of danger, Will?" he asked.

"They didn't say exactly, sir. But there were people looking for me yesterday, in our neighborhood, that we'd never seen before."

"Describe them for me."

"I didn't see them up close. Men in black cars, with un-marked license plates."

"Do you have any idea who they were or what they wanted?"

"No, sir."

"Was this before or after I saw you at your school?" asked Robbins.

"I saw them once before, briefly, but mostly after."

"Did your parents contact the police?" asked Rourke.

"They did," said Will, as close to making a lie of the truth as he could manage. "After I left for the airport. That was when I called you last night, Dr. Robbins."

"So this was the reason for the urgency," said Robbins. "Your parents felt these people represented some kind of threat to you."

Will nodded. His throat felt too tight to speak. He poured more coffee and hoped they wouldn't ask too many more questions.

"Have you spoken with your parents this morning?" asked Rourke.

"Not yet, sir."

"You need to let them know you've arrived safely, Will. And I'm sure you'd like to know they're safe as well."

"I do. I would."

"Do you have any idea what this could be about?" asked Robbins. "Or what their interest in you might be?"

"None at all," said Will. Then he asked the question he'd had in mind all morning. "Do you?"

Rourke and Robbins looked at each other. He seemed to ask for her opinion. She shook her head.

"We don't," said Rourke. "What you've told us is more than troubling, Will. But we're not without resources here. I'm more than willing to investigate the whole situation if you think that would be helpful."

"Thank you, sir."

"I'm truly sorry you've been through this. Hardly the ideal circumstances for your arrival. A new student's first day should be a much happier occasion."

"I'm happy to be here anyway," said Will.

Right now—straight up—I'm happy to be anywhere.

"We're happy to have you," said Rourke. "First things first: You can use the phone in my office to call home. Follow me."

Dr. Robbins stood as well, holding up Will's paperwork. "I'm going to expedite this and get your admission finalized," she said, heading to the office.

Will followed Rourke into a smaller office next door. Heavy leather couches bracketed wagon-wheel tables in front of another blazing fireplace. A substantial oak desk sat on a riser in front of a picture window. A bronze sculpture of a Native American warrior slumped on the back of his pony filled one corner, the work of a famous artist whose name Will couldn't recall. Portraits faced each other on the walls, paintings of two tall imposing men, in clothes and settings from different eras.

"My predecessors," said Rourke. "Thomas Greenwood, our founder and first headmaster, and Franklin Greenwood, his son." Rourke pointed Will to a console phone on his desk. "Hit nine for an outside line, Will. I'll give you some privacy."

Rourke stepped out. Will wondered if anyone would monitor his call. They would at least have a record of any number he dialed and could check it against the ones he'd put on his application.

He weighed the risk of being caught in a lie against the chance that whoever answered at home might trace his call to the Center. He decided to place the call but spend no more than a minute on the line. He punched in his home number. The phone rang twice before a bland male voice he didn't recognize answered. Will started the stopwatch on his iPhone.

"West residence," said the voice.

"Jordan or Belinda West, please," said Will, dropping his voice an octave.

"Who's calling?"

"Who am I speaking with?" asked Will.

"I'm a colleague of Mr. West's."

He didn't sound like any colleague that Will recognized.

"Can I tell them who's on the line?" said the man.

"Supervisor Mullins, Office of Family Services in Phoenix, Arizona," said Will.

The man muffled the receiver, repeated that to someone in the room, and a moment later another hand took the phone.

"This is Belinda West." Will felt the same sick ambivalence when he heard her voice. This *was* her, and yet it wasn't.

"Mom, don't say anything, just listen," said Will in his own voice. "I'm all right, don't worry. I'm in Phoenix—"

"They said Family Services. Are you in some kind of trouble?"

"I'm fine. They're helping me. Are *you* all right? Is everything okay there?"

"No, Will, we're worried sick about you—"

"Who just answered the phone?"

She hesitated slightly. "Someone from your dad's office is helping us—"

"What's his name?"

"Carl Stenson. So are you coming home? Should we fly over there?"

"Let me talk to Dad."

"He's sleeping right now."

That's a lie. Will checked his iPhone: fifty-five seconds.

"I'm going to Mexico," said Will. "Don't come after me. Don't try to find me. I'll call in a couple of days."

He hung up, then called the main switchboard for the science department at the University of California, Santa Barbara. A receptionist answered.

"Hi, I work for the school newspaper," said Will. "I'm trying to reach someone in your department. Carl Stenson. I think he works with Jordan West." He pictured the receptionist scanning a list.

"I'm sorry, we don't have anyone here by that name."

"You're absolutely sure about that?" asked Will.

"Yes. Would you care to leave word for Mr. West? He's not in"—Will started to hang up—"but the police were here earlier and I know they've spoken with him."

Will froze. "That's what I'm calling about."

"You mean the break-in last night?"

"That's right," said Will, going with it. "In Mr. West's office?" He heard reluctance in her silence. "This can be off the record if you like."

"All of Mr. West's work was taken," she said, lowering her voice. "Files and two computers. They're going through everything now to see what else is missing."

"Do they have any idea who did it?"

"Not so far. If you—"

Will hung up. Stealing Dad's research, on the same night. It had to be the Black Caps. But why? Was that what this was all about? What could Dad have been working on that would justify all this?

Will pulled out a business card and, using the cell phone Nando had given him, tapped in the number.

He answered after the second ring: "This is Nando."

"Nando, this is Will, you drove me to the airport last night?"

"Young fella, how you doin'? I was just thinking about you. You make it to Frisco okay?"

"Yeah, just wanted to let you know."

"So how's your pops feelin'?" Will heard a horn honk. Nando shouted something away from the phone in Spanish. "Sorry, bro, I'm working here."

"He's better, thanks. But I'm probably gonna be here for a while and we've got kind of an odd situation. Could you do me a small favor?"

"Absolutimento, whassup?"

"My dad's worried somebody might try to break into our house," said Will.

"Your house here in Ojai?"

"Yeah. I forgot to lock up and the doctor says he shouldn't have any stress right now. Could you swing by and check so I can tell Dad everything's okay?"

"I'm all over it. What's the address, bro?"

Will told him.

"See you're using that phone I gave you," said Nando.

"Untraceable is the way to go, bro. Gonna check this out and get back to you pronto."

Will turned and saw Lillian Robbins in the doorway. He worried she'd overheard, but as she moved forward, he realized she was focused on something else.

"Got to go," said Will. "Thanks, Mom. Check in with you later." He pocketed the phone as Robbins reached him.

"I have to ask you about this before I bring it up with Mr. Rourke," she said, concerned. "What you told me last night about the test in September. That you deliberately tried to fail. Is that really true, Will?"

"I didn't *try* to fail, exactly. I just didn't try to succeed."

"But *your* score topped results across the board. How could that have happened if you weren't trying?"

"I don't know."

"Will, the bigger question it raises is, *Why* would you do a thing like that?"

She looked at him searchingly with genuine concern, so he told her the truth. "A rule my parents had."

"What sort of rule?"

The words felt painful to say. He had never really questioned before why Dad put Rule #3 on his list. But now all bets were off.

"Don't draw attention to myself," said Will.

Robbins spoke carefully. "Why would your parents want people to think that you're not as smart—*exceptionally* smart—as you actually are?"

"You're a psychologist, right? That's the kind of doctor you are."

"Yes," she said.

"Then you tell me," he said. "Because I don't know."

"They *explicitly* told you to hold yourself back, with no explanations?" she asked.

"All they ever said was, 'We have our reasons.' End of discussion."

Dr. Robbins thought for a moment. "And then, after scoring off the charts, you discover you're being followed."

"Yes."

"Maybe they had some genuine cause for concern," she said.

"Maybe." Will flashed on his plane ride from hell and thought, *You don't know the half of it.*

"I can promise you you're safe here," said Robbins. "We have a lot of high-profile families and we take security very seriously."

Before Will could respond, Stephen Rourke walked in and moved toward his desk, giving no indication that he noticed any tension between them.

"Did you reach your parents?" asked Rourke.

"I did, thanks," said Will. "They're okay and they were real glad to hear I got here safely."

"That's every parent's job, Will: to worry about their kids. That never changes."

Rourke referred to a notebook on his desk, jotted something on a pad, and then handed the note to Robbins. She read it without reaction as Rourke put a hand on Will's shoulder and guided him to a door at the far end of his office.

"Now, Will, I need you to hear an abridged version of the Headmaster's Address—the one I use at the start of every year to welcome our new students."

Through the door they entered a long, narrow corridor sided

with windows from floor to ceiling on either wall. Gusts of cold wind whistled through open windows along the top. The room extended straight out the back of Stone House, pointing west toward the campus, which he could see in the distance over the ridgeline.

"This was the final addition Thomas Greenwood made to Stone House," said Rourke. "An observation deck that connects the house back to the Center. He wanted it to give a specific sensation to anyone who came here. That they'd feel suspended not just in space, but also in time. So he called this the Infinity Room."

The floor shuddered with every step. Will shivered when he realized they were passing over thick windows embedded in the planks. He could see straight to the ground a hundred feet down; cars parked below looked like toys. There had to be struts connecting it to the rest of the building, but he couldn't see any. The Infinity Room felt like it floated in midair. His balance wobbled like a top.

"Dr. Greenwood had the unorthodox idea that a visit here would serve as a crucial reminder to students," said Rourke, "to remain alert at all times to the reality of the present. Because all we have is right now."

Dad couldn't have put it better himself. In fact, he *did* put it that way, *exactly*. Rule #6.

"Why?" asked Will.

"He believed experiences that create intense awareness tune the self to a higher consciousness, like a signal amplifier for the soul. And that one of the most effective ways to induce this state is the perception, as opposed to the *reality,* of danger. Your recent experiences might have given you a sense of this."

Maybe that's my problem. Danger put the zap on my brain.

Will's eyes felt like they were revolving in their sockets. His palms swam in a clammy sweat. He didn't understand it. Heights had never bothered him before, but this uncanny place made him want to drop to his hands and knees and crawl back out the way they'd come. He raised his head to avoid looking down. The corridor dead-ended ahead in a room filled with blinding light.

"That's why Tom Greenwood founded the Center a hundred years ago: to introduce the future leaders of our country to each other, but more importantly to themselves. Or to quote him: 'to their *future* selves.' Think about that."

Will nodded as if he understood—he didn't, really—and moved robotically forward, feeling more brittle with every step. He realized the room at the end of the corridor was a circular observatory. Built around a large, elaborate brass telescope.

"The world's always changing, Will. But now it's accelerating at a rate almost beyond our ability to comprehend. Each generation faces bigger challenges and more responsibilities. If the human race expects to survive, we can't just evolve with it. We have to evolve fast enough to stay *ahead* of that curve."

They stopped at the end of the corridor. The observatory chamber opened ahead like a globe attached to the end of a stick. The walls, the ceiling, and the entire floor below the telescope were all fashioned from clear glass bricks.

Rourke walked onto the nearly invisible floor: "Are you with me so far, Will?"

Adrenaline pulsed in Will's gut. Keeping his eyes on Rourke, he stepped inside. He felt like he was tumbling through open air. He reached the antique telescope and tried to anchor himself by focusing on its intricate workmanship. Anything to stop his head from snapping off at the stem.

"When you look around, wherever you might be on the planet, fifty percent of the people you see are below average. The rest are, for the most part, only slightly *above* average. I'm not suggesting there's anything wrong with being average, because there isn't. But as a mathematician, I can assure you these numbers don't lie. Exceptional people are, by definition, exceptionally rare. We also know, from studying human history, that every innovation or adaptation that's allowed us to leap forward as a species has been made by less than one-thousandth of one percent of the people alive in that moment."

Will felt close to freaking out entirely, in a way that would make the worst impression on the one man whose goodwill right now he could least afford to lose. He leaned in and looked through the brass eyepiece. Expecting a dim view of the daylight sky, he couldn't identify what appeared: Blurry globes and fuzzed-out splotches of color floated through his field of vision, like a slide of microbial life in a drop of water viewed through a microscope.

Then he realized: The telescope was trained on the commons in the middle of campus half a mile away. He was watching the magnified faces of students as if they were a few feet in front of him, moving in and out of focus like a kaleidoscope.

"And in *this* moment, because the stakes for survival keep edging higher, the need is greater than ever to identify and educate and prepare this tiny percentage within each generation who are capable of meeting our future challenges."

He can't be talking about me. This is some ridonkulus cosmic joke. I'm not up for saving the planet. I couldn't even save my parents.

"So as you look around today . . . and try to imagine, Will, that you're in our auditorium with the rest of the student body—"

"Okay."

"All of these young men and women, like you, possess the talent and potential to become exceptional. Uncommon people who will one day do uncommon things. And if we do *our* jobs correctly, by the time you leave here for the wider world, you will be ready to realize that potential."

For the briefest moment, Will caught a glimpse of his *own* face moving through the crowd. He adjusted the eyepiece, trying frantically to find "himself" again. Instead, a startling image seared his mind: *Every face in the crowd was his.* Will closed both eyes and held on.

"In the meantime, make new friends. Connect. Learn from each other, and *for* each other. Because one day, much sooner than you realize, this will become your world. Your generation's time to put your hand on the wheel and navigate the way. But not yet. Until then, enjoy this part of your journey. Make friends with your hopes and dreams as well as with each other."

The headmaster took out an old wooden pipe, filled it from a worn leather pouch, and lit it with a safety match that he struck on the telescope.

"Godspeed, go in peace and so on, and here concludes my opening address," said Rourke as he puffed the bowl to life. "That wasn't too terribly painful, was it?"

"No, sir."

The sulfurous snap of the match and the savory, sweet smoke from Rourke's tobacco filled the air. Will couldn't catch his breath.

"I'm the third headmaster in our history. I've given that speech fifteen times. The same speech Tom Greenwood gave to the first assembly of his inaugural class almost a hundred years ago, and to the other forty-three classes he welcomed. As did his son Franklin, who succeeded him as headmaster for thirty-eight years."

"Really," said Will.

"I like to picture Dr. Greenwood in those early days. Standing out here alone on a warm summer night. Gazing at the stars, lost in dreams about this bold experiment he'd brought into the world. Right here, in the middle of the heartland, on the edge of the great North American plains. When our country itself was on the cusp of first realizing its own potential. What a perfect place to dream."

What a perfect place to die, thought Will.

With that, he pitched forward, unconscious, and face-planted on the transparent floor.

BROOKE SPRINGER

Will heard soft classical music, then voices murmuring nearby. He opened his eyes and found himself lying on a bed in a dimly lit room. Shades of white and gray appeared as the room gradually came into focus.

"He's awake," he heard someone say.

Dan McBride sat by his bedside, regarding him with gentle concern. Lillian Robbins joined him a moment later. A young female nurse in a crisp white uniform appeared on the other side of the bed.

"Where am I?" asked Will.

"The infirmary," said McBride. "You gave us quite a fright, young man."

"How are you feeling?" asked Robbins.

His head ached sharply when he tried to move. He raised a hand to the left side of his head where it hurt the most and felt a thick bandage. His left index finger wore a clip connected to a pulse monitor that the nurse was now checking.

"Okay, I think," said Will. "What happened?"

"An adverse reaction to the Infinity Room," said McBride. "You passed out and banged your head when you fell. Took six stitches to zip you up."

Will noticed a small bandage inside his right elbow. "What's this?"

"A blood sample," said Robbins. "Precautionary tests."

"If it's any comfort," said McBride, "you're not the first new student to find that place a bit overstimulating. I haven't set foot in there for years."

"Dr. Rourke sends his apologies," said Robbins.

Will closed his eyes against the pain. "How long was I out?" he asked.

"About twenty minutes," said Robbins. "Dr. Rourke drove you himself."

"How long do I have to stay?"

"Until they check under the hood," said McBride. "And no more rugby for you today, young man."

The curtain ahead was yanked aside, and a teasing female voice said, "You're definitely up for a Drama Club Award, though."

A girl about Will's age, wearing a school uniform skirt and blouse, held the curtain at the foot of his bed. She was slender, athletic, with shoulder-length, fair curly hair the color of wheat and cornflower-blue eyes. And she wore a wry, crooked smile slightly at odds with the rest of her delicate, freckled features.

"For Most Dramatic Entrance Ever," she said. "Bleeding all over the headmaster is a real attention-getter."

She's definitely got mine, thought Will.

"Will, this is Brooke Springer," said Robbins. "Brooke will be your student liaison for the first few days."

"She'll show you around and help you settle in," said McBride.

"They give me all the hopeless cases," said Brooke with the sweetest smile.

"I feel better already," said Will. "Is this going to leave a scar?"

"Your injury, or spending time with me?" asked Brooke.

"Guess I can always come back for more stitches," he said.

Brooke giggled. *Good sign,* thought Will.

They let him out of bed after the nurse rechecked his vitals. She told him to come in for a follow-up in two days, avoid strenuous exercise, and get plenty of rest. He didn't appear to have a concussion, but he was to call if any symptoms appeared. The nurse insisted he use a wheelchair, which Brooke insisted on pushing to the infirmary's back door.

#86: NEVER BE NERVOUS WHEN TALKING TO
A BEAUTIFUL GIRL. JUST PRETEND SHE'S A
PERSON, TOO.

"So this is your idea of a good time," said Will. "Pushing guys around."

"Hush," whispered Brooke. "They'll think you're still woozy."

"Let's meet in my office tomorrow morning at nine, Will," said Robbins as they stepped outside. "We'll go over your schedule and curriculum. Mr. McBride's volunteered to be your faculty counselor for now."

"If that's all right with you, Will," said McBride.

Will said that was more than all right. He stood up, shook

hands with both adults, and they walked the wheelchair back inside. Brooke pointed to an electric golf cart parked nearby, bearing the Center's crest and colors.

"Your chariot awaits, sir," she said.

Will's duffel sat in a basket in the back. He eased himself into the passenger seat while Brooke slipped behind the wheel. Will's forehead pulsed with pain, his side ached, his left ankle throbbed, and even though the sun had warmed the air into the low thirties, he was still absolutely freezing. But after all he'd been through, these discomforts rooted him firmly into his body and felt oddly reassuring.

"This is all you brought," she said. "You travel light."

"Habit, I guess."

"So tell me: What's your first impression?"

"At six I could do a pretty awesome Scooby-Doo."

She frowned at him. "How many head injuries have you had?"

"None that I remember. Is that a bad sign?"

"I meant your first impression of the school, you goof," said Brooke.

She twisted her hair into a ponytail, secured it with a clip, slipped the cart into gear, and steered them onto a crosswalk. She wore gray suede high-top cross-trainers with a school logo.

"Where are you from?" she asked.

"We've lived all over."

"Military family?"

"No. Where are *you* from?"

"I'll ask the questions, Mr. Newbie." She waved at some buildings they passed, like a model on a game show pointing out prizes. "Those are the kitchens. That's security, transportation. This, as you may have gathered, is the more quotidian side of the campus."

Like I don't know what quotidian *means.* A spike of irritation prompted Will to say, "Would you like to hear what I know about *you*?"

She glanced sideways at him and instead of "Oh, please"— which Will knew she was thinking—said, "What could you possibly know about me?"

"You're fifteen," said Will. "An only child. Wealthy family. You play the violin. You grew up in suburban Virginia, but you've lived in at least two Spanish-speaking countries because your father works for the State Department—"

Brooke slammed on the brakes and looked at him in alarm. "How could you know that? Did you read my dossier?"

Will shook his head and smiled. Brooke's eyebrows knotted, her eyes flashing. She drummed her fingers on the wheel, expecting an explanation, letting him know she didn't like waiting.

"I study regional accents," said Will. "You have calluses on the fingers of your left hand consistent with playing a stringed instrument. I speak Spanish, and you sound like you learned it as a second language. I put that together with proximity to DC and came up with 'State Department.' "

All of which would be much easier for her to accept than *My parents trained me to obsessively observe and assess every stranger I meet for reasons they never bothered to explain. And it's a hard talent to turn off, especially when the "stranger" is a beautiful girl.*

"How did you know I'm an only child?" she asked.

"Takes one to know one. Am I right?"

"Yes. And Dad was the ambassador to Argentina. But I don't play the violin. I play the cello."

Brooke drove on, pretending he hadn't freaked her out. But she didn't seem to be looking at him from quite as steep an angle down her narrow, patrician nose.

"There's the Administration Building—pay attention, Captain Concussion, you're meeting Dr. Robbins there in the morning."

"Got it."

"And this is the main campus coming into view on our left—"

Brooke kept up her museum guide patter, naming every building—including *three* different libraries—as they tooled around the commons. Will paid zero attention. The girl behind the wheel was much more fascinating, someone from a world of money, privilege, and power, a million miles from his own. He'd never met anyone like her. She was gorgeous, and her confidence was stunning, but not in the manipulative way of a girl who relied solely on her looks. Her poise and intelligence impressed him even more. He decided that since she didn't know the first thing about him—and how his pedigree paled in comparison to hers—it might be best to keep it that way.

As they made their way around, other students waved, regarding an obvious newcomer with friendly smiles. Brooke waved back, as serene and elegant as the Queen of the Rose Parade, even at the carts driven by smiling security guards, who all looked like Eloni: heavyset, with round faces and curly black hair.

"Is every security guard here Samoan?" asked Will.

"You noticed already," she said, then glanced at him again. "Not that I should be surprised."

"What's the reason?"

"Aside from the fact that they're huge and agile and strong enough to tear a bus apart with their bare hands?"

"Why? Is this a high school or an NFL team?"

"It's a *private* school for kids from high-profile families with legitimate security issues. Plus they're friendly, trustworthy, and incorruptible."

"What's the deal? Are they all from the same family?"

"They're from the same *aiga,* or clan," said Brooke. "My favorite theory, although it's probably an urban legend, is that they're reformed gangsters from South Side Chicago. Eloni is their *matai,* or chief. My father says that because of their great warrior culture, we should be glad Samoa is on our side. And if that ever changes, be grateful that Samoa's just a tiny speck in the South Pacific."

They followed a path away from the commons through a birch forest on a narrow plateau. Along a winding lane stood four identical redbrick buildings, each four stories tall with gabled roofs and lots of ornamental detail. They looked more postmodern in style than anything else Will had seen at the Center, pleasing to the eye and welcoming to the spirit.

"These are the residence halls," said Brooke. "Bring your bag."

Brooke parked in front of the last building in the row. He followed her to the front doors. A sign on the wall read GREEN-WOOD HALL.

"Looks different from the rest of the school," said Will.

"Big-bucks architect," said Brooke. "Winner of many awards."

He followed her down a wide empty hallway with stone floors and light pine woodwork to a door with a sign: GREEN-WOOD HALL PROVOST MARSHAL. She pushed the door open and pointed to a table in the square, wood-paneled room.

"Put your bag down there," she said. "And stand back."

LYLE OGILVY

Puzzled, Will did as he was told. Brooke knocked on an inner door, then stepped back beside him. Moments later a tall, slope-shouldered young man entered, wearing a blue blazer with the Center's crest on the pocket and a Windsor-knotted tie striped with school colors. He closed the door quietly and precisely behind him. He wore heavy black wingtips on big flat feet that splayed to the side as he walked. A helmet of oily black hair circled the crown of his unusually long head, and looked as if he ironed it every morning. His face was framed by an oversized brow and prominent jaw, creating an impression that the fleshy features jammed in between were fighting for space. Gray-green circles under his eyes added the only color to his deathly pale complexion. He sniffled constantly, fighting either allergies or a sinus infection. He looked at least eighteen.

"Will West, Lyle Ogilvy," said Brooke. "Greenwood Hall's provost marshal."

Ogilvy looked Will over with darting black eyes that radiated furtive intelligence. He took two measured steps forward, offering a moist handshake and an obsequious smile. Something about Lyle, his stooped posture and covert vigilance, reminded Will of an undertaker or a large bird of prey. Brooke edged back as Lyle advanced; she seemed more than a little afraid of him.

"So pleased to have you with us," said Lyle.

A surprisingly high-pitched voice for a person of his height and mass. Lyle affected a posh accent, halfway to British, the way actors in old movies talked when they wore tuxedos. His tone stayed polite on the surface, but a half-concealed sneer suggested he saw Will as his inferior.

"Likewise," said Will. "What's a provost marshal?"

Lyle seemed amused by the question. "We have rules in the residence halls. I don't make them, but I am charged with enforcing them. Reluctantly on occasion, but at all times, I can assure you, with alacrity."

He reached over and unzipped Will's bag. Will thought about stopping him, but a worried look from Brooke dissuaded him.

"You can start by giving me your cell phone and laptop," said Lyle.

"Why?"

"School policy," said Lyle. "They're not allowed on campus."

"No phones, no texting?" asked Will, addressing Brooke as much as Lyle. Brooke confirmed, with a subtle shake of her head. "I'd like to hear the reason."

"Students at the Center are encouraged to communicate through more traditional methods," said Lyle patiently. "Using the neglected arts of face-to-face conversation and the written word. Or, if need be, our system of courtesy telephones, placed conveniently throughout the facilities."

He pointed to an old-fashioned black phone on a corner cabinet that looked like it had been gathering dust since 1960.

"That seems, nothing personal . . . completely insane," said Will.

"Everyone feels that way when they first arrive." Lyle held out his hand, palm up. Dead serious. He wanted Will's gear, and he wanted it now.

Will tried to stall. His iPhone he could part with, but he couldn't afford to lose the phone Nando had given him. "Okay. The phone thing I can see in theory, but no *laptops*?"

Now Lyle sounded annoyed. "The school provides every student with a customized tablet for their personal use. Our IT staff will transfer all your data onto its hard drive—"

"What if I prefer my own?"

"—built with components and software developed in our labs. Considerably more sophisticated than this dreck from your trendy suburban retailer. Isn't that right, Miss Springer?"

"Yes." With her eyes, Brooke urged him not to press this.

"When do I get them back?"

Lyle made a visible effort to stay calm. "They're securely stored and returned to you at the end of term."

"I've got a bunch of stuff on my phone I need to back up to my hard drive," said Will. "Address book, calendar, personal files—"

"Go right ahead," said Lyle. "*Now.*"

Will's laptop was his most precious possession, a luxury his parents had scarcely been able to afford. He glanced at Brooke again. She looked panicked: *Please cooperate.* Will took out his MacBook and iPhone, cabled them, and started a sync.

With Lyle watching him, Nando's cell phone felt like it was burning a hole in his front pocket. He resisted an impulse to touch it while Lyle stared holes in him.

"Can I keep my iPod?" asked Will. "Or do we have to transfer everything back onto vinyl?"

A laugh burst out of Brooke, which she quickly stifled. Lyle didn't react. He moved to the cabinet in the corner of the room, unlocked it, and collected some printed material.

Will reached into his pocket and pulled out Nando's cell phone. While Lyle's back was turned, he pressed it into Brooke's hand and squeezed her fingers around it. Wide-eyed with alarm, she hid it behind her as Lyle walked back to Will and gave him a booklet and a letter.

"Your copy of our Student Code of Conduct," said Lyle. "And I need your signature on this release form, which stipulates that you will comply with and be bound by all the rules and regulations herein."

#68: NEVER SIGN A LEGAL DOCUMENT THAT HASN'T BEEN APPROVED BY A LAWYER WHO WORKS FOR YOU.

Lyle offered a pen from his pocket. Will ignored it.

"Great," said Will. "I'll take a look and get back to you."

Lyle studied him, searching for insubordination, but Will just smiled.

"I'm going to examine the rest of your belongings," said Lyle. "You'll find the legal authority for this on page six, article three: Arrival Inspection. Along with a detailed list of banned and forbidden objects and substances."

Will glanced at Brooke. She confirmed with an anxious nod.

"I've got nothing to hide," said Will.

"Empty your pockets," said Lyle.

Will turned the pockets of his sweats inside out. Lyle opened his bag and poked around, delicately, using the pen. He fished out Will's dark glasses, then came up with the ones Dave had given him on the plane. Lyle examined them avidly.

"Are dark glasses on the banned list?" asked Will.

"Why do you have two pairs?"

"Rule number ninety-seven: Regarding eyewear and underwear: Always travel with backups."

"Where did these come from?" asked Lyle, looking through the lenses.

"Boutique label."

"I don't *see* any label."

"That's what makes them so legit. It's a West Coast thing."

Not entirely convinced, Lyle put both pairs back in the bag. He brought out Will's Swiss Army knife and held it in the palm of his hand.

"Violation," said Lyle, smirking. "*This* is a weapon."

"Sorry to quibble, but that's incorrect. May I?" asked Will, lifting the knife from Lyle's hand. "It has a blade, yes, but that was originally included so soldiers could open cans of field rations." Will unfolded each tool. "It also has a chisel, scissors, a bottle opener, a screwdriver, an awl, a wire stripper, and a key ring. They give it to guys who already have rifles, bayonets, and hand grenades. It's not a weapon; it's a toolbox, and I'll call and argue that to the headmaster right now if you take it."

Fuming, Lyle set the knife back in Will's bag. After more probing, he lifted out the folded hand towel. Setting it on the table, he unrolled it, revealing the remains of the broken bird.

Damn. I keep forgetting that's in there.

Lyle held out a questioning hand, as if this time he didn't even need to ask.

"Science project," said Will. "From my old school. I'm still tinkering, so I couldn't bear to part with it—"

"What is this?" asked Lyle.

"What's it look like?"

"It *looks* like a mechanical bird."

"Yes, exactly what I was going for. Fist bump."

Lyle ignored him. Will sensed Lyle really wanted to confiscate the bird—wanted to confiscate *anything*—but was fishing for a reason.

"Don't tell me mechanical birds are on the banned list," said Will.

"Surveillance equipment is."

"*Surveillance* equipment?"

"That's a *camera*, isn't it?" asked Lyle, pointing to the eye.

"That's flattering, Lyle, but you have wildly overestimated my engineering ability. I couldn't even program the doggone thing to tweet, let alone fly. I'm hoping somebody here can teach me how to—"

Lyle drew himself up and locked eyes with Will. Will felt a strong, unpleasant pressure in his head, like a steel band had dropped and tightened on his skull, followed immediately by a sensation that someone was poking at the edge of his brain with a penknife. The wound on his head throbbed painfully and threatened to get a whole lot worse. Will didn't want to show he felt anything, so he turned to Brooke. She looked pale and sincerely frightened.

And suddenly Will understood why: Lyle Ogilvy played some kind of mind music, the way Will knew how to do, but unlike Will, he apparently felt no qualms about using his power on other people.

Will tried to evade Lyle's psychic prodding by pushing a blank picture at him. It didn't seem to affect him, but something stirred inside Will, like an electric current twitching to life. He sensed more power there but had no idea how to use it.

As he struggled, his perception of Lyle's pressure shifted, a new field of vision opening before him. It was as if he could see and hear whispered suggestions oozing out of Lyle, floating toward him like a volley of slow-moving bullets. Poisonous fragments of thought embedded in soul-piercing jackets aimed at his mind:

Let go . . . stop fighting . . . let me in . . . don't resist . . . I'm your friend . . . trust me . . .

Will recoiled. Instinctively he knew that once one of Lyle-the-Strange-o's "bullets" drilled into him, he'd find himself doing exactly what Lyle wanted, without a clue about why. No wonder he scared the crap out of kids like Brooke.

The thought of this arrogant cretin intimidating Brooke pushed Will over the edge. His anger ramped up the twitching circuitry in his mind into a unified surge of power, and the mind picture he'd been trying to project assumed the shape of a bright, impenetrable shield. It felt a little like trying to steer a runaway truck by kicking the tires, but somehow Will swung the shield in Lyle's direction.

Their energies collided. Lyle's bullets shattered as they hit Will's shield. At the moment of contact, Will knew that whatever mojo Lyle could throw at him was ten times stronger than his own. A violent shock wave ran back into Will, like he'd touched a live wire. But Lyle felt a kickback, too, and as his eyes lit up in shock, Will realized something:

He's never been challenged like this before.

Lyle's eyes redlined with anger. With his new awareness, Will could see Lyle's power regroup into a dark and dangerous mass. If his prior intent had been to probe, now he meant to punish.

Will knew he'd have no chance this time. So instead of trying to block him, Will feinted forward, then yanked his shield back and to the side. Like pulling a chair out from under someone halfway sitting down. The hammer blow of Lyle's fury blew past him, as if a freight train had missed him by an inch.

The faintest breath of wind rippled a few strands of Brooke's hair. On the wall behind them, a framed photograph of the Center sagged ever so slightly off center. The energy in the room sizzled and then vanished with a snap.

They stood there looking at each other, exactly as before. They'd hardly moved a muscle during their psychic jujitsu.

Lyle smiled confidently, showing his canines. "I'm quite certain somebody here can teach you something." He placed the bird back in Will's bag.

A tone sounded, indicating Will's iPhone and MacBook had synced. Lyle disconnected them and placed them in a plastic tray.

"As soon as the data transfer is complete," said Lyle, "your new tablet will be sent to your quarters. Miss Springer will show you to them now."

Lyle nodded at Brooke, who opened the outer door. She couldn't leave the room fast enough. Will zipped up his bag and winked at Lyle.

"See you round campus, pal."

Lyle didn't respond until Will reached the door.

"West. Let me offer some personal advice: At the Center, we say that problems exist only in order to inspire us to find solutions. Don't be an inspiration to me."

Lyle disappeared into his inner office. Will walked outside and joined Brooke. After a few steps, he staggered and had to brace himself against the wall. The same blackness and nausea he'd felt at the airport washed over him, although this time it was much worse.

"Are you all right?" asked Brooke.

He grunted, holding his head. She leaned against the wall beside him, close. Still afraid.

"How did you do that?" she whispered.

How much did she see, or sense, of what went on in there? Will wondered.

"Do what?" he whispered back.

"Stand up to Lyle that way. I've never seen anybody manage it before."

#91: THERE IS NOT—NOR SHOULD THERE BE—ANY LIMIT TO WHAT A GUY WILL GO THROUGH TO IMPRESS THE RIGHT GIRL.

"I don't like bullies," he said.

She pressed Nando's phone back into Will's hand. He slipped it into his pocket.

"Come on, let's get you upstairs," she said, taking his arm. "Your head's bleeding."

POD G4-3

Brooke decided Will shouldn't take the stairs, so a large, lumbering elevator conveyed them to the fourth floor. Will held it together for Brooke's benefit but felt as if someone had scooped out his insides and dumped him down a well.

The elevator deposited them into a central lobby full of light and brightly colored couches. Corridors ran out from the lobby like spokes from the hub of a wheel. She helped him down one of the corridors. Shorter passages fed off to either side. Turning down the last one on the left, Brooke took out a key card. They approached a white door marked with red raised letters: G4-3.

"Four floors to each hall. Twelve pods to a floor. Five students to a pod."

Will quickly did the math: *1,360 students at the Center.*

She scanned the card through a box above the handle. An electronic tone warbled. They entered a large octagonal central space, punched with wide skylights that cheerfully brightened the room. Clusters of comfortable couches and overstuffed chairs in muted colors softened the sharp architectural lines.

She guided him to a dining table with five chairs that sat outside a small, efficient kitchen.

"Sit here," she said, easing Will into one of the chairs. "Be right back."

She disappeared through one of five doors that led off the great room. Will looked around. Built-in bookshelves lined the walls. A single step led down to the heart of the room, where large pillows and throw rugs surrounded a round rock fireplace. Two old-fashioned black phones sat on opposite ends of the room. There were no TV or computer screens in sight, which made the room seem strangely timeless.

Classical piano music played from inside one of the closed bedroom doors. Someone was practicing, someone exceptionally skilled. Brooke returned with cotton pads and hydrogen peroxide. She opened the bottle and soaked one of the pads.

"You don't have to do this," said Will. "I can go back to the infirmary." His head still hurt, but the weakness had started to fade.

"Two years as a nurse's aide—I think I can manage," said Brooke. "My mom's a doctor. Tilt your head this way."

She leaned over, brushed his hair out of the way, and removed his bandage. When she set it on the table, Will saw it was solid red. She dabbed peroxide gently on his stitches; he willed himself not to react. She bit her lip as she concentrated.

"Looks like the stitches held . . . and the bleeding's stopped. . . . Doesn't that hurt like hell?"

"No," he said.

"Liar. I'd be screaming."

"Nurse's aide, huh?"

"Shut up." Brooke finished cleaning the wound and prepped a new bandage.

"How'd you end up here?" asked Will.

"My dad's an alumnus. We never really discussed my going anywhere else."

"So it had nothing to do with your test scores?"

"My scores were great, but legacy kids also have an inside track. I've known I was coming here since third grade." She applied the new bandage. "That'll do it. Don't tell another soul you have that cell phone."

"I won't if you won't."

Brooke looked seriously at him. "No joke, Will. I saw Lyle find a BlackBerry on a freshman last year. The kid got a nose-bleed that wouldn't quit."

And I'll bet Lyle never laid a hand on him. Will cringed at the memory of Lyle's attack. "The wrong people always get put in charge," he said.

"I should have warned you about Lyle. Next time you'll know better."

Next time I'll be ready.

"I'm sorry, did you say something?" she asked.

"No." *Okay, this is happening a lot lately.*

Brooke gave him a long look, then set the medical supplies on a counter and turned formal tour guide again. "So this is our shared space. Communal kitchen. Bedrooms are through each door. You're over here."

She led him to a door marked "4." Inside was a surprisingly large furnished room with irregular angles, pale blue walls, and dark hardwood floors. It was furnished with a single bed, nightstand, and sturdy desk with a futuristic meshwork chair. One of the black phones sat on the desk. A chest of drawers sat in an open closet. A large bay window looked out over the woods, away from campus. The only other door led to a private white-tiled bathroom.

"The blank canvas design is intentional, by the way," she said. "You're expected to make it your own. Are you hungry?"

"Starved."

"Take your time. I'll see what we have in the kitchen."

She closed the door behind her. Will set his bag on the bed. Tested the mattress. Firm but not too firm: the perfect balance. The room felt pleasant but utterly neutral. He might have been anywhere in the world.

This is where I live now.

He'd faced this moment many times before. He was used to starting over.

But never alone. Never without my parents.

Now that he was here—and safe—the enormity of his loss came rushing at him. He wrestled those feelings down before the anguish overwhelmed him.

I'm not going to grieve. I'm not going to give whoever did this to us the satisfaction. I know they're still alive and I'm going to fight until I find them.

He'd been dropped into this new life now. He had to stay strong and keep moving forward. That's what his parents would *want* him to do.

#50: IN TIMES OF CHAOS, STICK TO ROUTINE. BUILD ORDER ONE STEP AT A TIME.

Will dried his eyes, took a long look in the mirror, and didn't like what he saw: exhausted, pale, beaten down. He put away his few clothes in the closet. Set the mechanical bird in the top drawer of the dresser and folded the towel over it. The framed photograph of his parents and Dad's rules went on the bedside table. He hid the cell phone under the mattress and plugged in its charger behind the bed.

Will took a shower. Instant hot water blasted from an adjustable showerhead under solid pressure. Careful not to get his hair wet, he washed off the wear and tear of the road. Somewhat revived, he changed into his spare jeans, a white T-shirt, sweater, and his bomber jacket. Which more or less exhausted his wardrobe.

He heard raised voices from the great room and opened the door. An older boy stood near the front door. He was three inches taller and thirty pounds heavier than Will, all of it solid muscle. He was tan, ruddy cheeked, with short black hair, and he wore trim gray khakis and a tight navy blue polo. He held Brooke's left wrist in his right hand, twisting it slightly, pulling her closer.

"That's not what you said. That's not what we *agreed on*," he said, just short of yelling.

"Lower your voice and let go of me—" she said.

"Hey there," said Will. "What's the good word?"

The older boy looked at Will, surprised. "Who's this noob?" he asked Brooke.

"He just got here—"

Will walked over, grinning like a clueless goofball. "My name's Will West. And I'm from *out* west, too. Isn't that ironic? Really pleased to meet you. And you are?"

Will extended his hand, radiating nerd vibes. Some vestige of country club manners hit the front of the guy's brain. He let go of Brooke and shook Will's hand.

"Todd Hodak."

Hodak opened his eyes really wide, simulating interest, and clamped down on Will's hand as hard as he could. Will pretended it hurt a lot more than it did, bending over, trying to shake it off.

"Dang, that's some grip, Todd. Look, I'll never play the piano again." He held up his hand, hanging limply, and chuckled. Todd stared at Will as if he had leprosy.

"You must be an athlete, right? What sport? I'm guessing most of 'em! I just got here and I already miss my dog. Do you have a dog? Mine's named Oscar. He's a long-haired dachshund. You know, like 'Oscar *Mayer,*' 'cause he's a *wiener* dog—"

Todd turned to Brooke. "We'll talk about this later."

He slammed the door as he left. Brooke, flushed and upset, hurried to the kitchen. Will trailed her to the dining area. She came back out carrying a large plate, which she set down, noisily, on the table.

"Excuse me a moment," she said.

Brooke hurried into bedroom 1 and closed the door. A moment later, Will heard her crying. Unsure what to do, he went back to the table, where there was a pitcher of lemonade and tall glasses with ice, small earthen tubs of three different dips, a selection of sliced vegetables, and a dish of spiced olives.

And all he could think was, *She lives here. There is a God.*

The front door flew open. An elfin black-haired kid bolted in, arms full of boxes overflowing with electronic components. He stopped, startled, when he saw Will. His skin was the color of caramel, his eyes big, brown, and shiny. The kid studied him intensely but didn't change expression. Then he hurried to bedroom 3, transferring his load onto one skinny arm just long enough to unlock the door. He pushed it open with his butt, darted inside, and closed it behind him. Will heard multiple locks being thrown on the other side.

Brooke came out of her room. Eyes red, forcing a smile, determined to proceed as if nothing named Todd Hodak had jammed her frequencies. She sat at the table and grazed from the platter. Will sat across from her and dug in as well.

"We have a good group here, all things considered." She waved a carrot toward door 3. "You'll like Ajay. Everybody likes Ajay. He's indispensable."

She took a bite of carrot and pointed to door 2. "But Nick's a ginormous pain in the watusi. Do you like sports or Chuck Norris?"

"I like sports."

"Then who knows, you and Nick might be able to bond."

Will couldn't stop eating. The dips were all fresh and delicious: hummus, an artichoke mix, and something tart and gooey he couldn't identify.

"What is this?" asked Will, pointing to the third dip. "It's unbelievable."

"Baba ghanoush." The way she said it, with a slight lisp, sounded so adorable Will almost asked her to repeat it. Brooke waved her carrot stub at door 5, where Will had heard piano music earlier.

"Elise is in five. Elise is . . . well, you'll see for yourself." She popped the carrot into her mouth. "You may have something in common with her."

"What?"

"You're a big boy. I'll let you make up your own mind."

Will tried not to sound too interested. "So are all the pods co-ed?"

"Is that a problem for you?"

"No, no, not at all—" said Will.

"Because one of the halls is segregated by floors, if it is—"

"It's not—"

"—but you'd have to tell Dr. Robbins—"

"It's not a problem."

She leaned back and smiled. "You might feel differently when you meet Elise."

"I doubt that I'll feel differently."

She took a bite of red pepper. "You don't have a dachshund named Oscar."

"I don't even have a dog."

"So you were just messing with Todd."

"Doesn't everybody?"

"No. Not even a little bit."

"Yes," said Will. "I was messing with Todd."

Door 3 opened. Ajay stepped out and made sure his door was locked.

"Ajay, this is Will," said Brooke. "He's moving into number four."

"So I see," said Ajay with a small bow. "Welcome, sir. Misery is compounded by solitude, so it does, in fact and indeed, prefer company."

He had a deep, dignified voice and a refined Southern accent. He looked about twelve and sounded like he was running for president.

"Oh, fudge," said Brooke, glancing at the wall clock. "I've got to get to a lab. Ajay, could you take care of Will for a while? He needs clothes, groceries, books, and supplies—it's all really kind of desperate. Back in a bit."

Brooke hurried out the front door. Ajay helped himself to an olive.

"If that is indeed the case," said Ajay, "then I am exactly the man you need to see: Ajay Janikowski, entirely at your service."

Ajay reached behind his back, tossed the olive five feet in the air, and caught it in his mouth.

AJAY JANIKOWSKI

Ajay darted ahead of Will into the hallway and through a side door.

"We'll take the stairs," said Ajay. "The elevators date from the early days of the Harry S. Truman administration. They'd finish third in a race with a glacier and a deceased postal worker."

Ajay bounded down the stairs ahead of him, brimming with energy he hardly seemed able to contain. Will struggled to keep up with him.

"How badly are you injured?" asked Ajay.

"Not seriously."

"And you just arrived this morning. Where did you fly in from?"

"Southern California."

"Are those the only clothes you brought with you?"

"More or less."

Ajay stopped on a landing and assessed him. "You're going to die almost immediately from hypothermia."

"So I've been told."

"How much money do you have?" asked Ajay.

"What comes below abject poverty?"

"Tell me you don't already have a mad crush on Brooke."

Will finally caught up, his head throbbing. "What makes you think that?"

Ajay shook his head in disappointment and continued down. "Good God, man, we have our work cut out for us."

Ajay pushed through the ground floor door and set the same brisk pace outside toward campus. The temperature had warmed considerably, from crippling to just below disfiguring. Will zipped up his jacket and shivered.

"Why would you assume I have a crush on Brooke?" asked Will.

"Please, Will. Destiny clearly intends, by virtue of domestic proximity, some form of friendship for us, but you simply must acknowledge the danger of our situation."

"What would that be?"

Ajay's big eyes got even wider. "Why, the astonishing and nearly supernatural attractiveness of not just our two extraordinary roommates, but the school's entire *female population*."

"You mean . . . they're all like Brooke?"

"No, that's just it," said Ajay, gesturing expansively. "They're all as different as snowflakes. Beautiful, interesting girls, each capable, in her own delicious way, of driving you to madness. Any red-blooded male would swim shark-infested waters with a Bantu spear through his leg to change places with us. But if you don't control yourself, your nervous system will detonate like a string of firecrackers. A bomb-sniffing dog couldn't save you."

"How old are you?" asked Will.

"Fifteen. But chronological age is a most unreliable method of evaluation."

"Okay, so I think Brooke is a flat-out slammin' babe and will someday rule the world. That better?"

"Yes! We've established that you're not a robot."

Ajay slapped him on the back, laughed heartily, and led them into one of the larger buildings. A substantial sign read STUDENT UNION. It did nothing to prepare Will for what awaited inside.

The student union was the size of a shopping mall. A grocery store took up the southwestern corner. He saw a laundry and dry cleaners next door to a bank, a massive sporting goods store, and a store offering every art or academic supply imaginable. The school bookstore seemed to go on forever. It opened into a busy food court offering eight different cuisines, none of which looked fast, cheap, or unhealthy. Across from that was a duplex movie theater; one showed a film that was still in general release. Ajay explained the other theater ran only classics from the "Golden Age"—way back, before *Star Wars*—as part of a film studies course. The marquee read HITCHCOCK'S "REAR WINDOW." Next door was the six-lane bowling alley and soda fountain that he'd seen in the school's promotional materials.

Will followed Ajay into a clothing store as big as a football field, with row after row of every item you could imagine in variations of the school colors. Will felt overwhelmed and intensely aware he had only a hundred dollars left in his wallet.

"Start your engines," said Ajay, handing Will a wheeled shopping cart. "I'll be right back."

Ajay hurried off. Will pushed the cart to the winter wear

section. He didn't see any price tags, but the piece he wanted most—a heavy blue fleece sweatshirt with a gray CIL embroidered on the chest—had to cost half of what he had to his name. Reluctantly he tossed it into the cart. He was trying to decide whether to spend the rest on a pair of khakis or a rugby shirt when Ajay returned.

"This was waiting for you at the counter," said Ajay. "You didn't tell me you were on full scholarship, man. That's a horse of a different color."

Ajay handed him a thick plastic credit card. It was blank, with the same deep blackness he'd seen in Robbins's expanding tablet. Ajay ran a finger along its outer edge, activating a sensor. The school's crest appeared, floating in its center. Below that was a sixteen-digit code number and the name WEST.

Will turned it over. A standard magnetized credit card strip ran along the back. His parents had explained how these strips worked, how banks and companies used them to store confidential information they'd gathered about you. He wondered how much information was already embedded here.

"Do they take cash?" asked Will.

"Cash? For heaven's sake, man, you don't need cash anymore. You have the Card now. You can use it everywhere."

"Did they mention what my limit is?"

"If there is a limit, it will now be your job to find it," said Ajay.

Living expenses, books and supplies, all included. Once again, Dr. Robbins had delivered what she'd promised.

"Let's do it," said Will.

Will dropped the pants and the rugby shirt into the cart. He'd never shopped anywhere without the pressure of a budget.

The prospect made him giddy, but despite Ajay's encouragement to break the bank, he still felt like he was taking advantage. Ajay kept tossing things into the cart and Will kept putting them back.

#81: NEVER TAKE MORE THAN YOU NEED.

Three pairs of pants. Five navy and gray shirts. A week's worth of socks and underwear. A pair of heavy-soled winter boots. A navy watch cap. Fleece-lined gloves and a gray wool scarf. Two sets of long underwear. The only luxury he allowed himself was a dark blue winter parka with a fur-lined hood, but he easily convinced himself he needed that for survival.

A friendly cashier rang it up, asked for his card, and passed it over a scanner that made the card glow. Will didn't have to sign anything. He never saw a total. No prices appeared on the receipt she gave him.

"How long have you been here?" asked Will.

"My second year. As a freshman, I was roughly the size of this slice of chicken." Ajay laughed again, infectiously. Will found it impossible not to laugh with him, especially when he made jokes at his own expense.

They were seated in the food court, over teriyaki rice bowls and sunomono salads made to order, fresh and flavorful, and paid for with a single flash of Will's magic card. A full stomach did wonders for his mood. So did the fleece sweatshirt.

"So what's with the big noise about cells and laptops?" asked Will.

Ajay's brow knit together and his look darkened. "So you've met Lyle."

"Yes."

Ajay leaned forward. "At first I assumed it was a rule they imposed to show they're in charge and it would be more honored in the breach than the observance. That proved not to be the case. They take this very seriously indeed."

"But for what reason?"

"They don't want our faces buried in phones or our heads stuck up the Internet all the time. They really *do* want us to talk to each other."

"Texting is a *form* of talking," said Will. "And usually it's a lot more efficient."

"I wouldn't argue, Will, but I don't make the rules. And honestly, after a while you'll find that face-to-face communication works entirely to your personal benefit."

"How?"

"It forces you outside your comfort zone," said Ajay. "Refines social skills, in a good way. Believe it or not, I used to be quite the introvert."

"You're making that up."

"It's true, I swear to you! And now look at me, a regular chatterbox. I'm completely out of my shell."

Ajay took a small rectangular black box from the folder Brooke had given him and pushed it across the table.

"Clip that onto your belt. It's a pager. If anyone tries to reach you on the internal phone system, this beeps. Pick up any phone on campus and the operator instantly connects the call."

It was a bit bigger than a matchbox and had a metal clip on

the back. On the right front corner was a small grill, and there was one small recessed button in the middle. Otherwise it was seamless and solid, with surprising weight. He couldn't even find a slot for batteries.

"So I'll have to deal with the texting thing," said Will. "What about email?"

"You'll get an email address with your tablet. It's connected to the main servers for the school's internal network."

"Wait, you mean it only works on campus? What about Internet access?"

"Limited. No Wi-Fi or networks out here. You can sign on using ports in the libraries, for specific research, but outside websites are severely restricted."

Will's anger rose. "We can't even get on the Net from our own rooms?"

"No surfing, no social networking, no console or online games—"

"What about TV?"

"There's one in the student union, but I've never seen anyone watching—"

"But these are basic principles of free speech. The right to access useless information and mindless, mediocre entertainment—"

"The Center's a private institution; they can set any rules they like."

"This isn't Communist China. They can't just shut down the pipeline and cut us off from the rest of the world—"

"The point is there's hardly *time* for such things, Will. They work us like sled dogs, and in case you never noticed, sled dogs love the harness! You'll see. Don't underestimate the joy of being challenged or losing yourself in work. I'm talking one hundred percent immersion: classes, labs, homework, and field assignments. Add to that all the social activities: sports leagues, clubs, concerts, and dances—"

"Dances?"

Ajay lowered his voice so no one would overhear. "As part of the Fall Hayride festivities last month, I even attended a *square dance*."

"Get out of town."

"It was insanely fun! Call me crazy. The girls, man, the girls." Ajay jumped up and demonstrated his square dance.

Will's mind drifted to Brooke, and from her to Todd Hodak. He needed deep background on that situation, but for all he knew, Ajay blabbed like a talk-show host to everyone in their pod. He didn't want word of his "crush" getting back to Brooke.

When they finished eating, Ajay led him to the soda fountain by the bowling alley for a chocolate milkshake, which was handcrafted by a server wearing a white peaked cap, like the soda jerk in a Norman Rockwell print. Frost formed on the silver goblet as Will poured his shake into a tall fountain glass. He devoured the sublime concoction, which was laced with buttery nuggets of ice cream. Agreeable pop music issued from a jukebox. The muted swell of pins crashing next door sounded as soothing as a waterfall. Life, for whatever reason, felt worth living again.

Proving Rule #84: WHEN NOTHING ELSE WORKS, TRY CHOCOLATE.

"Why a bowling alley?" asked Will.

Ajay mimed throwing a bowling ball. "Apparently the headmaster read a study that tied the decline of American happiness to the disappearance of organized bowling leagues. A few weeks later, voilà."

"Are you on a team?"

"Yes. You'll love it. You even get a shirt, with your name on the pocket. Although for aesthetic purposes, I insisted that mine read 'Tony.'"

So far, everything about the Center looked and felt fine-tuned to perfection, as dreamlike as a movie set. Wherever Will turned, he saw nothing but content and happy faces, exactly as advertised.

"Ever wake up and feel like you're dreaming?"

"Will," said Ajay, suddenly serious. "My mother came to America from India at the age of nine. Her impoverished parents worked as domestics in an Atlantic City casino and eventually bought a dry cleaners. My father's from an old aristocratic Polish family that lost everything but their luggage in World War Two. He grew up in Milwaukee, a penniless immigrant. Worked his way through Duke University and eventually bought a small chain of drugstores in Raleigh, North Carolina, called the Pill and Puff. My mother attended community college at night to train as a pharmacist. She landed a job in one of his drugstores, where they met and fell in love. Which led to me, their only child.

"As a result of this unusual heritage, of which I'm immensely proud, I am an odd duck by any reckoning. I stand barely five feet tall, and if you think I'm puny now, you should have seen me at six. It won't surprise you to learn that I was bullied in school, unmercifully, from my first day of kindergarten all the way through junior high, by every redneck Neanderthal who ever laid eyes on me. Girls found me to be, throughout these years, invisible to the naked eye. I knew, secretly, that I was smarter than all of these knuckleheads and survived by my wits alone, with no way of knowing that I had anything worthwhile to offer any other living creature, that I was someone who could have friends and meet girls and experience something resembling a present or a future. Until the day I arrived at the Center."

Ajay held his gaze, openhearted and sincere. Will felt ashamed of any impulse he'd had to doubt him.

"If this is a dream, I'm begging you," said Ajay, "don't ever let them wake me."

NICK AND ELISE

When they left the soda fountain, Ajay excused himself to go to class. Will made a quick grocery run for staples like peanut butter, crackers, and milk. He saw no junk food on the shelves and tons of health foods; his parents would have approved. He bundled up in his new gloves, hat, scarf, and jacket for the hike back to Greenwood Hall. He felt like a sausage but didn't shiver once and covered the ground with surprising speed. So chalk up one plus for Nordic weather: It helped get you where you were going a *whole* lot faster.

Back inside, the door to the provost marshal's office was open. Will noticed a camera on the wall above the door. Inside the room, he caught a glimpse of Lyle speaking intently to Todd Hodak.

Somehow he knew: *They're talking about me.*

They saw him as he passed. Todd's eyes fired with anger. Will started upstairs and heard Lyle's door slam.

He reached his floor and used his key card to enter the

pod. As he carried his bags to the kitchen, he felt someone else watching him. He turned.

Stretched out on one of the sofas and propped up on one elbow, a book open in front of her. Jet-black hair cut in a sharp pageboy and bangs that framed her face like a chain mail helmet. Porcelain skin and arched black brows above almond-shaped eyes. Big eyes, a dazzling jade green that he'd never seen except in pictures of tropical waters. Her bone structure echoed some statue of a lost Egyptian queen. She wasn't conventionally pretty. There appeared to be nothing conventional about her. Words that came more immediately to Will's mind: *Commanding. Arresting. Intoxicating.*

She was dressed in dark blue from head to toe: a tight skirt, leggings, and a turtleneck sweater. She didn't move, secretly amused, still and regal as a Persian cat, and never took those unnerving eyes off him.

"You must be Elise," Will said finally.

One eyebrow rose slowly. "*Must* I?"

Will felt like a mouse. Being toyed with by a cat. "Yes. 'Must be.' Sticking with my original call."

"Well, then . . ."

She wants to know my name.

"Will," he said.

"Well, then," said Elise. "Advantage, Will."

Not for long, he thought. He snapped off a two-finger salute, then, on purpose, tripped over his own feet and sent his bags flying.

Elise rolled her eyes and shifted back to her book. *Dismissed.* Humbled, Will put his groceries away, coaching himself: *Just pretend she's a person, too.* He reentered the great room prepared to make small talk, but she held up a hand.

"Working," she said.

Whatever witticism he'd been preparing flew out of Will's mind. He hurried into his room and took some deep breaths. Brooke and Elise under the same roof? *You cannot be serious.* So far Ajay wasn't exaggerating about the girls at the Center.

Will noticed something sitting on his desk: his new "computing device." He examined it from every angle; it was nothing like a traditional laptop, more like a slightly thicker iPad. It was solid and metallic, with a soft black matte finish that looked and felt like velvet. Less than an inch thick, it weighed about a pound and a half and had no visible ports or drives. On the back, in the lower right-hand corner, stamped into the metal, was a sixteen-digit code number followed by WWEST. The same information that was on his black school card.

Will searched for a way to start it and found an indentation on the right side. He pressed it. Motors whirred. Legs unfolded in back and raised the entire unit to an ideal viewing angle. Then the thing expanded in size by a third—the way Robbins's magical slate had done—and powered on with a musical chord. The whole face sizzled to life, a screen, and in the middle words appeared: INSERT CARD.

Will took out his new school ID card. A slot had appeared along one side of the machine. He inserted the card, and the tablet read its metallic strip, then ejected the card.

Words appeared on the screen: AUTHENTICATE, PLEASE.

A pulsating outline of a left hand appeared on-screen, fingers spread, like the outlines he'd seen on Robbins's device.

Will extended his left hand toward the outline. An inch shy of it he felt a burst of warmth.

As he touched the screen, the outline locked onto his hand. Subtle currents flowed beneath his skin, then with a flash of light the outline faded. A majestic major chord filled the room. The display dissolved to a greeting screen that featured the Center's crest floating on a shimmering dark blue field. Moments later, a row of conventional interface icons faded in along the bottom of the screen.

Words appeared: WOULD YOU LIKE TO BEGIN THE TUTORIAL NOW? (RECOMMENDED) YES/NO.

Will tapped NO. A mailbox icon appeared. He double-tapped the icon, and the screen opened to a graphically familiar in-box.

There was one message inside: To wwest@thecil.org. From sroarke@thecil.org.

He double-tapped the message. A video file opened of Headmaster Stephen Rourke, at the desk in his office, looking straight into the camera. The image quality was so good he appeared to be on the other side of a window.

"Greetings, Will. I hope you're bouncing back from that bump on the noggin. Sorry I couldn't wait around, but the docs assured me you'd be okay. And I apologize for taking you in there in the first place. That one's on me: headmaster brain-lock. Hope you're getting settled. Let's catch up tomorrow. If there's anything we can do to make your first days here easier, all you have to do is ask. Have a good night now."

The mailbox came back up. Instead of using his finger as the cursor, Will tried another way to interact with it. "Close mailbox," he said.

The mailbox collapsed into the icon at the bottom of the screen. *Cool*.

"Open hard drive," he said.

A file cabinet icon opened in the screen's center. A drawer opened into a list of folders and files from the hard drive on Will's laptop. He verified that the data from his laptop had landed safely.

A muffled buzzing sounded somewhere in the room. He traced it to the bed, under the mattress. Nando's cell phone.

"Power off," said Will.

His tablet shut down. Will couldn't see one, but he worried there might be a video camera built into its frame. There was no way of knowing who might have remote access to its feed—Lyle, for instance. Will dropped his sweatshirt over the screen for good measure.

#83: JUST BECAUSE YOU'RE PARANOID DOESN'T MEAN THAT SORRY IS BETTER THAN SAFE.

Will pulled out Nando's phone and took it into the bathroom. He closed and locked the door, then turned on the faucet before he answered.

"Hey, Nando," Will whispered.

"Yo, Will," Nando whispered back. "I'm parked outside your house right now."

"Why are you whispering? Can anybody see you?"

"No, I'm cool, man. I'm down the street. Why are *you* whispering?"

Will thought a second. "You're not supposed to use phones in the hospital."

"So listen up, bro, your old man might be right. What's going down here's kinda freaky. Three black cars are parked out front. Identical makes and models, like undercover vehicles. Cops were here earlier, too. Two local cruisers."

"How long have you been there?"

"About an hour."

"Shouldn't you be working?"

"Nah, man, this is way more fun," said Nando. "Plus I got this little telescope my wife bought me at Brookstone? Puts you right up in somebody's grill. I'm watching these dudes from the sedans go in and out."

"Describe them," said Will.

"Black caps and jackets. Look almost like FBI, 'cept it don't say 'FBI' on the caps or jackets. They're loading suitcases into the cars. Boxes, too. All taped up, the kind you use for moving."

"How many Black Caps?"

"Six. Two in each car," said Nando. "And whoever these cats in the chapeaus are, they're in charge of whatever's going down: They were giving orders to the cops."

"Have you seen anybody else?"

"A lady came out a couple times. Black hair, kinda tall, good-looking. Tell the truth, first time I seen her, I thought she coulda been your mom."

Will felt bad about lying to Nando but didn't see an alternative. "Couldn't be. She's up here with us. Anybody else?"

"One other dude, *not* one of the Caps. Long hair and glasses, light brown beard. Only seen him once, through the window inside, talking to the Caps."

So Dad is still there. But in what condition?

"I took some snaps but didn't think I should send 'em till we talked."

"I have an email you can use." Will gave him the address of his new account.

"Okay, boss. Gonna stay on this. Looks like they're getting ready to move."

Nando hung up. Will heard a series of sharp knocks on his bedroom door. He went into the bedroom.

"Who is it?" he asked.

"House security," said a male voice. "Open the door *now*."

Not Lyle, but that didn't mean he wasn't out there with a whole goon patrol.

"One sec, I was in the bathroom."

He yanked the phone's charger from the wall and buried them both under the mattress. His heart thumping, Will walked over and opened the door.

A tough-looking kid with close-cropped blond hair stood outside. He wore a crested blue school blazer identical to the one Lyle had been wearing. A scalloped cowlick rose on the left side of his hairline like a nautilus shell. He stood four inches shorter than Will but occupied more space horizontally and radiated serious athletic vibes. His electric ice-blue eyes drilled straight into Will's.

The kid held up the rules booklet Lyle had given Will. "Are you familiar with Code of Conduct rule sixteen dash six, paragraph five, subsection nine?"

"No, I—"

"Mr. West, ignorance of the law is no excuse."

Glancing past the guy, Will saw Elise seated on the circular hearth. She'd changed into a short athletic uniform skirt, black cleats, and high blue socks, and she twirled a field hockey stick in her hands. Will thought she looked, oddly, like she was trying not to laugh.

"Since you've chosen to *ignore* the provost marshal's order to study the Code, let me read the relevant passage *for* you: 'New students are not allowed to ask other students about their personal lives for a period of six weeks—'"

The young man glanced back at Elise, indicating she had lodged this lame complaint against him. Will stared at them in confusion.

"Like I said, I didn't know the rules—"

"That is some weak sauce indeed, Mr. West. Do you have any idea what kind of trouble you're in? Would you like to know what *else* you don't know about subsection nine? Please tell me if I'm going too fast."

"No, go ahead."

The guy lifted the book and read again: "New arrivals may only ask time of day or directions to classrooms. Random comments about your playlists? Violation. Gushing about your favorite sports team? Violation. Any mention of homesickness for pets named Pinky or Gum Drop? Violation. And you are never, under any circumstances, to ever, in the same sentence, use the words *totally, freaking,* or *awesome.* Unless you're referring to me."

Elise bent over double, shaking with laughter. The blond kid cracked up and staggered back into a nearby chair. "Oh God, dude, you're priceless."

"Punked," said Will. "Nice."

"Pinky or Gum Drop," said Elise, and then shrieked with laughter.

"So you're Nick," said Will.

"That was so savage," said Nick. "I am feeling you right now." He turned and lifted off the arms of the chair into a perfect handstand: "Nick McLeish. Hope this doesn't mean we can't be buds." He flipped over the back, landed softly, and stepped forward to shake Will's hand. "Brooke told me you cracked heads with Lyle-Lyle-Crocodile, the Ogre of Greenwood Hall. Couldn't resist. Elise put me up to it."

"That's a complete and total lie," said Elise, suddenly not laughing.

"I'm okay," said Will. "No harm, no foul."

"Wow, you are being such a champ about this. Props, man, I'm majorly impressed. Aren't you, Leesy?"

"Don't let Nick's charm mess with your savoir faire," said Elise.

"She thinks I'm charming," said Nick, offering a wide and— Will had to admit—exceptionally charming grin.

"They used to burn witches at the stake for less," said Elise.

"Yo, we all know who the *witch* is, 'kay? And seriously, dude, I wouldn't be anywhere close to this nice about it if you'd pulled the same gag on me."

"I wouldn't pull the same gag on you," said Will.

"Right. I don't think you would," said Nick, looking at him searchingly. "You're a dude of honor and character. Not sure you'll fit in with us, but we're open-minded. Where you from?"

"Southern California."

"Shut up! So Cal, for real? You hear that, Elise? 90210. Hollywood. Surf City, USA, Lakers and Fakers—"

"Keep going," said Elise. "You missed a few clichés."

"You're from Boston?" asked Will.

"Close enough: New Hampshire."

"Celtics fan," said Will. "I knew it. I'm sorry, Nick. We can't be friends."

"Come correct now. You know the kelly green of our championship banners is like Kryptonite to your shallow left-coast powers—"

Will turned to Elise. "You a Celtics fan, too?"

"Hell, no, bro," said Nick. "She's from Seattle. Like they've ever *sniffed* a championship in anything 'cept *chronic depression.*"

"The correct term is seasonal affective disorder," Elise said.

"SAD," said Will.

"Yes, it is," said Nick. "Dude, let me tell you how life works in the pod. Our vixen-in-residence here, Miss Elise Moreau, is in charge of everything." He walked to Elise—shaking her head while she tied her cleats—and massaged her shoulders.

"Every five minutes you listen to him," said Elise, sighing, "you lose a point off your IQ."

"Elise, esplain to Will what you're like, girl," said Nick.

"No."

"Come on, you know I'll only mess it up—"

"Nick? *No* is a complete sentence," said Elise.

"Truth," said Nick. "Elise is a mad gypsy fortune-teller. She's got this spooked-out mind-ninja power. Once she locks on and gazes into your soul, you can't run, you can't hide, and you can't resist."

Will couldn't imagine why anyone would *want* to resist. Elise looked at him alertly, as if she'd heard him think it. He shivered and looked away.

"And, dude, imagine what it must be like for *her*? Knowing

she has the power to see into the deep, dark places peeps won't even admit to *themselves*?"

Is that why Brooke thinks Elise and I have something in common?

With a crisp swing, Elise cracked Nick on the shin with her hockey stick.

"Ow! Did I say that? No, what I *meant* to say is she's as harmless as a cheerleader with a Hello Kitty screen saver—"

"Please, ma'am, may I have another," she said, swinging her stick again.

Nick hopped out of range. Elise turned to Will. He avoided her big green eyes; right now, no one's soul held more secrets than his did. He also realized that if he was looking for *practical* answers, he'd been talking to the wrong person. "So should I really read Lyle's Code of Conduct?" he asked Elise.

"Yes," said Elise.

"Oh, no, *really*?" asked Nick.

"Don't be thick, Nick. Just because *you* never did. Forewarned is forearmed."

Nick sank back onto the sofa, rubbed his shin, and flipped through the booklet. "She's prolly right, dude." Heavy sigh. "It's just every time I try to slug my way through it, I . . ." Nick closed his eyes, fell back, and snored theatrically.

Elise shook her head again and started for the door, twirling her stick. She turned back to Will to say emphatically, "Read it. Did you get your tablet?"

God, her eyes were unnerving. "I just found it on my desk."

"Have you taken the tutorial yet?"

"No, not yet—"

"Take it."

"O-kay," said Will.

Elise left the pod. Nick stayed prone on the sofa, pretending to be asleep.

"I'm going to finish . . . unpacking," said Will.

Without opening his eyes, Nick flung his copy of the Code across the room like a Frisbee. It flew through the screen and right into the fireplace, where it began to smolder and burn. Nick waved at Will, eyes still closed, crossed his arms, and settled into a serious nap.

Will locked his bedroom door and lifted the sweatshirt off his tablet. The mailbox icon was blinking and had a question below it: WOULD YOU LIKE TO ADD "NANDO" TO YOUR OUTSIDE MAILING LIST?

"Yes. Open email."

YOU MAY NOW SEND AND RECEIVE MAIL FROM THIS ADDRESS.

The email from Nando opened. "FYI. AS PROMISED." Three photographs downloaded on-screen, one after the other. Will studied each as they came up. The first was taken from Nando's car as he drove past: three black cars parked in front of the house. The second showed three men in black caps loading boxes into the trunk of the first car. The third showed Belinda talking to one of them in front of the house. The man had taken his hat off. He was bald.

On instinct, Will tried something else. "Zoom in," he said.

His computer zoomed in on the photo until he could see Belinda more clearly. She hadn't changed physically, but she looked less like his mom in this shot. Like an actor in costume and makeup seen off camera; she wasn't *playing* Mom.

A tone sounded from the computer. On-screen, a new

message from Nando opened. It was a text, sent from his phone: caps on the move . . . I'm all over it . . .

There was another knock at his door. "Close all files," said Will.

The tablet instantly returned to its greeting screen, the animated school crest—angel, horse, knight—floating over shimmering black. The same message he'd seen earlier appeared: WOULD YOU LIKE TO BEGIN THE TUTORIAL NOW?

"Not right now," said Will.

AS YOU WISH, WILL. The screen went blank again.

Will had never owned a pet, but he had the oddest feeling about this new computer. It seemed—he didn't know how else to express this—*happy* to follow his commands. Like it was a dog.

Will moved to the door. Little Ajay stood outside wearing his school blazer, poised and formal.

"Will, we've decided you're joining us for dinner," he said in his deep voice. "And I'm afraid you have no choice in the matter."

THE DEAD KID

In addition to the soda fountain and the student union food court, there were four other restaurants on campus, including a formal dining room that required reservations and a coat and tie, for parental visits or faculty consultations, and a grillroom in the field house for team meals before or after games and practices. The cafeteria, by far the largest eatery, occupied most of the ground floor of a building near the student union and offered a perpetual buffet from 6:00 a.m. to midnight every day of the week. The fourth restaurant, where his roommates took Will for his first dinner, was the Rathskeller.

Down a flight of weather-beaten stone stairs, the restaurant was situated in the basement of Royster Hall, the oldest building on campus. A wooden sign, carved in a Gothic font from the Pinocchio era, swung above the door: THE RATHSKELLER ESTABLISHED 1915.

Inside was a surprisingly warm and intimate cellar space, divided by brick arches, with fireplaces at either end. The room was filled with long tables and dark hardwood benches. There

173

was sawdust on the floor and brass lanterns with fake flickering candles on the tables. The ends of enormous barrels studded the walls, stamped with insignias of old Milwaukee breweries. Will's roommates explained that the Rathskeller had been the faculty lounge back when the Center first opened, a gastronomic temple dedicated to Wisconsin's dominant Germanic cuisine.

The only menus were large rectangular blackboards fastened to the walls above the fireplaces. Written in chalk were strange words like *Kielbasa, Sauerbraten, Spätzle mit Schweinshaxe, Weisswurst, Bratkartoffeln, Hasenpfeffer, Spargelzeit.*

The others ordered for Will, who kept his mouth shut and watched his new roommates interact. Clever and nimble, Ajay directed the conversation and kept the tone light. Nick tossed jokes around like water balloons, sabotaging any topic that turned too serious. Elise hung back but joined Nick in firing barbed shots at the others, playfully, and at anyone outside their group who came up in conversation, *not* so playfully. Both specialized in keeping others off balance. Will couldn't tell if that was their way to conceal vulnerability, or if they were a bit mean-spirited.

All of which left Brooke stuck as the grown-up, herding the others back onto polite social ground when they crossed the line. Which they did constantly, if for no other reason than to provoke Brooke into correcting them.

Their food arrived, served by two cheerful, plump ladies in Bavarian-themed uniforms, and Will got a bigger surprise. It was a fantastic meal. The platters were piled high with five kinds of sausage, smothered in sauerkraut. There was a gigantic bowl of creamy potato salad that perfectly complemented the meat, and sharp, crisp pickle spears and jars of different mustards that redefined the word *mustard;* one was like velvet, another tart and spiked with spices, a third sweet as honey but hot enough to fire a blast wave through his sinuses. To wash it all down were pitchers of cold, fizzy apple cider, which the friends poured into big frosted mugs.

Ajay mentioned Will's dismay at the rule against texting, and everyone expressed how difficult they'd found it at first to adapt. Well, almost everyone.

"Never got into texting," said Nick.

"How could you?" said Elise. "It requires knowing how to spell."

"Go ahead, laugh, nerdlings," said Nick. "There's not even going to *be* texting in the near future. Which I know 'cause I happen to be sitting on the sickest, most awesome idea for a social network site *ever.*"

"Pray tell," said Ajay.

Nick lowered his voice and drew them in. "I take all the best parts of YouTube, Twitter, and Facebook, and combine them into a whole new service called . . . You*Twit*-face."

They laughed so hard Ajay snorted cider out his nose, which set off an even bigger laugh.

"May I propose a round of toasts," said Ajay, lifting his glass. "To our new companion: May the winds of fortune guide you, Will. May you sail a gentle sea. And may it always be the other guy who says, 'This drink's on me.'"

They laughed, then Brooke held up her glass and said, "Will, may you have all the happiness and luck that life can hold. And at the end of all your rainbows, may you find a pot of gold."

The others clapped. Nick stood up with his glass raised.

"Health and long life to you, young dude," said Nick. "Stay happy and well fed . . . and may you be half an hour in heaven before the Devil knows you're dead!"

They laughed again. It was Elise's turn, but she didn't stand or raise her mug or even look at Will. She rubbed her index finger around the edge of her glass until it sent an eerie, piercing note through the room. With the note hanging in the air, Elise shifted her eyes to meet Will's, with an intensity every bit as penetrating as the note. Her mesmerizing green eyes drilled into him.

"Never forget to remember," said Elise, barely above a whisper, "the things that make you glad. And always remember to forget . . . the things that make you sad."

Will turned away. *She looked straight into me. I felt it. Nick isn't exaggerating; she's got some witchy way of seeing about her.*

The happy mood at the table crashed.

"For goodness' sake, woman," said Ajay. "Do you have to turn every happy occasion into a werewolf movie? Warn him about the full moon while you're at it."

The others laughed, but Elise looked deadly serious. Trying to shake off a shadow, Will thought. Something she'd seen, felt, or remembered had disturbed her. Will let his intuition chase the idea, but he hit a wall. He couldn't read Elise at all.

"Hello," said Nick, miming answering a phone. "Suicide Prevention Hotline, can you please hold?"

Brooke shot a look at Nick: *Don't go there.* Nick protested, then got her point, and smacked himself on the head. They all looked subdued. No one would meet Will's eye.

"Okay, what's this about?" asked Will.

"What's what about?" asked Nick.

"Nick, you're a terrible liar. Whatever you all just flashed on that killed the mood."

"It doesn't have anything to do with you," said Brooke.

"Then why not tell it to me?"

"Because, well, obviously," said Ajay, "we'd rather not talk about it, old boy."

They all seemed to be waiting for Brooke to make the decision. A moment later she said matter-of-factly, "We had another roommate last year. And he died."

Will let that sink in.

#10: DON'T JUST REACT TO A SITUATION THAT TAKES YOU BY SURPRISE. *RESPOND.*

Elise turned away, her face ashen. *This* is what had upset her.

"At school?" he asked.

"No," said Brooke. "Over the summer. While he was away."

"While we were *all* away," said Nick.

"And before that he was living in my room," asked Will, knowing the answer.

"Yes," said Brooke. "And, as I said, it doesn't have anything to do with you."

"It didn't have anything to do with any of us," said Ajay.

"What happened to him?" asked Will.

"That's the thing . . . ," said Nick.

"What's the thing?" asked Will.

"Nobody knows," said Elise. "Get the check, Nick. We're outta here."

Elise had a way of ending conversations.

* * *

They walked back to Greenwood Hall, considerably more subdued than they had been on the trip over. Once in their pod, they spent only moments wishing Will good night before scattering to their rooms. Will grabbed some water from the kitchen and lingered in the great room. On a bookshelf near the fireplace he spotted a Center yearbook: last year's edition. He took it into his bedroom and closed and locked his door. Alone again, this time for the night.

In the dead kid's room.

The room had sat empty until they'd known for sure that he wasn't coming back. Did they change the furniture? Had the boy slept on this same mattress? Spoken on that black phone? Sat in this chair, worked and studied at this desk? Will nudged the desk, dislodging it to the right. The hardwood floor beneath the front legs was a darker color. This was probably the same desk the dead kid had used.

His name was Ronnie Murso. Will had gotten that much out of Ajay before they'd parted for the night. The five of them— Brooke, Ajay, Nick, Elise, and Ronnie—had spent freshman year in Greenwood Hall Pod 4-3. A momentous year, their first away from home, full of stress and upheaval. Will opened the yearbook to the freshman section. He found all their photographs, the usual smiling oblivious head shots. Except for Elise, who stared at the camera with a boldness suggesting she knew the photographer's every secret.

Then he found Ronnie Murso. He had a long narrow face, a delicate jawline, and straight blond hair as white as straw. His thin-lipped smile looked taut and a little forced. He had intelligent hazel eyes, a hint of vulnerability around them. He looked sensitive, clearly shy. An emo-geek most likely, a bit on the scrawny side. Below each photo sat a small block of text. Self-profiles. Ronnie's read:

Embrace paradox. Look for patterns.
Beethoven holds the key but doesn't know it yet.
Hiding inside your Shangri-la you might find the Gates of Hell.

Strange. This was the second mention of Shangri-la since he'd left home. And, wait, Dad also used that same phrase in his last message: "the gates of hell." To Ronnie's point: How many mentions in a short period of time constituted a pattern?

#26: ONCE IS AN ANOMALY. TWICE IS A COINCIDENCE. THREE TIMES IS A PATTERN. AND AS WE KNOW ...

There is no such thing as coincidence.

The mattress buzzed, startling him. Nando's cell phone. Will retrieved it, then stepped into the bathroom and shut the door.

"They're at Oxnard Airport, man," said Nando when Will answered. "They drove straight down here from your house. Pulled right onto the runway. They're loading up a private jet with the stuff from the house."

"Where are you?" asked Will.

"Parked across the street, watching through the fence. It's a twin-engine jet . . . looks like it seats seven or eight?"

"Can you see the tail numbers?"

A moment later Nando said, "N-four-niner-seven-T-F."

"Who's on board?" asked Will.

"The lady and that dude with the beard . . ."

Mom and Dad.

"And the bald dude just went inside with 'em. They're closing up the stairs. Rest of the Caps are back in the cars. Driving away, like in formation."

"Don't let 'em see you," said Will.

"They won't, bro. Taxis are invisible, especially near airports. The plane's moving now, ready for takeoff. You want me to stick with the Caps?"

"I can't ask you to do that, Nando—"

"Get real, man. I can haul Mr. and Mrs. Richie Rich and their potty-mouthed kids to LAX any day. You kidding me? Any hack in the world would kill for a thrill like this."

"I just don't know how to thank you," said Will.

"Give your pops a hug, man. We're good— Hey, here come the Caps on the frontage road. Gotta jam. Later."

Will called National Directory Assistance looking for private air charter companies that offered noncommercial flights out of Oxnard. On the third call, he got a hit on the tail numbers. The secretary who answered told him their company owned that plane: a Bombardier Challenger 600 twin-engine jet.

#34: ACT AS IF YOU'RE IN CHARGE, AND PEOPLE WILL BELIEVE YOU.

Will altered his voice to the flat institutional twang civil servants used when they wanted to let civilians know they meant business.

"This is Deputy Johnson, Ventura County sheriff," said Will. "We have reason to believe persons of interest may be on that aircraft. Do you have a passenger list?"

"No, sir." She sounded eager to cooperate.

"Was the aircraft engaged by Mr. or Mrs. Jordan West?" He heard papers shuffle.

"Yes. Mrs. West paid for it. With a credit card."

His parents didn't own credit cards. Everything he'd ever seen them buy they paid for with personal checks or cash.

"Was that the *name* on the credit card?" he asked.

"Yes. Jordan West."

"And what is their destination, ma'am?"

"They're flying to Phoenix. Scheduled to return tomorrow."

Phoenix. So his misdirection had worked. With a little luck, they'd go hunting for him in Mexico, too.

"And what was the charge for this flight?"

"Round trip from here to Phoenix is twelve thousand seven hundred twenty dollars," she said.

That put to rest any doubt his parents hadn't paid for this. They sweated out bills every month. They simply didn't have that kind of money. Will thanked the woman and said he'd call back with any further questions.

He went into the bedroom. His focus started to fade, the two most stressful days of his life dragging him down. His head ached dully along with half a dozen other body parts. Will climbed into bed. The mattress was firm but yielding, the pillow soft and cool.

Will looked at the photo of his parents on the bedside table, then picked up Dad's rules and browsed through them. Some were in his handwriting, but most were in Dad's, the way they'd collected them over the years. On the last page, Will noticed one he hadn't seen before, in Dad's handwriting, with no number attached. He must have put it there recently.

OPEN ALL DOORS, AND AWAKEN.

Why did that sound familiar? Will tried to track the connection but his eyes closed and he fell asleep with the book on his chest.

Climbing up through the walls of Greenwood Hall, the bug never varied its path or pace. Soon after Will fell asleep, a creature the size of a cockroach squeezed through a crack between the floor and baseboard of Will's room. Flat and armored like a beetle, the creature was studded with coarse black hairs. An unusual number of eyes bulged from its head. The creature trudged across the room, up a desk leg, and onto the surface to Will's tablet. The bug's forearms probed the sides until a port opened in the black seamless metal. The bug wriggled inside and disappeared.

Moments later, the computer turned on. Legs unfolded in back and slowly lifted the machine. The numinous black screen shimmered to life. Legs inching around in almost undetectable increments, the machine shifted until the screen faced the bed.

And it watched Will sleep.

There was no doubt this was the boy I'd seen in the dream. I recognized him instantly. Did he recognize me? I couldn't tell. But I knew he had secrets, maybe even more than I did.

He would start asking questions soon. No telling how that would turn out. One thing I knew for sure: Questions could be even more dangerous than secrets.

STUDENT-CITIZENS

The black retro phone on Will's desk rang with a musical but insistent trill. Will fumbled out of bed to the receiver.

"Hello?" he mumbled.

"Good morning, Mr. West. It's seven a.m. on Thursday, November ninth. Welcome to your first full day at the Center."

A female voice, pleasant, chatty, and cheerful. The squashed and hammered vowels of the upper Midwest.

"Thank you," said Will. "Who is this?"

He tried to pull the phone toward the bed, but its heavy-duty cloth cord ran only a few feet from the wall and wouldn't budge when he yanked on it.

"Dr. Robbins requested we give you a wake-up call today. And remind you, Mr. West, that you have an appointment with her at nine o'clock sharp—"

"I know, I know—"

"—at Nordby Hall. That's the main administration building. Room two forty-one. Would'ja like directions or maybe a map?"

"No, thanks, I know where it is."

"Great! It's gonna be a real nice day. Sunny, with light winds, and a high of thirty-eight degrees—"

"Wow. A heat wave."

"Oh, yah, you betcha. *Much* nicer. But cold weather builds character, ya know, so get out there and enjoy it now."

"What's your name?" asked Will again.

"I'm just one of the switchboard operators, Mr. West. So are you awake now, then? That time change deal can be a real bear—"

"I promise, I'm awake."

"Good, good, good. They're serving breakfast in the cafeteria if you want to grab a bite before your meeting. Have yourself a great day now, Mr. West."

The operator, whoever she was, ended the call. Will heard something like elevator music. He hung up and really looked at the phone for the first time. He lifted it; it felt inordinately heavy, at least two pounds. He couldn't find any seams or screws, as if it had been constructed out of a solid block of material. There were no numbers to push. Just one big round button in the middle of its face: glossy white enamel, with a black capital *C* in the center.

He picked up the receiver again and pressed that big *C* button. Instantly, an operator responded: "Good morning, Mr. West. How can I help you today?"

If this wasn't the same woman, it was someone who sounded exactly like her. Will hung up without speaking. He quickly showered and dressed in his new school threads: blue long-sleeved polo, gray khakis, and winter boots. He clipped the black pager onto his belt and slipped Dave's dark glasses into his pocket, then checked himself out in the full-length mirror on the back of the closet door. A shiver of strangeness ran through him; he looked like one of the kids in the school brochure.

That's me. I'm a student at the Center now.

"Good to be alive," he muttered.

Ajay was in the great room when Will came out, and offered to join him for breakfast. They walked outside together. The operator had been right; it was nowhere near as cold as yesterday. This time it took three whole minutes before Will felt like his face had frozen through to his skull.

"What's with the ladies on the phone?" he asked.

"The switchboard operators?" Ajay's eyes widened. "Oh, they're very mysterious."

"In what way?"

"No one knows who they are or where they work. They're always there, instantly, when you pick up any phone, but no one's ever *seen* them. And they never tell you their names."

"But they must be somewhere on campus. She sure *sounded* local."

"I know," said Ajay. "Like everyone's favorite auntie. You can almost smell the apple pie she's baking in the oven for you."

They entered the cafeteria. The room was as big as a department store, teeming with teenagers who seemed far more alert and energetic than any kids he'd ever seen this early in the day.

Maybe it's the coffee. They fell into one of two lines around a massive buffet that offered a staggeringly comprehensive breakfast. The roommates loaded up their plates and sat at a corner table. Will thought of himself as a big eater, but for the second meal in a row, he watched Ajay shovel enough down his gullet to power a Clydesdale. Pound for pound, the little guy ate at a championship level.

"Look at this," said Will. "Must cost a small fortune to go here."

"I'm told it's a *large* fortune, but I don't actually know. I'm here on full scholarship."

"You too?"

"I told you, old boy," said Ajay. "We're kindred spirits."

"How did they find you?"

"A test I took at my old school in eighth grade. Dr. Robbins showed up two months later—four-fifteen p.m., Wednesday, February fourth, 2009—and that was that."

"Did anything specific about you interest them?" asked Will.

"Not at the time. But since then they've shown some interest in an ability of mine." Ajay looked around furtively. "Do you want me to tell you?"

"Okay."

"I have unusually good eyesight," said Ajay, lowering his voice. "The standard for excellence is 20/20. Meaning one sees at twenty feet what most people see from that distance. Top-gun fighter pilots average 20/12, meaning they see at twenty feet what most people do at twelve. Mine, they think, is 20/6."

"Man, that's like an eagle."

"I'm told eagles are 20/4, but they've never persuaded one to take the test. And this doesn't run in my family. Both my parents wear glasses, and without them my father's blind as a bat." Ajay hesitated. "And that's not all."

Will waited patiently.

"I have a *second* ability," said Ajay, "but you have to *assure* me you won't tell anyone."

"Absolutely."

Ajay leaned in and whispered, "In the last few years, I've realized that I possess, quite literally, a photographic memory. I remember everything I see."

"Doubtful."

"That's the usual reaction. Hand me that newspaper."

Will handed him a copy of the school paper—the *Daily Knight*—that had been left on the next table. Ajay took a quick glance and handed it back. Then, as Will read along, he recited the entire page word for word, without pausing.

"You could have memorized this earlier," said Will, still skeptical.

"I could have. But I didn't."

"So you not only see everything," said Will, "but you also remember everything you see."

"I haven't even told them this part," said Ajay, leaning in farther. "I remember *everything that's ever happened to me.*"

"Really? Could you always?"

"I must have been able to, but I never really thought of it as out of the ordinary. Until I realized"—he tapped his head—"everything's in here, filed and stored by day, date, and time, like a hard drive."

Will asked carefully, "Why don't you want anyone to know about this?"

"I'm afraid that if word got out, other students would pester me to help them study. Or cheat. Or the school would start examining me. Perhaps I'm paranoid, but I'd just as soon keep it to myself."

189

"I know the feeling," said Will.

"Why? What brought them to your door?"

"That same test." Will hesitated again. "I got an . . . unusually high score."

"So we have that in common as well."

Will wondered if that was true about all his roommates—surely not *Nick*—and his mind drifted back to what he'd learned about their pod the night before. "What was Ronnie Murso good at?"

"Everything," said Ajay. "He excelled at excellence. Smartest kid I've ever known. He was designing computer games at seven. He spent most of last year in the labs working on some massive project but never told us what it was."

"Why?"

"He had hopes of selling it, I suppose. Students can patent anything they develop here, and a few have made piles of money. I got the impression Ronnie was afraid someone might steal his idea."

"Was it a game?"

"I don't know. I'm a hardware man myself. Give me a tool kit and a bucket of bolts and I'll tinker till the end of time. Ronnie was a dreamer, with a grand perspective. A visionary, really. Which makes his loss all the more painful."

Glancing around, Will noticed Brooke at a table on the other side of the room, sitting across from the same cocky jerk he'd chased off the day before, Todd Hodak. Brooke looked tense and, Will thought, unhappy. *This guy Todd is pressuring her.*

"Will, call me meshuggener but I have a good feeling about you," said Ajay, flashing his big bright smile. "You feel as solid to me as a beam of cobalt steel. I don't say this lightly, to anyone, but I know I can trust you."

Will wasn't used to people speaking so openly to him. Not even people he'd known much longer than Ajay. He liked Ajay a lot, but he'd never really had a close friend before. He wanted to say "I trust you, too," and felt like that was true, but his thoughts got so tangled up with his cautious past that he didn't know how to begin.

Before he could say anything, a weird look crossed Ajay's face. Like he'd just been *ordered* to do something. He stood up quickly, picked up his tray, turned around, and ran straight into someone.

Lyle Ogilvy had walked up behind him without a sound. When Ajay hit him, his tray toppled and the remains of Ajay's breakfast scattered. A partially eaten waffle plopped onto Lyle's right wingtip. Maple syrup oozed between the laces.

"I'm so terribly sorry," said Ajay, turning ashen.

"Yes, you are," said Lyle calmly, without moving. "Clean that up. Now."

"Of course, Lyle, right away."

The room grew quiet around them. Ajay fumbled a fistful of napkins from the dispenser on the table. Lyle never took his eyes off Will.

"You don't have to do that, Ajay," said Will.

"No, it's no trouble at all. My fault entirely."

Will reached out and stayed Ajay's hand. "Don't."

"Please, Will," whispered Ajay. "It's better if I do."

Will stood up as Ajay bent down to clean Lyle's shoe. Lyle looked at Will and smiled pleasantly.

"You didn't give him room to get up," said Will. "That was your fault."

"Why don't you clean it up for him, then?" said Lyle, his smile broadening.

Kids all around them turned to watch. Todd Hodak and a couple of other bruisers drifted their way. Ajay looked up at Will, from his hands and knees, silently pleading with him not to interfere.

Lyle leaned in and whispered, "I *know* about you. I know *all* about you."

Will picked up their table's maple syrup dispenser and stepped next to Lyle. He lowered his voice and leaned in so only he could hear, and grabbed Lyle's belt. "Question for you, Lyle," Will whispered back. "You ever sat through class with a pint of maple syrup down your pants?"

The smile left Lyle's face. Vivid red dots appeared on his cheeks.

"No?" asked Will. "Want to try?"

Ajay paused over Lyle's foot, looking up, unsure what to do.

"Sell 'scary hall monitor' someplace else," whispered Will. "I'm not buying."

Lyle turned abruptly and stalked away. The shoe with syrup on it squeaked with every step and made his odd splayed gait even more ungainly. Todd Hodak and the other older kids flocked around Lyle. Will caught Brooke's eye: She'd watched the whole exchange and flashed him a subtle thumbs-up.

"Put that down and follow me," said Ajay. "Fast."

Will followed him outside, where Ajay pulled Will around the corner. They sprinted out of sight. Glancing back, they saw Todd Hodak and two others run out of the union looking for them.

Ajay pushed Will back against the building, out of sight. "Good God, man, are you completely insane?"

"He was out of line," said Will.

"But you can't treat Lyle Ogilvy that way—"

"No, he can't treat *you* that way. And next time he'll think twice about it," said Will. "Why did you stand up so suddenly like that?"

"I don't know," said Ajay, looking confused. "I guess . . . I guess I thought it was time to go and . . . I don't really remember standing up, to be honest. Why?"

"Just curious," said Will.

"Anyway, my sincerest thanks for interceding. But next time, please, let's discuss these things in *advance*."

Will agreed. They shook hands as they parted.

"I trust you, too, Ajay," said Will.

Will found Nordby Hall without trouble and was outside Dr. Robbins's office when she hurried in at two minutes to nine wearing a fawn-colored suede skirt, brown boots, and a ribbed cream turtleneck sweater. Her cheeks were flushed from the cold.

"Dad's rule number fifty-four," said Will. "If you can't be on time, be early."

"I like that one. Come on in."

He followed Robbins into her office, which was full of morning light from windows that looked over the campus. Big canvases—seaside landscape paintings—dominated two walls, spare images of surf and sand in pale soothing colors.

Her desk was made of glass and stainless steel, her bookshelves thick chunks of glass suspended on cables. No clutter, everything clean and efficient, including a large relaxed sofa, a coffee table, and two chairs. Will wondered if she counseled students while they sat on that sofa; Robbins was, after all, a psychologist. He made a point of sitting in a chair instead.

"So how was your first evening? Did you meet all your roommates?"

He told her the other kids had taken him out to dinner and that they all seemed very nice. She sat across from him, holding two folders.

"I asked Mr. McBride to come by so we can discuss your schedule, but before I get to that . . ." She opened one of the folders on the table. "After what you told me yesterday, I requested a copy of the test you took in September."

Will read NATIONAL SCHOLASTIC EVALUATION AGENCY across the top of a bound text, about sixteen pages long. He recognized the questions on the first page.

"Is that yours?" she asked.

The proctor in charge had used a machine to stamp each copy when kids turned them in. The stamp on Will's read 11:43 a.m.

"It looks like it."

"The test began at nine o'clock. You had three hours to complete it. You turned yours in at seventeen minutes to noon— look at the time stamp. You told me you finished it in twenty minutes." She didn't sound mad, or accusatory, just neutral.

"I did," said Will.

"Why didn't you turn it in when you finished?"

"Same reason. I waited until half the group turned theirs in first—"

"So you wouldn't stand out. I get it. Do you have any way to *prove* that you finished it in twenty minutes?"

"No. But that's the truth."

Robbins took a moment, collecting her thoughts. She set a single page in front of him: the *results* of his test from the National Scholastic Evaluation Agency.

"You answered every question correctly," she said. "Four hundred and seventy-five questions. Science, math, logic, English, and reading comprehension. Explain how you could have done *that* in twenty minutes if you weren't trying—"

"I can't, I don't know—"

"—and how this was part of your plan to blend in?"

"I didn't *mean* to do that. I only glanced at it. I didn't try to get them wrong on *purpose*. I just checked the first thing that came into my head."

"So how *do* we account for it? Luck? Intuition? They've been conducting these tests for decades and this has never happened before. Not once, out of *millions*. You didn't see a copy of the test beforehand, did you?"

"No. They didn't even tell us ahead of time. They just showed up that day and laid it on us."

Robbins looked at him hard. "Well, I don't know what to think about this."

Will's heart raced to the edge of panic. "Do you think I cheated? Are you going to take back my scholarship?"

"No, Will. That's not even a consideration. As unlikely as this seems, I believe you. Not only do I think you deserve to be here, but also I believe you *need* to be. I can't tell you exactly why I feel that way, any more than I can explain how *this* happened."

Will thought about it. "Who else could have seen these results?"

"I don't know, outside of the Agency," she said, then looked up at him alertly. "You think the people who came looking for you had access to your test."

"Maybe," said Will. "I can't think of another reason why total strangers would take an interest in me. What do you know about this company?"

"The National Scholastic Evaluation Agency's been in business for over twenty-five years—"

"But who are they? A private company?"

"As far as I know they're a nonprofit foundation that receives some government funding—"

There was a knock at the door. Dan McBride opened it and looked in with a smile. "Hope we're not intruding?" he asked.

McBride entered, followed by Headmaster Rourke. Both shook Will's hand and exchanged pleasantries as they sat. "We spent hours discussing you yesterday, Will," said Rourke. "Your ears must have been burning."

"Why?"

"You present a dilemma for us," said Rourke. "With only five weeks left in the term, it's neither sensible nor fair to place you on a grading curve. So you'll just be auditing courses for now. It'll give you time to catch up before the new term, acclimate to life here. It's not just our goal to educate students; we want to create student-*citizens.*" Rourke nodded at McBride.

"Here, then, are the units we'd like to start with," said McBride.

McBride handed him a list with four classes that sounded nothing like any he'd ever taken before. All but the last had extensive reading lists:

CIVICS: PROFILES IN POWER AND REALPOLITIK
AMERICAN LITERATURE: EMERSON, THOREAU, AND
    THE AMERICAN IDEAL
SCIENCE: GENETICS—TOMORROW'S SCIENCE TODAY
PHYSICAL EDUCATION: FALL SPORTS

"One meets Tuesdays and Thursdays," said McBride. "The others on Monday, Wednesday, and Friday. The phys ed unit runs through the week."

Will pointed to American Literature. "Is this your class, Mr. McBride?"

"I'm afraid I couldn't resist," said McBride with a grin.

"As far as sports are concerned," said Rourke, "it's also too late for you to officially join teams, but no one objects to your *training* with them."

"Cross-country?" asked Will.

"I've already spoken to Coach Jericho. If you like, you can pick up your gear at the field house after class today and get back on the track."

After two days without training, Will couldn't wait to run again. His body and mind craved the relief. "Done," he said.

The headmaster stood up and shook his hand. "Now if you'll excuse me, Will, I'm late for a staff meeting."

Rourke took his leave. They were about to resume when Will's pager beeped. A red light flashed inside the grill. He pushed the button and the beeping stopped.

"I'm supposed to check with an operator, isn't that right?" asked Will.

"Use my phone," said Robbins. "Hit zero. An operator will put you through."

"I did have one question for you guys," said Will as he moved to the phone.

"What's that, Will?" asked McBride.

#59: SOMETIMES YOU FIND OUT MORE WHEN YOU ASK QUESTIONS TO WHICH YOU ALREADY KNOW THE ANSWER.

"My roommates mentioned something about a kid named Ronnie Murso?"

He could tell by their expressions that he'd caught them off guard. Will picked up the phone and dialed. The operator came on immediately:

"How may I connect your call?" said another flat, happy midwestern voice.

"This is Will West. I got a page?"

"One moment, please."

A clipped male voice came on: "Mr. West, this is Dr. Kujawa, over at the medical clinic?"

"Did you page me, sir?"

"I did. We met yesterday, but you were unconscious at the time. I put those stitches in your head. How are you feeling?"

"Much better, thanks."

"Glad to hear that. Mr. West, I've got some test results here that I need to go over with you. Could you come by my office right away?"

"Why, is something wrong?" asked Will.

"We'll discuss it when you get here. Please ask Dr. Robbins to come with you. I'd like her to see this as well."

Will hung up. "Dr. Kujawa wants to see us both," he said.

"We'll talk on the way," said Robbins. "And I'll tell you about Ronnie Murso."

THE MEDICAL CENTER

Will had to work to keep pace with Dr. Robbins as they crossed campus. A breeze had kicked up and the frigid air slapped at his face. Dr. Robbins hardly seemed to notice.

"Ronnie Murso came in as a freshman last year," said Robbins. "He had trouble adjusting to life away from home. A lot of new students do. He also had serious family issues; his parents had just divorced. When school ended, Ronnie was scheduled to split time with them over the summer. He took a vacation with his father first, at the end of the term. A fishing trip in a remote part of Canada. When their scout plane went back to pick them up, they weren't at the rendezvous point. Searches were organized. Police got involved. To make a long story short, they never found them. Ronnie and his father disappeared."

#92: IF YOU WANT PEOPLE TO TELL YOU MORE, SAY LESS. OPEN YOUR EYES AND EARS, AND CLOSE YOUR MOUTH.

"There are theories," said Robbins. "Ronnie was their only child, and his mother is convinced Ronnie's father kidnapped him to deny her custody. That he ran off with Ronnie to start a new life somewhere. If that is the case, no one's found them yet."

"What do you think?"

"It's possible, but I think it's more likely they got lost, or ran into trouble, and something tragic happened. But until someone finds them, we'll never know."

"Is that why you waited before putting anyone else into his room?"

"In part. For people involved in something like this, it's often harder not knowing what's happened than it is being told for sure."

"So why did you put *me* in there?"

She stopped, looked at him searchingly. "Why is this so important to you?"

"I guess I'm a little sensitive," said Will. "I just spent the freakiest twenty-four hours of my life getting here, only to find out I'm living in the room of a kid who mysteriously disappeared six months ago."

Robbins put a hand on his shoulder. "I understand your concern, Will. It's perfectly natural. But what happened to Ronnie doesn't in any way involve you."

There's something she's not telling me. Will didn't know how he knew it—instinct, intuition, whatever. But now wasn't the time to push her about it.

#60: IF YOU DON'T LIKE THE ANSWER YOU GET, YOU SHOULDN'T HAVE ASKED THE QUESTION.

They arrived at the medical center without another word. Set apart from the quad, it was the most modern building on campus—a six-story tower of blue-tinted glass and steel. Some donor had written a large check to put their name here: Large brushed silver letters identified it as the Haxley Medical Center.

They took an elevator to the fifth floor. Dr. Kujawa welcomed them and led them to an adjacent exam room. He wore a white lab coat with DR. KEN KUJAWA embroidered on the upper left chest. Kujawa looked trim and fit—early forties, Will guessed—with a close-cropped salt-and-pepper brush cut and a brusque, no-nonsense manner.

"Have a seat right there, Mr. West," said Dr. Kujawa, nodding to a table. "How's your head feeling?"

"Right now it feels fine," said Will.

"Let's have a look."

Kujawa bent over him, parted Will's hair, and examined the wound. "That's what I thought," he said cryptically. He waved Robbins over to see it; then they looked at each other.

"What's the problem?" asked Will.

"Come into my office," said Dr. Kujawa.

They followed him into his office, where Kujawa took a seat at his desk and punched up data on a sleek desktop version of a Center tablet.

"Your transcript said you're a runner. Is that right, Mr. West?" he asked.

"Yes. Cross-country."

"Have you ever, to your knowledge, taken, used, or been given any performance-enhancing drugs?"

"What?"

"They would have been classified as an ESA, or erythropoiesis-stimulating agent. Pharmaceutical product. Administered by injection."

"No," said Will, looking at Robbins with alarm. "Never. Absolutely not."

Kujawa continued matter-of-factly. "They stimulate the body's production of a hormone called erythropoietin. EPO substantially increases production of red blood cells, which radically increases the amount of oxygen carried to your muscles. Enables athletes to perform at a premium in sports demanding high endurance, like biking, rowing, or running."

Will's anger built steadily. "That's called blood doping."

"Have you heard of HGH or human growth hormone? Because your blood levels are also nearly double the average for your age and size—"

"If you're accusing me of taking drugs, I swear to you that has never happened."

Kujawa didn't react, just looked at him, neutral, appraising. Waiting.

"It's not that he doesn't believe you, Will," said Robbins calmly. "Go on, Ken."

"EPO and HGH also enhance the body's ability to heal, from life-threatening wounds down to micro-tears in muscle fibers. The obvious value to athletes is it speeds recovery. Not just from injuries but also from routine training."

Kujawa pulled a mirror from the top drawer of his desk and a smaller hand mirror from his coat. He walked over to Will. "You suffered a gash in your scalp that was an inch long. I needed six stitches to close it. Roughly twenty-four hours ago. Take a look at it now."

Kujawa positioned one mirror above Will's scalp and gave the other to Will to hold in front of his eyes. Then he moved Will's hair to the side so he could see the site.

The wound was gone. No scar, no scab, not even any stitches. Just a slight white discoloration.

"Not only is the wound healed, but your body's already assimilated the dissolving stitches, which normally takes more than a week. This, to put it mildly, is more than a little unusual." Kujawa put the mirrors away, took some printed pages off his desk, and handed them to Dr. Robbins.

"I ran a panel of routine tests with the blood I drew yesterday," he said. "The oxygen-binding capacity of your blood is off the charts, over *three times* the high end of normal. You'd make Lance Armstrong in his prime look like an invalid."

"I don't understand this," said Will. "It's not possible. This has to be some kind of crazy mistake."

Robbins was still staring at the results, pale, brow furrowed, deep in thought.

"I don't think so," said Kujawa. "To that end I'd like to run more tests, to determine whether your body produced these levels on its own or if they were synthetically created and, maybe by some method unknown to you, introduced into your system. Have you ever been given any injections?"

"No."

"What about any unusual vitamins or supplements?"

"Not that I'm aware of," said Will.

"It would be helpful to see your medical records. Yearly physicals, vaccinations, that sort of thing. Could you ask your parents to send them to me?"

"Of course," said Will.

The truth was a lot more awkward: *He couldn't remember ever visiting a doctor.* His father kept a weathered black leather bag in their bedroom closet that contained a stethoscope; exam instruments for ears, nose, and throat; a blood pressure cuff; and syringes for drawing blood. He used them to give Will a comprehensive checkup twice a year. For the longest time, Will had assumed that's what every family did. But there was another factor in this unusual routine: Will had never *needed* a doctor. Because as far back as he could remember—his entire *life*—he'd never been sick. Not once.

"Rather than have you worry, I want a more complete picture," said Kujawa. "Run more tests, cover all the angles, and see what they tell us."

"We'd need your consent, of course," said Robbins. "And your parents' as well. Would you ask them to okay this?"

"I'll call them today," said Will.

"The sooner the better," said Dr. Kujawa. "Use my phone if you like."

"They wouldn't be reachable now. I'll try later," said Will. "Does this mean it's okay for me to work with the cross-country team?"

"Mr. West, based on what I've seen, you could run from here to the border of Canada without even breathing hard."

PROFESSOR SANGREN

For the second day in a row, for different reasons, Will walked out of the medical center with his mind reeling. This time he hardly noticed the glacial air.

This explains the running, at least, but how on earth did it happen? Am I some kind of freak? No wonder my parents didn't want me on a cross-country team; I'd end up on Ripley's Believe It or Not. *And once they start poking around in my insides, what else will they find?*

As he walked toward the quad, bells rang nearby. Will tracked them to a tower atop Royster Hall, near the middle of the commons. Visible from anywhere on campus, the large clock on the tower's four sides read 11:00. Sounding the hour.

Will pulled out the schedule McBride had given him. The first of his five classes started at eleven. *Right now.* Room 207, Bledsoe Hall. He summoned the campus map in his mind and located Bledsoe Hall. He calculated direction and distance— over a quarter of a mile—and started running.

He reached Bledsoe before the bells stopped ringing. Will

hurried in, dashed upstairs, and found room 207. He saw shapes through the door's rippled glass window and heard a male voice. Will took a deep breath and stepped inside.

Six rows of curved mahogany desks on low risers ascended in a terraced half-circle amphitheater. A wall of windows was covered with louvered wooden blinds. Twenty-five students filled the desks, their tablets propped in front of them.

Every student looked attractive, poised, and physically fit. A diverse group of races and ethnic groups, all, without exception, put together and self-assured. If this sample was any indication of the Center's student body, Rourke was right; these kids were *way* above average. If they weren't already rich and famous, it was only a matter of time. Will felt like a skunk at the opera.

The instructor—a boyish, energetic man with a shock of long sandy hair—stood before a square blue screen that took up most of that wall. On a lectern in front of him sat some sort of built-in computerized control panel. The man stopped speaking as Will entered.

"And you are?" asked the teacher.

"Late," said Will.

"Only by . . . two months," said the instructor in a deep, resonant voice.

The class laughed.

Will glanced at his schedule: CIVICS: PROFILES IN POWER AND REALPOLITIK. *Professor Lawrence Sangren.*

"Really sorry, Professor Sangren," said Will.

#72: WHEN IN A NEW PLACE, ACT LIKE YOU'VE BEEN THERE BEFORE.

"Ladies and gentlemen, welcome if you would the *late* Will West," said Sangren, holding a hand toward Will like a talk-show host introducing a guest. "And did we bring our book with us today, Mr. West?"

"I was hoping I'd get the textbook once I got here."

For some reason the class laughed at that as well. Will's cheeks burned hot.

"Like primordial life emerging from the sea, learn to crawl before you walk," said Sangren. "And take a seat."

Will swallowed his anger and climbed the risers. He spotted Brooke in the middle of the third row. She winked at him, then nodded at an empty desk to her right. He slid in gratefully beside her, then noticed Elise sitting behind him, isolated, chin propped on her palm, staring at him. Shaking her head.

"Miss Springer," said Sangren. "Please explain to Mr. West why he should bring his *note*book to class."

"Current text, study guide, and notes are uploaded wirelessly onto your tablet during every class," said Brooke, then whispered, "That's why we bring them everywhere."

He hadn't brought *anything* with him: not even a pencil. Woeful.

#40: NEVER MAKE EXCUSES.

"How big a loser am I?" he whispered.

"We don't have units of measurement that size," Brooke whispered back.

"I am so doomed with this guy."

"Probably so."

"Thanks, I feel better now," said Will.

"Are we finding the accommodations satisfactory, Mr. West?" asked Sangren.

"Yes, sir."

"Good. Now please refrain from speaking unless you're struck by either an original thought or a meteorite. The odds of which I would estimate are about even."

An even bigger laugh. Even Elise gave a little smirk at that smack-down.

God. Just. Kill. Me. Now.

Sangren ran his fingers over the console on his lectern. Overhead lights in the room dimmed; the louvers on the windows closed automatically. The blue screen behind Sangren transformed into a map of Europe that took up the entire wall.

No, much more than a map, Will realized. Some kind of hybrid satellite image: intensely photo-real, with precise topographic three-dimensional contours. Engraved borders defined countries. Names of important places and geographic features conformed to the shapes of the ground below. Mountains jutted straight out of the surface toward them: The line of the Alps plowed south toward Italy.

Every detail looked startlingly vivid. Large cities—Rome, Vienna, Paris, London—appeared as broad flickering pockets of light, teeming with life. Currents and tides animated oceans, rippling and swelling around ports and shorelines. No map he'd ever seen more plainly showed the influence of geography on the creation of societies. Clouds drifted overhead, and sunlight and shadows played across the entire continent in a way that only an astronaut, or maybe God, could have seen them.

Will glanced around; the *same* map appeared on the tablets of all the other students. Astonishing.

"The name of the class, Mr. West, is Civics: Profiles in Power and Realpolitik," said Sangren. "The *point* of this unit is to look back and grasp what's relevant to us as Americans—at *this* moment in time—about the struggles of our human predecessors. Are you with me so far?"

"Yes, sir."

Sangren moved his hands on his console. Animated three-dimensional images blossomed all over the map; time came to life before their eyes. Roman legions advanced on barbarian camps. Napoleon's Grand Army rode toward Moscow. Dust rose from ancient roads to the drumbeat of hooves on paving stones, the clang of weapons, gunfire, and artillery. Merchants loaded sailing ships in harbors. Armadas clashed on open seas.

"We don't teach history here; we let history teach us. The way it did the people who lived it: the way you experience the present, as a living field you can reach out and touch. The human story. A long compelling tale fueled by one common theme: the lust for power. Driven by men and women who understood the tools and the rules of the *exercise* of power. What might those be, Miss Moreau?"

Elise glanced at Will as she answered. Biting off each word with a snap. "Brutality. Terror. Corruption. Greed. Bloodshed. Deception."

"Don't forget obsession, madness, and seduction," said Sangren.

"Oh, I never do," said Elise.

The class chuckled.

"In other words, we look for the *truth* behind the common assumptions," said Sangren. "And the truth isn't very pretty, is it, Miss Moreau?"

"No, sir. But it sure is interesting."

The class laughed again. All except Brooke, who rolled her eyes.

"Empty your mind, Mr. West. Forget those nice stories you've been told about history as 'progress' and the 'goodness' of humanity. Chock full of idealism, fairness, decency, the innate nobility of man, all that heartwarming flapdoodle. Nothing wrong with it, by the way. And if you're interested, you can learn all about it in another class just down the hall. It's called *fiction*."

The class laughed again. Will's eyes felt stuck wide open. He'd never heard a teacher chomp into the neck of a subject like this before. In the schools Will had attended, Sangren would have been banished for opinions this outrageous.

His floppy hair waving as he moved around, Sangren continued with the passion and energy of a conductor driving an orchestra to the end of a symphony.

"This is the big con of the ruling classes. The one they've convinced the masses to buy since the dawn of time, that submitting to the will of those in charge *is in their best interests*. Even if it costs them their cash, their livelihood, or their happiness. Even if it *kills* them, which more often than not is exactly what happens."

On the map, more images appeared: battlefields littered with casualties. Wagons carrying stacks of wooden caskets. Military graveyards. Rows of white crosses fading into the mist.

"So ask yourself, Which of these 'demographics' do you aspire to? Spending your life at the nickel slots in a cut-rate casino? Or at a table in the high-roller penthouse where the game's really played? That's the velvet rope of the great divide. Which side are you on?"

The question hung in the air. Sangren looked directly at Will.

"Don't answer yet. Pay attention. You'll be shocked by what you learn. Before the penny finally drops, there will be nights when you want to cry yourself to sleep. Then, one fine morning, you'll wake up, look around, and see the world the way it really is. Lucky, lucky you."

The dire images faded away and a breathtaking image of the earth floating in the dark void of space appeared on-screen.

"After all, this lovely, fragile little blue sphere is going to be *your* amusement park someday," said Sangren. "Isn't it in your best interest, before that comes to pass, to learn how it really works?"

When class ended, Will staggered down the risers toward the door. In one hour, Sangren had stretched his mind in directions no teacher had taken him before. He felt invigorated, but overwhelmed: He had a *world* of catching up to do. Brooke waited for him outside, but before he reached her:

"Mr. West!"

Professor Sangren, packing his valise at the lectern, beckoned Will over.

"We'll talk later," said Brooke, squeezing his arm. "Hang in there."

Will walked back to Sangren and realized he was actually taller than his teacher.

"I frightened you today," said Sangren.

"That's all right, sir—"

"I'm not apologizing. That was my intention." Sangren regarded Will with a patronizing smile. "We need to determine, rather quickly, if you belong here. Not many do, and there's no shame in that, but this will be trial by fire. Get that through your head: The Center is a meritocracy, not a charity day-care facility."

Will felt his guts churning and struggled to hold in his anger.

"Do you know what's at stake? We're in a global knife fight. Will America and the Western democracies remain the most powerful, resourceful, and innovative force on earth? Or are we just going to wave China and India on ahead and say, 'Yo, catch you later.' Your generation's going to make or break this battle. You're either smart enough and strong enough to lead on the front lines, or you're not. As teachers, we need to state the stark reality of what's expected and demanded of every student. You'll have to do whatever it takes to survive here, and it is going to be *hard*."

Will noticed something peculiar about Sangren's eyes. His left iris was solid black, as if dilated by an optometrist. Something about this weird contrast made it feel as if two different people were looking at him through the same set of eyes.

Sangren smiled again. Will didn't like it. "I'm guessing none of our cuddly old softies in administration explained it this way."

"Not in so many words."

"Then let me be the first to use *this* many words: You have five weeks to make the grade. Best of luck to you. It appears you're going to need it."

Sangren strolled away, lifting onto his toes with each step, swinging his case, whistling "Singin' in the Rain."

Will watched him go. The little professor had just dumped ice water all over his sense of security. If Sangren was telling the truth, what if he *didn't* make the grade? If they showed him the door five weeks from now . . . where in the world would he go?

Will wandered out into the hall. His only class for the day over, he felt lost and a little helpless, and paid no attention to where he was. He heard piano music from down the hall, classical, expertly played. A woman joined in, singing in a foreign language—French, he thought. Her voice stopped him cold; powerful but restrained, it was deeply emotional. He tracked it to a room and opened the door.

A grand piano stood in the center of the room. Sitting at the piano, both singing and playing, was Elise. She stopped when she heard him come in.

"Sorry," said Will. "Please, don't stop."

She scowled at him. "You've never heard *Lakmé* before?"

"I've never heard anything like that before."

"Well, don't get all moony over it, Jethro," she said. She started again, improvising the classical phrase she'd been playing into effortless jazz.

"Where did you learn . . . ?" he asked, astonished by her skill.

"Dad's a first violin. Mom used to headline at a nightclub in Hong Kong. So it's not as if I had a *choice*, okay?"

"You sound embarrassed about it."

"If you're not embarrassed about your parents at our age," said Elise, "you've got a plate in your head."

Will listened as she riffed the same melody into pop, R & B, and hip-hop idioms. Dazzling.

"You ought to just turn pro," said Will. "I mean it. Right now."

Elise laughed. "And then what, spend my life giving piano lessons to the tone-deaf spawn of suburbia to subsidize my passion? No thanks."

"So what is your passion?"

"The usual," she said, running glissandos up and down the keyboard. "Writing. Recording. World domination."

She looked straight into him with that wide-open unnerving gaze, but this time Will didn't look away and he was struck by a feeling he'd seen her eyes before. . . .

"I saw Sangren grab you after class," she said, turning back to the piano. "Did he gut-punch you?"

"What do you mean?"

"Don't play dumb, West. You know what I'm talking about."

Will fidgeted. "I guess he said a few things that caught me off guard—"

Elise slammed down the cover on the keys. "Would you just *stop*?"

Will jumped. "What? Stop what?"

She locked eyes with him. He tried to make himself blank, unreadable, which only seemed to make her angrier. "Stop *hiding*. Maybe that's how you survived with the hicks back at Nowheresville High, but you're not the only smart kid in the room now. And you're not gonna make it unless you come out from under your *rock*."

He realized she was trying to be helpful, reach out to him in her own complicated way, just as Ajay had earlier at breakfast. He took in a deep breath and tried to let down his guard as he exhaled: "I'm not sure how to do that."

"Show yourself," said Elise urgently. "Trust somebody. Lose your game face. Figure out who your friends are—that would be *us*, by the way—and ask for help. Be real with us, be who you *are*, or be gone."

Part of him appreciated the advice. But the way she so effortlessly sliced through his defenses infuriated him. Before he even knew what he was saying, he heard himself lash back at her: "Is that what happened to Ronnie Murso?"

Elise flinched, as if the question had cut her physically. It came as a surprise that Miss Above-It-All could be wounded. Will immediately regretted it. He braced for a counterattack, but instead of baring her claws and striking back, she just looked at him, completely unguarded, and let him see how much he'd hurt her.

"Someday you'll realize just how unfair that was," she whispered.

Elise left the piano and brushed past him, out of the room, leaving him holding a big bag full of *What the hell did I say that for?*

"*Damn* it," he said.

Will looked at his watch: He was due at the field house to meet the coach. He needed a run more than ever. He hurried outside and struck out across the commons for the field house. Elise's voice echoed in his head: "*Show yourself. Trust somebody.*"

He'd been taught, trained, and conditioned to never trust *anybody*. Drop his game face? He'd been living with his guard up for so long that if his game face was taken away, he wasn't completely sure who he'd find underneath.

After everything he'd learned the last two days, he wasn't even sure he could trust himself.

THE FIELD HOUSE

The field house stood on the far edge of the practice fields, and it was bigger than an airport hangar. It was made of sturdy weathered red brick, supported by latticed black wrought-iron struts and stately colonnades surrounded by a concrete plaza. The style reminded Will of an ancient ballpark, like a place Babe Ruth might have played. LAUGHTON FIELD HOUSE EST. 1918 was carved into the brick near the front doors, but everyone on campus called it the Barn.

A life-sized bronze statue of the school's mascot, the armored knight pictured in the Center's escutcheon, stood outside the entrance. Coiled and menacing, poised to attack, it carried a short sword and shield, and a hatchet hung from its belt.

The coat of arms was carved on the knight's shield. The knight was depicted in the bottom panel, pointing its sword at the neck of a defeated foe. But the fallen figure on the statue's shield had demonic horns growing out of its head and a forked tail, details missing from images of the crest he'd seen before.

And up close, the knight's armor didn't look medieval at all, but sleek and fitted like a second skin. A shiny brass plate fixed to its pedestal said THE PALADIN.

Will wandered inside, into an immense, cavernous space crisscrossed by exposed steel beams. It was lit by casement windows near the roofline and circular spotlights suspended on long steel cables. An artificial turf field occupied half the structure, circled by a four-lane running track. A lacrosse squad practiced on the turf. Hardwood basketball courts filled the other side. Expanding wooden bleachers on rollers were collapsed and stacked against the walls on three sides. Spirited pickup games filled smaller courts subdividing the main one.

Following signs to the locker rooms, Will went through a door beyond the courts and then down a corridor filled with the pungent smells of liniment, ancient sweat, laundry soap, and, from somewhere, swimming pool chlorine. Framed black-and-white photographs of old school sports teams lined the walls: football, baseball, basketball, hockey, soccer. Each one bearing the school's nickname: the Paladins. Will found the men's locker room and felt as if he'd stepped back in time.

Long wooden benches fronted row after row of tall, battered steel cage lockers. The concrete floor was worn smooth and scalloped by a century of use. Wide-bladed fans hung overhead beneath an arched ceiling. He passed showers and an open restroom, tiled in pale blue, dotted with piles of plain white cotton towels. He heard footsteps moving through the room ahead of him, then hung back when he realized they belonged to Lyle Ogilvy. Lyle was alone, moving toward a small door around the corner from the showers. He took a quick look around before exiting through the door. *Curious.* Will moved on to the far side of the showers. Around that corner he found a wire mesh wall, painted white, with a sign that read EQUIPMENT ROOM.

A wide stainless-steel counter ran the length of the cage. A desk bell on Will's side and one of the black phones on the other were the only objects on the counter. A substantial padlock secured a gate to Will's left. On the far side of the counter, honeycombed walls were filled with every variety of sports equipment. The shelves extended away until they disappeared in shadow. Somewhere back there, an overhead light flickered silently.

Will rang the bell. It echoed through the empty cage. Moments later, he heard rhythmic squeaking as something rolled through the shadows at the end of the hall. As it got closer, Will realized it was a motorized wheelchair with a squeaky wheel and a very unusual passenger.

He couldn't have been more than four feet tall, twisted and contorted by some sort of neuromuscular disease. He wore an oversized sports jersey and a baseball cap with the Center's logo. A cargo vest with multiple pockets covered the jersey. His arms looked weathered, but he had large, expressive hands. His right hand operated a joystick that drove him forward. His twisted legs splayed to either side of the chair, his feet shod in spotless blue and white Nikes.

The guy's square, oversized head tilted left and shook slightly, a constant tremor. Will couldn't tell how old he was. He didn't see any hair under his cap. He seemed both youthful and ageless. A name tag on his jersey read JOLLY NEPSTED, EQUIPMENT MANAGER.

"I know what you're thinking," said Nepsted, his voice high and slightly garbled.

"What's that?" asked Will.

"What does he have to feel jolly about?"

Will laughed as he realized Nepsted was grinning at him. "You tell me."

Nepsted's hand moved to his waist. He pulled out a crowded brass key ring—holding every sort of key imaginable—on a zip line from his belt.

"I'm the guy with the *keys*," said Nepsted. He released the keys and they jangled back to his belt. He grinned again.

"Then you're the guy a new guy needs to meet," said Will.

"Will West," said Nepsted.

"How'd you know that?"

"How many noobs you think we get this time of year?" Nepsted looked him over. "Shoes: nine and a half. Waist: twenty-nine. Inseam: thirty-one. Sweatshirt: medium."

Nepsted pushed a button at the base of the joystick. A steel drawer slid open below the counter beside Will. A black rectangular wicker box sat inside. Will took out the box and set it on the counter.

Inside were two pairs of running shorts and color-coordinated jerseys. A dozen pairs of white quarter socks. Two sets of new gray sweats with the name of the school above the Center's logo: the helmeted head of the Paladin, eyes visible through slits in the steel, two hot sparks of light. One set of sweats was lined with fleece for cold-weather work. Everything was in the exact sizes Jolly had mentioned.

At the bottom, Will found a pair of Adidas Avanti ultra-lightweight distance spikes. Gunmetal-gray mesh with three royal blue Adidas stripes. They were the road shoes he'd always wanted. Will knew just by holding them they'd be the perfect balance and fit.

"Your locker key's there, too," said Nepsted.

Will found it in the corner of the box. A single brass key on a wire ring, with a faded number engraved: 419.

"Buy a combination lock as backup if you're not the trusting type. Sign that form for me, please, and drop it in the drawer."

Will took out a clipboard holding a receipt. He signed at the X with an attached ballpoint and set it back in the drawer. "The trusting type," said Will. "I'm getting that a lot. Do I seem like the trusting type?"

Jolly tilted his head to the side. "How should I know? I'm alone in a padlocked cage. Do I *look* like the trusting type?" He pressed the button on his joystick and the drawer slammed closed with a resounding thud. Nepsted collected the receipt and stuffed it into his vest.

As Will gathered up his gear, he asked, "How'd you get your nickname?"

"It's not a nickname."

"Your real name is Jolly?"

"No, my real name is Happy. Jolly's my middle name. Happy Jolly Nepsted. Happy and jolly, but only on the inside," said Nepsted, his expression never changing. "Let me know how the gear works out. You looking for Coach Jericho?"

"Yes, where can I find him?"

"He'll find you," said Jolly.

"Thanks, Jolly," said Will. "Something tells me if I want to know what's going on around here, you're the guy I need to talk to."

Nepsted stared at him. "You don't want to know what's going on around here." He nodded at the gear Will carried in his arms; the sweatshirt with the logo of the Paladin was on top. "You know what a paladin is?"

"Some kind of knight," said Will. "In the Middle Ages."

"A holy warrior," said Nepsted pointedly. "Dedicated to fighting evil."

"Speaking of evil," said Will, pointing to the crest on the sweatshirt. "On all the versions of the crest I've seen, like this one, the Paladin has beaten down some generic bad guy. But on the crest on the shield of the statue out front, the Paladin's opponent has horns and a forked tail. More like a demon."

Nepsted blinked twice. "A new kid's never noticed that before."

Will stepped closer and pointed to the front of the sweatshirt again. "So why'd they take the demon off the logo?"

Before Nepsted could answer, the black phone inside the cage rang so loud the steel counter rattled. Jolly picked up.

"Equipment room, Nepsted. Hang on." Nepsted hung up and looked at Will. "Come see me again. When you're *ready.*" Nepsted turned his chair around and squeaked off down the aisle into the flickering shadows.

Ready? Ready for what?

Will followed the numbers until he found his locker at the end of a row in a remote corner. He eagerly changed into his new sweats and shoes. Remembering that he was not a trusting person, at least when he was in locker rooms, he shoved his wallet and dark glasses into his pockets.

From the corner of his eye, he caught a glimpse of someone

moving between rows of lockers nearby: a big guy with broad shoulders, in a leather flight jacket and military boots.

"Dave?" said Will.

"Follow," he heard Dave's voice say in his head.

Will hurried after him around the lockers to the same door he'd seen Lyle pass through earlier. It was standing slightly ajar. He peered inside into a long, dark hallway.

"Dave?" Will whispered. "Dave, you there?"

Will stepped tentatively forward, his new spikes crunching on concrete, trailing his hand along the wall as he waited for his eyes to adjust. The air felt twenty degrees hotter than it had in the locker room—steamy, almost tropical. He soon reached a flight of stairs and edged down them, passing under a slight hissing that sounded like steam from a leaky pipe.

"This way," he heard Dave say.

At the base of the stairs, the corridor turned left ninety degrees. The door behind him slammed shut with a loud metallic bang. Will froze. When he heard no one behind him, he continued, feeling his way through the dark down a long endless corridor. Eventually a line of light came into view ahead at floor level. He realized it was spilling out from under a door. Will heard voices on the other side.

"They're moving faster than we thought, mate," said Dave. "Serious juju. You need to see this, so you know what we're up against. Put the glasses on and open it."

Will didn't like the sound of that, but he put the dark glasses on anyway. The last line Dad had written in his rulebook came back to him:

OPEN ALL DOORS, AND AWAKEN.

Will closed his hand around the doorknob, cracked open the door, and peeked inside. A blinding white light issued from something in the center of the room. A group of people stood in a circle around it, focused on the object. It was hard to see how many there were—the light made it hard to see anything—but Will could tell there was something wrong with their features. They didn't have human faces.

The round object they stared at hung in the air at eye level. Its surface appeared to be covered by a pale, translucent membrane. The circle's edges glowed like hot embers, vibrating black, red, and green.

A window, Will thought. *A window in the fabric of the air.*

"That's where the monsters come from," whispered Dave.

Through the membrane, Will could make out a blasted alien landscape of crimson and ash. Black skies streaked with poisonous shades of lavender and green arced above a desolate, volcanic wasteland. Fires raged along the far horizon. A stink of sulfur and festering rot issued from it in blinding waves.

"That's the Never-Was," said Dave.

Will saw movement through the membrane. Something came around a cracked pile of rock and lurched toward the window. It looked like a tall woman, severely beautiful, naked as far as he could tell, her shapely breasts hidden by her long gleaming black hair. She reached the glowing circle and raised her hands to the membrane. Her eyes found Will.

"Uh-oh," said Dave. "That's not good."

The creature's hands pushed at the membrane, stretching it until they finally broke through. Other limbs, dark and slippery like tentacles, tore the remnants of the membrane away. The creature's head and upper body slipped through, and Will saw now that her hair was as wet and ragged as seaweed. Her black eyes flickered and twitched, lids clacking, lit up with pitiless hunger. A foul odor reached him; Will felt sickness wash his guts.

"Run, damn it!" Dave roared.

Terror pulled rank on paralysis. Will slammed the door shut and sprinted headlong back down the corridor. Running in the dark, he heard the door behind him burst open and then the dry rattling slither of something sliding across the concrete after him.

Dave appeared ahead of him in the corridor and drew his hybrid gun. As he opened fire, Will glanced over his shoulder. The corridor was strobing with blasts of hot white light. Will saw the creature closing on him, her spidery limbs reaching for him, her head tilted back, jaws hinged wide open, hideous fangs—

"Don't look at it!" shouted Dave. Standing his ground, Dave fanned the hammer of his gun, firing an explosive barrage of light at the thing. As Will sprinted past him, Dave called, "That's three!"

Howling shrieks echoed down the corridor. Will ran through the stygian darkness for what felt like forever. As he finally turned the corner, he heard yelling and footsteps behind him, human voices—the group he'd seen when he'd first opened the door.

Will stumbled up the stairs, desperately feeling his way along the wall. Hissing filled his ears. He fumbled open the door to the locker room and scrambled through it, spikes skidding on the concrete as he turned a corner.

Two strong hands yanked him back into an alcove. A steel

cage door closed silently behind him. He saw brooms, a mop and bucket, cleaning supplies.

And his roommate, Nick McLeish, in sweats, crouching beside him inside the door, holding a finger to his lips. Moments later, his pursuers burst through the door into the locker room and rushed by their hiding place. There were at least ten of them, moving so fast it was impossible to tell who they were.

The last person in the group came to a halt just outside their door. Through the gaps in the mesh, Will saw a pair of Adidas running shoes, black with three red stripes on the instep. He looked up and saw a hand reach for the doorknob. Nick silently pushed the lock button just as the knob began to turn. Whoever was outside rattled the knob, then moved off. The voices and footsteps faded. Nick covered his mouth with one hand, trying to keep from laughing.

"What's so funny?" whispered Will.

"Dude, the look on your face. When you skidded around that corner, rocking the full Scooby-Doo windmill? Oh my freakin' God, I nearly lost it."

"They were freakin' *chasing* me, Nick."

"I know, I know—"

"Who was it? Did you see?"

"No, bro. I'm at my locker, you go flying past, and I hear them coming, so I pulled you in here. What the h-e-double-hockey-sticks did you do, man?"

H-e-double-hockey-sticks indeed. Will hesitated, then remembered Elise's advice: If he was going to make it, he needed *all* his roommates' help.

"I don't know," said Will, his entire body shaking. "I opened a door. And saw something I wasn't supposed to see."

"Well, give it up. What was it?"

"I don't even know how to describe it."

"Awesome. Which door? Come on, you got to show me, man."

"No way. No *freaking* way, Nick." Will buried his face in his hands.

Nick paused, then patted him on the back. "Okay, chillax, slackasaurus. Don't drop a litter of kitties about it. We better slip you out of here. Before the townsfolk come back with torches and pitchforks."

SUICIDE HILL

Will followed Nick as they snuck out of the broom closet to an undersized door hidden between two rows of lockers. Down a dark flight of stairs, along a low, narrow corridor, up another flight of stairs, out another door, and they were outside the field house, on the side facing away from campus toward the thick leading edge of the woods.

Will gulped in deep breaths of cold air, hands on his head as he walked off the stress and tried to make sense of what he'd seen.

A window in the air . . . like the one in the hills behind my house! A window into the Never-Was . . . That's where the monsters come from and that's how they get here . . . burbelangs and gremlins and whatever the hell that last horror was.

Nick watched him the whole time, arms folded, leaning against a tree, rolling a toothpick around in his mouth. "What'cha doing at the Barn anywho, dawg?"

"I'm supposed to hook up with the cross-country team and Coach Jericho."

"Jericho? Aw, man, that is tragic," said Nick, shaking his head.

"Why, what's the matter with him?"

"Ira Jericho's a classic death-dealing crush-your-spinal-column hard-ass. And by the way, about said dude? He's watching you right now."

Will turned. A tall, rail-thin man in formfitting dark blue sweats stood forty yards away, where a dirt path from the field house entered the woods. Jericho wore his long thick black hair in a ponytail. His face was so bronzed it almost looked carved. He had severe cheekbones and a thin severe mouth. His dark eyes stared intensely at Will. He inserted two fingers in his mouth and let out a shrill, piercing whistle. He pointed a finger at Will, then at his feet: *You. Right here, right now.*

#88: ALWAYS LISTEN TO THE PERSON WITH THE WHISTLE.

Will waved to him. He glanced back and saw that Nick hadn't budged from his spot against the tree.

"Aren't you coming?" asked Will.

"Meh."

"Why?"

"Dude, I'm a *gymnast*. Jericho's got no authority over us *jumpy-springy* types."

"Come on, Nick, give me some cover here. I'll pay it back."

Nick calculated. "Show me that freaky room you found—tonight—and I'm in."

"Okay, okay."

Nick pushed off and joined him. The two jogged to where

229

Coach Jericho waited by the woods. Arms folded across his chest, motionless as stone, the man towered over them; Jericho had to be at least six foot five. Everything about him was pared clean to the bone. Not an ounce given to waste on his body or being.

"West," said Coach Jericho.

"That's me," said Will, raising his hand slightly.

"That's him," said Nick, pointing.

"That's helpful," said Jericho. He still hadn't moved. "Are you two clowns awake?"

"Yes, sir," said Will.

"I don't understand the question," said Nick.

"My practices start at one forty-five," said Jericho. "Sharp."

Will looked at his watch: 1:40.

"O-kay," said Will.

"That means *ready* and *at your marks* at one forty-five," said Jericho.

"I warmed him up, Coach," said Nick. "He's good to go."

Jericho stared at Nick. Nick tried one of his charming smiles.

"Well, aren't you Susie Citizen. Our greenhorn needs someone to show him the trail, McLeish. We're running a five-K. You're going with him."

Nick's smile went ker-splat. "But—"

"Wait, don't tell me: You have practice now. With the *gymnasts.*"

"Why, yes, Coach, as a matter of fact, I do—"

"That's a crock of spit. I know the schedule. You want to go for ten K instead, candy cane?"

"Five K sounds good," said Nick.

"My squad gathers at the Riven Oak," said Jericho. "That's our rally point, outbound and inbound. Rain, sleet, snow, or shine. Show him, McLeish."

"Can do, Coach," said Nick. He tugged Will's arm, eager to get away. But Jericho stopped them.

"West: You're a sophomore and a scrub. Scratch that: You're what a scrub scrapes off his spikes in a cow pasture. Don't get in our way. Trip up any of my frontline guys and I'll bury you in these woods. Stay on the trail. I don't want to waste a search party. Drag your sorry butts back here, if you can manage, before dark."

"Come on, Will—"

Will shook him off. Jericho's tone irked him. "I'll do better than that, Coach," said Will.

For the first time, Jericho looked at him with something other than steel-eyed contempt. "Is that a fact? You think you can compete with my team?"

"Yes, sir."

"Not with this screwball as your wingman."

Nick laughed, and then stopped abruptly when Jericho beamed his death-ray stare at him again.

"I can do better than compete," said Will. "I can win."

Jericho gave Will one last almost-interested look. "Move it, McLeish."

"Showing him now, Coach."

Nick ran away, fast, and Will sprinted to catch him. They followed a cinder trail until it crested a slight rise. Down below, looming over a clearing on the edge of the forest, stood the massive, towering sprawl of an ancient and ghostly white oak.

Its branches formed a canopy that spanned fifty yards. In its center, the heart of the trunk had to be at least fifteen feet thick. Some ancient injury had badly damaged it; a gap ran through its belly from front to back wide enough to drive a motorcycle through.

The Center's cross-country team waited at the base of the tree. They didn't look anything like boys. A dozen ripped, wiry, impossibly fit young men, hardly the slight, greyhound body mass prototype of the distance runner. Only a few were Will's height. The rest stood taller and outweighed him by at least twenty pounds. None wore the heavy fleece-lined sweats that Will had put on. They were stripped down to singlets and shorts, socks, and shoes. Their exposed arms and legs were flushed by the numbing cold, but they seemed immune to it. They were warmed up and restless, kicking out excess energy like Thoroughbreds at the starting gate. Sharp snorts of vapor-ized breath trailed away all around them.

The Paladins. Eyes lit by the same competitive fire as the logo. Road warriors.

As Will joined them, they sized him up, in that aloof, disdainful way runners throw down before a race. Dismissing him: *Just another scrub.* In the mix at the front, Will saw Todd Hodak staring at him. Will checked the squad's body language, the way they conceded space to Todd, deferring to him.

He's their leader.

Will glanced down at Todd's shoes: black Adidas with three red stripes. The shoes he'd seen outside the closet minutes ago. When Will looked up, he saw something else color Todd's look: an alarm that he just as quickly tried to still.

Is this the group I stumbled on in that weird room? The ones who chased me back into the locker room? He'd seen Lyle go through the door to that corridor, too. *What the hell was going on?*

The team turned away, as if drawing a curtain over the idea. The sharp crack of a starter's gun shattered the silence. Jericho stood back on the rise, smoke circling from the pistol he held in the air.

With Todd Hodak in front, the team thundered single-file through the hole in the oak and uphill toward the woods. Jostling for position, they reached cruising speed on the cinder track in less than fifty yards. Will and Nick were slower to react and by the time they found their stride, the pack had opened up a lead of fifty yards. At the top of the hill, they passed by Coach Jericho.

"That all you got, scrub?" said Jericho, looking at a stop-watch.

Nick pulled next to Will when the path widened as they approached the woods. "Yo, Will-the-Thrill . . . you forgot to tell me you were Dumpster-dog crazy."

"What are you talking about?"

"You just told Jericho you were gonna win this race."

"I guess I kind of did."

"Lame. Well, lots of easier sports to choose from, after Coach Buzz-kill bounces you out on your hein-dorf . . . volleyball, water polo, golf—"

"Not for me."

"Dude, trust me, you'd be doing yourself a favor. I'd rather inflate myself with helium and start a sumo wrestling team . . . than this." Nick spit into the woods.

"What's Jericho's deal? Why's he such a hard-ass?"

"Dude's full-blood Oglala Lakota, man," said Nick. "Back

in the day, this whole part of the state belonged to his peeps. Think he's still cheesed off about it. There's a rumor he's a direct descendant from Crazy Horse."

"Really?"

"So if that's true . . . dude's great-great-great granddaddy killed Custer."

"Holy crap," said Will, slowing so Nick could keep up with him.

"They say he inherited some whacked-out warrior-shaman skills from his bloodline . . . like he gets visions, talks to the Great Spirit."

"Is that why he makes his team run through the oak?" asked Will.

Nick shook his head. "His ancestors kicked off buffalo hunts riding through that old split tree . . . so Jericho starts and ends every race that way."

That was cool, but Will thought of a more practical explanation: There was only room for one runner through there at a time, which set the stage for last-minute heroics and built competitive instincts. There'd be no photo finishes on this course. Whoever made it to that finish line had to win flat-out.

"But first you have to survive Suicide Hill," said Nick.

"What's that?"

"Dude, you'll spoil the surprise."

Will eyed the pack ahead, calibrating the gap, holding it steady. He thought he could handle their pace from back here as long as he stayed at striking distance, but they were all strong, confident runners. The weakest man on the Center's squad was better than the best he'd ever faced. On any other day, this might have felt like a bad dream that had dropped him into the state finals without warning, the kind of nightmare where the gun's up and you can't find your shoes or you don't know how to tie them.

He didn't stress about it. Kujawa's test results had changed all that. *Don't hold back.* Screw it, no reason to now. For the first time in a real race, he could bust out the full RPMs of his turbo-charged system. But to make it count, he still had to run smart and wait for his moment.

#73: LEARN THE DIFFERENCE BETWEEN TACTICS AND STRATEGY.

Will loped along as if they were walking, but Nick was already in distress. He was incredibly cut and buff, but his body was trained for different challenges: short bursts of power in the vault or floor work, the controlled propulsion of the rings and bars. There was almost no overlap with the demands made by the pounding animal drumbeat of a road race.

"I hate you for this," said Nick. "Hope you know that . . . if you don't, I'll be sure to . . . remind you every few hundred feet."

"Have your legs always been that stubby?"

"Hey, Laughing Boy, you try a dismount from a static hold . . . into a flyaway double back salto . . . with a five-forty somersault . . . and see if you can stick the landing . . . without snapping your neck like a chicken wing."

They followed the path into the woods, where it rose and fell over a series of rolling ridges. The trees grew deeper and darker, marching into the shadowy distance in every direction. Will had never been in woods so thick or seen trees with so much life, variety, and character. The smells startled him, a savory mix of damp dirt, decaying leaves, and molds. The earth preparing for winter.

His new shoes felt light on his feet, every bit as good as he'd hoped. He kept the pack in sight as they kicked up the pace at the first kilometer.

"Tell me about Todd Hodak," said Will.

"Dude, Todd's real name should be Richard . . . because he's a dick. His picture's on the cover of the dick-tionary. He registers a constant nine-point-five on the Dickter Scale. In other words . . . if I'm not making this clear, Todd's a massive dick, on the highest order of dick-titude."

"Yeah, I'm getting that."

Nick sucked in a huge gulp of air, wincing in pain. "Dude was born on third . . . and thought he hit a triple."

"What's the deal with Todd and Brooke?"

"Families know each other . . . old money, like Moby Dick old . . . Daddy Ho-Dick's a big Wall Street dude . . . runs one of those hedgehog funds."

"A hedge fund?"

"Yeah, for hogs . . . so Brooke gets here and silver-spoon Todd comes on strong . . . with the moose jaw, Ranger Rick vibe. . . ."

"Please tell me she didn't fall for it."

"Dude, Brooke can handle the full-court press . . . but Todd's so helpful, showing her around . . . introducing her to his fellow ass-hats . . . that he covers his stink with Old Spice . . . but once she catches a whiff of the *real* Todd? Thanks, but no thanks . . . Todd won't take 'no thanks' for an answer . . . but Brooke won't give it up . . . stupid, meet stubborn . . . game on, baby!"

Nick nearly stumbled. Will caught his arm and kept him upright. "So did they get together or what?"

"That's the weird part . . . *doesn't* happen . . . she does everything but nail a crucifix to her door but . . . fourteen months later Todd's still trying to crack the safe . . . he keeps harassing her . . . and Brooke's too proud to blow the whistle."

"You're right," said Will. "Dick with a capital *D*."

"Todd puts the dick in *dick-tator* . . . which is an insult to *dictators*. And why . . . pray tell . . . do you ask?"

Will tried to sound casual. "No reason."

"That was awesome . . . who'd ever suspect that . . . beneath your chill So Cal facade . . . beats the heart of a hopeless Romeo."

Will scowled at him. "Don't be a dick, Nick."

"By the way, Ho-Dick owns every cross-country school record . . . the one place where he really is . . . the cast-iron stud monkey he sees in the mirror. . . ."

They climbed the last ridge, and the body of water Will had seen on the maps came into view: Lake Waukoma. The running trail led down to the shore and then snaked along the edge just inside the tree line. The lake looked much larger than Will had pictured, half a mile across at its widest and more than a couple of miles long. The sky had turned a slate gray, cloud cover rolling in, and the water mirrored it. A fresh wind stirred up whitecaps, tossing around lines of red buoys that marked a racing course on the surface. They passed an old wooden boathouse stacked with sailboats and various rowing sculls.

The pack rounded a corner ahead of them, Todd Hodak cruising just off the lead. He ran strong, with textbook form: even stride, perfect balance, upper and lower body working in unison. He was drafting off a tall thin kid who had gone out as the rabbit. Probably on Todd's orders.

"Ever had your blood tested since you've been here?" asked Will.

"Yeah," said Nick, wheezing. "Once or twice . . . Do we have to run this fast?"

"Yes. Did they find anything?"

"Lemme think . . . oh, yeah. It was red . . . why?"

"They want to give me a physical," said Will.

"They do that every year with the athletes," said Nick, staggering like he was about to keel over. "Did I mention . . . that I hate you?"

"Not in the last twenty seconds."

To their right, away from the lake, the land rose abruptly beyond the trees into a long limestone ridgeline, broken by tall ribbed columns of rock. Each column was striped with horizontal striations of vivid reds, yellows, and creams.

This whole gorge must have once been an ancient riverbed, thought Will. *The water carved its way down over the ages, leaving these strange artifacts behind.*

On the face of the ridge above them, Will noticed a number of black pockmarks. "What's up on that ridge?" asked Will. "Are those caves?"

"Sacred Lakota burial grounds . . . ask Jericho about it . . . maybe it's a casino and outlet mall now . . . and I hate you."

"And this is all school property?"

"Over twenty thousand acres," gasped Nick. "Bigger than my hometown . . ."

The island in the middle of Lake Waukoma came into view, along with the strange structure rising from its center. Will had seen photos of castles on the Rhine in Germany, and apparently so had whoever built this joint. Gray stones and concrete formed a high solid wall surrounding the central core that branched into two towers. Lights burned in the windows. A bridge from the entrance led to a landing and dock at the shore, where powerboats bobbed in the choppy water.

"That's called the Crag," said Nick.

"Does the school own it, too?"

"Private residence," said Nick. "*Crag* is a Scottish word . . . that means big-ass house . . . in the middle of a lake."

"Tell me you're not trying to do homework with that brain," said Will.

"Some bazillionaire lives there . . . big-time donor to the school. Haxley."

"That's the name on the medical center," said Will.

"But he's never around . . . that's like his fourteenth home."

"Somebody's there now," said Will. "Ever been out there?"

"Hell, no," said Nick, huffing. "Private property . . . trespassers verboten . . . guarded by vicious dogs and . . . snipers . . . and I really . . . really . . . hate you."

Will glanced at his watch, calculating time, pace, and distance. "We've got a click and a half left. Will you be all right getting back to the Barn from here?"

"Nuh-uh. I just bonked," gasped Nick. "Total lactic meltdown."

"What's the worst that could happen?"

"I'll go blind. Die from hypothermia. Then bears will eat me."

"Good," said Will. "So I won't worry."

"Where are you going?"

#13: YOU ONLY GET ONE CHANCE TO MAKE A FIRST IMPRESSION.

"Hammer time," said Will.

Will took off, hard, leaving Nick behind as if he were walking on a treadmill. Will barely heard his roommate's last feeble protest.

"Curse you, Will West!"

The trail turned left, rounding the northern end of the lake. Will churned up the track, digging into every stride. Quickly and methodically he closed the gap. Fifty yards. Then thirty. At this point in the race, the pack had spread out, less fluid runners filtering to the back. He zipped by the first trailer, then the second; they looked stunned as he passed and couldn't even respond.

Vaporized.

Through a gap in the trees ahead, Will saw Todd Hodak and another powerful runner, an African American kid, pushing the pace, about to pull away. The rabbit, his job done, was about to surrender the lead.

One kilometer to go.

The track straightened and widened as it moved inland, then stretched toward a dead uphill climb to the Barn and the Riven Oak. It was steep enough to function as a ski run once winter arrived. The whole length of the severe slope was visible for a quarter mile before you reached it, inflicting maximum damage on a tired runner's mind. Designed to scare whatever life was left out of you at the toughest point of the race. A fiendish finish.

Suicide Hill.

The tall kid working as the rabbit hit the base of the hill and fell away like a discarded booster rocket. Hodak and the other senior jammed past him and attacked the grade in lockstep.

Will accelerated as he approached the slope. Suicide Hill would have mentally terrified him in the past, back before he knew what he was capable of, but today it didn't faze him. He cruised by another trailer, slipped outside and torched three more, flashing by them in a blur. Focused. Mind and body meshed.

Go for it. No reason to hold back anymore, right, Dad? For the first time ever.

Will hit the hill at full throttle, without pain, strain, or effort. He hurtled by another trailer, and then the rabbit, still in free fall. Only two runners left between Will and the leaders. Deep steady breathing. He could feel how much energy each breath delivered to his core, fueling him to push harder and faster, still nowhere near his limit. Exhilarated. Liberated.

The two runners ahead heard him coming and glanced over their shoulders. Big guys, seniors, running side by side. Only the squad's elite would be near the front this deep into a race. Seasoned competitors who had won major races and who on any given day could be leading this one.

Shock hit their faces. A faceless scrub in heavy sweats trying to pass them on Suicide Hill? WTF! They looked at each other and called on their kicks. They spread out to narrow and protect the trail, determined to block this punk from getting past them. Will altered his path and made a move toward the middle. They wanted him to split that gap between them; they were inviting him in.

A trap.

As he drew even, the kid on the right slammed a vicious elbow into Will's shoulder, knocking him off stride. The kid on the left stomped at his foot, trying to spike him. Will swerved away; the spikes grazed his calf, shredding the leg of his sweats. Will was forced to drop back for a beat and regroup.

The two gatekeepers glanced at him again and at each other. Hard grins. Thinking they'd delivered the message and protected their leaders, forty yards ahead. The grade went vertical another degree, halfway up the hill. Merciless now.

A structure came into view on top of the hill, a tall wooden viewing stand, like a ranger's fire watch station. Coach Jericho stood on top near the rail with binoculars, watching them finish. Watching him.

Check this out, Coach.

Will darted to the left side. The kid on the left shifted to block him. Will spun a 360 back to the right without breaking stride and darted between them. The kid on the right grabbed at his sweats, but Will shot past him untouched. Off balance, the kid stumbled and went down hard. The other kid tried to hop over his buddy but clipped his foot and crashed. They shouted a warning to the leaders as they tumbled.

Hodak and the African American kid looked back and saw Will ten yards behind them and closing fast. Both put their heads down and dug harder.

Fifty yards from the top of the hill.

Will's lungs finally began to burn. He was nearing his red line—Suicide Hill and the squad's rough tactics had cut into his reserves—but he felt exhilarated. Hodak glanced back and then pulled away from his partner; the team's alpha dog still had something left in his tank. The African American kid labored, steadily losing ground, and by the time they reached the crest, Will had passed him.

Once they topped the hill, the track flattened. Will took a few strides to adjust to level ground again. Only two hundred yards left, a two-man dash to the Riven Oak. The trail passed right by the viewing platform. Coach Jericho darted to the opposite rail to watch them finish.

Will felt doubt stab him for the first time. This was Hodak's home course. He held the school's records. He was running freely ten yards in front. He probably had a whole wing of the family mansion devoted to his trophies, and Will had never won a single race in his life; he'd never even been allowed to try. On any other day, in any other race, he would have been happy to finish the way things stood right now. But he wasn't going to settle for second today. He doubled his breathing and dialed up every emotional trigger he could think of to spur him on.

Images flashed: Sedans. Black Caps. Monsters. Everything they'd done—whoever they were—to his parents and to him. Deep red anger. Projecting it all onto the one man left in front of him. *Rocket fuel.*

One hundred yards to the opening in the oak.

Raw fury gave Will what he needed for one last attack. He rode it hard and pulled up just behind Hodak's left shoulder, drafting off him, and then with another push drew up beside him. Hodak glanced over. He was straining at max effort, furious at Will's challenge but prepared. Determined to beat him. He threw an elbow but Will dodged it.

Sprinting, dead even, stride for stride. The opening in the oak zoomed at them. Only room for one of them to pass through.

RUN, WILL!

His father's voice, as real and clear as if he were standing right next to him.

With a final burst, Will veered right and cut in front of Hodak on the next-to-last step, spikes nipping his heels. Cool air swirled around him as he passed into the hole in the oak—his sweats brushing the sides—and then he was through.

Will ran on, letting momentum carry him, powering down with each step, legs melting to rubber. Hodak went down on his hands and knees as soon as he cleared the tree, heaving for breath. Will turned, bent over, and struggled for air. The rest of the team came in and gathered around their captain. The two thugs who'd tried to take Will out on the hill pulled Hodak to his feet.

His face white, fists bunched at his side, Todd Hodak stalked toward him. Will straightened and stood his ground. Hodak stopped a foot away, still trying to catch his breath. Pointed a finger at Will's face and stuttered, speechless.

"That was great, wasn't it?" said Will, breathing deeply. "I've got an awesome buzz going right now."

Now Todd just looked confused.

"I'm sorry, what was your name again? Dick?"

Hodak's eyes went haywire. Losing it in every possible direction. "You're dead," said Todd. "You are *dead*!"

"It's not Dick? I'm sorry, I'm really terrible with names."

His teammates had to jump on Todd to hold him back. He flailed around, shouting threats until that piercing whistle sounded again. Everyone stopped. Coach Jericho stepped around the tree and narrowed his eyes at the scene.

"Cool down," he said to his team. "Inside."

The rest of the squad dragged Todd toward the field house.

Will stayed behind. He felt his pulse dropping back to normal, his respiration evening out. He was already recovering! He waited for Jericho to speak first, but the coach just stared at him.

"How'd I do, Coach?" he asked.

Jericho looked at his stopwatch; he wanted Will to see that he'd clocked his time.

"Don't be late tomorrow," said Jericho. "We'll talk then."

Jericho pocketed the watch and strode off toward the field house.

Will turned back to Suicide Hill and saw a solitary figure stagger over the ridge, weave sideways, then fall to his knees and tip over. Will trotted to where Nick was lying, just off the track, moaning and wheezing melodramatically for air.

"Flopper," said Will.

"Suck-up," said Nick.

"I beat Ho-Dick."

"Really? That's great . . . and I'd offer my . . . heartiest congratulations . . . but I just remembered . . . that I still . . . really, really hate you."

A MISUNDERSTANDING

Will waited for the rest of the team to leave before he showered and changed. He found a first-aid kit in his locker and cleaned the spike wounds on his left calf. A quiet pride filled him like he'd never felt before. He'd called his shot in front of their stone-faced coach, handled everything Todd Hodak and company had thrown at him on their home turf, and delivered.

It was four-thirty and nearly dark by the time the roommates made it back to the pod. Nick limped in moaning about his legs, then flopped onto a sofa and instantly fell asleep. No one else had come in yet. Will locked himself in his room, then fired up his tablet and checked his email. Nothing. He pulled the cell phone out from the mattress and took it into the bathroom.

Three calls in the message log from Nando. All in the last two hours. Two click-offs, one voice mail: "Will, where you at, man? Breaking news. Gimme a shout."

Will punched the RETURN CALL button. Nando picked up after the second ring.

"Hey, Nando, where are you?"

"On the road. Hectic day. Followed those sedans last night all the way to LA. The Caps checked into a hotel near UCLA, so I crashed at my cousin's."

"You haven't even been home?"

"I tole you, man, I'm like a dog with a bone. Greased one of the valets so he tipped me when the Caps called for their rides. Seven a.m.: All three sedans drove to the Federal Building, holmes. On Wilshire in Westwood. Took the ramp into the private parking garage."

The Federal Building . . . Will's mind leaped to something Robbins had told him: *They're a nonprofit company that receives government funding.*

"Check the lobby directory," said Will. "See if there's an office for a company called the National Scholastic Evaluation Agency."

Nando paused, writing it down. "Getting right back to you on that, boss."

Nando ended the call. Will punched up the number for the air charter company at the Oxnard Airport and hit REDIAL. The same young woman quickly answered.

"This is Deputy Sheriff Johnson," said Will. "We spoke yesterday about the Bombardier Challenger your company chartered to Mr. Jordan West?"

"Yes, sir, I remember."

"They were scheduled to fly into Phoenix. Have they returned yet?"

She hesitated slightly. "No, sir."

"Can you confirm for me that they did, in fact, *land* in Phoenix?"

247

"Yes. As scheduled, yesterday evening."

And with any luck they spent the rest of the night running around Phoenix looking for me at bus stations and youth centers.

"Have you heard anything from them since then?"

"No. The plane took off from Phoenix about two hours ago, but we don't know where they're headed."

"So they're not on their way back to Oxnard?" asked Will.

"No, sir. We don't know where they are."

"Well, didn't your pilot file a flight plan?" he snapped.

"We haven't been contacted by the pilot, sir."

"What about Phoenix air control—shouldn't they have a destination?"

"We're trying to obtain that information," she said.

The woman put her hand over the mouthpiece and spoke to someone, then came back to ask, "What do you need to speak to Mr. West about?"

Will tried to sound calm and in control. "That's confidential."

She paused again. "Would you hold a moment?"

A male voice Will hadn't heard before came on, authoritative, no-nonsense. "This is Inspector Nelson with the Federal Aviation Administration," the man said. "Who am I speaking to?"

Will ended the call abruptly.

Federal Aviation Administration? What the hell? What got the FAA into this? Wait: These days if you rent a private jet and don't bring it back, wouldn't that automatically attract their interest? Not to mention Homeland Security.

He didn't know how he felt about that, but the whole last

few hours weighed on him heavily as he walked back into the bedroom.

Dave was sitting at his desk holding the glass cube, looking at the black "dice" swimming lazily inside, suspended in a weightless vacuum.

"Cheers, mate," said Dave with a grin. "You look surprised to see me."

"I'm funny that way; it startles me when you keep breaking the laws of physical science."

"Wanted to make sure you'd recovered from our expedition—"

"Why didn't you warn me that thing would be down there?"

"Didn't know myself. I just wanted you to see the Weasel Hole." Dave held up the cube. Strange symbols and glyphs appeared inside it, followed by a projected image of the monster they'd just seen. "That was a lamia, by the way. Part female, part snake, part spider, and smokin' ponies, can those things make a mess."

"Is it still after me?" said Will, his eyes wide.

"Naw, mate, I turned its lights out after you shook a leg, no worries."

"But did the Caps send it after me, specifically, like the other ones?"

"I don't think so," said Dave. "Just bad timing is all, and I blame myself for that."

Will felt a thump in his chest. "Listen, what I'm asking is, does this mean the Caps know I'm here at the school?"

"Put it this way, the lamia didn't have time to tell anybody. Depends on who else saw you. Did you get a good look at who summoned it?"

"No, but I have a few ideas," said Will, pacing. "But even

if they weren't targeting me, I'm assuming this means there's some connection between the Black Caps and whoever they were. Am I right?"

"So it seems," said Dave gravely.

"So we have to find out, for certain, who was down there." Will sat on the bed, took out the dark glasses, and twirled them around, thinking it through. "This Weasel Hole, that portal or window, that's how these things come across from the Never-Was."

"Right," said Dave. "Here's how it works."

He held up the cube: The dice stopped moving and unleashed a powerful burst of light. Out of its brightness, a striking visual projected onto the wall, of cows grazing in a sunny meadow. In a corner, a milky window like the one Will had seen in the locker room burned in, like someone cutting a hole through a wall. Once the circle was completed, shapes pushed at it from the other side until the skin burst open, unleashing a cascade of invisible force that bent the air.

Will put the dark glasses on and saw a roiling mass of hideous black slugs pouring across the meadow. They swarmed over the cows, consuming them, reducing them in seconds to bony carcasses.

Horrified, Will took off the glasses. The image disappeared. "Why can't I see these things without the glasses?"

"Electromagnetic frequency issue," said Dave. "Takes a while for 'em to enter our visual spectrum once they cross over. The lenses compensate. We don't usually hand 'em out, but you need a sniff of what you're up against."

"Of what *I'm* up against?"

"Bringing you up to speed at the right pace is my goal at

this stage of the game. I've seen strong men collapse under the strain, but you're doing a bang-up job."

Will took a deep breath. "Can they come across on their own?"

"Starve the bloody lizards, there's a heart-stopper. If the Fuzzy-Wuzzies could carve open a weasel hole by themselves from *their* side of the membrane? We'd be hip-deep in creepers by now."

"Did you just call them Fuzzy-Wuzzies?"

"Not a *technical* term, more of a nickname."

Will swallowed hard. "So this is how they brought over that . . . *thing* they used on my mom."

"The Ride Along. One of the nastiest buggers in their playbook."

"Show it to me," said Will.

Dave raised the cube and another image projected on the wall: a vile tube-shaped "bug."

"A small but vicious infestation unit," said Dave. "It loads into a mechanical tracker that carries it to the target, where it deploys and attaches like a parasite on the back of the neck. They're usually mistaken for an insect bite."

Will remembered the red mark he'd seen on Belinda's neck in the kitchen back home. His skin started crawling.

"It drills in and hatches into the bloodstream. Its spawn infiltrates the nervous system, spreads up to the brain, and starts to influence behavior."

The image illustrated the infestation Dave described, as the implanted bug attacked a generic three-dimensional human "model."

"You're saying . . . this thing can take over a person's mind?" asked Will.

"That's right. The part we don't understand yet is that it seems to work on more than just *people*. They can latch on to *anything*—animals, plants, even inanimate objects. Some of which, under laboratory conditions, have become . . . animated."

"Can you get rid of them? Do the victims survive?"

"Not that we know of," said Dave gently. "I'm sorry, mate."

There was a loud knock at the door.

"Keep your voice down," whispered Will.

"I told you they can't hear me—"

"Just a second!" said Will. He opened the door to the closet. "Then would you mind stepping in here?"

"Not necessary."

"They can't *see* you either?"

Dave smiled. "Not unless we want them to."

There was another even more urgent knock on the door. When Dave turned to it, Will noticed the back of his jacket again.

"By the way," said Will, lowering his voice, "I know what ANZAC is."

"Good on ya, mate. And what's that got to do with the price of pancakes?"

"It's on the back of your jacket? Hello?"

"So it is. I'd be well advised to never underestimate your powers of observation."

Dave extended a finger and tipped over the open bottle of water on Will's desk. It hit the ground and began pouring out onto the floorboards. Will rolled his eyes in annoyance, unlocked the door, and opened it a crack.

Brooke. Still wearing her coat and scarf, a little out of breath.

Tiny beads of sweat dotted her freckled nose and forehead. She had an urgent look in her eyes.

"Sorry, can I come in?" she asked.

"Sure. Just pay no attention to . . . oh, never mind."

Brooke slipped inside. Will closed the door. She clearly didn't see Dave, who perked up in his chair as soon as Brooke breezed in. In fact, Dave wolf-whistled.

"Sweet raspberry tea cakes," said Dave appreciatively.

"Shut up," said Will.

"What?" said Brooke, turning to him.

"Nothing. I said, 'What up?'"

"Will, listen, I came in downstairs just now and the door was open to Lyle's office, and I saw *Todd* in there talking to *Lyle*. In a very intense way that I can only describe as *conspiratorial*."

"What a stunner," said Dave. "She is a serious beauty, mate."

"Todd and Lyle," said Will, shooting an angry look at Dave behind Brooke's back and drawing a finger across his lips: *Zip it.*

"That's right, and then I got up here and Nick just told me about what happened with you and Todd at *practice* today—"

"All in good fun—"

"No, Will, you don't understand: If you made a mess in his sandbox, Todd is coming after you. The shortest distance possible, point A to point B—"

"What is this guy's problem?"

"The problem is that Todd has no fuse. When he gets angry, he just detonates, without warning, and you need to get out of his way."

"And he needs to leave *you* alone," said Will.

"That's the spirit, kid," said Dave.

"We're not talking about me," said Brooke. "I'm talking about you. They're probably on their way up here *right now*."

"So?"

"So haven't you read the Code of Conduct? Do you want to hand them a reason to kick you out of school?"

"What reason?"

Brooke's eyes went wide with alarm: "Your *cell phone*?!"

"Oh, right." Will took it out and held it up to her. "Here, you take it."

"No! Will, they can search the whole pod if they don't find anything in here—"

"Better listen to her, mate," said Dave.

"Lyle has the authority to do that?" asked Will.

"Yes, and you'd know that if you'd read the manual. Why is there water all over your floor? Get a towel—"

The front bell to the pod rang repeatedly.

"They're here," she said. "I'll try to stall them. Toss that phone out the window. Lock the door after me. *Now*."

She rushed out of the room. Will closed and locked the door. He looked at the phone in his hand, then looked at Dave, who hadn't budged from his seat at the desk. He didn't look particularly concerned.

"I really need to hang on to this," said Will.

"Roger that. Better find a place to stash it, then," said Dave.

Dave rocked back and tapped his boot on the floor. Will was surprised to see that nearly all the spilled water had disappeared. He dropped to his hands and knees for a closer look and realized the remaining water was draining into a nearly invisible crack between floorboards under the rear left leg of the desk.

He heard raised voices in the great room: Brooke, possibly Nick. *Definitely* Lyle and Todd. They were already inside.

Will shifted the desk a few inches over, then knelt down and felt around the edges of the crack, digging in with his fingernails. He grabbed hold and pulled; the board shifted slightly upward but wouldn't give any farther.

He retrieved his Swiss Army knife, opened the thinnest blade, and wedged it between the boards. He levered the loose board up a fraction of an inch until he could grab hold, then yanked it out, a three-by-six-inch chunk of wood, clean edges, finely cut. Seamless. Undetectable to the naked eye.

"Nice craftsmanship there," said Dave, leaning in for a look.

Below the gap in the floor was a hole a foot deep and half a foot wide.

There was a pounding knock on his door.

"Open up, Mr. West! Right this minute!"

Lyle Ogilvy.

Will set the cell phone and charger in the hole, then replaced the loose board and wedged the heavy desk back on top of it.

"Feel free to pitch in anytime," whispered Will to Dave.

"You're doing aces, mate."

"I have a master key with me," said Lyle. "And I'm going to use it as soon as I count to—"

Will unlocked and opened his door. "Ten?" asked Will.

Lyle stared down at him, livid with anger. Todd stood behind Lyle, glaring, hands on his hips, flanked by the two lugs from the running team who'd tried to take him out on Suicide

Hill. Both had multiple cuts and scrapes on their faces from the spill they'd taken. Behind them in the great room were Brooke and Nick, who was cool and unconcerned, tossing another log onto the fire.

"You *can* count that high," said Will. "Can't you, Lyle?"

Lyle held a copy of the Code of Conduct in front of Will's face and thumped it for emphasis: "Page five, section seven of the Code of Conduct," said Lyle. "Suspected possession of contraband objects or materials is grounds for immediate search of said student's entire residential area." He turned to Brooke and Nick. "You two open your doors, sit down, and do not *move* until I tell you to."

They did as they were told. Lyle lowered his shoulder and brushed past Will into his bedroom. Todd and his posse swept in after him, Todd pausing long enough to eyeball Will with a sneer. Dave had moved from the desk; he leaned on the edge of the bay window, watching calmly. None of the newcomers noticed him.

Just then Ajay came in the front door. He stopped when he saw Will in his room. Will caught his eye, mimed holding a phone, and slowly mouthed, "Call Mr. McBride."

Ajay nodded, backtracked out, and silently closed the door behind him. Will turned to Lyle and the others, who had begun methodically tearing apart his room. Todd rifled through his desk, while the other two checked the bathroom and closet. Lyle flipped over the mattress, feeling for sinister lumps in the bedsprings.

#65: THE DUMBEST GUY IN A ROOM IS THE FIRST ONE WHO TELLS YOU HOW SMART HE IS.

"Todd, buddy," said Will. "If you're this serious about busting my chops, you should check out my awesome hiding place. Under the desk. You're practically standing on it."

Todd stopped long enough to scowl again. "You think I'm some kind of *idiot*?"

Dave nodded, winked, and gave Will an enthusiastic thumbs-up.

"Hey, just trying to help," said Will.

"Go in the living room and wait with your roommates," said Lyle. "Per the Code of Conduct, page nineteen, subsection six—"

#96: MEMORIZE THE BILL OF RIGHTS.

"No. I'm not doing that."

"Sorry, *what*?"

"I'm staying here to watch," said Will. "Per the Bill of Rights, Fourth Amendment. Protection from unreasonable search and seizure. In case any contraband 'accidentally' finds its way into my room."

Lyle glared at him. "Are you accusing me of planting incriminating evidence?"

"Just make sure nothing falls out of anybody's pocket."

The goons came back from the bathroom empty-handed and Todd shook his head. Frustrated, Lyle picked up Dad's rules from the bedside table. "What is *this*?" asked Lyle as he paged through it.

The sight of his father's book in Lyle's hands enraged Will.

#30: SOMETIMES THE ONLY WAY TO DEAL WITH A BULLY IS TO HIT FIRST. HARD.

"That's *private property*," said Will, walking over to him. "I don't care what your damn rulebook says. The next time you decide to get all gestapo up in here, bring a warrant signed by a judge. Because if you *ever* come in here again without one? I will roll up my copy of the Constitution and knock your teeth out with it."

All four intruders froze. Will ripped the rules out of Lyle's hand. Lyle turned pale, livid spots blossoming on his cheeks.

Dave hopped down from his perch in the window and went into what looked like a touchdown dance.

"You can't talk to him like that," said Todd, stepping between them.

"What are you good at, Todd?" asked Will.

"*Excuse* me?"

"What are your big talents in life? I mean, aside from 'second fastest' and 'inheriting'?"

Todd's eyes went as red as brake lights; his whole body vibrated. Lyle put a hand on Todd's shoulder, but Todd shook him off and got in Will's face.

"You are so completely gone from here," said Todd.

#76: WHEN YOU GAIN THE ADVANTAGE, PRESS IT TO THE LIMIT.

"Get out," said Will. "Now. All of you."

Will stood chin to chin with Todd, who flexed his fists, then reached over and knocked the photo of Will's parents off the bedside table. It crashed onto the floor, and the glass cracked. Fury spread through Will like a time-lapse sunrise.

I'm going to wipe that smirk off your face.

Wild energy rumbled through Will's chest and throat, an electrical charge firing up his spine, but just as he was about to let loose, Dave leaned in beside Todd and blew lightly into his ear. Todd swiped at his head, completely spooked, spinning around to look for whoever or whatever could have done that to him.

"What the hell . . . ?" said Todd.

Will saw a puzzled, inward look steal over Lyle's face. *He has no idea what to make of it—but he* felt *Dave's presence just then.*

"Search the other rooms," said Lyle.

Todd put his head down and stormed out. His running mates fell in behind him. Lyle leaned toward Will and levered his face into a gruesome version of a smile. Will caught a whiff of foul breath and sour body odor. Lyle's voice was raspy and dry with adrenaline, spittle forming at the corners of his liverish lips.

"I've got you all figured out," said Lyle.

"Do you?"

"You think being *good* is all that matters. That *goodness* and *virtue* have something to do with *value*. That's the false comfort losers always fall back on. The pathetic fallacy of the weak."

Will's heart beat faster. The blood drained from his face.

"We don't like you," said Lyle softly. "We don't like what your being here means: charity for nobodies. The false promise of a 'level playing field.' This field isn't level. It never has been. It isn't *supposed* to be."

"Who's 'we'?" asked Will.

"Your superiors," said Lyle viciously. "You're an *oik*. *Oiks* don't belong at the Center. And you won't be here for long. Count on it."

Lyle straightened his jacket over his slouched shoulders and left the room. Will followed him out. Brooke and Nick were watching the others try to open the door to Elise's room. Lyle took out his master key and headed over to open it. Will picked up the nearest black phone and pushed the button.

"Good evening, how may I direct your call?" said the operator.

"Send an ambulance to Greenwood Hall," said Will loudly. "Fourth floor, pod three. Right away. There's been a terrible accident."

Lyle, Todd, and their two goons stared at him. Will picked up the black phone, hefted it in his hand, testing its weight and feel. Seeing that, Nick lifted an iron poker from the fire pit and tapped it into his palm.

Todd took the key from Lyle and inserted it into the lock. Elise threw open her door from inside and blocked his path. She held her field hockey stick, spinning the blade in a confident, businesslike way.

Emboldened by the others, if not quite as committed, Brooke picked up a pillow from the sofa. Reared back. Totally prepared to throw it.

"Excuse me?" asked the operator.

"One sec," said Will. He lowered the phone and made a show of counting Lyle, Todd, and the two goons—*one, two, three, four*. He lifted the phone again: "Make that two ambulances."

Todd signaled his sidekicks. Both lunged at Elise. With the reflexes of a cobra, Elise smacked their wrists, a sharp precise crack from her hockey stick. They backed away, shaking their hands in pain. Everyone tensed, both sides waiting for the other to react, the prospect of violence heavy in the air.

Standing in the doorway to Will's room, Dave took out a cigarette lighter, fired the wick, and held it in the air like a concertgoer listening to an '80s hair band. He disappeared a moment later when the front door burst open. Dan McBride hurried in, followed closely by a breathless Ajay.

"What's going on here?" said McBride. "Mr. Ogilvy? Please explain."

"Searching the room for contraband, sir," said Lyle.

"On what basis?" asked McBride.

"He doesn't have one," said Will.

"I do so!" said Lyle, eyes blazing with anger, then he seemed to instantly regret that he'd said it.

Will could read it in Lyle's eyes: *He's seen something but he can't reveal how. There's more to this creep hassling me than just bullying. Maybe a lot more.*

"Let's hear it, then," said McBride.

"I'm afraid I can't prove anything," said Lyle, backing down. "Yet. Let's call it a misunderstanding."

Lyle gestured to the others and they quickly followed him to the front door. Nick, politely, opened the door for them and waved as they left.

"Ta-ta," said Nick quietly. "Have a safe trip back to Douche-bagistan."

Todd gave Nick a last poisonous glare on his way out. McBride headed after them into the hallway.

"I'll be right back," said McBride as he left.

"Hello? Mr. West, are you still there?" said the operator. "Mr. West?"

"Sorry. Wrong number." Will hung up the phone.

"Da-yem, that was classic," said Nick.

He asked for a fist bump. Will gave him one. Brooke dropped the pillow and wrapped her arms around Will, who didn't object. Leaning against the door frame, twirling her hockey stick, Elise offered a crooked smile and a raised eyebrow.

"*Two* ambulances," she said. "Nice."

"Nice?" said Ajay, jumping around. "*Nice?* Are you kidding me? That was totally fa-rouking *awesome!*"

McBride came back into the room. "Will, step outside with me for a moment," he said.

WAYFARER

Once they were in the hall, Dan McBride confided that this wasn't the first complaint he'd heard about Lyle Ogilvy. He explained that the Center gave provost marshals authority because it reflected their philosophy of students governing themselves. This had occasionally led to a few marshals abusing their position. McBride promised to bring the incident to Headmaster Rourke's attention.

"I'm glad you called me, Will. You let me know if he troubles you again. You're certain you have no idea what Lyle could be looking for?"

Will felt bad about lying to him but didn't see an alternative. "No, sir."

McBride bade him good night. Back in the pod, Will found his roommates seated at the table. Elise sat apart from the others, staring at the ceiling. He realized they were waiting for him to speak first, and he took a deep breath.

"Anybody have a problem with how that went down?" he asked.

"You're clowning, right?" asked Nick.

"I know you're afraid of Lyle," said Will. "For good reason. He's messed with you before, and he's going to keep messing with you." He made a point of not looking at Brooke when he added: "The same goes for his pit bull, Todd, and those other chuckleheads."

"Tim Durgnatt and Luke Steifel," said Ajay.

"Unless we put a stop to it. Right now." Will waited. No one responded. "Come on, the headmaster wants us to talk to each other. So let's talk."

"Our concern is this, Will," said Ajay cautiously. "As delicious as it was to see them all eat a large helping of crow, we're afraid that now it may only get worse."

"This is supposed to be a democracy," said Will. "Who wrote this Code of Conduct Lyle keeps yapping about?"

"Dr. Greenwood and the school's first class," said Brooke. "Students helped draft it, and they've been in charge of it ever since."

"Can we change it? To put the brakes on Lyle, or any other kid who throws his weight around?"

"You can propose amendments," said Brooke, "but they have to be approved by the student council."

"Small problem," said Elise. "Lyle, Todd, and their minions— all seniors—*control* the student council."

"And Lyle and Todd just put you on their Major Shit List," said Ajay.

"Along with the rest of us," said Brooke.

"Big whoop," said Nick. "We were on it already."

"Well, now we're number one," said Brooke. "With a *bullet*."

"Thank you, Miss Congeniality," said Elise caustically.

Time to make it real. Stop worrying about what they think of you and speak your truth.

Will stood: "Everybody *shut up*!"

They all looked shocked. Particularly Elise. But she didn't look angry.

#98: DON'T WATCH YOUR LIFE LIKE IT'S A MOVIE THAT'S HAPPENING TO SOMEONE ELSE. IT'S HAPPENING TO *YOU*. IT'S HAPPENING RIGHT NOW.

"Fighting among ourselves is *exactly* what they want," said Will. "What's the worst they can do if we stick together and stand up to them? Throw us out of here?"

"Isn't that bad enough?" asked Brooke.

"You tell me," said Will. "The day before I got here, back home, a group of men in black sedans tried to kidnap me three times." He paused to let that sink in. "And I'm starting to wonder if Lyle and Todd are mixed up in it somehow."

They all stared at him, stunned. "You can't be serious," said Ajay.

"What's your evidence for that?" asked Brooke, her eyes wide.

"Let him *talk*," said Elise intensely to the others, and then to Will, an order, not a request: "Talk."

"I can't *prove* they're part of this yet," said Will. "But I saw something today that strongly suggests the kidnappers have people here who are working with them, or for them. I have an idea about where to look to confirm this, and if I'm right, if Lyle and Todd are involved . . . then we're all in danger."

Will looked around: *Now* he had their attention.

"You have to tell the school," said Brooke.

"I told them some of this already," said Will. "But I can't tell them about Lyle because I don't know who to trust. Here or anywhere. Aside from the four of you."

"Dude," said Nick sympathetically. "So what can we do?"

"What does that have to do with this?" asked Brooke, looking nervous.

"You heard him," said Will. "Lyle just declared war on us and he has the Code on his side. If the system's rigged against us, we have to fight back any way we can."

The others kids shared cautious looks around the table. Will had struck a chord in everyone but Brooke, who sat upright and rigid, alarmed.

"You mean we have to break the rules," said Brooke.

#55: IF YOU FAIL TO PREPARE, YOU PREPARE TO FAIL.

"Whatever it takes," said Will. "Unless you want to let Lyle and his jackals keep using you as a chew toy. But I'm not lying down for that and neither should you."

"Old saying in my neighborhood," said Nick. "Don't show up for a knife fight with a Hostess Twinkie in your hand."

"Professor Sangren said the same thing today," said Will to Brooke. "The hell with morals and ethics that are supposed to be the basis of civilization. Life is just an iron cage death match and only the strong survive."

"He's right, and I'll tell you why," said Elise emphatically. "Do you know about the Dunning-Kruger effect?"

"Never heard of it," said Will.

"Scientific fact," said Elise. "Part one: Idiots and incompetents grossly overestimate their intelligence and abilities. In fact, they're *so* stupid they're unable to see what complete morons they really are. So they end up with a false sense of superiority, which in turn creates a false sense of confidence, which perpetuates the cycle that constantly reinforces their fake superiority. Part two: Genuinely smart and skillful people chronically *under*estimate their own abilities and end up suffering from equally false feelings of self-doubt and inferiority."

No one responded for a moment.

"I think I can speak on behalf of everyone," said Nick, "by saying . . . *huh*?"

"She's saying ignorance encourages confidence," said Ajay. "Intelligence creates insecurity. Therefore, the stupid act with blind assurance, while the smart are crippled by self-doubt."

"And that's how the lizard brains end up in charge," said Elise. "How messed up is that?"

"Totally," said Nick. "You can't teach 'stupid.'"

"No, it's a gift," said Elise, staring at Nick. "You're just born with it."

"It does help explain what we're up against," said Ajay thoughtfully.

"And we're putting a stop to it," said Will, banging a fist on the table. "Starting right now. Tonight."

Brooke's face flushed. "I'm sorry, this is too much for me to process." She stood abruptly and headed to her room. "I just have to think about it." She quietly closed her door.

"Damn," said Will, kicking himself. "Should I say something?"

"Don't you dare," said Elise.

"That's how she deals," said Nick. "Coloring outside the lines makes her *crazy*."

"She'll come around," said Ajay.

"Dream on," said Elise. "We're talking about insurrection? Ten bucks says she's never even jaywalked."

"Well, if she ever does," said Nick, "look out, 'cause traffic's coming to a screeching halt—"

Elise kicked him, hard, under the table.

"What?" protested Nick.

Will held out his fist, inviting the others to put their hands on top. "Let's do this. Right here, right now."

Nick and Ajay put their hands on top of Will's. Elise raised an eyebrow.

"Really?" asked Elise.

"Come on, chick-a-boom," said Nick. "Get with the program."

"I'm not a big joiner," she said, wincing.

"Oh, for God's sake, get over yourself," said Ajay. "Do you think you can break the vicious cycle of the Dunning-Kruger effect by sitting on your hands?"

"At last," she said dryly, putting her hand on theirs, "a way to channel my inner fifteen-year-old."

"You *are* fifteen," said Nick.

Elise looked at Will and shook her head: *You see what I have to put up with?*

"Let's open up a nine-pound can of *extra-crazy*," said Nick.

"Nick, Ajay, get your coats," said Will, getting up. "Ajay, we need flashlights and a map of the campus."

"What are we looking for?" asked Ajay.

"Evidence that connects Lyle to the men who came after me," said Will. Then to Nick he said, "We'll start in that room you wanted to see."

"Awesome," said Nick.

Nick and Ajay scattered to their rooms. Will lowered his voice and turned to Elise: "How'm I doing? Like me better without my 'game face'?"

Elise assessed him coolly. "I've seen worse."

Will hurried to his room. Dave was sitting on the bed, poking at the mattress. At this point, Will would have been more surprised *not* to see him.

"You're not planning on spending the night, are you?" asked Will.

"I've just been authorized to give you a bit more information," said Dave.

"One second." Will slid the desk to the side, removed the floorboard, pulled out his phone, and checked for messages. A text had just come in from Nando: Call me. Will speed-dialed him. Nando picked up immediately.

"Yo, Will," he whispered. "That place you asked about, the National Scholastic Evaluation Agency? It's in the Federal Building."

Will stopped cold. "Really? You're sure?"

"I'm looking at it, bro. Seventeenth floor, name on the door. I'm going in—"

"Wait a second—"

"An unemployed Latino walks into the wrong office in the Federal Building. What could go wrong?"

Will heard a door open. Will felt like hiding, as if people there could see him by looking at Nando's phone.

"Can I help you?" he heard a woman say.

"My brother Frankie says I'm s'posed to meet him here?" Nando replied, thickening his accent, dumbing down. "This is the passport office, right? Oh, he musta got it wrong." Nando spoke into the phone again. "Wrong floor, bro. Passport's on *seven*." Then, to the lady, "So what's this place? The *what*?"

The woman answered, losing patience.

"National Scholastic Evaluation Agency," Nando repeated. "Is that a federal program? 'Cause my niece, my sister's kid Claudia, who's like super, super smart, goes to one of those, wha'chu call 'em, magnetic schools?" Then, in the phone again, "Hey, Frankie, she says it's a private company, but they get federal funding, and all they do is testing."

"Ask if they have brochures," said Will.

"He says to ask if you got any brochures," said Nando to the woman. "Okay, thanks for your help, lady. Sorry to bother you." Will heard Nando open the door and walk back into the hall. He used his normal voice again. "No brochures. Normal office, front counter, civil service types. And two Black Caps—"

Will gripped the phone. "Where?"

"In a back room . . . Whoa, they just came out in the hall. Gotta bounce."

The call ended. Will slapped the phone shut and turned to Dave. "That's *it*," said Will, excited. "That's how they knew to come looking for me. The Black Caps are hooked in with the agency that gave me the test!"

"Sounds reasonable," said Dave, still testing the mattress.

"Now if I can tie Lyle and Todd to that hole in the basement, maybe we'll figure out how this all fits together," said Will as he plugged the phone into the charger and slid it under the mattress. When he turned around, Dave was by the door.

"You were spot on about ANZAC, by the by," said Dave.

"Another time, okay?" said Will, grabbing his coat, scarf, and hat.

"Thought you wanted to know who I am," said Dave.

"No, I've figured that out, too. You're my 'imaginary friend.' A phantom or hallucination—a really convincing one, I'll give you that—that my brain cooked up after it was shattered by a nervous collapse."

"So you're as mad as a meat ax and I'm just a bit of random gristle stuck to the blade," said Dave.

"Very much something like that, yes."

"Hmm. Worth a rethink."

"I *have* rethought it," said Will, "and it's the only possible explanation."

"You might want to have another gander at that room in the basement before you count your chickens—"

"As a matter of fact, that's where I'm headed right now," said Will, putting on his winter duds. "So, no offense, in the interest of my mental health, I can't pay attention to you. You're a 'symptom.' A stress-related coping mechanism—"

"Fascinating theory."

"But things *are* going to settle down, eventually—because they *have* to—and when they do, you're just going to disappear. *Poof.* For good."

Will headed for the door. But this time Dave didn't dematerialize out of his path. Will ran right into him. Dave felt as real as a slab of industrial steel.

"Think what you like, mate. I'm just trying to give you the straight guff."

"Please get out of my way," said Will.

"You've had your two bobs' worth; now you'd better hear me out before I lose my temper—"

"I'm leaving now." Will reached past him for the doorknob.

A blinding light filled the room. Will staggered back as Dave transformed into another, much larger, being. His head touched the ceiling. His broad frame obscured the door. He looked like he could crush a Mini Cooper in his fists. His whole body glowed with a white-hot righteous fury that was impossible to look at, but Will couldn't turn away. The towering figure wore what looked like platinum armor and he held a gleaming blue sword in one hand.

Dave leaned over and roared in Will's face, "Sit down and shut yer bloody *yapper!*"

The thunderous blast of his voice lifted Will off the floor. He flew backward into his desk chair, which rolled across the room and crashed into the far wall.

"Okay," said Will, stunned, ears ringing.

Dave disappeared. Suddenly he was leaning against the wall next to Will's chair, calm, collected, and back to his usual dimensions and physical appearance.

"Here's ground zero, mate: You're not half-cracked. On the contrary, this is all on the level and you're up to your neck in the mullock. And you're not the only one they're after. I'm at risk, too. We all are, our whole side of the field. There's a war going on, and you're smack in the middle."

Dave reached down, gripped Will's shoulder, lifted him

gently in the air, and spoke right in his face. Will shrank back, going limp.

"You're in a riptide, Will, and the power and scope of forces at work here are as far beyond your comprehension as eternity is to an earthworm."

"Uh-huh."

"Our usual policy is to let the client figure things out afterward, but given the urgency of your situation, they've given me the green light to tell you who I am."

Dave deposited him on the bed and showed him a partially burned identification badge. "Staff Sergeant Dave Gunner. I was a chopper pilot with ANZAC, as you've correctly inferred. Special Forces. Vietnam."

Dave pointed to the insignia on the back of his flight jacket and the three images inside: the helmet of a knight, the red kangaroo, the silhouette of a helicopter. "Flew sixty-five combat missions," he said. "Went down over Pleiku in 1969. Rear rotor came a cropper. Catastrophic mechanical failure."

"So what are you saying?" asked Will, his whole body shaking involuntarily.

"We didn't make it," said Dave, and for a moment he seemed almost wistful. "Me, Digger, Fat Philly, the whole crew. And wouldn't you know it, buzzard's luck—two days after the best weekend of my life, when I fell in love on the white sand beaches of Nha Trang with Miss Nancy Hughes, Ensign First Class, US Navy Nurse Corps, from Santa Monica, California."

Will had no idea why he said what he said next. "But you drive a hot rod."

"Once you reach my rank, you're allowed a personalized vehicle. After my chopper went down, I opted for something lower to the ground."

"So you're saying . . . you're a ghost?"

"No, mate," said Dave. "Categorically speaking, dead, yes, insofar as I've had that experience, but we're still material beings. Or we *can* be, depending on the circumstance. Not a ghost. Entirely different kettle of fish."

"What are you, then?"

Dave took out his cube; three-dimensional images of what appeared to be heavenly warriors materialized in the air before Will. "Neither here nor there, but somewhere in between. They've coined a number of terms for us down the ages: Wayfarers, Secondaries, Celestial Templars."

Will finally took in a breath. "So you're . . . not just a dead helicopter pilot?"

Dave heaved a sigh. "Let's keep it simple," he said patiently. "This is a high-priority assignment. We caught wind of it two days ago: The Other Team was looking hard and wide for a particular kid. One, it turns out, whom we had our own good reasons to be interested in. And *they* were moving heaven and earth—for reasons not yet entirely clear—to find him before we did."

Will was afraid to move. "You mean . . ."

"I mean you. You may have chanced to notice this already, Will, but the nasties from the Never-Was are trying to kill you," said Dave gently. "In the rare instances we're allowed to tell the client who we are—and this is a first for me personally—they encourage us to use a simple term that you can better relate to.

Common parlance. Even though it's completely inadequate to convey the exact nature of our relationship."

"So what are you, then?" asked Will, filling with more dread than at any time in the last two days.

"I'm your guardian angel," said Dave.

Someone knocked softly on the door.

"That'll do for now," said Dave.

Then he disappeared.

THE OTHER LOCKER ROOM

Will unlocked and opened his door. Ajay and Nick stood just outside, wearing coats, hats, and scarves.

"You ready, Will?" asked Nick.

"Yes," said Will, still numb. He stumbled past them toward the kitchen, and they tagged along. "Where are we going?"

"The Barn," said Nick. "You're gonna show us that spooky room in the basement."

"Right," said Will.

"I'm bringing some gear along that I think might be useful," said Ajay, studying him. "Are you all right, Will?"

Will picked up a bottle of water and drained it. "I'm good. I'm fine."

"You look kind of . . . sketchy," said Nick.

"You look, actually, like you've seen a ghost," said Ajay.

Good guess. "I'm your guardian angel." *Yeah, close enough. I'm in shock. Not a good time to be alone. Go with them. Stay calm.*

"Did you guys hear anything?" asked Will. "In my room just now? Like thunder, or . . ."

"No," said Ajay.

"Okay," said Will, and moved to the front door.

"Uh, dude, you might want to grab your coat?" said Nick.

"How would a person know if they're going crazy?" asked Will.

"The usual," said Ajay. "Hearing disembodied voices. Rampant paranoia. Visions of hallucinatory figures, often of an overtly religious nature."

How reassuring.

Will, Ajay, and Nick hurried across the commons, hands shoved in their pockets, huddled against the frigid night air. Will had broken out his new blue winter parka, wearing it over his fleece pullover, a shirt, and long underwear. And he was still freezing. The big clock atop Royster Hall said it was nearly nine, but the halogen streetlamps along the paths lit the grounds like daylight.

"I always fall back on the Robin Williams rule," said Nick.

"What's that?" asked Will.

"Seeing ninjas on your front lawn," said Nick. "Totally dependable nutball indicator."

"Why do you ask, Will?" asked Ajay.

Will wanted to say, *Because my guardian angel thinks an army of monsters is trying to assassinate me and we don't know why.* Not exactly breaking news, but hearing Dave say it in so many words was a throat-grabber. Which left Will feeling he couldn't decide which was worse: if Dave was real or imagined.

But either way, how much more should I tell these guys? If I spill the whole story, they'll think I'm riding the express train to Crazytown.

"No reason," said Will.

"Have you been using that phone in your room?" said Ajay.

"A couple of times," said Will.

"It's possible that Lyle has some kind of scanner or tracking device," said Ajay. "That could be why he decided to search our quarters. You should definitely limit your use of it."

"I'll do that," said Will.

Streetlights thinned out as they reached the athletic fields. In the distance, the Barn lit up the night. A Samoan guard buzzed by in a security golf cart. He waved and smiled. They waved and smiled.

"Do the guards always smile like that?" asked Will.

"Try sneaking out after curfew," said Nick.

"Eleven on school nights," said Ajay. "Midnight on weekends and holidays."

"What happens if they catch you out after curfew?"

"They politely escort you back to your room," said Ajay.

"Unless you're walking around with a severed head and a bloodstained chain saw," said Nick.

When they reached the field house, Will stopped to examine the statue of the Paladin and the crest on his shield. *Fighting a horned demon. Coincidence? Maybe I should ask Happy Nepsted about monsters in the tunnels.*

They moved inside. Interior lights burned bright, but the practice field and basketball courts were deserted. The unsettling silence made the cavernous building feel even bigger. Will led them down the corridor lined with old photos of school sports teams toward the locker room.

Will gestured for silence as they entered. Lights had been switched off, so they flicked on their flashlights. With the room emptied of life, the air felt as cold and still as a meat locker.

They walked past the shower room, where dozens of drips plinked and echoed onto tile. Their beams caught the white grill of Happy Nepsted's equipment cage. They flashed their lights inside, glancing up and down the long aisles behind the counter.

"What are you looking for?" asked Nick.

"Nepsted," said Will. "The equipment manager. I had a question for him. He seems a little . . . mysterious . . . by the way."

"What, a surly dwarf who talks in riddles and never leaves the basement?" asked Nick. "Yeah, I'd say that's mildly odd."

"The door I saw Lyle use is over here," said Will.

He led them to the door, their beams bouncing off the painted metal into the air around them with a ghostly glow.

"I never even noticed this was here before," said Ajay.

"Let's rock this joint," said Nick. He barged through the door and slammed it behind him. Moments later they heard a strangled scream: "Oh, no, oh God, help!"

Will and Ajay threw open the door and rushed in.

"Nick? Nick?! Where are you?"

Nick flicked on his flashlight, pointing up under his chin, and his face popped out of the darkness in front of them.

"Nepsted got me," he croaked.

Ajay jumped back against a wall, hand on his chest. "You incorrigible numb nut. You almost gave me a heart attack."

"Dude, no worries. I almost learned CPR once—"

"Seriously, Nick," said Will, his own heart racing. "It's a miracle nobody's murdered you yet."

"Yeah, I know, right? Now brace yourselves. Not sure you can handle this . . . 'cause it turns out we're in a pretty horrifying . . . *utility corridor.*"

Nick flashed his light around to show them a square feature-less concrete corridor. A cluster of insulated pipes ran along the ceiling. A few feet farther in, a small jet of steam escaped from one of them.

"That must've been the hissing I heard," said Will. "The room's this way."

He led them down the staircase and around the sharp left turn. They pointed their lights down the long straight passage ahead until the beams died in the darkness. Ajay took out his pager and pressed the button on it.

"This," said Ajay, clearing his throat, "is a very long hallway."

"The room's at the far end," said Will.

"How far is that?" asked Nick.

"I don't know. Far. Let's go."

They started walking. A chill descended around them. Hazy motes of dust hung suspended in their light beams, lazy particles in a murky sea. Vague shapes appeared to float in the distance. Their lights started to wobble.

Ajay stopped and shivered. "I've got chicken skin," he said. "Goose bumps. All over."

"Ditto," said Nick.

"Do you want to see this or not?" asked Will.

"Aye," said Nick.

"So what are we," asked Will, "men or mice?"

"Pass the cheese," said Ajay.

"Keep going," said Will.

"Sure, the way you can motor, what are you stressed about?" said Nick. "It's Ajay and me who'd be dragged down from behind . . . and have our brains eaten by ravenous bloodsucking ghouls—"

"Would you please for the love of Mike stop *talking*?" said Ajay.

"Mike? Who's Mike?" asked Nick.

Will continued edging forward. The others followed a step behind him. They kept their lights pointed ahead, piercing the thickened gloom with one united beam.

"Would anyone care to join me," said Nick in a shaky voice, "while I sing the National Anthem?"

"The first good idea you've had all night," said Ajay.

Nick quietly cleared his throat. *"Oh, say, can you see"*—his voice wavered, barely above a whisper—*"by the dawn's early light . . ."* The others joined in, no louder than Nick. *"What so proudly we hailed . . ."*

A loud metallic bang sounded in the corridor behind them. They stopped singing and froze. No one wanted to turn around.

"That happened before," said Will. "That was the door we came in."

"And that's not a problem *because*?" said Ajay.

"Because it shut by itself," said Will. "Keep going."

They crept along again.

"Come to think of it, dude," said Nick, "you never did tell us what you ran into down here."

"You really don't want to know," said Will.

"That is, uh, incorrect," said Nick.

"Yes, Will," said Ajay. "Pray tell."

"It's . . . hard to describe. And even if it showed up again, you wouldn't be able to see it anyway. Since you don't have the . . . special glasses."

"You need special *glasses*?" asked Ajay. "Oh God, I really have to pee."

"How far do you think we've gone?" asked Will.

"A hundred yards," said Ajay. "Maybe more."

"You think we're still under the Barn?" asked Will.

"I have no idea," said Ajay. "I'm so turned around I'd need a compass just to tell you on which end my buttocks are attached."

"We're headed due east," said Nick.

"How could you possibly know that?" said Ajay.

"I have a sick sense of direction," said Nick.

"You said your dad was a wrestler, right?" asked Will.

"Dude, he won the New Hampshire Junior College Championship."

"How many times did he drop you on your head?" asked Will.

"Wait. Your father went to *college*?" asked Ajay.

"Junior college," said Nick. "For a year. And you don't have to sound so surprised."

Ajay took the school pager off his belt and pressed the button again.

"What do you keep doing with that thing?" asked Will.

"Recording intermittent GPS coordinates," said Ajay. "I'll use them to map the tunnel when we get back."

"*If* we get back," said Nick.

"You're using the school's pager as a GPS?" asked Will.

"I modified the processor," said Ajay. "Reverse engineering."

"Dude," said Nick. "I can't even figure out where they put the batteries."

The darkness folded around them like a heavy shroud. Their footsteps echoed, every sound magnified in the endless void. Finally, their beams glinted off something that sent back a burst of light.

"What's that?" asked Nick. "Is that a door?"

"Yes," said Will as they trained the lights on it. "That's the door to the room."

"With any luck, a bathroom," said Ajay.

"The room where I saw the people who chased me," said Will.

"People were *chasing* you?" said Ajay. "Oh dear God."

"Not just people. There was that 'thing' that only you can see," said Nick sarcastically. "With your 'special glasses.'"

"You didn't say there was a *thing*," said Ajay.

"Didn't I?"

"I don't know about you," said Nick, "but I'm feeling *excellent* about this."

They stopped ten feet shy of the door at the dead end of the corridor. This time no line of light leaked out from under the bottom of the door. They heard distant rumblings issue from somewhere, perhaps the old building's ancient furnace.

"Inspired effort. Good show all around," said Ajay. "Our work here is done. Let's retrace our steps." He turned to leave, but Nick hooked him with an elbow and stopped him in his tracks.

"Not so fast, Professor Plum," said Nick. Then to Will he said, "Aren't you going to open it?"

"Yes," said Will. "Yes, I am."

"Are you going to put your glasses on first?" asked Ajay.

"I don't think so."

Will stepped forward and gripped the knob. It turned freely. He took his hand away, wiped the sweat off his palms, and gripped it again. He opened the door. Their flashlight beams poured past him into the room, and Nick chased them inside.

"Oh my God," said Nick. "This is incredible, dude. You've done it."

"Done what?"

Nick hit a light switch. Overhead fluorescents flickered on. "You've found the auxiliary locker room," he said, pointing to a sign that read AUXILIARY LOCKER ROOM.

They followed him into a small L-shaped room with a paneled drop ceiling. Lining one wall were metal lockers fronted by benches. In a mirrored corner, a weight bench sat on a rubber mat, surrounded by an assortment of free weights. Will stepped forward, sniffing the air.

"Do you smell anything?" he asked.

"Definitely," said Nick, pocketing his flashlight. "Stale socks and rotten jocks. Dude, it's a *locker* room."

"Dear God, let there be a toilet," said Ajay, hurrying around the corner. "Yes!"

"So, Nick, you knew about this place before?" asked Will.

"Heard rumors," said Nick, picking up a dumbbell and doing curls. "It's practically mythic. For good reason, as you can see. Right up there with Atlantis and Bigfoot."

Will took out his dark glasses and put them on. Nothing appeared out of thin air. No sulfurous smells, blinding lights, or gleaming portals slicing through time and space. No windows to the Never-Was or screeching, menacing monsters.

"*And the rockets' red glare,*" belted Ajay from around the corner, "*the bombs bursting in air—*"

"So it's a fail, but at least it's an epic fail," said Nick. "Hey, are those the glasses? Let me have a look."

"No," said Will, putting them away. "What do they use this place for?"

"Dude, take a wild guess. It's the *auxiliary* locker room," said Nick, yawning and stretching. "And if I knew what *auxiliary* meant, I could tell you."

"Providing help or support in a secondary capacity," said Ajay from around the corner. "As in the *backup* locker room. Which, given that the main locker room covers half an acre, probably means it isn't used for anything."

"Why would they build it all the way down here?" asked Will. "Why all the secrecy?"

"Honestly, dude?" said Nick, yawning again. "I wouldn't even trip about it."

"Check the lockers," said Will, opening the one nearest to him. "Come on, Nick, get off your butt."

Nick dragged himself over as Ajay came around the corner, zipping up.

"That is definitely enough passion fruit iced tea for one night," Ajay said, beaming with relief. "We're searching lockers? What are we looking for?"

"I don't know," said Will. "Clues."

Ajay pitched in, opening lockers. Most were empty. A few held bent wire hangers or wads of discarded sports tape.

"Well, maybe if you'd share *exactly* what you saw here the *first* time, we'd have a better idea what to look for *now*," said Nick.

Will thought about it. *What the hell. If I can't trust these guys, who can I trust?*

"Okay. I'd describe it as a portal," said Will, matter-of-factly. "Or a window carved in the air to a nasty, horrible place. They call it a Weasel Hole."

"Aren't you glad you asked?" said Ajay, shooting a worried look at Nick.

"Right," said Nick. "And so was there, I'm just taking a shot here, a giant weasel involved?"

"Not a weasel," said Will. "Something else came through. It looked more like—this is going to sound even more wacko, okay—a hybrid human-spidery-snake thingy with hypnotic eyes. Only a lot more disgusting and dangerous."

"No, that doesn't sound crazy at all. Oh, look what I found," said Nick, pointing into an empty locker. "A cuckoo clock: *Cuckoo-cuckoo-cuckoo*."

"Behave yourself," said Ajay.

"He called what I saw a lamia," said Will. "I don't expect you to believe me."

"A lamia?" asked Ajay, who froze in place. "Are you certain of that?"

"Yes."

"Sounds bogus," said Nick. "What's a lamia?"

"A lamia is an ancient mythological demon," said Ajay, looking a little green. "Half-female, half-serpent. A monster that creeps silently through the night and . . . devours children. Allegedly."

"That sounds about right," said Will.

"Refreshing," said Nick.

"And the gentleman who told you this," said Ajay. "Who might he be?"

"The same one who gave me these glasses," said Will, reluctant to say more.

Ajay leaned against the lockers, and a concealed panel on the wall above the lockers slid open.

"What did you just do?" asked Will, jumping up onto the bench to take a look.

"I must have activated some kind of pressure plate," said Ajay, pushing the same spot on the side of the locker again.

The panel closed. Ajay pressed it again: It opened.

Nick jumped up beside Will. "Secret compartment. Awesome."

Will reached into the recessed space. "There's something back here. I can't reach it; it's shoved way inside."

Ajay jumped up beside them. "Give me a lift up. I can get to it."

They grabbed Ajay and boosted him above the lockers. He wriggled inside to his waist and with both hands dragged a midsized black steamer trunk out of the compartment. They lowered him and set the trunk on the bench.

"Not very heavy," said Ajay.

"It's locked," said Will.

"I'm on it," said Nick. "This requires years of intense training, natural talent, and incredible finesse. . . ."

Nick picked up a dumbbell and smashed it repeatedly and violently into the lock, which shattered into pieces.

"Works for me," said Will as he flipped up the lid.

Inside was a strange assortment of old hats. Will lifted them out one at a time. A pirate hat adorned with a big flouncy feather, cavalier style. A floppy red beret. A conical dunce's cap, inscribed with strange glyphs. A bishop's miter. A bronze crown, set with large fake gems. A garland made of olive branches. Two tricornered American Revolution–era hats. An iron knight's coif, made of real chain mail. A cowboy hat. A long feathered Indian headdress. And finally what looked like a steel welder's mask, inset with a small thick window for the eyes. All substantial pieces, blocked and solidly constructed, none of them shoddy or cheap.

"Amazeballs," said Nick, astonished. "You know what this means, don't you?"

"No," said Will.

"The Village People are getting back together," said Nick.

"Apparently at a Renaissance fair," said Ajay.

"Hold on, there's more," said Will.

Will lifted the false shelf on which the hats had been resting, revealing an equally eclectic collection of heavy molded plastic masks, with thick elastic bands in the back. The kind you might have found on the shelves of an old-fashioned toy store. The masks were hand painted, designed and crafted with an attention to detail seldom seen anymore. A diverse group of faces, stark and more than a little unsettling: a clown, a devil, a fox, a horse, a tusked wild boar, a pigtailed girl, a grinning jack-o'-lantern, a snarling grizzled man wearing an eye patch, a ghost, a menacing wolf, and two human faces. Will lifted one of them: a heavy-jowled, middle-aged man with pursed lips, with long silver strands of hair hanging on either side of his balding head.

"Who does that look like to you?" asked Will.

"Dude on the hundred-dollar Benjamin," said Nick.

"Benjamin *Franklin*," said Ajay.

"Whoa. *That's* a coincidence," said Nick.

Will lifted the last mask. "And this one?"

"George Washington?" asked Ajay.

"The father of our country?" said Nick, then with mock outrage, "Okay, now they've gone too far."

"The people I saw down here were wearing these," said Will, realizing. "That's why their faces looked so weird. Twelve hats. Twelve masks."

"So what does it mean?" asked Ajay.

"I don't know yet," said Will.

Will searched the trunk again and found a yellowing envelope in a small net fastened to the side. He removed an equally aged piece of paper and unfolded it. An embossed insignia topped the sheet, a round cluster of tightly arranged flower blossoms, topped by a square formed by four crossed tools or weapons. In their center was a grinning death's head. A headline below the insignia read THE PEERS. Below that, in graceful, exquisite calligraphy, was a list of names that filled the rest of the page.

> Orlando
>
> Renaldo the Fox
>
> Namo the Duke
>
> Salomon the King
>
> Turpin the Archbishop
>
> Astolpho of the West
>
> Ogier the Dane
>
> Malagigi the Enchanter
>
> Padraig de Mort
>
> Florismart the Friend
>
> Ganelon the Crafter
>
> Guerin de Montglave
>
> "The Old Gentleman"

Will, Nick, and Ajay looked at each other.

"The Peers," said Will. "You recognize any of these names?"

"No," said Nick. "But then I don't own a phone book from the fourteenth century."

"Any guesses?" asked Will.

"The French national soccer team?" said Ajay.

"The Twelve Musketeers?" said Nick.

"Okay, okay," said Will.

"Twelve hats, twelve masks," said Ajay, "but thirteen names on the list."

"What's up with that?" asked Nick.

"I'd venture a guess that a hat and mask correspond to each name," said Ajay. "Except for the last, which is in quotes and is really a description, not a name."

"'The Old Gentleman,'" said Will.

"So let's take all this stuff with us and brainiac it later?" asked Nick, yawning again, glancing at his watch. "I really need to crash."

"No," said Will. "We should put it all back exactly as we found it. Spread everything out first—I want to take pictures."

"I'm quite certain I can *remember* them, Will," said Ajay pointedly.

"I know. We may need to show them to someone else."

Nick and Ajay laid the masks and hats on the floor. Will pulled out his cell phone and activated the camera. "Can we get more light in here?" he asked.

Nick tried more switches by the door. None turned on fixtures in the locker room, but one activated lights in the corridor outside. He stepped out to look at them. Will took shots of the hats and masks, then leaned in to snap close-ups of the paper with the insignia and the list of names.

"So the people you saw were wearing *both* hats and masks?" asked Ajay.

"Which could explain why it took them so long to come after me," said Will. "They had to put all this away first."

Nick slowly backed into the locker room, looking pale. "Uh, hate to harsh your mellow. We need another way out of here."

"Why?" asked Will as he took the last photo.

"Bad guy. Far end of the hall. With a big-ass knife . . ."

"What?!"

". . . and a medium-sized hatchet," said Nick.

"Are you high?" asked Ajay.

Will and Ajay stuck their heads out into the hallway. A long row of single bare lightbulbs had come on, suspended from the ceiling down the full length of the corridor, creating small sharp pools of light that didn't quite blend. In a last splash of light at the far end, just before the distant corner, stood a lone figure.

The figure was tall, wrapped in a black cloak, and wore an iron helmet. He looked up, appeared to see them, and drew something from his belt: a short sword that gleamed in the light. The figure headed their way, picking up speed as he rushed from one pool of light to the next. A harsh, bloodthirsty cry echoed down the corridor.

"Thank God I already peed," said Ajay.

Will yanked them both back into the room and shut the door. "Look for another way out," he said.

Nick and Ajay frantically searched the room and adjoining bathroom. Will turned the lock on the inside knob and rattled it to make sure it was secure.

#15: BE QUICK, BUT DON'T HURRY.

"Anything in the bathroom?" shouted Will.

"Not unless we flush ourselves," said Ajay.

"You might fit," said Nick. "Then you could go for help."

Will studied the lockers. They were welded in groups of three, stacked against the wall. He dropped to his knees and saw that the section in the middle was missing the small strip of wood that attached to the floor.

"Give me a hand here," said Will. "Now!"

The others ran to him as a teeth-gnashing howl sounded outside. Will threw open the lockers in the middle group—all empty—then grabbed the shelves and pulled. The lockers shifted toward him slightly.

"This section isn't fixed to the wall," he said. "Something's back here."

"See if you can find a button or a switch of some kind," said Ajay.

They each searched a locker. Nick found ventilation holes punched in the back of the middle one and put his eye to it. "I don't see a wall," he said. "It's open back there."

The doorknob rattled, then fierce pounding on the door began.

"There must be another concealed button. Look for unusual shapes or indentations," said Ajay, pressing every inch of metal. "Could be anything, a pressure or kick plate of some kind . . . oh God, oh God . . ."

"Stay calm, Ajay," said Will. "He may just be trying to scare us."

There was a loud crash, metal on metal, as the figure assaulted the door.

"It's working!" shouted Ajay.

"Pull the whole freakin' thing off the wall," said Nick.

"Count of three," said Will. "One, two, three!"

They each grabbed hold of a locker and pulled as hard as they could. The lockers moved an inch and seemed ready to yield more but hung up on something.

"There's a bolt and spring latch here at the top," said Ajay, feeling around the inside of the middle locker. "Definitely a locking device. There's got to be a hidden mechanism that'll release it."

Another smashing blow to the door, then three in succession with increasing speed and power. The inside of the plate around the knob started to warp.

"He's chopping down the freaking door," said Nick.

Ajay climbed completely into the locker, grabbed hold of the metal hooks in its ceiling, and twisted them. "Okay, I think I've got it," said Ajay.

"Any time," said Will as another blow landed, pushing the knob inward.

Ajay jammed one foot against a bulge in the metal on the left side, lifted his right foot, and pressed it against a similar bulge on the right. Then he grabbed and turned the hooks as hard as he could. They heard a snick as a catch gave way.

"Now pull!" shouted Ajay.

Will and Nick grabbed the lockers and yanked. This time they gave and the section fell toward them, with Ajay still inside. Will and Nick jumped out of the way as it crashed to the floor. Directly behind where the lockers had stood, a rough hole in the cinder-block wall led to a dark narrow passage.

"Little help here," said Ajay, muffled, from inside the locker.

Another furious blow landed on the door; Will glanced back

and saw the hatchet punch through next to the knob. A second blow doubled the size of the gash.

"This dude's serious," said Nick.

"Nick!" said Will. He grabbed the bottom of the lockers, and Nick took the other side. Lifting with all their strength, they leveraged the lockers to a standing position. Ajay came into view, upside down in the middle one, squashed in a pile.

"That was most unpleasant," Ajay croaked.

As Ajay tumbled out, Will and Nick shoved the section of lockers toward the door. A hand in a black metallic glove ripped through the hole by the lock plate and felt around for the lock. Ajay jumped in to add his weight as they slammed the lockers against the door. They heard a snarl of pain from outside.

"You like that?" shouted Nick, eyes lit up, hopping back and forth. "Come get some, fool, bring it!"

"Nick, are you insane?" asked Will. "Don't yell at the guy with the hatchet."

"Look on the bright side," said Nick. "At least it's not a lamia."

Will wedged a bench between the barricading lockers and the nearest wall, anchoring it in place. The roommates glanced at each other, breathless, then turned to the narrow opening in the wall.

"Who wants to go first?" asked Will, and switched on his flashlight.

DÉJÀ VU

Ajay darted through the hole in the wall, with Nick and Will close behind. Through the first few turns, the walls of the passage were reinforced by concrete, which gave way to a structure of broad timbers. Fifty feet later, they were in a tunnel of solid rock that looked as if it had been dug with chisels.

"Did he get through? Is he coming after us?" asked Nick.

"Not yet," said Will, glancing back. "Don't hear anything."

"Are either of you claustrophobic?" asked Ajay, shining his light ahead.

"I'm not," said Nick.

"Never have been."

"Let's hope you're right," said Ajay. "This would be a bad place to find out otherwise."

The tunnel closed in quickly around them from that point forward, until it was wide enough for one person and only Ajay could move freely without crouching down.

"Who was he? Did you get a good look at him?" asked Will.

"He's wearing a big helmet," said Nick. "And a black cape

and a belt with an iron buckle and awesome chain mail armor and an iron mask."

"He's got to be one of the Peers," said Will. "But how did he know we were down here?"

"I can feel air moving around us," said Ajay. "I think that's good."

"Where the deuce are we?" asked Nick.

"I'll be able to tell you when we get back to the pod," said Ajay, pressing the GPS button on his pager again.

"What good will it do us *then*?" asked Nick.

"We're in a secret passage," said Will. "Emphasis on *secret*. Keep going."

"It seems surprisingly clean," said Ajay, feeling the walls. "Without the overwhelming number of insects and vermin you might expect."

"That may mean it's used frequently," said Will. "By whoever the Peers are."

"Agreed," said Ajay.

"I don't think so," said Nick.

"Oh? Why's that?" asked Ajay.

"Dude, it's not wide enough for them to get through here with those hats on."

"I'm sorry, my bad," said Ajay. "I forgot you were an idiot."

"Whoa, I just had a mind-blowing flash," said Nick. "You know the statue of the Paladin in front of the field house? *That's* who Ax Dude looked like."

"Honestly, Nick? I don't find that at all helpful," said Ajay, creeping ahead.

"I'm serious. He's wearing armor and a helmet like the statue, and he had the cape thingy and he's carrying a sword and hatchet like the statue, too—"

"You're alleging that a *statue* made of metal came to life and chased us like a homicidal maniac," said Ajay, coming to a stop.

"I didn't say the dude was *made* of metal—"

"He's saying," said Will, "it was somebody dressed up to *look* like the statue."

"*Thank* you," said Nick.

"At least now you've moved from the ridiculous to the merely implausible," said Ajay, going forward again. "Why would any person do such a thing?"

"Maybe the Peers are pissed off we found their playhouse," said Nick. "And the treasure chest with their Happy Meals hat collection."

"They wanted to scare the living hell out of us," said Will.

"*Because . . . ?*" asked Ajay.

"Because," said Will, annoyed at his tone, "I saw them earlier today with the Weasel Hole and now we know what they call themselves. *Okay?*"

"Forgive me," said Ajay, glancing back at him. "I get grumpy when being chased by an ax murderer."

"It was a hatchet," said Nick.

"Otherwise known as a *hand ax*," said Ajay.

"But, dude, I gotta give you props," said Nick. "You're amazingly chill about it."

"I *seem* calm from years of meditation," said Ajay. "But I assure you it's taking all my self-control to restrain an irresistible impulse to shout for my mommy."

Will pointed his flashlight into the darkness behind them,

light glinting off the rocks. "Can you see anything up ahead?" he asked.

"The walls are getting wider," said Ajay. "And we're moving slightly downward. Can you feel the change in the grade?"

"Yes," said Will. "Keep going."

The tunnel gradually widened as they trudged on, until the walls fell out of sight. They stopped and shined their lights into the heavy gloom. The ceiling lofted high above them and the walls were shored up by rows of ancient timbers.

"Damn, who built all this?" asked Nick, looking around in wonder.

"I don't know," said Will. "But it's been here a long time."

"This would have taken years, if not decades," said Ajay, examining the timbers. "Controlled blasting, all this shoring up, it's a massive operation."

The air felt humid, fresh, and much warmer than expected. Somewhere they heard water trickling. A surprising heat enveloped them, emanating from the walls. About an inch of water splashed underfoot as they moved along.

"We must be getting close to the lake," said Ajay.

They passed a few dark openings, leading off in either direction. As they neared the far end of the big chamber, the walls narrowed down again, until finally they reached a finished wooden door frame leading to another tight, carved tunnel. They followed the twisting tunnel and fifty feet farther on, the corridor dead-ended in a T-intersection, with two tunnels heading off at ninety degrees.

"Which way do we go?" asked Nick.

At that exact moment, they heard voices and footsteps

echoing from far back behind them and erratic beams of light glanced off the rocks in the tunnel.

"Let's try this way," said Will, pointing to the right. *"Run."*

They sprinted, single file, but the passage soon widened enough to move side by side. The tunnel dipped down even deeper, leveled off for a long stretch, then rose sharply again. Fifty yards farther on, it ended abruptly in a small rock chamber.

These walls had been shored up with timbers that looked newer than any they'd seen so far. A sturdy steel ladder climbed straight up the far wall, into a narrow round chute. Without a word, they pocketed their flashlights, jumped onto the rungs, and climbed with desperate speed into darkness. Fifty feet, then a hundred, losing track of where they were, impossible to see how far they had to go.

"There's no end to the damn thing— Ow!" said Ajay, in the lead, just as his head bonked into something hard. He stopped and the others piled into him. "Check that—I've found the end. Nick, please be kind enough to withdraw your head to a reasonable distance from my hindquarters."

"Sorry," said Nick, then turned to Will. "Back up, dude."

Will dropped down a rung, hooked an arm around the ladder, brought out his flashlight, flicked it on, and pointed up. A wooden hatch, just above Ajay, covered the tunnel where the ladder stopped.

"Open it," said Nick.

"Many thanks for your helpful suggestion," said Ajay.

Far below, at the other end of the ladder, they heard shouts. Moments later, someone pointed a flashlight up the chimney. The beam didn't reach them but if their pursuers began to climb, it wouldn't be long before they were spotted, and trapped.

"*Can* you open it?" asked Will, whispering.

Ajay pressed his shoulder against the wood and pushed as hard as he could. It rose slightly but he couldn't lift it. "I need help."

Ajay slid over to make room as Nick climbed up beside him, and they applied all their weight; this time it lifted a foot, hinging on one side.

"Put your back into it," whispered Nick. "Come on, bro, we've got this."

"On three," whispered Will, shoving his shoulders into their rear ends.

At the count of three, they pushed together. The door swung up to the hinges' balance point, hung there precariously, then fell backward with a muffled thud. They scrambled out onto long, wet grass.

"Close it fast," said Will.

They scuttled over, lifted the hatch, and dropped it over the opening.

"Is there a lock on it?" asked Will.

"I don't see one," said Ajay.

"If we stand on it, they can't follow us," asked Nick.

"Yes, you two wait here," said Ajay dryly. "I'll go buy a hammer and nails."

"Where are we?" asked Nick.

"I have no idea," said Will, looking around.

They were in a small clearing in the middle of some woods. Ajay turned and looked up; his eyes went wide.

"Uh, guys," said Ajay. He pointed. "It appears we're on the island."

Nick and Will turned. The Gothic-style Crag loomed above them, less than a hundred yards away. They were practically in its backyard. The forbidding castle looked enormous from this distance, stone ramparts arching high above them. Dogs were barking, and lights came into view, bobbing toward them from a nearby gate.

"They know we're here," said Will.

"How could they possibly know that?" asked Nick.

"Someone must have told them we were in the tunnels."

"Probably that Paladin fellow," Ajay said. "He must have alerted the rest of the Peers—"

"Dudes, discuss later?" Nick said. "Those guards are nobody we want to mess with."

They ran away from the lights, the hatch, and the Crag. A waning moon had risen in the east, offering enough light to dimly show the way. Within minutes, they had passed through the woods and reached the water's edge. The closest shore stood a quarter of a mile away across the lake. Will put a hand in the water.

"This is the western shore," said Nick, pointing across the water. "School's that way."

"Should we swim for it?" asked Ajay.

"Water's too cold," said Nick. "And the guards have powerboats."

"Let's grab one ourselves," said Will.

"There's a dock on this side of the island," said Ajay, pointing to their right. "Over this way."

Behind them they heard shouts and saw lights twisting in

the dark as the Peers exiting the tunnel hooked up with the guards from the Crag.

"Hurry," said Will. "That's where they'll look first."

They ran along the shoreline to their right. A small dock came into view, with a rowboat and motorized tender tied at the end. Two guards stood near shore, under a light on a pole. Will bent down and retied his shoes.

"Wait for me here," he whispered. "Don't make a sound. Be ready when I come for you."

"Where are you going?" asked Ajay.

"To get a boat."

Will pumped in a few deep breaths and launched toward the dock. The rocky beach provided poor footing but he reached cruising speed quickly. As he neared the dock, Will slowed and waved at the sentries: grown men wearing dark uniforms.

"Hey, how ya doing?" asked Will.

Will sped by the dock. The sentries ran after him, shouting warnings to stop. Will stepped on the gas and turned right, heading inland, narrowly avoiding collisions with the densely packed trees. The sentries gave chase, crashing clumsily through the brush, calling out to the others.

The lights of the group to Will's right, who had nearly reached the dock, turned and backtracked toward them. Will zigzagged through the woods, dodging and jumping obstacles, making a lot of noise to let the group join up behind him and find his trail.

Will broke into an opening near the castle. He dropped into a crouch when he saw a single silhouette with a flashlight thirty feet to his left. Will recognized the figure's shape and its awkward, lurching gait:

Lyle Ogilvy.

Can't say I'm surprised to see him, thought Will. Lyle moved with purpose instead of thrashing around in the dark. He came to a stop and raised his head like a dog catching a scent. Will sensed Lyle was about to turn. He did, but by then Will had ducked behind a tree.

He knows I'm here. He can feel my presence.

Will felt around for a fallen branch and hurled it deep into the woods. Lyle whipped his flashlight in that direction. Will's other pursuers turned toward where it landed. Will pivoted 180 degrees and sprinted back the way he'd come.

Silently this time. As he focused on quieting his footsteps and tracking the sounds of his pursuers, Will felt his senses tune up to a higher level of awareness. A sudden, specific sense of distance and vector of the sounds all around him, a 360-degree scan. Almost like a grid of the surrounding area forming in his mind's eye.

As Will let himself drop deeper into this heightened perception, time seemed to slow. He saw his own footfalls before each touched down, and was able to make minute adjustments to avoid anything that might make a sound. He increased his speed, entering a zone where a preview of every move appeared on the "grid" before he committed to it. He felt like a weightless beam of light shooting through space.

Just like that, Will was back at the western shore, fifty yards from the dock. The dock was empty, his pursuers scattered all over the woods behind him. Without breaking stride, Will angled toward the dock.

He "saw" the move before he made it: leaping onto the pier from over ten feet away. As he ran, he pulled out his Swiss Army knife and flicked open its longest blade. Reaching the end of the dock, he soared out over the water. The blade sliced cleanly through the securing line as he landed, perfectly balanced, in the bow of the motorboat. Cut loose from the dock, the boat shot into open water, propelled by his momentum. Two steps to the stern, one pull on the starter, a rev of the throttle, and he was off, banking hard left.

Nick and Ajay splashed out to their knees as Will sluiced a path toward them. He slowed enough for the boys to haul themselves over the gunnels. Will ruddered hard right and zoomed off for the western shore.

Will felt his heightened state of awareness recede as they made their way across in silence. He felt shaky inside, similar to how he felt after "pushing pictures."

So they're related, he thought. *The speed, the stamina, pushing pictures, and now this. I can do more. I can do a lot more.*

Their pursuers didn't reach the water until they'd nearly crossed the lake. By the time they heard a powerboat behind them, Will had gunned the tender up onto a stretch of mainland beach. They ditched the boat as it stopped in the sand. With the flashlights, they quickly found the running track.

"What time is it?" asked Ajay.

"Ten-fifty. We'll never make it back before curfew," said Nick, panting. "Well, *Will* could make it."

"We'll make it," said Will. "Guys, I just saw Lyle on the island."

"*What?*" said Ajay.

"I don't know if he was in the tunnels or with the guards that came from the Crag, but he was looking for us."

"Busted," said Nick, pumping his fist.

"Whatever the hell's going on," said Will, "Lyle's right in the middle of it."

They ran in silence, fiercely. Will hung behind, pushing their pace as he listened for signs of pursuit. He heard a power-boat sweep by near where they'd landed, but it didn't come ashore. They passed the Barn without incident.

Minutes later, they passed a security guard driving back in his cart outside Greenwood Hall—for once *without* a friendly smile—who watched them plow through the front doors, breathless, at exactly 10:59 p.m.

"First things first," said Will as they ran upstairs. "We're going to need a lot of coffee."

PUZZLES

"These are French names," said Elise, looking at the list.

"Duh," said Nick.

"Eat your cake, Nick," said Elise with a withering look.

"Lees, babe, I think we figured out they were *French* already, okay?" said Nick. "Except for that first one. Orlando."

"And, pray tell, what kind of name is Orlando?" she asked.

"Hello?" said Nick. "It's from *Florida*?"

Four of the roommates sat around the dining table; Ajay had gone to work on something in his room. Everyone but Will had their tablet on in front of them, although Nick was more focused on a slice of chocolate cake. They'd woken Elise and Brooke as soon as they returned and made coffee, and Will told them the whole story about the Peers and the Paladin, Lyle, and the tunnels to the Crag. Minus the monsters—Will thought it best to leave out any supernatural details until he was sure the girls were on board, and Nick and Ajay agreed. When Will was finished, Ajay transferred the photos Will had taken of the masks onto everyone's tablets. Elise had lit up with interest throughout their account, but Brooke looked and acted remote. At least she was at the table, studying the photographs.

"You're not here on scholarship, are you, Nick?" asked Will.

"I am totally on scholarship," said Nick, taking another bite. "Man, I *loves* me some chocolate cake."

"For gymnastics, not geography," said Elise. "I'm half French, you nitwit. I speak and read French. My father's French."

"Oh, yeah? Well, what about your mom? She's not French."

"She's Vietnamese, and she *speaks* French, and these are all, take my word for it, French names. Or more specifically, Frankish. From the Middle Ages."

"Wicked," said Nick. "So we know this much, then: They're a bunch of middle-aged French dudes."

Brooke touched Nick's arm gently. "Please don't talk anymore."

"Guys," said Will. "Concentrate. Once we figure out who the rest of the Peers are and what they're up to, we may have the whole picture."

"But it's safe to say they're *not* a bunch of middle-aged French dudes," said Elise, glowering at Nick.

"Let's focus on this insignia at the top of the list," said Will, pointing to the photo he'd taken of it on Brooke's tablet.

Brooke studied the image closely. "These look like they might be white chrysanthemums. We need a reference book on flowers."

"Where will we get that at this time of night?" said Will.

"I'll go to the library," said Brooke, but she made no move to get up.

"How?" asked Will, puzzled.

307

"On my tablet," she said.

"I thought they put the clamps on Internet access," said Will.

"To outside servers," said Brooke. "Not the ones on campus."

"You *still* haven't taken the tutorial?" asked Elise, incredulous.

"I haven't had time," said Will.

"Show him," said Elise.

Brooke angled her tablet around for Will to see. The image on-screen—a high-def re-creation of their pod's great room—didn't startle him. He was getting used to these vastly superior graphics. This was something else.

Around the table sat three incredibly lifelike versions—virtual doubles—of Brooke, Elise, and Nick. And they were *looking* at him with all the poise and attention and—he didn't know how else to put it—*personality* of their living counterparts.

"What in the world . . . ," said Will.

Elise, Brooke, and Nick laughed. The figures on-screen laughed along with them. None of their actions exactly synchronized with their real-life counterparts' but they seemed eerily similar; it was like watching three pairs of big/small identical twins.

"What are those things?" asked Will.

"They're called syn-apps," said Brooke.

"Short for 'synchronized synthetic applications,'" said Elise.

The fourth chair, where Will was sitting in real life—and where a version of "Will" would have completed the group—sat empty.

"So where am I?" asked Will.

"You haven't taken the tutorial yet, dummy," said Elise.

"Go to the library," said Brooke to her screen. Brooke's syn-app stood up from the table. The walls of their pod on her screen morphed seamlessly into towering stacks of a vast library. "Find a book on the symbolic significance of flowers."

Her syn-app waved okay, in a way that seemed utterly Brookeian. Then she walked toward the stacks to find her objective. Will guessed that he was seeing nothing more than a sophisticated "waiting" screen while the computer searched a database, but the effect still floored him.

"Is that the real library?" asked Will.

"A *virtually* real one," said Brooke. "A replica of the Archer Library, the main one on campus. With digital versions of all its books and archives."

Will pointed to the figures of other "students" that Brooke passed, seated in chairs or at tables, browsing through shelves.

"So those are other students' syn-apps, doing research online," said Will.

"Exactly," said Brooke. "All in real time. Like a chat room."

"Only nobody's *chatting*," said Nick. "'Cause it's a *library*."

Will looked at Elise's tablet. Brooke was gone from her screen as well. And Elise was staring out at Will with the same cocky, sardonic smile the *real* Elise usually wore.

"So if I take that tutorial—" said Will.

"Your tablet will create your own syn-app," said Brooke.

"And people used to think photographs stole your soul," said Will, shaking his head.

"Nya-ah-ah," said Nick.

Elise sighed. "It's just a graphic stand-in for an intuitive user interface."

"Yeah, whatever," said Nick. "Check *that* at the door, 'cause let me tell you what: having your own little dude is freaking *massive*."

"How do they make it look so much like you?" asked Will.

"Sophisticated character-based three-D modeling," said Elise. "Rendered from your appearance and behavior. The software learns from observing you."

"To be more *like* you," said Nick. "How shwhacked is *that*?" Nick turned his tablet around. Nick's character was walking around the table on his hands, making goofy faces. Nick got up and walked around the table on *his* hands.

"Yep," said Will. "That's you, all right."

Back at work, Elise was examining the insignia on the letterhead above the names with a magnifying glass. "These might be weapons around the edge of the bouquet," she said. "Or maybe tools."

Ajay hurried out of his bedroom to join them, carrying his tablet. "Good news. I've collated the GPS data I grabbed from the tunnels. Now let's lay it over a grid of the campus and see what we find."

Ajay set his tablet on the table. Will snuck a look at it and saw the syn-app version of Ajay moving images around on-screen. Ajay's double appeared even more elfin than he did, almost like an anime character, with enormous brown eyes.

"Okay, that's just freaky," said Will.

"Good gravy, man, haven't you taken the tutorial?" asked Ajay.

"Not sure I want to," said Will. "Not after seeing this."

"I've got it. They're weapons *and* tools," said Elise, studying the insignia through the magnifying glass. "The two on top are a sword and a hatchet—"

"Hello," said Nick. "Just like *Paladin* dude."

310

"And the two on the bottom are a builder's square . . . and a compass. . . ."

"A *compass,*" said Nick. "That could be a clue. What direction is it pointing?"

"Not a navigational compass, a *drafting* compass. The kind architects and draftsmen use to draw circles," said Elise, showing them her screen.

"All four objects could also be something else," said Brooke, scrutinizing the insignia on her screen. "I think they might be letters."

"What kind of letters?" asked Nick, trying to drink coffee while balancing upside down on one hand.

"Calligraphy of some kind," said Brooke. "From an archaic alphabet."

"Let's check it out," said Elise. She held the Peers list in front of her screen. Elise stood up from the table on-screen to study the page, then reached to the top of the screen and brought down an *exact copy* of the list.

"Okay, what the heck just happened?" asked Will.

"The tablet used its camera to scan the letter, rendered a virtual copy, and delivered it into the simulation," said Elise. "So my syn-app could go find a match."

Elise on-screen looked up at Will and said, "Pretty spooky, huh?"

Will fell over backward on his chair. "It talked!"

"Boo-yah," said Nick.

"They all can," said Brooke. "Once they get to know you."

"Oh, they can do a lot more than *talk,*" said Nick, helping Will up while still walking on his hands. "If you know what I'm saying, wink, wink."

"There's a difference," said Elise, "between using a tool and *being* a tool."

"Touché, my lady," said Nick, flipping back to his feet and giving a small bow.

Elise rolled her eyes, then spoke to her syn-app. "Library."

The environment on-screen around Elise shifted to the same academic library. Elise started toward the stacks, and on the way passed Brooke, coming back with a large open book. The syn-apps waved to each other.

Will peeked over Brooke's shoulder at her screen as her character ported back to the pod. She looked at them, held up a book about flowers, and moved close to the screen. Brooke read the entry her double had found: "The white mum is the city flower of Chicago . . . and the flower of the month of November. . . ."

"Step back now," said Nick, snapping his fingers. "Dudes, we're not that far from Chicago . . . and . . . it's *November right now.*"

"Take a deep breath," said Ajay slowly. "And try to prevent your mind from working altogether."

"The white mum is also the emblem of a mysterious organization called the Fraternity of the Triangle," said Brooke, still reading. "A secret society of scientists, architects, and engineers. Its origins reach back to the Middle Ages . . . and they're aligned with the Freemasons."

"Now you're on to something," said Ajay, excited. "The compass and builder's square, which you found in this insignia, are both Masonic symbols."

"Freemasons?" asked Nick. "Is that a fraternity, too?"

"Neither is a 'fraternity,' Nick," said Brooke wearily. "At least not the kind you're thinking of."

"And what kind might that be?" asked Nick.

"College pledges, Greek Week," said Brooke.

"Frat house keggers," said Elise. "Horny knuckleheads projectile vomiting."

"My point *exactly*," said Nick, banging his fist on the table.

"Don't be a nincompoop," said Ajay. "These are centuries-old organizations with notorious reputations for secrecy and violence."

"For real?" said Nick, sitting back down. "I am so *stoked*."

"Okay, found it," said Elise, swinging her tablet around. Her syn-app transported from the virtual library to their great room and held a leather-bound volume to the screen, displaying a page of calligraphic letters.

"The letters are from the Carolingian alphabet," said Elise, reading from the screen. "The standard script used for handwriting in western Europe between about 800 and 1200 AD."

"*Carolingian* means 'under the leadership of Carolus,'" said Ajay. "The Latin name of the emperor Charlemagne, who united Europe for the first time since the Romans and was eventually crowned emperor by the pope."

"Which suggests that whoever the Peers are, they were inspired by some group that originated during the reign of Charlemagne?" asked Brooke.

"Perhaps so," said Ajay.

"So which letters are *these*?" asked Will.

Elise put the insignia next to the ancient alphabet and said, "T, k, o, c."

Nick grabbed a pen and paper and wrote them down. On his screen, his syn-app did the same.

"Okay, I'm officially confusiated," said Nick, scratching his head at what he'd written. "T-k-o-c doesn't spell anything."

"Maybe it's an anagram," said Brooke. "Mix up the letters."

"Interestingly, although Charlemagne was exceptionally tall and imposing for that era," continued Ajay, "roughly six foot two, his father was apparently a dwarf."

"Dude . . . how can you possibly remember all that random stuff?"

Ajay glanced nervously at Will. "Well, I do study a great deal, and I take copious notes, and I guess I have above-average retention—"

"Okay, *scoreboard*," said Nick, who triumphantly held up his list of words and pointed to the last one. "Check it out."

"Tock," said Brooke. "That's the best you could do."

"Tock could mean something," said Nick.

"Yes. If you were a clock," said Ajay.

"At least a clock can tell time," said Elise, scowling.

Nick looked discouraged, but his on-screen counterpart held up to the screen the page he had written, whistled, and waved his arms excitedly to catch Nick's eye.

"Hold on, hold on," said Nick. He then tried to pronounce the variations on his syn-app's page. "Ktoc, cokt, ockt . . . crap, I sound like a cat with a hairball—"

Nick started choking on-screen, like a cat.

"Amazing," said Ajay, shaking his head. "Even his cartoon is a moron."

"Somewhere," said Elise, drumming her fingers on the table, "there's a tiny little village that's missing its idiot."

"Screw it, where'd we stash the Scrabble set?" Nick got up and rifled through the kitchen. He returned with a bag of letter tiles, fishing out the four he needed.

"Have a look at this," said Ajay as he laid his tablet on the table. A three-dimensional view of the campus appeared in midair, floating above his screen. Ajay used his hands to expand the image until it covered most of the table.

"Now let's track the coordinates I entered. . . ." Using his fingers to scroll the image, Ajay moved their point of view until it hovered over the field house. The building turned transparent, revealing a detailed re-creation of the men's locker room. "We entered the tunnel from the locker room . . . went down these stairs, turned hard left . . . and followed the hall to here. . . ."

He moved his finger down a long straightaway, outlining the path of the tunnel, until he reached another blinking point at the end.

"The door to the auxiliary locker room," said Ajay. "Exactly one-quarter of a mile under the athletic fields." He touched his screen again; the smaller locker room appeared, and inside it another doorway. "We entered the *second* tunnel here behind the lockers. Now watch."

Their point of view rose back into a bird's-eye view as he tracked the tunnel to the east. "By the time we moved through that large chamber and reached the T-intersection, we were over two hundred feet underground."

Two corridors branched off at ninety degrees. The one to the right ran directly under the photo-real waters of Lake Waukoma.

"We followed the right fork to here," said Ajay. The blinking spot moved under the lake to the island and came to a stop at the hatch behind the Crag.

"The Crag was built in the early 1870s," said Ajay. "It's my opinion that these tunnels were built at the same time. A rough geologic network of caves probably existed here already."

"Like the ones on the bluff across the lake," said Will.

"Correct," said Ajay, "but it took enormous effort to extend and finish them, as we saw. The required resources would have been on hand when the castle was being built, and I believe only a person rich and eccentric enough to create such a folly in the first place could have built those tunnels. Therefore, I think whoever put up the Crag also created these tunnels. Over fifty years *before* the Center was built."

"So who built the Crag?" asked Will.

"I'll find out," said Brooke. "But why were the tunnels built in the first place?"

"We can't answer that yet," said Will.

"Do you think the people who chased you from the castle have something to do with the Peers?" asked Elise, looking concerned.

"I'm not sure," said Will. "We know the guy who owns it now, Haxley, keeps heavy security on the island. Maybe they were just guards reacting to the presence of intruders."

"Will, they were practically waiting for us when we came up that ladder," said Ajay.

"And that tunnel leads directly to the Peers' meeting room," said Elise. "There must be *some* connection."

"I think she's right, Will," said Ajay.

"Then let's keep looking for that," said Will.

"Okay, all that's awesome and totally sick," said Nick,

obsessing over the Scrabble tiles. "But these four frickin' letters still don't spell frickin' anything."

"That's because they're not an anagram," said Brooke, excited, staring intently at her screen. "They're an *acronym*."

"You mean something that means the opposite of something?" asked Nick.

"No, that's an *antonym*," said Brooke. "An acronym means they're the first *letters* of words or a phrase that mean something." She rearranged Nick's tiles to their original order. "T . . . K . . . O . . . C."

"You mean like LOL?" asked Nick skeptically.

"Yes," said Brooke. "Like an *acronym*."

"LQTM," said Nick.

"What's *that* mean?" asked Ajay.

"Laughing quietly to myself," said Nick.

"So what's the phrase for TKOC?" asked Will.

Brooke turned her tablet around. Her syn-app opened another leather-bound book from the library and held it to the screen. They were looking at a lavish two-page color illustration, a heroic painting of twelve heavily armored knights on horseback.

"The Knights of Charlemagne," said Brooke. "The twelve greatest warriors who served under Emperor Charlemagne. They called themselves the Peers, and every name on that list you found is here: Orlando, Renaldo, Namo—"

The others crowded around her to take a look.

"—Salomon, Turpin, Astolpho, Ogier, Malagigi, Padraig, Florismart, Ganelon, Guerin de Montglave—"

"Dude," said Nick. "My head's about to asplode."

"That's why the Peers used Frankish letters for this acronym," said Ajay. "A hidden clue to their origin and identity, concealed in the insignia."

"The first twelve names are here," said Elise, scanning the list from the book. "But not the *last* one: the Old Gentleman."

"So who is he, then?" asked Will.

"I have an idea about that," said Brooke, paging through her online book. "Give me a second."

"Let's put this together," said Will, pacing as he thought it through. "The locker room and those tunnels are being used by members of a group called the Knights of Charlemagne. A modern incarnation of an ancient order that may have some connection to the person who built that castle."

"Or the person who lives there today," said Elise.

"And the Knights are definitely connected to the Black Caps who came after me," said Will.

"Maybe they're all part of the same organization," said Ajay.

"Maybe," said Will.

"So what do we freakin' do about it?" asked Nick, pacing opposite Will.

"Our mission hasn't changed," Ajay said. "We have to find out who the Peers are. Who did Will see down there with the hats and masks? Who chased us through the tunnels tonight?"

"We know who one of them is," said Elise.

"Lyle," said Will. "We'll start with him."

Brooke gasped and stood up abruptly, holding her tablet. "Listen to this," she said, alarmed.

"Don't scare me like that," said Nick.

Brook urgently read another passage from her syn-app's

book: "Charlemagne's twelve knights accompanied him on two different crusades when the emperor led his army across Europe to capture Jerusalem and the Holy Land for the 'civilized' western kingdoms."

"And what's the significance of that?" asked Ajay.

"Charlemagne had another name for these guys," said Brooke. "His twelve knights . . . were the original Paladins."

I'd stopped dreaming about him as soon as he got here. But the danger he was in hadn't vanished with the dreams. If anything, I sensed it was worse now, and drawing closer. Had he brought it with him, or had it been waiting for him all along?

He should be safe here. The school has ways. Should I tell him what I know? Maybe he hasn't learned any of it. Would it help? How can I be sure that telling him won't make it worse?

Sleep is becoming impossible.

THE TUTORIAL

The roommates packed it in after one in the morning, satisfied that they'd at least put a name to what they'd found. But Will lay awake worrying about the implications of the last piece Brooke had discovered: The original Knights were all Paladins. One of the contemporary Knights, dressed as a paladin, had come after them with an ax. The Paladin had been the school's mascot since 1915.

Did this suggest that the school was somehow involved?

Then there was the even crazier stuff he *hadn't* told them yet: The connection Nando had found between the Caps and the testing agency that had brought him to the school. The repeated appearances of his guardian angel, the monsters from the Never-Was, and this paranormal "war" that Dave said he was smack in the middle of.

Will heard a soft knock, moved to the door, and opened it a crack.

It was Brooke. "I need to ask you something," she whispered.

She was close enough for him to catch a sweet hint of

323

peppermint on her breath. He stood aside, inviting her in. She wore an oversized white men's dress shirt and floppy socks. She crossed to his bed and sat down, folding one bare leg underneath her. Will sat nearby, but not too close. She leaned toward him, her big eyes wide and bright with alarm, caught in a fragment of moonlight through the window.

"I'm lying there, staring at the ceiling," she said, her voice low and trembling, "and I can't stop asking myself, why did the Paladin show up down there?"

"Maybe he followed us," said Will.

"But how did he know you were down there in the first place?"

"Maybe we set off a silent alarm—"

"I think Lyle has some way of watching you," she said with conviction. "The same thing used to happen to Ronnie. Lyle always seemed to know where he was."

Will shivered as he thought about it.

"And, Will, think about this." Brooke put her hand on his. "If Lyle really is part of the Knights, and they're working with the men who tried to kidnap you . . ."

Will felt a chill run down his spine. "Then there's a good chance that word's gotten back to them and they know I'm here."

"I'm sorry if I haven't been more supportive," said Brooke sincerely. "I really don't believe that rules are made to be broken. But this is different. You're in real danger and I want to help in any way I can."

"I'm really glad to hear that," said Will. "There's something I need to tell you, too. Chances are good that Todd's part of this. With some of the other seniors from the cross-country team."

She looked away and sighed. She seemed more saddened than surprised.

"I'm sorry," he said. "Whatever's going on between you is none of my business."

"Nothing's going on between us," she said, eyes flashing. "Our families are close, that's all. We've known each other our whole lives."

"If you need me to help, I will," said Will.

She looked at him again, her eyes full of concern. "All this is going down, and you want to help *me*?"

Will got lost in her eyes for a second before he looked away. She reached out with her other hand and held his.

"Seriously, Will. I don't want you to get hurt."

"Don't worry about me," he said.

"But I am worried," she said. "I knew you'd been through something awful the moment we met."

"Well, I *was* lying there with stitches in my head."

She punched his arm lightly. "The technical term is *emotional intelligence*? Give me some credit. I don't want to help just because it's the right thing to do. I want to because I like you. Because you're smart and nice and kind of, well, brave."

Will had to look away.

"You haven't heard that a lot from other kids before?" she asked.

"No," he said quietly.

She tried to meet his eyes. "What about friends back home? People you're close to?"

Will shrugged. "Don't have any."

"Not *ever*?"

Will shook his head.

"Okay, that's just wrong. And not because there's something wrong with you," she said gently. "What were your parents thinking? Your life should have been filled with friends. From now on it will be."

He hoped she couldn't hear his heart beating because it was about to bust through his ribs.

"And if you ever want to talk about . . . whatever you've been through or football or eighteenth-century English poetry, just know I'm up for that. Because that's what friends are for."

She said it like someone explaining the concept for the first time in human history. She squeezed his hand and headed for the door.

"I'll work on Todd and see what I can find out," she said at the door.

"You be careful, too."

She seemed amused. "You really don't know much about girls, do you? Get some sleep, champ."

Fat chance. After flopping around for half an hour, Will noticed that his tablet had turned on. He was certain he'd switched it off and laid it flat before he'd gone to bed. Now it was standing on its legs, pointed directly toward him with a message floating on-screen:

WOULD YOU LIKE TO BEGIN THE TUTORIAL NOW? (RECOMMENDED)

"I surrender," said Will. He stumbled to the desk and sat down. "Yes, I'd like to take the tutorial."

The screen dissolved into a curtain of bubbling effervescence that gave Will a strange visceral impression: *It's happy.*

A series of questions appeared, dissolving in and out at an increasingly rapid pace as Will responded:

WHAT IS YOUR HEIGHT? YOUR WEIGHT? YOUR BIRTHDAY? YOUR FAVORITE COLOR? YOUR FAVORITE SPORT?

When that ended, it asked him to put his hands on the screen, one at a time. A bright blue light issued from it each time. It instructed him to move his face six inches from the screen, hold still, and shut his eyes, and when he did he felt a symmetrical grid of intense light moving slowly across his features—

It's mapping me.

One last message appeared: THIS DEVICE WILL BE ACTIVATED FOR YOUR SECURE AND PERSONAL USE. DO YOU STILL WISH TO PROCEED?

"Yes," he said.

The screen dissolved to a deep, shimmering blue. A faint pulse began beating, creating rippling disturbances like pebbles dropped in a still pond. A tiny round pale dot appeared in the center. With each successive heartbeat, the dot grew in size. Then Will realized that the pulse on-screen was keeping pace with the beating of his own heart.

He couldn't take his eyes off it; within minutes the spot grew to the size of a dime. Something about its rhythmic regularity relaxed his mind enough to finally let go. When his chin sagged onto his chest, he dragged himself to bed and instantly fell asleep.

A few hours later, he woke in sunlight. Will looked over and saw that the dot on-screen had continued growing while he was asleep. The pale shape that had formed overnight looked like the outline of a human body lying on its back, suspended in space. Vague, unfinished, but evolving.

That's me. It's growing my double.

After he'd showered and dressed, Will reached down to pick up the tablet and take it with him, but a harsh tone sounded and a warning appeared on-screen:

DO NOT ATTEMPT TO USE THIS DEVICE UNTIL ACTIVATION IS COMPLETE.

"The ancestor of every action . . . is a thought."

Will jolted awake, instantly guilty. Thirty minutes into his first class with Dan McBride, the one teacher whose opinion of him mattered more to Will than any other, and he was fighting to keep his eyes open. He glanced around at the twenty other students in the amphitheater. No one seemed to notice his struggles.

"This is Emerson's central idea," said McBride at his lectern. "That everything starts in the mind. Everything you perceive, everything you create, everything you experience or believe . . . begins here. Inside of you."

Will squirmed in his seat. A swampy mass swirled in his head. Sinister masked faces swam toward him as he struggled to stay awake.

A group that calls itself the Knights of Charlemagne. Named after the original Paladins from the Middle Ages. Members of a secret society within the school. Connected to the Black Caps and the Never-Was.

What's their purpose? *How long have they been here? It can't just be coincidence that the Center's mascot is a paladin, but how does this all fit together?*

"You have to trust yourself," said McBride. "Learn to trust your instincts when the world is telling you not to. 'Trust your *self* beyond the reach of reason, or the opinions of others.' That's how Emerson insisted we live. Because *your* lives must first and foremost make sense to *you*."

McBride's words sounded as if they were meant just for him. One of Dad's primary rules: #11: TRUST YOUR INSTINCTS.

That snapped Will back awake. He gazed over at Brooke, seated in the corner and watching McBride, listening intently. Looking so effortlessly beautiful it made Will's chest ache. Then he felt a pair of eyes drill into him from behind.

Stop gawking. Show some restraint, you nimrod.

He turned and saw Elise staring at him. Busted. *God, are my feelings so ridiculously transparent now?*

Elise used her fingers to prop her eyes open, mocking him in his efforts to stay awake. He also noticed something else in Elise's eyes—some unresolved pain *behind* the attitude—that made him feel like he was seeing her for the first time.

"Here's what I believe Emerson wants us to do," said McBride, moving away from the lectern, as sincere as if he were saying this for the first time. "He wants us to think for ourselves, without fear of ridicule or judgment. He wants us to make up our minds and ignore what the rest of the world is saying. Pay no attention to fads or fashions, and listen, always, to the voice of your innermost self. Learning who you are is your primary task. There are no mistakes in life, as far as Emerson's concerned, only lessons. Once you master one lesson, you move on to the next. And the only place you can learn is right now. In the everlasting present."

All we have is right now. McBride was really channeling Dad today. Will felt his spirits lift. When the class ended, McBride waved Will over to the lectern.

"Will, great to have you in class. Hope you didn't have too much trouble staying awake." McBride winked as he packed up his briefcase.

"Sorry, sir," said Will. "Still adjusting to the time zone. Couldn't sleep."

"No worries. That reminds me, Dr. Robbins asked if you've connected with your parents. About your medical records and those additional tests."

"Yes," said Will, scrambling internally. "We spoke last night. They'll mail them out right away. And they're fine with more tests."

"Splendid," said McBride.

As they walked out together, Will decided to trust McBride with this question: "Sir, do you know anything about the . . . possible existence of any secret clubs or societies here at the school?"

McBride stopped in the hall, curious. "What prompted your asking, Will?"

"I heard a rumor. About some group called the Knights of Charlemagne."

McBride nodded. "Well, I don't recall one by that name specifically, but you could try the Archer Library. They keep an extensive archive on school history."

"Thanks, that's a good idea," said Will.

"Check in over the weekend," said McBride, putting a hand on his shoulder. "And try to catch up on your sleep." McBride winked again. Will watched him hobble off, gamely battling his brittle knees.

Damn. Forgot all about the medical records. That was a problem. But there was one place he could look.

* * *

"Hey, Nando, Will. Is this a good time?"

"Hey, Wills, yeah, it's good."

Will was locked in his bathroom, whispering into his cell. "Got worried when I didn't hear back from you yesterday. The Black Caps were headed your way."

"I'm cool, my brotha. Me and Freddie gave 'em the slip. Made the run to Ojai last night. Back to the grind, doing my cab thang. Whassup?"

"They need some medical records for my dad and we think they're at our house. Any chance you could swing by and pick 'em up if the coast is clear?"

"Happy to."

"We've got a key stashed by the back door. Let's get on the phone when you go in and I'll tell you where to look."

Will pictured their house in Ojai. It had been only three days since he'd been there, but it seemed like months ago already. That version of him—Will West 1.0—felt shockingly out of date.

"If you can receive it, I'll figure a way to stream you some video," said Nando.

"Great idea," said Will. "I'll work on that from my end, too."

Will ended the call and went back to his bedroom to prepare for his last class of the day. The figure on his tablet had continued to grow, like a sculpture emerging from rock. Hair had appeared—the right color and length—and muscles gained definition with every passing second.

Another few hours and this little homunculus will be me.

Will moved the desk and opened the hiding place. As he set the phone inside, he noticed that the hole extended a few inches under the floor toward the wall. Will stuck his hand inside and probed around. He felt nothing until he turned his wrist to check under the floorboards and found an angular lump under a strip of duct tape. He eased the tape away and brought the object up into the light.

It was a small strip of silver metal, the length and about half the width of a domino. He replaced the floorboard and slid the desk into place. At that moment the black phone rang, startling him. He answered on the second ring.

"Will, it's Dr. Robbins," she said, crisp and efficient. "Mr. McBride tells me you got permission from your parents for the tests."

"Yes, I did."

"Excellent. Dr. Kujawa's scheduled you for tomorrow morning. It's Saturday, so you won't miss any classes. Meet us at the medical center at eight o'clock?"

"I guess so, sure."

"Good. We'll see you then," she said, and hung up.

Will didn't know how he felt about that. He'd learned a lot from their first tests, but what would they reveal this time?

Heading out for his next class, Will stopped to knock on Ajay's door. "Ajay, it's Will."

He heard locks thrown, the door opened a crack, and Ajay stuck his head out. "Yes, Will?"

Will held up the strip of metal. "Can you tell me what this is?"

Ajay eyed it suspiciously. "Where did it come from?"

"I'll tell you later. Just take a look and tell me what you find?"

"All right." Ajay took the metal object. "Anything else?"

"I need a live two-way video link with a buddy in So Cal later," said Will. "Can you handle that?"

"Does he have access to a phone with streaming video?"

"I'm sure he does," said Will.

"Consider it done," said Ajay, and started to close his door.

Will glanced over at Elise's door and decided to play another—slightly more obscure—hunch. "So when did Elise hook up with Ronnie Murso last year?"

Ajay turned back, his eyes wide. "How did you know?"

"I think that's why Elise is so sawed off at everybody all the time."

"Very perceptive, old man," said Ajay, impressed. "How'd you figure it out?"

"The way she reacted when we first talked about him," said Will. "See you later."

RULAN GEIST

For the second time since he'd arrived at the Center, Will had fallen into deep water in a classroom. Genetics—Tomorrow's Science Today. Eighteen students wearing lab coats and goggles worked in two-person teams at stations on long benches.

Their instructor, Professor Rulan Geist, wore a lab coat that hung down to his black ankle boots, like a cowboy's duster. He roamed the aisles as he talked them through the day's procedure: gene splicing and DNA extraction from some creature called a nematode, which wasn't a "toad" at all, Will learned, but a tiny primitive worm they were dissecting. Geist might as well have been speaking Iroquois.

Geist was tall and bulky, with long arms and big thick hands that he clutched behind his back or gestured with awkwardly. His deep, resonant voice had the hint of an accent. Maybe Scandinavian or Dutch. Geist was one ugly dude. He had dark circles under his eyes and rough bronzed skin, the lower half of which he tried to improve with a trim Van Dyke beard and mustache. The beard looked as if it would grow back, if he shaved, in less than an hour. Short, curly salt-and-pepper hair carved a sharp widow's peak into his receding hairline like a dorsal fin. Bristly hairs sprang from his ears and bushy eyebrows like a row of corkscrews. A pair of heavy, square black glasses perched on the end of a ski-slope nose and magnified his dark liquid eyes when he looked down at you.

He stopped a few times to do that at Will's station. Will gamely tried to pretend he was helping his partner, a serious redheaded girl named Allyson Rowe, who was polite enough not to rub Will's face in how hopeless he was. Geist smiled kindly at Will each time, unconvinced but appreciative of his effort. The last time, he patted Will's shoulder and leaned in to say, "Let's speak after class."

After the room emptied, Will and Geist sat down on tall stools. Smiling and friendly, Geist hooked his boots on the bottom rung and spread his hands on his knees. Patches of black coarse hair sprouted between the knuckles of his long thick fingers.

"Science is a foreign land for you, I think," said Geist.

"Where they speak a different language," said Will.

"Most assuredly. But it's more than language. A different culture altogether. One that seems very strange to anyone who first sets foot in it."

"That obvious, huh?"

"I don't mean to be critical, Mr. West. I've seen your transcript. You were taking geometry, and you've had only a year of biology. No chemistry or algebra. That puts you far off our pace. I also noticed your father works as a researcher."

"Yes, sir. Neurobiology."

"And none of his interest in science rubbed off on you?"

"I didn't even know what he did for a living until a few years ago."

"So he never brings his work home or discusses it with you."

"He never did," said Will, then remembering to keep everything in the present tense, added, "He never talks about his work."

"That's surprising. Neurobiology is an *adventurous* discipline," said Geist enthusiastically, "with high rates of discovery and thrilling themes. I'd have thought you might *inherit* some residual interest."

"Maybe I have and don't know it. Maybe it's just a recessive gene."

Geist laughed. "So you do know a little about our subject."

Will held his fingers a millimeter apart.

"Well, I'm a firm believer that before you visit a new country, it's very useful to have a look at a map. Let me draw one for you. Metaphorically speaking."

Geist led him to a large blank whiteboard on the wall. Will felt grateful for Geist's kindness in response to his cluelessness. As opposed to, say, Professor Sangren melting his face off in front of the whole class.

Geist picked up a stylus and flipped a switch on it. The brightness of the board intensified; light beamed out of the stylus.

"Genetics," said Geist. "From the same root word as *genesis*, meaning 'origin.' The beginning of all things. The branch of science in which we study the role played in the development of living organisms by two factors: heredity and variation. Traits either inherited from biological predecessors—our parents and ancestors—or influenced by a multitude of factors in nature."

"Nature versus nurture," said Will.

"Exactly! The philosophical polarities that define our field." Operating the stylus, Geist somehow made the words *fate* and *nature* appear on one side of the board and drew a circle around them.

"Over here," he said, tapping the circle, "think of heredity as a form of destiny. What the Greeks liked to call fate. Everything that happens to us in life is predetermined, because the *definitions* of our character are set in advance by the limits of what's in our individual genetic code. While over here is the other extreme . . ."

On the opposite side of the board, Geist stamped the word *nurture,* then added the words *free will* and circled them.

". . . which argues that people have *complete autonomy* in how they develop. Embracing the idea that as unique creatures, each of us evolves into what we become in life because we *choose* to do so through the unfolding expression of our character, regardless, or in *spite* of, what's written in our code. These two positions and everything in between, in the simplest terms, constitute our map."

"I'm with you," said Will.

"Good. Where do you suppose we'll find objective, scientific *truth*?"

"Somewhere in the middle."

"A fine answer."

Geist used the stylus again and the center of the board opened like a window looking into a three-dimensional aquarium. A graphic of twin multicolored spirals of DNA strands twisting around each other spanned the length of the window. Around it appeared clusters of animated boxes, filled with letters and symbols pointing to different sections of the strands.

"The human genetic code," said Geist. "The blueprint of life. It contains over twenty-four thousand individual genes and three *billion* chemical base pairs, each one capable of thirty thousand variations. All of which contribute to the existence and persistence of human life. Over seven billion humans alive today carry their version of what you see here, inside trillions of cells in their body. And all these blueprints are as unique as the stars in the sky. Now turn your mind to the difference between a *map* . . ."

The screen zoomed in and hovered over magnified sections of the double helix, as large, detailed, and dimensional as the surface of an alien planet.

". . . and the *territory* it describes. And *this* territory, Will, is as dark and unknown to us as the Great Plains were to Lewis and Clark when they set off to find the Northwest Passage. As mysterious as space exploration was to my generation.

"Every generation finds its own frontier, and this one is yours, Will," said Geist with an evangelist's zeal. "It may well be the *last* frontier. Someone from your cohort, maybe even a person you know, will become the Magellan, Cortés, or Columbus of this world. They won't be in search of a new trade route or commodities like spice or sugarcane. The possibilities of discovery here are infinitely more profound, because we can now say with certainty that somewhere on this map all the answers to the mystery of human existence—of creation *itself*—are waiting to be found."

Images of plant and animal life, boundless varieties of both, flashed across the screen, around the twisting strands of DNA and four letters: A, T, C, and G. Will was mesmerized by the elegant spectacle.

"All life on earth owes its existence to the secrets of these simple, elegant forms, but for most of nature, their fates are written in their code—as limitations—with the finality of stone. This flower blossoms in purple; that small mammal mates exclusively during two weeks each spring; this bird's life is ruled by rigid migrations.

"Less than seven percent of the building blocks of life are unique to human beings. Seven percent that allows our species to 'transcend' in a single generation what, to every other form of life, are unbreakable boundaries. Seven percent that, in ways we don't yet understand, is responsible for the phenomenon of 'human consciousness.' The phenomenon that in only a few thousand years has given us . . ."

A cascade of images flowed on-screen, familiar faces, mathematical formulas, engineering blueprints, musical notes.

". . . Shakespeare, Newton, Mozart, Leonardo da Vinci, Jesus, Beethoven, Dickens, Michelangelo, Edison, Einstein, Gandhi, Galileo, the Buddha, the Beatles . . . With this map in hand, we will one day, soon, crack the secrets of that seven percent. You and your contemporaries may awaken as an evolutionary generation that leads humankind to a brighter future."

Geist tapped the stylus and a sea of young faces appeared, students at the Center gazing up at something dazzling and unseen. "And here lie wonders to behold."

Will walked away from class lost in thought. If Geist's intention had been to make him think, he'd succeeded: His primer on genetics focused Will's mind in a new way on these mysterious abilities he'd been discovering almost every day. They had to have a genetic basis, but as far as he knew, Jordan and Belinda West had never demonstrated anything like these talents he now possessed.

If he didn't inherit them from his parents, where the hell had they come from?

THE WEIGHT ROOM

Will rang the bell on the counter by the cage in the locker room. He'd picked up his laundry bag from his locker, leaving time to change before practice.

"Hey, Jolly, you there?"

"You again," said Nepsted.

Will heard his wheelchair before the dwarf rolled out of a small room on the side of the cage that Will hadn't noticed before.

"I forgot to ask," said Will, holding up the mesh bag. "What do we do with our laundry?"

"Drop it in a shower room hamper," said Nepsted. "It'll be delivered to your locker in two days. Except Fridays. Drop it Friday, you get it back Monday."

Nepsted rolled up to his side of the cage and held Will with his strange round, unblinking eyes.

He said come back when I'm ready. Am I? Only one way to find out.

"We were talking about the mascot the other day," said Will carefully. "I learned something I want to ask you about."

341

"Oh?"

"Did you know the original Paladins were the Knights of Charlemagne?" asked Will.

"Do I look stupid?" asked Nepsted, neutral. "If you know so much, tell me how many there were."

"Twelve," said Will. "They called themselves the Peers."

"Twelve is a sacred number," said Nepsted, his voice a mesmerizing drone. "Wholeness. Unity. Twelve signs of the zodiac. Twelve tones in the musical scale. Twelve face cards in a deck. Twelve on a jury. Twelve nights of Christmas. Twelve labors of Hercules. Twelve men on the moon. Twelve petals of the unfolding eternal lotus. Twelve hours of darkness, twelve of light. Twelve tribes of Israel—"

Will instantly regretted asking him anything. The guy sounded as nuts as a conspiracy freak broadcasting from a mobile home in the desert.

"Months, inches, eggs," said Will. "I get it—"

"Twelve *Paladins*," said Nepsted emphatically, then paused before adding, "Twelve *disciples*."

"Disciples . . . ," said Will. "You're saying . . . the Paladins are disciples? Of who? The Old Gentleman?"

Nepsted's head wobbled as he grinned crookedly. "The Knights *follow* the Old Gentleman, but they're *disciples* . . . of something *else*."

"Something? Not someone? You mean like the Never-Was?"

Nepsted's eyes lit up, but he just shrugged. *He* likes *toying with me,* Will thought. *Time to stop talking in circles.*

"Does the school know about the Knights?" asked Will.

Nepsted grinned at him. "Would they pick a paladin for our mascot if they didn't?"

"But do they know about what's down in that auxiliary locker room?" asked Will. "Do they know about the tunnels?"

"What makes you think *I'd* know that?"

"You told me you're the one with all the keys."

"All but one," said Nepsted cryptically.

"You know what's really going on down there, don't you?" Will insisted.

Nepsted suddenly looked frightened. "If you've got business there, you know what goes on. If you don't know what goes on, you've got no business there."

Knowing he'd touched a nerve, Will moved closer to the cage and pointed a finger at Nepsted. "*You* know what's down there, and you know what it's for. The hats and the masks and the tunnels that run under the lake and come out at the Crag. I think you even know about the Never-Was. You told me you're the one who knows everything that goes on around here. Or were you just lying?"

Nepsted's face contorted, turning an alarming beet red. "How many locks do you see around here, kid?"

"What's that supposed to mean?"

"Bring me *that* answer," said Nepsted, hissing with venom. "Or don't come *back*."

Nepsted pushed a button on his side of the counter. A screen of articulated metal siding began to slide down from the ceiling on Nepsted's side of the cage. He turned around to ride away.

Will called after him, "What do the Knights want? What are they doing here? Why are you afraid of them?"

This time Nepsted whipped his chair around and zoomed to the counter with startling speed. He pointed a long bony finger at Will as the metal lowered past his face. "You've got a right to put your own life in danger, but don't you *dare* mess with mine, boy. Do you hear me? It'll go far worse for you than you can imagine."

The screen crashed onto the counter with a resounding clang. Will heard the squeak of Nepsted's chair retreating into the cage.

"Great," muttered Will. "I pissed off the sociopathic dwarf."

"How many locks do you see around here, kid?" What the hell did that mean? It was like trying to talk to a fortune cookie. Rumpelstiltskin clearly held the key to more than just doors, but the *first* challenge was unlocking *him*.

Maybe next time I should use my "enhanced" powers of suggestion, thought Will.

He dropped his laundry into a hamper and glanced at his watch. Eight minutes to get to Jericho's cross-country practice. He hurried to his locker and changed into his sweats. The spike wounds from Suicide Hill had nearly disappeared already. Only faint red lines remained from yesterday's long nasty scrapes.

Will glanced in the mirror at the end of the next row. Staring back at him, behind his own reflection, was *Dave*. Will whirled around, but Dave wasn't there. He turned back and stepped closer to the mirror. Dave smiled, looking substantial and real, standing beside him in the aisle. Will turned again: empty space.

Dave was *inside* the mirror.

"How am I seeing you right now?" asked Will.

"If you want to get technical, 'astral projection.' I'm back at headquarters. Good news: You've been cleared for the next level of classified info."

"Whatever you say, Dave," said Will, sitting to tie his shoes. "I don't want to get you mad again."

"I work for the Hierarchy," said Dave. "Have a gander."

Will looked up from his shoes and his jaw dropped.

An image had appeared beside Dave in the mirror: a vast cityscape of gleaming towers, spires, and pavilions floating in midair above an endless snowcapped mountain range. As Dave spoke, the image rotated slowly.

"Imagine seven interlocking divisions of a global corporation whose only purpose is to do good. I know: not humanly possible. That's why the Hierarchy exists on the etheric level. It's that big, Will: *Epic* can't convey its real scope." Dave pointed to some of the gigantic buildings. "The Personnel Department alone could cover Kansas—caseworkers, managers, counselors. Architects and builders. The Legion of Thoughtforms. The Hall of Akashic Records. Our offices are up here, near the Council of Mahatmas."

Dave pointed to a high ivory tower rising above the center of the complex. Will saw thousands of people at work in gargantuan halls.

"Are all those people alive?" he asked.

"Alive, absolutely. Not in the earthbound sense of the word—that is, like me, not strictly physical, but they can be, depending on the need."

"What's it all for?" asked Will, his voice barely a whisper.

The image faded. Dave looked kinder than Will had ever seen him, as if he knew how impossible this was to absorb. "We look after the whole planet, mate. Caretakers for all the forms of life, according to department. I'm with Security. We keep eyes peeled for funny business from the Other Team, provide special services for the chief of operations, upon whose desk the buck comes to a complete stop."

"He wouldn't be 'the Old Gentleman,' by any chance?"

Dave cocked his head. "No, that bloke's *captain* of the Other Team. Wrong side entirely. Our CO is nothing of the sort. He doesn't have a name, really, although folks on the job sometimes use the term *Planetary Logos*."

Will felt his whole body tingling. "You mean . . . God?"

"God?" Dave almost laughed. "Not hardly, mate. *That* one's a thousand orders of magnitude removed from us. The Hierarchy's a strictly local outfit with local responsibilities. No need to overreach. Trust me, the Other Team's enough to keep us locked and loaded, with every man and his dog tending to their station."

Will gulped in air, his head swimming. "So all these monsters, bugs, and 'Fuzzy-Wuzzies' from the Never-Was are part of the Other Team?"

"Absolutely. Minions of our deadliest enemy."

"And they're not human," said Will.

"Nowhere near. But they've got plenty of human collaborators."

"Like the Black Caps and the Knights of Charlemagne?"

"That's right, mate," said Dave admiringly. "You seem to be taking all this rather in stride."

"Well, you know, after you hit me with 'guardian angel,' the rest just seems like 'sure, whatever.' How'd you get into all this?"

"The usual way," said Dave. "I was recruited."

Dave disappeared. Will saw only his own reflection in the

mirror. A couple of younger students, who'd just wandered in behind him, stared at him warily.

"That's right," said Will. "I'm the new kid who talks to himself in the mirror."

Shocked at how calm he felt, Will hurried out and went looking for the weight room. He found it near the far end of the Barn's central corridor. It was a long, high-ceilinged space filled with gymnastic stations at one end—rings, bars, horses—and training machines and free weights at the other.

There were about a dozen athletes—about half from the cross-country team—stretching on rubber mats in the middle. As Will entered, the few who noticed—Durgnatt, Steifel, and the African American kid Wendell Duckworth—gave him the cold shoulder. Todd Hodak trotted on a treadmill nearby. No sign of Coach Jericho.

Will assessed his options. He could lower his eyes, go submissive, and try not to provoke them. Hope that Todd and his pack ignored him. But if some of these kids—maybe all of them—were the Knights . . . ?

Maybe now was a good time to find out.

Will grabbed a towel and jumped on the treadmill next to Hodak. He nudged up the speed until he was running at Todd's pace, then looked over at him and grinned.

#31: IT'S NOT A BAD THING, SOMETIMES, IF THEY THINK YOU'RE CRAZY.

"We should just drop the *masks*," said Will.

Hodak shot a wary look at him. "What did you say?"

"Let's stop pretending," said Will casually. "You can bully

me every single day I'm here, and even if you succeed? I will still take you down on the course. I own you there, and you know it. I am the CEO of Beat Todd Hodak, Incorporated Dot Com."

Todd turned off his treadmill and stepped away. Breathing deeply, his upper body rippling with stress.

"You seem tense, Todd," said Will, stepping off the treadmill and following him. "Did you have a rough . . . *knight*?"

Todd's face flushed bright red when he heard the word. He balled his fists. Will moved right next to him.

"I don't care who you are," said Will quietly. "If you ever take another shot at me, or if you or your stooges hurt any of my roommates, including Brooke—*especially* Brooke—I'm painting a bull's-eye on you. And I will tear you up."

That ought to do it.

Will turned his back on him. From the corner of his eye, he saw Todd give the nod to Durgnatt and Steifel. Both stood up and jammed straight at him.

Here comes the pain.

Durgnatt, the dark-haired one, lunged at Will, grabbed him by the elbows, and pinned his arms behind his body. Steifel went for Will's legs. Together, they lifted him off the ground. Will didn't resist. The rest of the team reacted as if they'd rehearsed. Two went to the doors as lookouts. The others gathered around the mat in the middle, where Durgnatt and Steifel forced Will to his knees.

Todd grabbed Will by the sweatshirt and cocked back his fist. Will focused his eyes between Todd's eyebrows. With a lot more confidence than he'd felt the last time, Will pushed a picture at him:

Hit Durgnatt.

Todd's right hand flew right past Will's chin and slammed Durgnatt in the nose. The big kid let go of Will and cradled his face, blood leaking between his fingers as he crumpled to his knees. Todd stared at his fist as if he couldn't believe what it had just done. He cocked another punch.

Hit Steifel.

Todd's left hook nailed Steifel flush on the side of the head. Dazed, Steifel staggered away. Will hopped to his feet, danced around shaking his hands, then added a Bruce Lee shuffle for fun.

"What the hell, Todd?" said Durgnatt, looking at the blood.

"Hold him still next time, idiots," said Todd. "Get him!"

Every guy in the room rushed at Will. They collided from all directions with Will smack in the middle. Their momentum carried the entire scrum to the floor. Will tucked and landed under them. Lowering his head, he tunneled toward daylight, struggling to breathe with their weight squirming on top of him. He summoned his energy into focus again and pushed a picture at the whole group:

Hit him in the package.

A short rabbit punch got thrown by every man in the pile at the crotch of the man closest to him, in perfect unison. Will heard a chorus of yelps as the shots connected. Everyone fell sideways, moaning and writhing in pain.

Will snaked out from under the pile, shoving a few groaners aside, and scrambled to his feet. Halfway up, something slammed hard into his back and knocked the wind out of him. He fell forward, turned, and saw Todd staring at him savagely, holding a weighted hardwood club. Will gasped for air like a fish flopping on a dock. His thoughts scattered, veering toward panic.

Todd threw his legs out, dropped his rear end on the mat, and hammered his elbow into Will's ribs, driving what little breath he had left from his body.

Oof. That really hurt.

Still bent over and moaning, the others gathered in a circle around them. Todd straddled Will's chest, then knocked his arms away to take a free shot at him. Others grabbed Will's arms and pinned them to the mat. Will gasped for air. Short of oxygen, he couldn't summon the energy to defend himself.

This was about to get completely out of hand. *What the hell, Dave? Good time for the guardian angel to put in an appearance, don't you think?*

Through the crowd, Will caught a flash of movement as the nearest door flew open. A shape soared up onto the hanging gymnastic rings nearby, whipped around in tight circles, and then streaked toward them.

As Todd prepared to rearrange Will's face, a pair of feet slammed into Todd's shoulder and sent him tumbling into his teammates. About four other kids went flying. A familiar face popped into view in front of Will.

"Whose happy fun-time idea was *this*?" said Nick, grinning.

Nick launched a series of backflips across the mat as the team gave chase. Nick hopped up out of the last flip, landed on top of a pommel horse, then *reverse* somersaulted back toward Will. He landed on three of the kids. They crashed into each other, and the ones behind them scattered like bowling pins.

When Durgnatt and Steifel ran at him, Nick sprinted to the uneven bars. He caught the low bar, spun all the way around, let go, flew up, and grabbed hold of the high bar. He circled twice, doubling his speed, then let go, extending his legs and power-kicking both kids into a padded wall, where they crumpled and lay still.

"Next, please," said Nick.

With most of them disabled—including Todd, on his hands and knees, dazed and wobbling—the few who could still walk slunk away. Nick yanked Todd to his feet.

"Run *that* down, Ho-Dick."

Nick pushed him with one finger and Todd keeled over. Nick flipped backward onto a springboard, arced into the air, dove to the ground, tumbled across the mat, and landed next to Will. He knelt down and helped Will to his knees.

"You all right, bud?" asked Nick.

Will nodded, still trying to catch his breath.

"Twelve against one. Slick move, ace. Lucky I came in when I did."

"Hey," said Will, finally able to speak. "*Forget* geography, man. Stick with gymnastics."

Coach Jericho came through the door, clipboard and whistle in hand. He stopped cold when he saw his squad lying on the ground, moaning, bleeding, or cowering in fear. Todd saw Jericho and staggered to his feet.

"Hey, Coach," said Todd.

Todd stumbled a few steps toward him and collapsed face-first. Jericho's gaze settled on Nick and Will, the only uninjured bodies in the room. His eyes flashed with anger.

"McLeish, you chuckwagon, what the hell are you doing here?"

Nick and Will grabbed hands and pretended they were stretching.

"Just stretching out my roomie, Coach," said Nick.

"What happened?" asked Jericho.

"Not real sure, Coach, we just came in," said Will. "But if I had to guess . . . it looks like they overtrained."

COACH JERICHO

Coach Jericho took them into the hall and chewed them out for two minutes. The man could cuss like a drill sergeant, but they both stuck to their story. When the coach realized this was going nowhere, he dismissed Nick and walked Will to a room down the hall. It was carpeted, hushed, and three of its walls held massive trophy cases. Jericho didn't speak as Will looked around. Every competitive sport imaginable was represented. There were cups and medals, ribbons, and trophies going back nearly a hundred years.

"These all your teams, Coach?" asked Will.

"Wiseass," said Jericho. "What does it tell you?"

"That they've always been competitive. For a bunch of over-privileged jerks."

"Tradition. Tradition and history," said Jericho. "Dishonor the past, and you disgrace the present and destroy the future. Where'd you come from?"

"California."

"I know that. Where you'd *come from*?"

"I don't know," said Will honestly.

"Kids show up here full of ego, self-importance, and the foolishness of the culture that raised them. It's not their fault. If they leave here that way, that's *our* fault."

Will realized, with surprise, that he felt comfortable speaking openly to Jericho. Beneath his fierce appearance and temperament, the man seemed to be a straight shooter.

"I'm on board with that," said Will.

Jericho moved closer, his eyes focused on Will's. "All that matters once you're here is what you have inside and how well you listen to what it wants to teach you. Learn that and you harmonize with *Wak'an*. The Great Mystery. Then you'll know where you come from."

Jericho's dark eyes stared into him like an X-ray. The hairs on Will's arms stood on end.

"Mysteries reveal purpose," said Jericho, calm and conversational. "Life without purpose is its own punishment. You ever think about your purpose?"

"I have lately."

Jericho walked over to a large globe on a stand, turning it as he spoke. "One of our purposes, collectively, is to serve as the guardians of our world."

Now he's starting to sound like Dave, thought Will as he followed him.

"Do you know how terrible it is to watch your civilization lose its way?" asked Jericho.

"I'm sorry, you're talking about . . . ?"

"*My* people. Our beliefs, gods, culture. All that's gone now," said Jericho. "We know every civilization gives way to another.

354

Every animal, every species, yields to one that takes its place. Impermanence. That's reality."

"So I've been told," said Will, thinking of Sangren's lecture.

"But that doesn't mean you just surrender to evil. We can't afford 'you' and 'I' anymore. Red, white, black, yellow—those distinctions no longer matter." Jericho gave the globe a spin; all the colors blended into one. "We're all one people or we're not going to make it. You think there weren't others before us? You bet there were. Before even my people walked this ground. Long before. Right here."

Will felt the room go alarmingly still. "You mean . . . in Wisconsin?"

"They weren't *like* us," said Jericho as he stopped the globe. "But the same dangers destroyed them: Madness. Distraction. Disharmony. Societies catch diseases, too. Why do you think that is?"

"I have no idea," said Will.

Jericho opened a carved wooden box on a shelf beside one of the trophy cases. He took out a bundle of four round sticks, with groups of feathers attached to the ends. He made some small circular gestures with them as he looked at Will.

"Because no one's immune; imperfection's part of being alive," said Jericho. "What this world needs isn't new ideas. What it needs is old wisdom. If you develop your *vision*, you'll see a way forward. Become a warrior in the fight between dark and light. Do you have a favorite animal?"

"I've never really thought about it," said Will, mystified.

"Think about it. Look for an animal in your dreams," he said, lightly touching the feathers to Will's forehead. "Then tell me if you dream of bears . . . or weasels."

"Bears or weasels?" asked Nick. "Give me a freakin' break."

"That's what he said," said Will.

They were trudging back to campus after finishing their workout, afternoon light fading fast. The wind had picked up, smacking them in the face, a different kind of cold. Dark clouds bunched on the western horizon and a deep barometric disturbance was massing in the air. The pressure was falling fast; heavy weather was headed their way, maybe the first winter storm of Will's life.

"Weasel Holes, now weasels?" said Nick. "That's so random. I mean, why not monkeys or chickens?"

"He said weasels are the only animals that kill more than they need to survive," said Will. "They kill because they *like* it."

"Okay, that sucks," said Nick. "Speaking of weasels, you think Todd ratted us out? Does Jericho know we're the ones who kicked his team's butt?"

"I don't think Todd would want to admit it, do you?"

"Don't know," said Nick. "Never been in that situation."

"Seriously? How many fights have you had?" asked Will.

"Including today? Thirty-one."

Will stopped in his tracks. "You've had thirty-one fights?! And you're undefeated? Thirty-one to zero."

Nick shrugged, a little embarrassed, as they walked on. "Dude, there's no point *being* in a fight if you're gonna lose. You didn't grow up in my neighborhood. Townies learn to throw down before they can walk. My dad says I clocked a four-year-old from my crib when he tried to steal my blankie. How many you had?"

Will stuttered, "Uh, fights? Besides that one? None."

"You never had to fight, moving around as much as you did?"

"I've had to *outrun* a few guys," said Will.

Nick gave him a fist bump. "That works, brother."

"I just had no idea you were such a hard-core badass," said Will.

"Let's keep it that way," said Nick, lowering his voice. "That's the first scrap I've been in since I got here. I promised Pop I'd change my ways. He hears about this he'll freakin' *kill* me."

"I'm sorry you got mixed up in it, then."

"Naw, don't be. Truth is, I miss letting the beast loose," said Nick, shadow boxing. "Not that I went *looking* for trouble, but in my world when guys hear you're a gymnast? You might as well be a *florist* who's into ballroom dancing."

"How'd you learn to . . . bounce around like that?"

"Started gymnastics when I was five," said Nick. "The same year Pop got me into boxing. Then wrestling. Then tae kwon do and karate . . . later on aikido and kung fu . . . wing chun for defense . . . and recently this Brazilian jujitsu style, capoeira, that's the total bomb."

"Damn. No wonder you never learned how to run," said Will. "How'd your mom feel about it?"

Nick looked away. "My mom died when I was five."

Will stopped. "I'm really sorry, Nick."

Nick nodded. "Thanks. I'm still pretty bummed out about it myself."

"Any brothers or sisters?"

"Just me and Pop."

A security guard drove by and waved as they reached the quad.

"So how'd you end up at the Center?" asked Will.

"Got the invite after I won gold at the New England high school gymnastics finals," said Nick. "Which was kinda unusual, seeing how I was in eighth grade."

"I'd say so," said Will. "Which event?"

Nick shrugged again modestly. "All of 'em."

Will's eyes bugged out. "*All* of them? So you really *are* on athletic scholarship."

"Dude, look around," said Nick. "We couldn't afford this joint without it. My dad's a motorman for the MTA. He takes a *train* to work so he can drive a frickin' train. Kind of guy who never gets the dirt out from under his fingernails, you know? So who says the only kind of luck you have is bad?"

"I hear that."

"Dude, case you ain't noticed, I'm not exactly the sharpest Crayola in the box. I can't even *spell* dyslexia. I thought ADHD was some kind of plasma screen."

Will laughed so hard he doubled over.

"But the day I get a *college* scholarship, nobody's laughing," said Nick, looking around at the ivy-covered halls. "A *real* college, not some juco vocational joint. Big Ten, Ivy League, ACC. That's our plan, Pops and me, and we're stickin' to it."

Will found Nick's story hard to square with what he'd heard about the Center's imposing academic standards. Could athletic ability mean that much in their selection process? And if so, why?

"I should talk," said Nick. "You run like a freakin' antelope. That how you got here?"

"No. Something to do with a test I took," said Will vaguely.

Will stopped under a streetlamp a block from Greenwood

Hall. He wanted to tell Nick everything, all the rest of what he'd been through, what had happened to his parents, the things Jericho had just told him, Dave's tour of the Hierarchy and the Never-Was. Keeping all these secrets straight made his head feel like it might split in half. And Nick was the right guy to trust, an honest, good-hearted scrapper from the wrong side of the tracks. Will wanted him as a friend more than ever.

Do I really need any more convincing? The guy just launched himself into a one-sided stomping and saved my rear end. And, by the way, he hits like a dump truck.

But Rule #5 floated into his head like a tile in the eight ball: TRUST NO ONE. And this time it pissed Will off.

Why did my parents discourage me from making friends? Why tell me I could never trust anyone outside our family? Why work so hard to isolate me from people?

"You're the real deal, Nick," said Will. "I don't know how to thank you for helping me. I mean that. I don't know how."

Nick seemed almost bashful. "No big thing, Chilly Will. I'm sure you'd'a done the same for me."

"I'd want to, but I'm not sure I could pull it off," said Will.

"You could always run for help," said Nick with a crooked grin.

"I think I've got all the help I need right here," said Will. "Nick, I'm pretty sure Todd and most of those guys are part of the Knights. I dropped *mask* and *knights* on Todd while we were talking, and he flinched like I hit him with a rock."

"Awesome work," said Nick, and gave Will a high five. "What's our next move? Do we blow the whistle on these bad boys?"

"Not without proof, something that totally nails them to the

Black Caps," said Will, looking over at the lights burning in Greenwood Hall. "So we need to do something totally illegal."

Nick got a very serious look. "I'm all over that."

"We're going to search Lyle's quarters," said Will.

They tried calling him from the house phone in the lobby. No answer. Then they knocked on Lyle's door.

"Think he's in there?" asked Will.

"You know the old saying," said Nick. "Keep your friends close and your enemies dead and buried in the basement."

Nick turned the knob; they looked at each other in surprise when it opened.

"Lyle?" said Nick, calling inside. "You in the house, buddy?"

They moved into the wood-paneled inspection room. Empty. Nick knocked on the inner door. "Yoo-hoo, Marshal Lyle!"

No response. Nick tried the door. Locked. He took a device from his pocket and picked the lock in less than five seconds, then smiled sheepishly at Will.

"Kind of a neighborhood skill," he said.

They entered Lyle's suite. The front room centered on an L-shaped desk lined with six monitors showing views from security cameras around Greenwood Hall. A bookshelf filled with rows of twelve-inch spiral notebooks stood against one wall. Above that, a metal rack screwed into the wall held sealed plastic containers. Will found one with his name labeled on it and saw his iPhone and laptop inside.

Nick opened the door to Lyle's bedroom and switched on the light. He recoiled from something inside. Will joined him and caught a whiff of foul air.

"You ever smell anything that disgusting before?" asked Nick.

"Three times now," said Will, stepping inside. *When the monsters show up.*

"Either he stuffed a dead fish with rotten eggs marinated in raw sewage," said Nick, "or this dipstick needs a shower worse than anyone on the planet."

Will tracked the smell to the bedroom closet. He opened the door. Behind a rack of clothes, Nick uncovered a poster-sized sheet of superthin metal attached to the wall, embossed with rows of small, indecipherable glyphs. When Nick waved a hand near it, the closest glyphs lit up, illuminated from within.

"What the hell is this thing?" asked Nick.

"No idea," said Will. He snapped a picture of it with his phone camera.

Sticking out from under a pile of Lyle's stuff deeper in the closet was the corner of a trunk made of high-tech black carbon fiber. "Check this out," Nick said.

He pulled the trunk into the open. It was rectangular, fairly shallow, with a handle on top. Will leaned over to look at it and his eyes started burning.

"That smell's coming from here," said Will.

"Let's leave him a note: 'Dude, bad news: Your ferrets died. Buy some Lysol.'"

They had to cover their noses and mouths against the stink. Will undid the catch and opened the lid. Inside were neat rows of black mesh containers in three sizes: some the size of matchboxes, others shaped like thermoses, others long and skinny like spaghetti boxes. All had more of the strange glyphs on them.

Nick reached for one of the thermoses and something jumped at him inside it with enough force to dent the mesh. "What the hell," he said, yanking his hand away.

Will slammed the trunk shut and kicked it into place. "We're out of here."

Nick followed him back into the office. "What's in those canisters?"

"I'm not sure, but I saw a Black Cap carrying one outside my house in Ojai."

"Maybe we should ask *him*." Nick pointed at one of the monitors on Lyle's desk.

Lyle Ogilvy had just stepped inside the building.

They dashed outside and made it into the hallway as Lyle came around the corner. He looked deathly pale, his eyes red and strained. His winter coat increased his bulk, and he had a thick wool scarf wrapped around his neck. He carried a paper bag that was soaked at the bottom, greasy liquid oozing through the seams. Strangest of all, instead of shooting them the evil eye, Lyle didn't even look at them.

"Hey, Lyle, how's it going?" asked Nick.

Lyle stopped and turned. He barely seemed to register they were there. He walked into his office, quietly closed the door, and locked it from inside.

"What is up with Uncle Fester?" said Nick softly, spooked.

"Beats me," said Will. "Looks like he's got the flu. Let's go talk to Ajay. We've got a long night ahead of us."

"I'll make a food run," said Nick, heading for the door. "Chinese takeout?"

"Yes," said Will.

FLASH

It was five-thirty when Will entered their pod. Ajay sat at the table scarfing a bowl of cereal. Will filled him in about Todd and the other seniors on the cross-country team and the likelihood that they might be the Knights. He also told him about what he and Nick had just found in Lyle's closet.

"What's in those containers?" asked Ajay.

"I think it's more of the . . . you know," said Will, suddenly self-conscious.

"Monsters?" said Ajay, his eyes widening. "You know, Will, I *want* to believe everything you've told us, but you're the only one who's seen any of them so far."

"If you're lucky, that won't change," said Will.

"Well, I have a lot to show you, too," said Ajay, taking his dish to the kitchen. "Meet me in my room. Bring your tablet."

Will hurried to his room. His tablet sat up on his desk, a screen saver of the crest floating in a liquid blue field. He stopped when it dissolved to black, then faded up on a replica of his room. A young man sat at the desk with his back to Will, working at his tablet.

The figure turned. It was Will's syn-app, fully fleshed. He had the same face, hair, and clothes as Will, except for a different-color shirt, light gray to Will's blue. Then—after the syn-app *saw* Will—his shirt changed color to match his exactly.

It was like looking in a mirror, but not quite. The figure appeared smooth around the edges, slightly vague, like a nearly finished sketch. Computer Will met Will's eye and smiled, as if he had been waiting for him.

The syn-app waved. Will hesitated, then waved back. He thought about asking the figure to stand, so thrown by this eerie thing that he felt the syn-app needed to move so he could reach his *real* tablet. "Will" stood and stepped away from the desk, smiling agreeably and awaiting Will's next instruction.

Did he just hear me think *that?*

"Okay, that's a little creepy," said Will. "Shut down."

"Would you like me to run a system security check, Will?" asked Will in a spooky simulation of his own voice.

"Not right now—"

"I highly recommend you let me perform a—"

"I said not *now*. Shut down."

"Will" snapped his fingers and the screen went black. The legs folded into the frame and the tablet settled down flat on the desk. Will warily picked it up. Holding it like a ticking bomb, he hurried to Ajay's room, knocked, announced himself, and heard Ajay open the locks before the door opened.

"Come in quickly," said Ajay.

Ajay closed and locked the door behind them, noting the cautious way Will carried in his tablet.

"I take it your doppelgänger has finally arrived," said Ajay.

"This thing's freaking me out."

"Perfectly natural reaction. I couldn't even stay in the same room with mine at first. Set it on the desk next to mine. We'll need it."

Gauzy sheer panels of material hung down from the ceiling of Ajay's room. Big soft throw pillows covered the floor. An animated wall poster of the periodic table adorned one wall, molecules lazily circling around each other. Ajay's desk stood under a suspended muslin pyramid covered with bright red satin. A printed banner spanned the bookshelf above the desk:

GOD DOES NOT PLAY DICE WITH THE UNIVERSE.
—EINSTEIN

Will set his tablet next to Ajay's. Ajay's double sat on-screen in a precise reproduction of Ajay's room, working at his desk.

"Power on," said Will to his tablet.

His screen lit up. Will's double reappeared, now in the same virtual version of Ajay's room. "Ajay" greeted him with pleased surprise, hurried toward him—moving from his screen to Will's!—and shook "Will's" hand.

"Weird," said Will. "They just met each other."

"Yes. They'll be friends, just as we are." Ajay spoke to the screens. "Go big screen." The image on their small screens now also appeared on the large screen on Ajay's wall, replacing the animated periodic table.

"This thing you gave me is a flash drive," said Ajay, holding up the mysterious metal strip Will had given him earlier. He held it to the side of his tablet; a port opened and he plugged it in.

A large square steel box materialized on Ajay's big screen, resting on the floor of his virtual room. DO NOT OPEN was printed on its top and sides. "Ajay" and "Will" walked over to take a look.

"Open it," said Ajay.

Ajay and Will opened the top; it hinged back like a real box. Ajay reached inside and lifted out a smaller box—another solid graphic object, with FILE stamped on the side—and placed it on the desk.

"Open file," said Ajay to his double.

Ajay's syn-app opened the smaller box, revealing a small photograph. "It's a JPEG," said Ajay. "Expand to full screen, please."

The photo grew until it filled the big screen with a landscape unlike any Will had ever seen. Craggy snowcapped mountains were threaded with waterfalls that dropped hundreds of feet into a network of geothermal pools in a lush green valley. Weird rock formations rose abruptly, angular pinnacles shrouded in mists that drifted up from the pools. It was as majestic and ghostly as an alien world.

"Ajay" and "Will" looked up at it from the small screens on the desk, which still showed the simulation of Ajay's room. Will heard them make faint "oohs" and "aahs," equally captivated.

"Where is this?" asked Will.

"I have no idea," said Ajay. "It's the only item on the drive."

"No captions or information, no other clues?"

"Correct, but I found something strange. A digital image like this shouldn't occupy more than thirty megs. This file is over nine gigabytes."

"How is that possible?" asked Will, looking closer.

"Additional layers of data embedded in the image would be

the only way to account for it. I started to poke around and was able to extract a bit more." Ajay said to his double on his tablet, "Show MPEG."

The image on the big screen sprang to life. The water ran in the streams and rippled in the pools. The ghostly fog swirled around the rocks, and clouds drifted overhead. They could hear birds, the crash of the waterfalls, and wind rustling tall stands of bamboo.

"So it's a video file, not a photo?" asked Will.

"It's both," said Ajay. "Which still doesn't come close to accounting for its size. Now that it's in motion, does it look any more familiar to you?"

"No," said Will. "I've never seen this place before. I'm sure of it."

"Nor have I. I'll keep trying to hack it, but I need more info. When are you going to tell me where you found this?"

Before Will could answer, someone knocked on the door in a rhythmic pattern.

"That's Nick," said Ajay.

Ajay opened the door. Nick strolled in carrying boxes of Chinese takeout, paper plates, bottles of water, and a stack of fortune cookies balanced on his nose.

"For God's sake, don't make a mess," said Ajay.

"Lighten up, broheim. When have I ever made a mess?"

Nick juggled everything he carried into the air—Ajay nearly had a coronary—before setting it deftly down beside their tablets. Nick dished them each a plateful: kung pao shrimp, chicken pot stickers, red pepper beef, and Singapore rice threaded with chunks of barbeque pork and raw scallion.

"I see Ajay's getting his geek on. Will, check it out—is that your little dude? Sa-weet sassy molassey!" Then he noticed the video on the big screen. "And what the hay is *this*?"

"That's what we're trying to figure out," said Will.

"It's a bit of a mystery," said Ajay.

"No mystery, dude," said Nick, stabbing a pot sticker. "That's only the most awesome shot of Shangri-la *ever*."

Shangri-la. Something clicked for Will. First Nando mentioned it, now this . . . Rule #26: ONCE IS AN ANOMALY. TWICE IS A COINCIDENCE. THREE TIMES IS A PATTERN. AND AS WE KNOW . . .

"What do you mean, Shangri-la?" asked Will.

"You know," said Nick, chomping on a shrimp. "That Asian joint on top of the Hima-hoo-zee-whatzees."

"The *Himalayas*," said Ajay.

"Right. Totally famous place, where the heavyweight spiritual dudes hold conventions. Like Comic-Con for mystics. An awesome green valley way up in the mountains, like *this*—" Nick jabbed his chopsticks at the image. "Where monks and llamas go to do what mystical dudes do when they're . . . you know . . . doing it."

"Monks and llamas," said Ajay.

"Hello? How do you think the monks get *around* up there? Riding *llamas*."

Ajay shook his lower jaw like an annoyed cartoon character. "While they're doing what, for instance? What do they *do* at these 'conventions'?"

Will ignored them, leaning in to study the video, trying to remember: *I came across a third reference to Shangri-la recently . . . what was it?*

"Do I have to spell it out for you?" asked Nick. "They *mind-*

368

meld. They play catch without a ball. They talk to the cosmos and . . . get . . . cosmic answers."

"Shangri-la is not a real place, you ninny," said Ajay. "It's a *myth.* Utter bilgewater. A silly Western legend that sprang up about the 'mystical Orient' from the wishful thinking of some hare-brained early-twentieth-century travel writers. A dozen expeditions went looking for it and never found so much as a teakettle."

"Says you," said Nick, gnawing on a dumpling.

"And you know *why* they didn't find it? Because it doesn't exist!" said Ajay, too agitated to eat. "Even the name Shangri-la is wrong. A pop culture bastardization of what these morons called it in the first place. The *accurate* name for such a *make-believe* place is *Shambhala,* if you must know, not Shangri-la."

"Step back," said Nick. "Like that old tune *'How does your light shine in the halls of Shambhala?'"

"Three Dog Night," said Will, still staring intently at the video.

"I don't know how many dogs they have, but that is the place!" said Nick.

"Yes, that's the place," said Ajay. "And it's a big wad of New Age hooey. You will not find 'heavyweight spiritual dudes' juggling cigar boxes with their brain waves, and certainly not in an 'awesome green valley' that couldn't possibly exist at an altitude of fourteen thousand feet. Because Shangri-La is no more real than Bigfoot or the abominable snowman—"

"Oh, really? Well, it so happens that Bigfoot is a yeti, and yetis *are* abominable snowmen, and abominable snowmen are like the *watchdogs* at Shangri-la."

"Good God, where do you absorb this drivel? More importantly, why are you repeating it?"

"'Cause you can't figure this out with just your *brain*," said Nick, pointing to the banner above Ajay's desk. "Like it says, right there, in the immortal words of Norman Einstein: God does not play dice with the universe."

"I desperately need an aspirin," said Ajay, putting his head in his hands.

"Where's your yearbook, Ajay?" asked Will, finally remembering. "I need to show you something."

Ajay pulled his copy from a shelf by his desk. Will flipped through to the page with Ronnie Murso's freshman photo and read the text below the photo:

"'Embrace paradox. Look for patterns. Beethoven holds the key but doesn't know it yet. Hiding inside your Shangri-la you might find the Gates of Hell.'"

"Dude," said Nick triumphantly. "Tol'ja."

"I'm sorry, but I don't see the connection—" said Ajay.

"Ronnie Murso left that flash drive behind," said Will. "Stashed in a hiding place he built under the floor of his room. In the hope, I think it's safe to say, that the next occupant would come across it. Like I did this morning."

"Say *what*?!" said Nick, his mouth full of food.

"Ronnie wrote *that* message in the yearbook and put *this* image on the drive," said Will, folding his arms. "Draw your own conclusions."

Ajay studied the image on-screen: "I agree that if Ronnie embedded something in this image, it would also be in character for him to leave clues about how to unlock it."

"In his yearbook," said Nick, between bites. "Staring at us the whole time. Like one of his games. *Way* Ronnie-esque."

"Or something much more serious," said Will.

"I have an idea how we can crack this," said Ajay, energized. To the syn-apps on the tablets he said, "Integrate into image."

Their syn-apps disappeared from their tablet screens, and a moment later appeared in the image on the big screen, standing at the base of the mountain.

"What did you just do?" asked Will.

"Exactly what I think Ronnie wanted us to do," said Ajay. "I hacked us into the file's code to get to the bottom of it. Or rather, the top."

Will noticed the syn-apps were now carrying backpacks. He watched, astonished, as they took out an assortment of mountain-climbing gear.

"But that's the *computers* doing all this, right?" asked Will. "Our syn-apps entering the image is just a visual version of what you're telling the software to do?"

"If it makes you feel more comfortable to think of it that way," said Ajay with a sly smile, "be my guest."

"Little dudes doing *work*," said Nick, sucking in a last noodle. "Getting 'er *done*."

Will glanced at a clock on Ajay's desk: six. "Are you ready to make that phone call to California, Ajay?"

"Let's do it," said Ajay, rising from his desk. "This will take a while anyway."

Will held out his phone to him.

"I won't need anything but the number," said Ajay. "I've rigged an alternate device. Come with me."

Ajay led them toward the door to his closet. Will glanced back. On the big screen, Will and Ajay began climbing the mountains of Shangri-la, using ropes and spikes to scale the sheer rock wall beside the tallest waterfall.

THE HOOKUP

Ajay opened the door to his closet. A light winked on, revealing an ordinary space filled with clothes and a wall of shelves. They stepped inside. Ajay closed the door, flipped a switch on the wall twice, then activated a small remote he took from his pocket. The shelves rotated ninety degrees, revealing a cramped space with a saddle chair and a tiny workbench, packed with tools, electronic components, and stacked rows of Altoids tins, labeled and sorted by color.

"Please don't touch anything," said Ajay.

On one shelf sat six handmade electronic gadgets plugged into chargers. Will recognized four as walkie-talkies but the other two were unidentifiable: two curved and lethal-looking blue metallic loops.

"What are those?" asked Will, pointing to the loops.

"A pair of electrified brass knuckles," said Ajay. "I came across something similar on the Net and thought I could improve on the design. I haven't had occasion to use them yet."

"Dude," said Nick eagerly, "I am *so* going to field-test those for you."

Ajay pointed to something bulky on the bench, covered by an orange scarf. "This is it. Cobbled together from cannibalized parts but it should work." Ajay yanked away the scarf, revealing a curved oval green screen connected to a hodgepodge of wires, plugs, circuit boards, and a rotary dialer from an ancient telephone.

"Awesome," said Nick. "What is it, like a death ray?"

"It used to be an old TV," said Ajay. "Now it's a video phone."

"No way," said Nick.

"Now I see why you have so many locks," said Will.

"And why, needless to say, preventing Lyle from searching our rooms when you did saved my bacon," said Ajay.

"So this is completely against the rules," said Will admiringly.

"Guilty as charged, sir," said Ajay with a grin.

"Did you know about all this?" Will asked Nick.

Nick put a hand on his shoulder. "Dude, I helped build the room."

"What's your friend's number, Will?" asked Ajay.

Will read it to him. Ajay dialed it on the ancient rotary device. A moment later they heard ringing on a speaker, and then Nando answered: "This is Nando."

"Nando, how's it going? Where are you?" asked Will.

"Parked behind your garage, compadre."

"Any Black Caps in the area?" asked Will.

"Negativo, all clear. Where you at, bro?"

"With my friends the tech experts," said Will. "They've set it up so we can receive video from your end."

"Cool," said Nando. "I'm on a four-G smartphone with hi-def and the signal's flying five bars. You ready to stream?"

Ajay gave Will a thumbs-up.

"Switching now," said Will.

Ajay flicked on a power switch and a green dot appeared in the middle of the tube. The dot exploded into waves of ghostly interference, and then an image materialized from a cloudburst of static: a shaky handheld shot of Will's garage in Ojai in living color.

"How's it lookin'?" asked Nando. "You getting this?"

"Coming in clear," said Will.

Nando turned the phone around and held it at arm's length so they could see his face. He wore glasses and a hipster's Heisenberg hat. Wires trailed from the phone to buds in his ears. "*Buenos tardes,* my friend," said Nando, tipping his hat.

"Good to see you, Nando," said Will. "You can't see us but say hi to Nick and Ajay."

"*Hola,* friends of Will."

"Good evening, sir," said Ajay.

"What's cracking, Nando?" said Nick.

"It's all good. I improvised a rig for the phone, holmes," said Nando, holding up a red elastic loop. "My wife got the idea from watching some reality show. Looks goofy, but it'll let you see what I'm seeing."

"Go for it," said Will, then to Nick and Ajay: "We're looking for some medical records my dad left in the house."

"How'd you meet this guy?" asked Ajay.

"He helped me escape the Caps," said Will. "Totally solid guy."

The picture jostled around as Nando attached the phone to the strap and fastened it to the front of his hat. Fragments of images whooshed around—the garage, the backyard, Nando's taxi, late afternoon sky—until the camera stabilized on the back of Will's house.

"How's that lookin', guys?" asked Nando off camera.

"Perfecto," said Will.

"Now tell me where to find that key."

"In a magnetic key box," said Will. "Attached to the window by the back door."

"Copy that," said Nando.

On the tube they watched as Nando approached the house. They heard his feet crunch on gravel and the sound of his breathing. He pulled on a pair of thin black gloves.

"So it's sixty-five degrees, a lovely autumn evening here in Southern California," said Nando, doing a TV weatherman impression. "How is it up there in San—"

"Cold," said Will, remembering how much he hadn't yet told either Nando *or* his roommates. "Colder than that. Much colder."

"You find anything out about that rented jet?" asked Nando.

"Nothing so far. Still checking."

"Jet?" said Nick. "What jet?"

Will held a finger to his lips at Nick and mouthed, "I'll explain later."

"Not like they walked out of Costco with a toaster under their arm. That's a multimillion-dollar takedown, homie. Surprised I ain't seen nothin' on the news. Say, how's your dad doing?"

"He's feeling better. Thanks for asking."

Ajay looked askance at Will; Will held up a hand, gesturing for patience.

Nando reached the back door. His hands came into view and searched around the window.

"Hey, my cousin Freddie tracked down a website for that National Scholastic Whatever Agency," said Nando. "I emailed you the link. You get that yet?"

"I'll check when we're done," said Will.

"Got something here." Nando lifted a small metal box into view, slid open the lid, and pulled out a house key.

"That's it," said Will.

Nando moved to the door and inserted the key. The door swung open. "Going in," he said. Nando stepped inside and closed the door. The floorboards creaked.

Seeing the inside of his old house sent queasy waves of unreality through Will. Sweat dripped under his arms.

"No lights on. Gonna leave it that way, case the Caps got it scoped out."

"Where are your parents?" whispered Ajay.

"Not home," whispered Will. "Still at work and . . . out of town. Out of town on work."

Nick and Ajay glanced at each other. Nando moved down the hall into the living room. Will's heart sank when he saw it.

It was completely trashed: Books scattered, chairs broken, wallpaper ripped from the walls. Floorboards had been pried up and left in jagged stumps. The sofa had been torn apart and the stuffing pulled out. Dad's plaster bust of Voltaire had been shattered. They'd smashed his prized turntable, too, dumped out his record collection and stomped most of the priceless old disks into shards.

"Dude," whispered Nick. "You been *robbed*."

"Doesn't look too good, holmes," said Nando.

"The *bastards*," said Will, gritting his teeth.

"Did you know about this, Will?" asked Ajay, more wide-eyed than usual.

"I had a pretty good idea," said Will. "Check upstairs."

Nando backed out of the room and climbed the stairs. The light grew dimmer; all the doors on the second floor were closed.

"Hang a left at the top," said Will.

Nando rounded the corner. The whole house was deathly quiet. All they could hear was Nando's breathing. "Hot up here, man," he whispered. "A *lot* hotter. They must've left the heat on."

"My room's straight ahead of you," said Will. "Look in there."

The hallway flooded with light as Nando opened the door. It took a moment for the camera to adjust and then Will saw his room. Or what was left of it. It looked like wreckage caused by a hurricane. Everything had been chopped to pieces. The banner over the window—THE IMPORTANCE OF AN ORDERLY MIND—hung to the floor in tatters.

"Oh, Will," said Ajay in sympathy.

They were looking for something. Something Dad must have hidden. But what?

"Dude," said Nick. "All kidding aside. This is serious."

Will felt sick, hoping and praying that the same kind of violence hadn't been done to his parents. *What do these people want from us? From me?*

"Check my parents' room," said Will. "Down the hall, last door on the left. There's a shelf of files next to my dad's desk."

Nando padded down the hall. When he reached the door,

the camera tilted down. Nando's hand came into view, turning the knob. He pushed the door open.

As he walked through the doorway, a thin gossamer strand of filament that had been stretched across the threshold snapped. Nando never noticed. And in the furnace room under the basement stairs, a ring on a round steel mesh drum the size of a beer keg rotated slowly to the left. A plug rose out of the barrel with a hiss, and a thick yellowish vapor began to fill the room. . . .

Upstairs in Will's parents' bedroom, Nando surveyed more of the same destruction. Will's parents' bed had been slashed and stripped to the coils. His father's desk had been emptied, drawers pulled out and smashed.

"The shelves are all empty, man," said Nando. "Maybe the Caps took the files out in those boxes." The camera focused in on a thermostat near the door. "No wonder it's so hot in here. Thermostat's turned up to eighty-five."

"Check the closet," said Will.

Nando moved to the open closet; it was a walk-in, deep and spacious and dark. He raised a pocket flashlight and switched it on. The camera followed the flashlight beam around the closet. Clothes and hangers had been pulled off the rails and tossed into a big pile on the floor.

"There's nothing in here, man," said Nando. "And they've searched it."

"There's a false panel in the ceiling," said Will. "Near the back right corner. Try looking there. You'll need a chair."

Nando dragged a chair from the bedroom to the rear of the closet. He stood on it and examined the ceiling, which was covered with a layer of sprayed white insulation.

"Think I see it," said Nando. "There's a seam here." He

poked around until a panel, about a foot square, shifted out of its frame. Nando pushed it up and out of the way. "I can see the rafters. There's like a crawl space. And there's something up here."

"Can you reach it?" asked Will.

"I'll try," said Nando. The screen went blurry as Nando tilted his head to the side. "I got it." He brought a black bag down into view and pointed his light at it. "It's like a doctor's bag. Real old leather."

"That belonged to my dad," said Will.

"Something's printed near the handle, kind of faded. It's initials, I think."

Will didn't remember seeing lettering on the bag before. "Is it *J. W.*?"

"No, man. That's not it. Looks like . . . *H. G.*"

"That can't be right," said Will.

"Take a look," said Nando. He held the bag in front of the camera. They saw faded gold letters on the worn pebbled leather below the handle: H. G.

"Open it," said Will.

"Hold on a sec," said Nando. "Thought I heard something."

A moment later they heard a muffled boom, as if something heavy and metallic had hit the floor downstairs.

"What was that?" asked Nick.

"Maybe the furnace?" said Ajay.

"No," Nando whispered. "I think somebody's in the house."

Will leaned in, alarmed. "You need to get out, Nando. Get out of the house."

Nando jumped off the chair and started toward the open door. "Oh, man," he said. "What is *that*? Something really *stinks* in here." Then he stopped at the door. "I hear something moving in the crawl space."

Will shouted at the screen, "Nando, get out of there now!"

Nando spun around. His flashlight whirled and found the hatch in the ceiling. Something stood on the edge of the opening. Will's first thought was that it looked like a huge version of an insect kids called a potato bug.

But this thing was worse. Much worse. It had a tiny head on a pale stalk; pincers sprouted from its jaws. Big bright eyes protruded from an almost human face. It reared up on its hind legs, revealing a waxy segmented belly and the rest of its limbs, wriggling rows of what looked like black, stubby fingers.

"Aw, *sick*!" said Nando.

The thing emitted a high-pitched rattling screech and leaped off the ledge at the camera. Ajay, Nick, and Will jumped back from the screen. Nando swatted it away, turned, and jumped out of the closet, slamming the door behind him.

"Did you see that?" Nando asked.

"Yes!" yelled Will, Nick, and Ajay.

They heard the bug hit the inside of the door, then watched as its pincers speared straight through the wood like twin drill bits, secreting an acidic red-orange fluid that quickly liquefied a pulpy wet hole.

"What is that thing?" shouted Ajay.

An automatic pistol appeared in Nando's hands.

"Dude's got a *gat*," said Nick.

Nando fired three shots, point-blank, as the thing wriggled through the hole it had made. The creature exploded into loose fluids that splattered and burst into flames. Liquid fire flowed down the door.

"That is *not* a bug native to Southern California," said Ajay, shaking.

"Ya *think*?!" yelled Nando.

"Get out!" yelled Will.

"I'm getting," said Nando.

Nando ran out the door as the fire quickly spread. They saw another bug just outside, perched on top of the banister. It leaped and attached itself to Nando's leg. The camera spun frantically as Nando hopped down the hall, trying to slap the thing away as it crawled all over him, jaws snapping wildly.

Ajay and Nick jumped as if it had landed on them, slapping at their legs.

"Get to my room," said Will. "Use the window—"

"Damn, it's on my back," said Nando.

Nando slammed backward into a wall. They heard a hideous screech and a loud crunch. Nando quickly turned. The black smear and gooey debris that had splattered from the thing burst into flame.

"Go, go!" yelled Will.

Nando had reached Will's door when they heard a sickening skittering sound. When Nando turned, they saw a stampede, hundreds of the monsters pouring upstairs, scrambling over each other. Nando fired a burst at the head of the swarm, setting off the combustible bugs like a string of firecrackers, flames erupting.

Nando threw himself into Will's room, slammed the door, ran to the window, and pushed up the sash. They heard a chorus of band saws behind him. Nando whipped his head around, tilting the phone sideways: A thousand bugs were chomping their way through every inch of the door, all at once, dissolving it before their eyes. Nando emptied the clip at them and what was left of the door exploded.

Then he was on the roof, breathing heavily as he crunched across the shingles. "Somebody call the damn Orkin man!" shouted Nando.

He reached the edge of the roof and jumped into the air. The camera jerked. They heard him grunt as he broke his fall on the branch of a tree, then groan as he dropped to the ground. He scrambled to his feet and limped for his taxi.

He opened the door and turned just as the whole house went up, flames bursting from every window. Nando climbed in behind the wheel and slid his key into the ignition, then jammed the taxi into gear and pulled into the alley.

"Are you okay?" asked Will.

"I'm a long way from okay," said Nando. "But I'm *alive*—"

Another bug dove straight into the windshield, screaming. Nando shouted and swerved hard right.

The screen went blank.

A TINY PIANIST

A message came up on-screen: CALL DISCONNECTED. When Will turned around, he saw Nick and Ajay with their arms wrapped around each other.

"Monsters," said Ajay faintly.

"Dude," said Nick. "I am believing anything else you ever tell us for the rest of my life."

They separated, a bit self-consciously. Nick staggered out of the closet, gulping in some deep breaths. Ajay and Will followed.

"You think Nando's all right?" asked Ajay.

"I'll try to call him," said Will, taking out his phone.

"So those bugs are from the same place as the other ones?" asked Nick.

"Yes." Will hit Nando's number. The call went straight to voice mail.

"Well, we didn't need special glasses to see *these*," said Ajay.

"No," said Will. "I think that means they came across a while ago."

"From this place you called the Never-Was," said Ajay.

"Right," said Will.

"And they get here through those Weasel Holes," said Nick.

"Yes." Will punched REDIAL. "Damn, he's not answering."

"Dude," said Nick. "Your *house* is on fire. Call the local fire department."

"And tell them what?" asked Ajay. "That we saw it burning from *Wisconsin*?"

"I don't know," said Nick, throwing his hands up. "If they hurry, maybe they can catch one of those crazy cock-a-roaches."

"They won't find anything," said Will. "It'll all be wiped out by the fire. That was a trap set to go off if I came back. That's how the Caps planned it."

"You mean . . . they want to kill you?" asked Ajay.

The hell with rules or what my parents wanted. My friends are involved now, in harm's way, and I put them there. Time to come clean.

"Yes. Did you record any of what we just saw?" asked Will.

"All of it," said Ajay.

"Get the girls," said Will. "Let's meet in the great room."

Five minutes later, Elise and Brooke had joined them, huddled together on the couches in the great room, listening as Will told them the whole story about how the Black Caps had chased him that morning in Ojai. He showed them the mechanical bird they'd used to spy on his family before his parents had been kidnapped, or worse. He told them about the monsters in the hills and on the plane, about Ride Alongs and Weasel Holes and how people at the school were now summoning monsters from the Never-Was. He didn't mention Dave or the Hierarchy—he didn't want them to think he was *completely* crazy—but he did say that Todd and some of the seniors on the cross-country team, along with Lyle and the rest of the Knights, appeared to be the ones who were bringing monsters over.

"Monsters?" asked Elise skeptically. "That's laying it on a bit thick."

"I want to believe you, Will," said Brooke, wide-eyed and a little shaky. "Do you have any proof of all this?"

"Show them," said Will to Ajay.

Ajay played back Nando's phone call on his tablet for them. When it ended, Brooke and Elise looked stunned. No one in the group said anything for a moment. Wood crackled in the fire.

"So basically," said Elise slowly, as if intrigued by the idea, "everything we know . . . is wrong."

"One question, Will," said Brooke. "Why are they coming after you?"

Will shook his head. "I think that my parents must have known, considering how much we moved around." He told them how they had ordered him to stay under the radar, how he'd always pulled back in school and in athletics. "Then I aced that test," he said. "If it hadn't been for that, my parents might still . . ."

Brooke scooted over and took his hand. "Whatever's going on," she said softly, "I'm really glad you told us. And we're *all* going to help you."

Will's chest tightened; his eyes burned. Elise sat on the other side of him and patted his shoulder. There wasn't much of his game face left now.

"So it's all connected," said Ajay, on his feet, pacing. "The

Knights, the locker room, the tunnels to the Crag, and what happened to you back home. Now if we can just find out the reason for all of it."

Will looked at Elise and when their eyes met, he could swear that he heard her thinking something. Almost as if she'd "pushed" a thought into *his* head.

Ronnie knew about this.

"I'll tell you what *I* think," said Nick, pacing and agitated. "I think that the bastards who did all this to you are in for a prime-time *ass*-kicking—"

"Take it easy, Tarzan," said Brooke.

Ajay knelt beside Will to look at the bird. "May I examine this later, Will?"

Will nodded. Ajay folded the bird into the towel and picked it up.

"I need to talk to Elise," Will whispered to Ajay.

"Brooke, come to my room, please," said Ajay. "I want to show you something. You, too, Nick."

"What?" snapped Nick, still pacing.

"I need your help," said Ajay. "In *here*."

Will caught Ajay's eye and nodded thanks. As soon as they left, Will sat in front of Elise.

"Tell me," said Will gently. "What did Ronnie know?"

Elise's eyes widened. "How did you . . . ?"

"I'm not sure," he said. "But I'm right, aren't I? Ronnie knew something about this and he told you."

Elise put her hands on her temples and rubbed hard, like she was fighting off a migraine. Her fine black hair hung down over her eyes.

"They picked on him relentlessly," she said. "Todd and Lyle and the rest of them. He was so shy, whining about how homesick he was all the time. We'd decided he was hopeless, *V* for 'victim' stamped on his forehead like a license plate. Then he started crushing on me. *Way* beyond awkward. He played the *flute*. He wrote poems, for crying out loud."

"He wrote them to you?"

She put on a tough face. " 'How do you measure the distance traveled by a smile?' Gag me with a deer rifle, do I seem like the kind of girl who likes *poems*?"

He saw the answer behind the protest in her troubled eyes. "Yeah, you must have hated that."

"*Please.* We knew he was brilliant, in a dorkus malorkus sort of way. And funny and self-deprecating, and that was . . . unexpected. He didn't find his confidence until he started his project in the labs. They even stopped picking on him then. But he never told us what he was working on."

"Not even you?"

"Why would he tell *me*? It wasn't like we were *seriously* hooked up. I mean, we spent some time together, and I—" She saw he wasn't buying it. "Okay, so we got tight. Then something changed a month before end of term. He just cut me off."

"Why?"

Her jade eyes blazed with pain and anger. "I don't know. I *tried* to find out. About him or me or what was wrong or *any of it*. And I don't know if you've picked up on this or not, but I'm kind of skilled at finding out what people are feeling."

Will gulped. "I can see that."

"But I couldn't read the faintest signal from Ronnie. Instead of this cute warm goof, an iron curtain came down. And I had told him things about myself . . . stuff I'd never told anybody. I *trusted* him, and I couldn't get a *hello*."

Will had to tread carefully. One wrong word might shut her down again. "So what did Ronnie know, Elise?"

Elise shot a fierce, penetrating stare at him. Will tried to open his mind, let her look inside him if she needed to, show her that he trusted her.

"The last day of term," she said, "we're packing to leave for the summer. Ronnie stops me in the quad with this . . . sweet, openhearted look he used to have for me, so I know it's *him* and his guard is down and . . . I caught a glimpse inside."

She looked away. Will tried to keep eye contact. "What did you see?"

"Something that scared him. Something he'd seen in the labs. Something deep and dark and terrifying that he couldn't handle."

"Did he tell you what it was?"

Elise shook her head. "He just hugged me and said that if anything ever happened to him, he'd find a way to tell me . . . so I'd understand. And then he whispered a question in my ear: 'Are you awake?'"

"Awake?" The word sent a shock through Will; he'd been hearing it a *lot* lately. "What did he mean?"

She shook her head. "I don't know. That was the last time I ever saw him."

She looked away, deeply wounded but too proud to cry. Will racked his brain, trying to think what to do. But this wasn't a *thinking* problem. Then he remembered: #87: MEN WANT COMPANY. WOMEN WANT EMPATHY.

"Did you ever tell Ronnie how you really felt about him?" he asked quietly.

"Of course I didn't," she said, twisting her hair.

"And that's what you're mad at yourself about."

"Isn't that painfully obvious?"

"Kind of."

"Well it's *kind of* a stupid question."

"I guess we all have a game face, don't we?" asked Will.

Elise's eyes went soft. She mimed pulling out a knife, then stabbed herself and fell over. Will laughed. A moment later, so did she. Will stood and held out a hand. When he pulled her up, they came face to face.

And suddenly Will couldn't move. A prism of light from her dazzling eyes shot through him as if he were made of glass. She could have told him, in that moment, to rob a bank or jump off a building and he'd have done it without thinking. He couldn't break away, and in that moment he didn't want to.

"I think I might know how Ronnie planned to tell you," he said. "Come on."

He took her by the hand and led her to Ajay's room. When they entered, Brooke looked up from the desk and saw them holding hands. Elise didn't notice, but Will felt like he'd been caught pickpocketing. He let go. Brooke quickly looked away.

Nick had set up chairs for everyone. Elise sat beside Ajay in front of the animated mountain image on the enlarged screen. In the half hour since they'd started, the syn-apps had climbed all the way to the top of the rocks onto a narrow ledge above the tallest waterfall. The figures waved to Will and Elise as they came closer.

"What is this?" asked Elise.

"This image was on a flash drive Ronnie hid in his room," said Will. "I found it this morning."

"I hacked our syn-apps into it," said Ajay. "We think Ronnie hid something in the file; the syn-apps have been trying to uncover it. Zoom in."

The point of view zoomed in on the ledge where the two figures stood.

"Go on now," said Ajay to the figures. "Follow the path."

The two syn-apps worked around the corner. As they made the turn, the image opened into a peaceful green glade. Sprays of colorful wildflowers dotted long grass swaying in the breeze. A still pond sat in front of a pagoda-like structure built into the face of a sheer rock wall.

"What is this place supposed to be?" asked Elise.

"I've been telling 'em all along," said Nick. "They're in *Shangri-la*."

The figures walked across a bamboo bridge that spanned the pond, where sparkling, jewel-like white and golden koi swam lazily. They climbed the stairs toward the pagoda's imposing double doors. The doors opened and two human figures in long white coats stepped out before them. The doors closed.

"Who are those guys?" asked Will.

"They look like doctors," said Brooke.

"So go inside," said Elise.

"Let's try," said Will. Then, to their doubles, "Enter."

But as the syn-apps advanced, the doctors locked arms and blocked the doors. Each time they moved, the doctors moved in their way.

"Losers," said Nick. "Do I need to jump in there and kick their butts *for* you? Let me get my munchkin—"

"Sit down and shut up," said Brooke.

"Read his passage from the yearbook again," said Ajay.

Will picked up the book from the desk: " 'Embrace paradox. Look for patterns. Beethoven holds the key but doesn't know it yet. Hiding inside your Shangri-la you might find the Gates of Hell.' "

"Ronnie wrote that," said Elise.

"Yes," said Will.

"We think he built all of this," Ajay said. "That it's like one of his games."

"It's more than a game." Elise leaned closer to the screen. "This was how he saw the world: a maze of interlocking mysteries. If you solve this puzzle, you unlock the next one and eventually reach the heart of things."

"Where he hid what he wanted to tell you," said Will.

"Maybe," said Elise, studying the passage in the yearbook.

"So this is his version of an extremely elaborate password," said Brooke.

"I keep telling you," said Nick, biting a nail. "Type in Shangri-*la*."

"Your contribution has been duly noted," said Ajay.

Elise looked up sharply. "Tell them to hug those two figures on the porch."

"That's limp," said Nick.

"Do you want my help or not?" said Elise.

Ajay and Will looked at each other, shrugged, then both said, "Hug them."

Their syn-apps looked at each other, shrugged, then walked toward the figures at the door with their arms outstretched. The figures in white looked at each other, then stepped forward and allowed themselves to be hugged by the syn-apps.

The doors behind the doctors immediately swung open. The figures in white stepped back, bowed, and faded away.

"Embrace the 'pair-o-docs,'" said Will.

"Now you're starting to get it," said Elise.

"ROTFLMAO," said Nick, his jaw hanging open.

"You are *not* rolling on the floor laughing your ass off," said Ajay.

"I am on the inside."

"Tell them to go in," said Elise.

They did and their doubles walked into the building. The walls faded away and the small figures entered a vast empty gray space. Near them, a sharp circle of blinding white light snapped on from high overhead. More circular beams appeared, polka-dotting the space with a rainbow of colors as far as they could see.

The syn-apps stepped into the first white circle. Without warning, all of the floor untouched by light dropped away. Only the colored circles remained. The circles were now the tops of tall round columns that rose out of a bottomless void.

"Uh," said Will, unnerved. "What happens if our syn-apps die?"

"My guess is that if we die, we'll lose access to the program," said Ajay.

"Ronnie probably rigged it to self-destruct," said Elise. "To protect whatever he hid in here. We have one shot at this."

"What did he write next?" said Brooke, picking up the yearbook.

"Hope it wasn't 'Plunge to a meaningless death,'" said Nick.

"'Look for patterns,'" read Brooke.

"What patterns?" asked Nick.

The circles began blinking on and off, one color at a time. Each of the seven colors corresponded to a single loud tone that repeated with each blink, until the whole space filled with cacophonous music. The syn-apps covered their ears.

"How does this work?" asked Ajay. "What should we do?"

Elise closed her eyes and listened closely. "It's a Phrygian scale. The fifth mode of the harmonic minor scale."

"How do you know that?" asked Nick.

"Because I *told* him about it," said Elise, scowling. "You need to jump to the color that corresponds to the next note in the scale." Elise struggled to concentrate; the music was nearly deafening.

"Blue," she said.

The two syn-apps hopped from their column to the closest blue circle. As they landed, every other blue column crumbled and fell out of sight. The "blue" notes disappeared with them, slightly simplifying the music.

"What's next?" asked Ajay.

Elise concentrated, then said, "Purple."

The syn-apps jumped to a purple circle, and the rest of the purple columns collapsed. Then all the columns, including the one they were standing on, began rising up and down like titanic pistons, making further leaps infinitely more dangerous.

"Now red," said Elise.

The syn-apps waited until the nearest red column rumbled up out of the darkness, timing their jump to land on it as it rocketed past them. The rest of the red columns disintegrated.

In addition to rising and falling, the columns began moving horizontally, sweeping rapidly from side to side. The syn-apps struggled to stay on top, clinging to each other as their red column whipped around.

"It's like some kind of insane carousel," said Brooke.

"What's next?" asked Will.

Three colors remained: orange, yellow, and green. "Orange," said Elise. "Will" and "Ajay" had to wait longer for an orange column to pass, and then made the leap together. Will landed cleanly, but Ajay stubbed a foot on the edge and nearly fell backward. Will grabbed his belt and hauled him to safety as the pillar whirled around.

"Why didn't we bring Nick the Human Goat-Boy along for this?" said Ajay.

"Dude, I offered," said Nick.

"Yellow," said Elise. A yellow column whipped by, and they made the leap. Now only green columns remained. The columns picked up speed. The syn-apps threw themselves on top of a green one as it sailed past. The green column gradually slowed, then ground to a halt with an alarming shudder.

A single white column appeared ahead of them. The syn-apps were stranded ten yards away from it, too far to jump.

"What now?" asked Ajay.

"Think it through," said Will. "There's no rush."

A message appeared on-screen: YOU HAVE THIRTY SEC-ONDS. The message was replaced by the number 30, which changed to 29, then to 28. With each passing second, the syn-apps' green column slowly crumbled. The syn-apps moved to the center, looking out at them for help.

"You were saying?" asked Brooke.

"*Damn* it, Ronnie," said Elise.

"Jump, dudes!" said Nick.

"Use your ropes," said Ajay to the screen.

The syn-apps huddled for a moment and agreed on something. "Will" opened his backpack and took out what looked like a flare gun. "Ajay" attached a spike to the end of his rope and dropped it into the barrel of Will's gun, and Will fired it down at the white circle. The spike embedded in its surface near the edge. Ajay secured their end of the rope to the center of their shrinking pillar with a piton.

"Zip lines," said Will.

As the countdown hit 10, they attached clips from their belts to the rope, then launched off the column. They soared over the void and tumbled onto the white column just as what was left of the green column collapsed into the bottomless dark. Slipping off their climbing gear, they just escaped being dragged over the edge. Everyone, including the syn-apps, stopped to catch their breath.

"Now what?" said Brooke.

The light slowly brightened and the white circle of light became part of a ledge at the bottom of a tall smooth cliff.

"Keep going," said Elise. "You're getting close."

The syn-apps moved along the ledge until they reached an open doorway in the cliff. As they moved through it, the space transformed into a large chamber containing antique furniture, a blazing fireplace, and geometric parquet flooring. Tall hunting tapestries hung on the walls.

An ornate grand piano sat in the center of the room. A man sat on the bench with his back to them. He wore a high-collared white shirt and neckerchief, breeches, buckle shoes, and a long tailcoat. The man was leaning forward, with one arm on the piano, resting his chin on his hand. A feathered quill and bottle of ink sat beside him on a small wooden stand. Two blank pages of musical composition paper rested on the piano's rack.

The doubles walked around the piano until the point of view shifted and Will could see the man. He looked about forty, stocky and powerful. A wild shock of thick gray hair swirled around his head. His face was heavy and grave, lined with care, almost tormented. He didn't seem to notice them, his intense, steely blue eyes staring into the distance.

"You know who that is?" asked Ajay.

Will had seen this face on dozens of record covers in his parents' collection. "Ludwig van Beethoven," said Will.

"Oh my God," said Nick. "The dude who wrote the 'Star Spangled Banner.'"

"Beethoven did not write the—" said Brooke.

"Don't bother," said Ajay.

"The last puzzle," said Brooke, reading from the yearbook. "'Beethoven holds the key but doesn't know it yet.'"

"Then tell him," said Ajay to his syn-app.

"*Guten Tag, Herr Beethoven*," said Ajay's syn-app on-screen with a polite bow. "May we have a word with you, sir? *Dürfen wir mit Ihnen sprechen, bitte?*"

"Your dude speaks *Russian*?" whispered Nick.

"*I* speak *German*," said Ajay.

But Beethoven didn't respond. Didn't even look at them.

"He can't hear you," said Brooke. "He's deaf, remember?"

"Ajay, does your little dude know sign language?" said Nick, then slapped his forehead. "What am I saying? Sign language hadn't been *invented* yet."

Brooke stood up suddenly and asked, "Do either of you play the piano?"

"I can a little," said Ajay.

Brooke leaned in and hummed a melody in his ear. They looked at each other.

"How?" asked Ajay.

"Tell him to play it by ear," said Brooke.

Ajay leaned in to his syn-app and said, "Play this on the piano." He hummed quietly. Ajay's syn-app moved to the right side of the keyboard and played the notes.

Dah-dah-dah-du-dee-da-da . . .

Elise gasped and touched her hands to her face, her eyes filling with tears.

Beethoven came to life, his face lit up as if inspired by "hearing" the notes in his mind. He brought his right hand to the keys and picked up the melody, adding his left hand in the third measure. Every note he played appeared in ink, as if *he* were writing them, on the notation paper.

"I've heard this before," said Will. "A hundred times."

"It's one of his most famous compositions," said Ajay.

"Maybe so," said Nick, disappointed. "But that is definitely *not* the 'Star Spangled Banner.'"

"No," said Elise, quietly wiping away a tear. "In German it's called '*Für Elise.*'"

"For *Elise*," said Brooke, with a look at Will.

As Beethoven continued, a full invisible orchestra joined in. The wall in front of the piano transformed into the door of an enormous bank vault, covered with intricate locks, bolts, and steam-powered gears.

The notes of the tune lifted off the page as if animated and floated through the air toward the vault. They poured into a slot near the center. Gears and immense levers went into motion all over the vault's surface. Bolts gave way, bursts of steam spurted, wheels turned, a bar drew back with a heavy thud, and the door swung slowly open.

"Beethoven holds the key," said Brooke softly.

And out walked the syn-app of Ronnie Murso.

RONNIE

The syn-apps backed away from Ronnie in alarm. Elise moved closer to the screen, while the rest of the roommates grouped behind her. Ronnie blinked and looked around, confused and disoriented. To Will he looked exactly like Ronnie's yearbook photo, except that the syn-app's straw-blond hair was filthy and his face was covered with grime. His clothes were disheveled and dirty, his pants ripped at the knees.

"Ronnie?" said Elise, almost in a whisper.

The syn-app looked up, saw Elise, and recoiled, looking frightened.

"Ronnie, do you know where you are?" asked Elise.

He shook his head.

"Do you know *who* you are?" she asked softly.

The syn-app hesitated, then shook his head again.

"What's wrong with him?" Will quietly asked the others.

"Don't know," said Ajay. "I've never seen a syn-app behave like this before."

"Little dude looks homeless," whispered Nick.

"He *acts* like he's got amnesia," said Brooke.

"Ronnie . . . do you know who I am?" asked Elise.

After hesitating, Ronnie shook his head, sweet and utterly vacant. Elise buried her face in her hands. Brooke stepped forward and put a steadying hand on her shoulder.

"What does this mean, Elise?" asked Will, mystified.

"It means he's *alive*," said Elise.

"Perhaps," said Ajay thoughtfully.

"Ajay, his syn-app is *right there*," she said, pointing at the screen. "Ronnie's alive. He said he'd find a way to reach me if something happened to him. Something has, just look at him. He's not *right*. He's injured or lost, but he's alive—"

"Hold on a second," said Will. "You're saying he's alive just because his syn-app is here?" No one responded. The roommates looked at each other uncomfortably. "You're not seriously suggesting they have some kind of physical *connection* to what's happening to us in real life?"

"That's just a . . . theory, Will," said Ajay.

"That's *exactly* what I'm saying," said Elise.

"That's impossible," said Will. "These things are just billions of ones and zeros strung together. No matter how many tricks they can do, it's only a simulation."

"One would suppose," said Ajay warily. "But then, we didn't write the original program."

Will didn't push the argument. He remembered the uncanny feeling he'd had when his own syn-app had come to life: *There's something to this. I did* feel *a connection.*

"'There are more things in heaven and earth, Horatio, than are dreamt of in your philosophy,'" said Brooke.

Ronnie absentmindedly took something from his pocket. He seemed surprised to find it there. Ronnie cradled it in his hands and examined it closely.

"Nick," said Elise. "Get my tablet."

Nick darted out of the room. Ronnie held the object to the light.

"What have you got there, Ronnie?" asked Elise gently.

Ronnie shrank back from her, hiding the object behind his back.

"It's okay," said Elise. "I won't hurt you. I just want to see what you found."

Ronnie shrugged; he didn't know either.

"Can you show me?" asked Elise. "Maybe I can help you figure out what it is."

Will's and Ajay's syn-apps moved toward Ronnie.

"Not too close," said Elise to Ajay. "We don't want to spook him."

Ajay and Will stopped a short distance away. Nick rushed back in with Elise's tablet. She powered it up on the desk next to the others and moments later, Elise's syn-app materialized with the others on the big screen.

"Elise" walked toward Ronnie and held out a hand. Ronnie took a step backward.

"You're perfectly safe," said Elise. "We won't hurt you. Can you show me what you have there, Ronnie?"

Ronnie slowly opened his hand. A virtual flash drive rested on his palm. "Elise" took the object from him.

"Ajay," said Elise. "See what that is."

Her syn-app held out the flash drive behind her. "Ajay"

darted over and took it like a relay baton. He took a virtual tablet from his backpack and inserted the drive into it, just as the real Ajay had with the real one.

"So let me see if I've got this straight," said Will. "A virtual flash drive . . . inserted by a virtual character . . . into its virtual computer."

"Think of it this way," said Ajay quietly. "They're all levels of the same file on a *real* flash drive, being read by a real computer. Now that we've cracked his puzzle, maybe this flash drive represents the final level and contains what Ronnie wanted us to see."

But "Ajay" was frowning. He looked out at the real Ajay and shook his head.

"It's not opening," Ajay said. "We missed something."

"Damn it," said Elise under her breath.

The image of Beethoven's salon disappeared and was replaced by the Himalayan meadow in front of the pagoda. Ronnie seemed more alert. "Elise" took his hand; this time Ronnie didn't shrink away.

Will had an idea and leaned in past Elise toward the screen. "Ronnie, this is *Elise*," said Will firmly. "She was your best friend."

As he listened, Ronnie's brow furrowed, in a struggle to comprehend.

" 'How do you measure the distance traveled by a smile?' " said Will.

The line sent a jolt through Ronnie. He turned, looked out at the *real* Elise, and seemed to recognize her. Ronnie reached out and Elise touched the screen. As their fingers met, Ronnie suddenly looked alert, revived, glowing with spirit.

"Show us what you hid on this drive, Ronnie," said Elise. "Show us what you wanted us to see."

Ronnie nodded, then pointed to the top of the screen. A moment later, an iron-banded transparent barrel dropped into the screen from above, landing with a heavy thud on the wooden bridge over the pond. The barrel began to fill with a viscous red liquid rising from the bottom.

"What's that?" said Nick.

"It's working," said Ajay. "The file's uploading to my tablet."

Elise was still holding her hand to the screen, completely still, locked onto Ronnie. Will got the odd impression they were communicating without words.

"I think he's a prisoner," said Elise.

"What?" asked Nick. "How could you know that?"

"I just do," she said. "I think what's on there will tell us who did this to him."

Ajay looked at Will with a raised eyebrow. "We'll know soon enough," he said, as the upload reached 50 percent.

Brooke had a funny look on her face. "Does anybody else hear that?"

"Hear what?" asked Nick.

"Yes," said Ajay. "It's a—"

"Buzzing sound," said Elise. "It's coming from the image on-screen. Near the top of the mountain."

Now Will could hear it, too.

It was a droning sound, and as they listened, it grew louder and more menacing. A trickle of scalloped black shadows dripped into the upper right corner of the screen and gyred lazily around, like cottonseeds blown by the wind. As they drifted toward the meadow, the shapes melded together into a pulsating mass that began to spin in place, counterclockwise, picking up force. The sky darkened as it gained strength and size, forming into a funnel cloud.

"What is that?" asked Nick.

"I think someone's hacked into the program," said Ajay.

"But how?" asked Brooke.

"I don't know," said Ajay. "We're not online. It must be coming from one of our tablets."

The syn-apps retreated toward the bottom of the screen. Will's syn-app pulled a virtual Swiss Army knife from his pocket, expanded one of the blades, then stretched the handle out until it was as long as a harpoon.

"What's your dude doing?" asked Nick.

"No idea," said Will.

"I don't like this," said Elise. "We need to get out."

Their eyes moved to the barrel, which had filled to nearly 90 percent.

"We almost have it," said Ajay.

The surging vortex hit the ground, destroying everything it touched, tearing up the meadow, smashing through the pagoda. The syn-apps dodged a rain of debris.

"Ajay, it's not *safe*—" said Brooke.

"If I terminate this download, we'll lose what Ronnie wanted us to see," said Ajay, "probably forever."

Ronnie suddenly ran toward the cyclone. The syn-app shouted and waved his arms, then dashed away from the barrel. The twister changed direction and chased him.

"What the hell is he doing?" asked Nick.

"Buying us time," said Will.

"Will" followed Ronnie toward the ledge they'd come in on.

As the funnel cloud cornered Ronnie on the rocks, it morphed into a swarm of what looked like locusts. They descended on Ronnie and tore into him; he turned to Elise, his face a mask of pain. The pixels of his disintegrating image flew up into the cyclone.

"No!" shouted Elise.

As the funnel cloud consumed Ronnie's syn-app, it took on the rough outline of his screaming face. "Will" reared back and cast his harpoon into the heart of the vortex; it swayed and weakened, but it was too late. Ronnie's cries faded as the ravenous swarm swallowed the last of him.

The barrel on the screen filled, crimson slopping into the pond.

"We've got it," said Ajay. "Shut down!"

"Shut down!" said Elise and Will.

Their tablets powered off. The syn-apps vanished and all their screens went blank. At that same moment, the lights in the room flickered and dimmed, then went out, plunging them into darkness.

Nick rushed to the window. "The whole campus is dark!"

"A power failure," said Ajay, stepping beside him. "But campus-wide? Never seen that before."

Will turned his tablet back on, and the room filled with ghostly light. Will's syn-app appeared on-screen, holding his Swiss Army harpoon.

"You should have let me run that security check, Will," the syn-app said.

"Will" raised the harpoon and showed them a creature impaled on the blade, a black beetle the size of a small dog, covered with coarse black hairs. It had distorted semihuman features on its hideous, squashed face.

"What the hell is *that*?" asked Nick.

"A virus infected your tablet," said Will's syn-app. "Origin unknown."

"Will" shoved the bug toward the edge of the screen. A port opened on that side of Will's tablet and the body of an identical bug—this one an inch long—plopped out onto the desk.

Brooke turned pale. "That's what went after Ronnie?"

"So it appears," said Ajay. He used a pencil to sweep the dead bug into an empty Altoids tin.

"Run the rest of that check now," said Will to his syn-app.

"Can do," said the syn-app.

"Where did this come from?" asked Elise, staring at the bug.

"Lyle," said Will.

"Dude, Lyle's trunk, these things were in those *boxes*," said Nick, staring wide-eyed at the dead bug.

"This is how he was watching me," said Will. "How he knew about my phone and our visit to their locker room."

"But where did *Lyle* get it?" asked Brooke.

"The same place all the rest of them came from," said Will. "The Never-Was."

Ajay activated his tablet. His syn-app held up a large file icon. "It's intact; we've got Ronnie's file," said Ajay, excited. Then to his syn-app, "Open it."

The screen opened to the grainy image of a video file, with a PLAY arrow in its center. They appeared to be looking through a hole into a dimly lit room, where a briefcase sat on a bench, with documents visible inside. There was a time stamp in the corner.

"It seems to be a video," said Ajay, reading the time stamp. "Shot last April."

"That's the auxiliary locker room," said Will, leaning in. "I think we're looking out through one of the lockers."

Ajay clicked the PLAY button. The image jumbled around a bit; then a face slid into view: Ronnie Murso.

"Auxiliary locker room," whispered Ronnie. "Watch this."

The image moved as Ronnie, camera in hand, stepped out of the locker into the room. He moved to the briefcase and rummaged around. Ronnie pulled out a thick gray metallic rod, held it up to the lens, then spoke into the lens again: "I think this is what they use to—"

He looked toward the door in alarm, as if he'd heard something outside. He dropped the rod into the briefcase, hurried back into the locker, and closed the door. He put the camera lens up to the hole in the locker looking into the room again.

A tall, heavyset man wearing a dark suit and hat entered the room. They couldn't see his face. "Put it here," he said.

Lyle Ogilvy followed him in, laboring as he carried a black metal footlocker like the one Will and Nick had seen in Lyle's closet. He set it on the bench beside the briefcase. The man took three things out of the briefcase and set them on the bench: the metal rod, a rectangular silver box with some writing on it, and a rolled-up sheet of thin metal. He unrolled the metal first. It was poster-sized and covered with strange glyphs.

"We saw that on the wall," said Nick. "In Lyle's closet."

"Did they show you how to use this?" the man asked Lyle.

"Yes, sir," said Lyle.

The man picked up the rod. "What about the Carver?"

"No, not yet," said Lyle.

"We only have two of them. You'd better take care of it,"

said the man as he checked some kind of gauge on the rod's side. "It takes time to build up a charge. Give me a canister."

Lyle opened the footlocker. Inside they saw rows of the same black carbon-fiber containers they'd seen in Lyle's closet. Lyle removed one of the thermos-sized ones. The man activated something on the metal rod he'd called the Carver; a line of glyphs on the rod lit up and the tip of it glowed white-hot.

"They're called by the glyphs," said the man. "The holes are unstable and only stay up long enough for one to cross over. Make sure you use the right-sized canister. Open it."

Lyle slid open the end of the canister. His hands were shaking. The man raised the Carver and pressed some of its glowing glyphs, in order, as if entering some kind of code.

"Hold it flush to the hole or you'll lose a hand," said the man.

The white tip of the rod grew blindingly bright, illuminating the man's face for the first time. Will gasped.

It was the Bald Man, the one he'd seen at his house with the other Black Caps.

Using both hands, the man moved the tip of the rod in a tight circle, which traced and then carved open a small hole in the air. "Now," said the Bald Man. "Quickly."

Grimacing, Lyle held the open canister up to the hole, covering it. The canister jerked as something appeared to slip through the hole and into the container.

"Close it!" shouted the man.

Lyle snapped the lid shut. The camera suddenly jolted, as if Ronnie had lost his balance.

"What was that?" said the Bald Man.

The screen went dark as the video ended abruptly.

"Oh my God," said Brooke, sitting down. "Oh my God."

"That's the leader of the men who were chasing me in California," said Will. "Do any of you recognize him?"

They all shook their heads.

"Damn, Ronnie," said Nick.

"That's why they took him," said Elise grimly. "They knew what he'd seen."

"But not before he had time to bury that video in all of this and leave it behind," said Ajay.

"Lyle has that same footlocker in his room," said Nick. "And, dude, the canisters are *full*."

"I want to check something else," said Ajay. He reversed the video to the moment when the Bald Man set the metallic box on the table. "There was some writing on that box. Isolate and enhance."

The image tightened and clarified around the silver box on the table. It was about the size of a legal pad. The writing on its surface was engraved in the metal:

THE PALADIN PROPHECY

MCMXC IV

"What's the Paladin Prophecy?" Ajay wondered aloud.

"Those other letters don't spell anything," said Nick.

"Those are Roman *numerals*," said Elise.

"Were the Romans all stupid or what? Why didn't they just use *numbers*?"

Elise and Ajay looked at each other and shook their heads.

"Nineteen ninety," said Brooke, looking at the screen. "And four."

"Does this mean anything to anyone?" asked Ajay.

Everyone shook their head.

"Bring your tablet, Ajay, and everybody grab a flashlight," said Will, determined. "We're going to track down Lyle, right now, show him this, and nail him to a wall until he tells us what he knows."

Lights had gone out all over the campus. Will noticed a cascade of white falling outside the windows, glowing in the pale light of the moon. Using flashlights, the five roommates made their way down to the first floor. A lot of students were poking around, buzzing about the blackout and the coming storm. There was just enough confusion for them to slip unnoticed into the outer room of Lyle's suite.

Will listened at the door but heard nothing. Nick picked the lock again and moved inside. Lyle's rooms were empty, and the vile smell was gone. Will quickly moved to the open closet door and searched inside.

"Everything's cleared out," said Will.

"So's Lyle," said Nick.

THE MEDICAL CENTER

As they reentered the pod, the black phone by the fireplace in the great room shattered the silence. Ajay walked over and answered.

Ajay listened, then turned to Will. "For you."

Will took the receiver. "This is Will."

"Hold, please, for Headmaster Rourke," said an operator.

Will mouthed "Rourke" to the others. Then Rourke came on the line: "Good evening, Will."

"Hello, sir."

"The storm took out a relay station to the east of us," said Rourke. "The whole area's lost power. We'll have emergency generators up shortly. But that's not why I'm calling."

"Okay."

"I got a call a short time ago from your parents. Don't be alarmed, Will, nothing to worry about. They're flying in for a visit tomorrow afternoon."

"Really." *So Brooke was right. They know I'm here now.* Will's stomach flipped. "That's great news."

"They asked if you could clear your schedule."

Will swallowed hard. "I will. Thanks for letting me know, sir."

"How's the rest of your week gone? Enjoying yourself so far?"

"Yes," said Will, looking at his roommates. "Never a dull moment."

Will hung up and told the others just as the lights came back on.

"What are you going to do?" asked Elise.

"I don't know," said Will. "I want to think about all of this before we do anything. It's late. Let's get some rest."

"Everyone give me your tablets first," said Ajay. "I want to run tests and make sure they're all clean."

"I'll stand sentry," said Nick. "In case Lyle or any of his goons try anything."

With tired farewells, the roommates headed for their separate rooms. Will tossed in bed for an hour. His parents were on their way, and he had to assume they were bringing the Black Caps with them. What did these people want? Dave had talked about a war between the Hierarchy and the Never-Was, but what did it have to do with him?

The words they'd seen on that silver box kept kicking around in his mind: The Paladin Prophecy. They didn't know what it meant, but it seemed to be more evidence that somehow the school or some faction within it was involved.

Will managed a couple of hours' sleep, then relieved Nick at the door just after dawn on Saturday morning. Will was getting ready to leave for the medical center just before eight, when Brooke came out of her room, dressed for cold weather, crisp and purposeful.

"I'm going to the library," she said. "Walk out with me?"

"Did you sleep?" asked Will as they headed out of the pod and down the stairs.

"Are you kidding? After all that? Where are you headed?"

"Kujawa's going to run some tests at the medical center," said Will. "Shouldn't take long."

"At least one of us should go with you," she said.

"I'll be okay. It's Kujawa and Robbins. I trust them."

"I do, too," she said. "But I still want security to take you over there. Have you thought about what you're going to tell them about Lyle?"

"Not a lot," said Will. "Enough to get them looking for him."

"Will, be careful," she said, putting a hand on his arm. "I trust Robbins, too, but it's impossible to know who might be part of this."

"Agreed," said Will. "Do you know anything about who owns the Center?"

"A private trust called the Greenwood Foundation," she said. "Named for the founder, Thomas Greenwood."

"Who runs it?" asked Will.

"A board of directors—CEOs, philanthropists. All high-powered alumni. My dad used to be on it. I can't believe they'd be involved in anything like this." She chewed on her lip. "What are we going to do when your so-called parents get here?"

She said we. "I haven't worked that out yet," said Will.

"I have," she said. "You're going to introduce me to them. I'll be your date at dinner. You're not spending one second alone with those people."

"My *date*?"

"That's right. And if they try anything, I'll scream. Unless you'd rather blow them off and go bowling." She smiled, and Will's heart skipped a beat.

"Fake date or real date?" he asked.

"As real as US Steel."

"Milk shake and a movie after?" asked Will.

"Not unless we can sit in the back row and make out." They stopped at the bottom of the stairs and looked at each other. Brooke stood on tiptoe and kissed him. "Moving too fast for you?"

"You've never seen me run," he said.

"Run, Will, run."

Brooke opened the door and they walked out into a world of white. Over a foot of snow had fallen, and it continued to tumble down in a howling wind, blowing and swirling into massive drifts around the buildings.

So this is what snow looks like.

Brooke waved down a Bobcat with a snowplow attachment and spoke to the driver, who threw back the hood of his parka. It was Eloni, the head of security.

"Eloni will drive you over," said Brooke. "Page me when you're done. I'll be digging for deep background on the Knights and the Crag. That's spy lingo, by the way. I met mucho CIA types when Dad was posted overseas." She punched him on the shoulder. "Later, West."

Will climbed into the Bobcat beside Eloni. He couldn't stop grinning, which made the big Samoan laugh.

"Medical center?" Eloni asked.

Will nodded and they plowed forward, the blade cutting through drifts like the prow of a ship.

Kujawa was waiting for Will when he stepped off the elevator on the medical center's third floor. He walked Will into a medical suite with a small locker room and asked him to change into running gear. Dr. Robbins knocked and came in as he was finishing up.

"You look tired," she said.

"I'm okay," said Will.

"I heard your parents are flying in today," she said.

"So did I," said Will.

"I was told they're coming in by private plane," said Robbins, watching him closely. "Could they afford something like that, Will?"

Will shook his head, trying to keep his anxiety hidden.

"Will, I've been thinking about how you could have scored so high on that test when you weren't trying to," she said, moving closer to him. "I think that maybe, unconsciously, you were trying very hard indeed. Because you knew something was wrong in your life and that you needed someone, anyone, to notice you."

Hearing her say it, Will had to admit to himself that might be true, which made him feel a whole lot worse.

Robbins lowered her voice. "I can act as your advocate here, if you need me to, but to do that I need you to level with me."

"Okay," he said.

"Has something gone wrong between you and your parents?"

Will chose his words carefully. "You could say that."

She took a step closer. "Do you think there's any possibility that they're coming here to *remove* you from school?"

415

Will looked into her eyes, wanting to believe she could help but afraid to say too much. "Yes. I think that's possible."

"If that turns out to be the case . . . do you want to leave with them?"

"No. I want to stay."

She studied him. "Then I want *you* to know that I'll do whatever I can," she said.

Dr. Kujawa stuck his head in. "We're ready for you, Will."

Will and Robbins followed him into a lab filled with exercise machines and an array of large and complicated medical devices. At the far end of the room, a panoramic picture window looked out over the snowy campus. Will sat on a bench and stared at the wintry landscape as Kujawa attached dozens of self-adhesive electrodes and polymer dots to points on his torso, neck, and forehead.

"These are wireless sensors that transmit data to computers on the other side of that window," said Kujawa, pointing to a small interior window. "We'll observe you from the control booth and go over the results with you afterward."

Kujawa led Will to a high-tech treadmill and fitted him with a blue plastic mouthpiece that looked like a horizontal snorkel, connected by a long tube to a nearby computer deck.

"Wear this for me while you run," said Kujawa. "We're going to measure a couple of functions, like the efficiency of your oxygen consumption. The mouthpiece lets you breathe normally. You won't even know it's there."

"Sounds easy enough," said Will.

Kujawa clipped a pulse monitor to the tip of Will's right index finger and put a blood pressure cuff on his arm. He swabbed the back of Will's right hand and painlessly inserted a small catheter, which he fastened down with tape.

"We'll also take a few blood samples to grab real-time oxygen uptake." He connected the catheter to another long tube, which split to a couple of different machines. Will saw a small stream of red run from his hand down into the tube.

Kujawa set some controls on the treadmill. "Hop on. The belt will adjust to your pace so don't hold back."

Kujawa and Robbins retired to the control room and through the window signaled him to begin. Will started walking and the treadmill belt rolled with him. He quickly advanced to a trot and then a steady run. In spite of the mouthpiece and electrodes, he found his rhythm, breathing easily. He let go of his worries and, as Kujawa had requested, held nothing back. The belt underfoot whined as he increased his pace, his legs pistoning faster and faster. Will felt eerily weightless, nothing but green lights ahead of him.

Will glanced into the control room and saw that his friendly genetics teacher, Dr. Rulan Geist, had joined Kujawa and Robbins. Kujawa was showing him a readout.

Good. Maybe he can give me some answers. Let's show him maximum speed.

Will pressed a button that tilted the nose of the treadmill bed upward until he was running on a six-degree incline. He pushed faster and faster, until the treadmill's gears and motors groaned in protest. When he saw sparks rising from the belt and smelled burning rubber, Will slammed a red emergency stop button on the arm. The belt screeched to a halt, and before he could tell his legs to stop, Will sprinted into midair off the raised front end. He landed on his feet, turned, and saw flames spreading from under the elevated bed.

Kujawa rushed into the room, grabbed a fire extinguisher, and doused the fire. Will saw Robbins staring at him from the doorway, curiosity mixed with serious worry. Dr. Geist was still in the observation room, looking dumbfounded as he stared at the monitors.

Will took out the mouthpiece as Kujawa gently removed the catheter from his hand. "Uh . . . sorry about that, Doc."

"No, it's all right," said Kujawa, making an effort to stay calm. "You did what I asked you to. Let's move over here."

Kujawa led Will to a large white machine, an open cylinder of molded plastic set on its side. Kujawa operated a control panel, and a flat waist-high platform slid out of the cylinder.

"Lie down here, Will, faceup and your head toward the machine."

"What's this?"

"It's an MRI machine," said Kujawa. "We're going to take some pictures of your brain. This time you don't have to move. In fact, it won't work if you do."

"Good. I don't want to break this one, too."

"Please don't. It's a lot more expensive."

As Will lay down, Dr. Geist rushed in holding a Center tablet, with Robbins trailing behind him. He showed Kujawa and Robbins results from the treadmill test, gushing with excitement.

"This VO-two rate is astonishing," said Geist. "Higher by three basis points than any I've ever seen—hello, Will, forgive me, but this is incredibly impressive. Hematocrit level is low triple figures; that's unprecedented. Watts expended steady at over six hundred but pulse never got above one-fifty—are your leg muscles sore?"

"No, sir."

"I'd venture to say he's not even producing lactic acid," said Geist to Kujawa. "His cellular rate of exchange is a kind of self-cleaning engine."

"Any evidence of PEDs?" asked Robbins.

"No, his blood's pristine," said Geist. "Glucose levels are steady without spikes. He's generating EPO in response to stress in an extraordinarily efficient homeostatic loop." Geist again remembered Will was lying there. "I'm sorry, Will, this must all sound like gobbledygook to you."

"What does it mean?" asked Will.

"It means you have remarkable aerobic and metabolic capabilities," said Kujawa.

"To say the least," said Geist, shaking his head at the numbers. "This is marvelous. Absolutely marvelous."

"Do we have a plausible explanation?" asked Robbins, concerned.

"It's awfully early to speculate," said Geist, deferring to Kujawa.

"Maybe the MRI can shed light on that," said Kujawa. "Let's take a look."

Geist smiled, patted Will's shoulder, and walked back to the observation room. Feeling even more unsettled, Will tilted his head back and looked warily into the dark center of the machine as Kujawa entered commands in the control panel.

"How does this work?" asked Will.

"An MRI machine immerses you in a harmless magnetic field, which we flood with radio waves pitched at different frequencies. They're loud, by necessity, so wear these." Kujawa handed Will heavily padded headphones, equipped with an adjustable bayonet mic. "Close your eyes, lie completely still for ten minutes, and we'll have a picture of your entire nervous system."

Kujawa headed for the observation room. Dr. Robbins stepped forward and took Will's hand; her palm felt smooth, cool, and reassuring.

"Have you ever been in one of these before?" she asked.

Will shook his head.

"Just breathe and relax," she said. "That mic is voice activated. If it feels like too much, let me know and I'll pull the plug."

"Let's get it over with," said Will.

Dr. Robbins squeezed his hand and moved away. Will put on the headphones and settled back. A moment later, the platform slid slowly into the narrow aperture. The headphones muted the motorized whirr. Will kept his eyes closed and tried to stay calm by focusing on his breathing. He felt another jolt when the sled came to a halt, leaving him in muffled silence inside the machine, encased down to his knees in what felt like a plastic coffin.

Kujawa came on the headphones. "Are you all right, Will?"

"I'm okay," he said.

"I'm going to start the sequence," said Kujawa. "Lie as still as you can."

After a short silence, a rhythmic, insistent electronic bass note pounded through the chamber around him, sound waves clanging through Will's skull. While the bursts continued, another sound blended in, a familiar voice hitchhiking inside the gravelly frequency. Then it emerged—clear as sunlight—deep in his brain.

"'Stay calm. Breathe deeply,'" the voice said. "What a load of hog slop. Easy for them to say. They're not the ones packed in there like bloody sardines in a ten-cent tin."

Dave.

TESTED

"Are you're actually here?" asked Will. "Or am I talking to an 'astral projection'?"

"What was that, Will?" asked Dr. Kujawa in his headphones.

"Nothing," said Will in the mic, and then whispered, "What do you want?"

"I left you with a snoot full to cogitate last time," said Dave. "Now that you've had a chance to cleanse the mental palate, you're ready for the rest of it."

Back in the control room, Kujawa, Geist, and Robbins were watching images of Will's brain on a monitor. Dr. Geist pointed to multiple flares of orange and bright red. "He's neurally hyperactive all through the frontal lobe . . . and here in the corpus callosum, both sides are firing in unison. The hemispheres are almost in perfect sync."

"And look at this," said Kujawa, tapping the screen. "His posterior hippocampus is enlarged to nearly twice normal size, and not at the expense of the *anterior*."

422

"What would that mean?" asked Robbins.

"His spatial comprehension must be almost beyond belief," said Geist.

Lillian Robbins cocked an ear to the speakers and listened. "Is he *talking*?"

"When we're finished here," said Geist, "I need to run a full genetic profile."

The MRI machine switched to the next frequency burst, this one long and high-pitched. Will tried to keep his voice as low as possible.

"Go on," said Will.

"Our executive council's been called into emergency session," said Dave. "All hands on deck, round-the-clock discussions—"

"I'm tired of hearing about this, okay?" Will hissed. "Those thugs set some kind of freaky roach motel that burned down my *house* and tried to kill my friend. My parents, or what's left of them, are on their way here right now, in a stolen jet with the feds on their tail. The Black Caps are hooked in with a secret society at the school that's bringing creatures over from the Never-Was, and they killed or kidnapped the kid who was living in my room—"

"Wow," said Dave. "You *have* been busy."

The frequency changed again, clobbering the chamber with sound. With his eyes closed, Will realized he could now see Dave walking around the MRI machine. He even noticed writing in the helicopter patch on the back of his jacket: ATD39Z.

Am I seeing him right through this machine?

But when Will opened his eyes, the only thing in front of him was the white plastic ceiling an inch from his face. Will's heart hammered. He closed his eyes again and tried to ride it out. Dave moved into sight, leaning on the MRI machine.

"That's it, mate, keep breathing," said Dave. "Here's the word: You've been given our highest security clearance, Level Twelve. Cards on the table. You need to know the background on the Other Team."

Will struggled to stay focused. "Okay."

"The Other Team is what we refer to as the Older Root Race," said Dave. "Have a squiz at this."

Dave walked *through* the MRI machine until he was standing right in front of Will. He took out the glass cube with the floating dice. The dice slowed to a halt. A beam of light shot from the die on the left and refracted through the other like a prism. The split beams shot directly into Will's eyes. His mind filled with tumbled, disturbing flashes of the narrative Dave proceeded to tell him.

"They were here eons before humans," said Dave. "They're our distant predecessors. Not ancestors. *Ancestor* implies lineage. They're *not* human, but a different breed altogether. Hence *predecessors*. As in, prior *inhabitants* of Earth."

An older race. Someone else told me something like this recently. Coach Jericho.

"Back in their day," said Dave, "these Old Ones made a thorough bollocks of the premises and ran afoul of the Hierarchy."

"How?"

"They were smart. Wicked smart. They built empires and wonders that make humans' great achievements look like squiggles in a sandbox. And the bigger they dreamed, the further they sailed off course. They lost their moral compass a million miles at sea, which led them into wrong thinking and the development of what we call *aphotic technology*."

"What's *aphotic* mean?"

"Without light," said Dave.

In the flickering light of the dice, Will saw strobing images of vast laboratories filled with towering slabs of unfathomable machinery, manned by huge, shadowy inhuman figures.

"That's when they stuck their skizzers in where they shouldn't have mucked about. With their infernal tinkering, they abused the primal tool kit and brought all manner of unnatural creatures into this world that were never meant to be."

Will saw row after row of transparent canisters filled with rank, roiling substances. Suspended in them grew shockingly deformed creatures of all shapes, species, and sizes.

"They twisted the earth's flora and fauna into a catalogue of nightmares: bugs, beasts, bacteria, whatever they could lay their hands on. They tainted codes, perverted blueprints, and made the world a butcher's picnic beyond the end of madness. Unable to stand idly by any longer, and in spite of our eternal hands-off policy to let locals sort things out for themselves, the Hierarchy intervened."

"What happened?" whispered Will

"Suffice it to say, these bad boys did not go quietly."

The visions bombarding Will shifted. Now he looked down on a grim, befouled earth where explosions erupted from a surface rent by titanic storms, earthquakes, and massive tidal waves. A global cataclysm.

"After a period of time referred to as the Great Unpleasantness, we banished the whole rotten horde of them to the confines of an interdimensional holding area. Or, if you will, a prison."

Above a barren arctic landscape, a gigantic shimmering scythe slashed open a hole in the sky, revealing the hellish wasteland Will had glimpsed once before.

"Otherwise known as the Never-Was," said Will.

"Yes," said Dave.

Dark demonic legions driven by a gleaming host of warriors passed through the glowing, fiery portal. When the last of their shadowy masses had gone through, the portal slammed shut and vanished with a finality that made Will's blood run cold.

The Gates of Hell.

"So this lot isn't *from* a different dimension; they're from *here*. They're now *in* a different dimension, very much against their will. Most of their misbegotten handiwork went with them, but we missed a few lurking in dark corners. When a new apex species emerged from the primordial kettle, the *human* race, those last, fugitive remnants became the monsters of all our early myths and legends."

More images appeared, mythical creatures of land, sea, and air terrorizing primitive man: flying serpents, werewolves, deepwater leviathans, a complete zoology of horror.

"Over the last millennium," said Dave, "the Old Ones have been trying to restake their claim on the planet. And they've recruited some of our own—*human* collaborators—to help them."

"The Black Caps," whispered Will. "The Knights."

"The latest in a long line of strong men and women with weak minds," said Dave. "For hundreds of years, the Old Ones have corrupted them with gifts of aphotic technology, ideas and inventions that make them worldly fortunes. That's how they turn them against their own kind. And with every betrayal, the Other Team moves closer to breaking through and regaining control of Earth."

The bright light and visions ended abruptly, withdrawing into the black dice. Dave stuck the cube back in his pocket and walked through the other side of the MRI machine.

"Okay, fine," said Will. "But what do they want with *me*? I'm nobody. I'm just a kid. I have nothing to do with this—"

"That's where you're wrong, mate," said Dave, leaning in. "Turns out they've got a bloody good reason that was in front of us this whole time."

"Which is . . . ?"

"You're one of us," said Dave. "What we call an Initiate. A member of the Hierarchy."

Will's mind froze. He couldn't even respond.

"Think about it, Will. All those nasty bits sent across to take you out, all this relentless pursuit. There's big doings in store for you before you're home and hosed, my friend."

"That's why you're here? To protect me because I'm an . . . an . . ."

"*Initiate,*" said Dave. "And the baddies know that once you're in training, as your case officer I can only intervene a limited number of times—"

"Training? What training? I haven't started any *training*—"

"Don't be thick, mate. The Hierarchy doesn't hand out Level Twelve security clearances like raffle tickets. You've started whether you know it or not—"

"Don't I have any say in this?"

"Not anymore," said Dave. "And as an Initiate, there's two

427

rules you need to mind. One, you're now bound by a strict confidentiality agreement. Don't even tell your pals about the Hierarchy, and beyond them, I wouldn't trust another living soul at this point."

Will glimpsed a flash of the avenging angel in Dave's eye. "What's the second rule?"

"Stay alive," said Dave. "During your probationary period, I'm allowed to save your bacon nine times. And since we're nearly halfway through your allocation, you'd best learn how to look after yourself, and fast."

"But we're not 'nearly halfway,'" Will protested. "We're only at *three;* that's a *third* of the way—"

"Not anymore." Dave held up four fingers and drew his long hybrid sidearm from its shoulder holster.

The lights went out.

BATTLEFIELD CONDITIONS

The computers and monitors in the lab and observation room went down with a dying thump. Kujawa hammered on the keyboard of his control panel.

"Another power failure?" asked Dr. Geist.

"Apparently so," said Kujawa.

"Is everything backed up? We can't lose this data."

Robbins spoke into the mic. "Will? Will, can you hear me?"

Will opened his eyes. Only a dim gray glow from the window on the far side of the room penetrated the depths of the machine.

His body was pinned above the knees. Will choked back the impulse to flail around. He flexed and extended his feet, gripped the edges of the sled and dragged himself toward the opening. The pad on the sled bunched up beneath him, making progress nearly impossible. Within seconds he was drenched with sweat.

He heard a door swing open behind him on the other side of

the machine. Not the one to the control room. A door he hadn't noticed before.

Will closed his eyes and called up that grid into his mind's eye. It fanned open and a sensory image of the room appeared all around him. He found the door, leading to a back staircase. He saw a tall, stooped figure standing on the threshold, holding a long tube in its hands. He heard a vacuum seal being broken.

Lyle.

When that familiar nauseating odor reached him, it became much harder to hold on to anything like calm or sanity. A bright light exploded as Dave fired toward the front of the machine. Another beam shot across the room . . .

. . . toward long thin forms skittering across the floor with the sickening patter of a thousand feet. Dave retreated and kept firing, but there were too many, more than a dozen, and they were moving too fast. The things leaped onto the sled, bodies coiling with squishy plops around Will's ankles. He felt vicious rows of serrated teeth all along the length of their moist bodies. Will kicked frantically with his limited range of motion but he couldn't shake them off.

He opened his eyes as they crawled into the cramped cavity of the tube and saw them in the dim light, sliding over his thighs and hips, inching toward his upper body. They looked like three-foot-long flat worms crossed with millipedes, and they were heading for his face.

Will sensed Lyle's image pulse in the darkness beyond the door, sickness, pain, and rage radiating from his malignant form. Will "saw" him draw up and fire a thudding hammer blow from his twisted mind, aimed straight at his. If it landed,

Will knew he'd have no chance; by the time these crawlies choked him, they'd be strangling a senseless shell.

Time slowed to a moment of nuclear focus. Will closed his eyes and searched with his mind for the largest nearby object he could find: Just outside the big picture window, he "saw" what looked like a tall, bare tree. Will hooked into it and yanked it toward him with all he had. There was a bright flash and a tremendous explosion of breaking glass as air pressure in the room plummeted. Wind and frigid cold reached his legs.

"We've got to get him out of there," said Robbins in the darkness of the control room. She felt her way to the door.

At the moment Robbins opened the door from the observation room, a blinding flash of electricity arced across the length of the lab. A dark mass flew out of the storm toward the picture window and crashed through the glass, shattering it. A blast of snow and howling wind knocked Robbins back against the wall. At first she couldn't make sense of this incongruent object thrusting into the room. Then she recognized its shape.

It was a telephone pole.

The shock of the explosion broke Lyle's concentration. His kill-shot dissolved before it reached Will. Lyle turned and scurried down the stairs, but his creatures crawled closer, four of them slithering over Will's chest, closing in on his face. Screaming with super-human effort, Will gripped the sides of the sled and pushed a blank mind picture at the back of the tube behind him. With a wrenching crack, the sled's armature gave way.

The sled shot out of the machine and hurtled across the room. Will rolled off toward the ground, slapping the worms away as he fell. He landed, turned, and saw Dave standing his ground, a still figure in whirling snow. It was snowing *inside*. Dave fanned the hammer of his gun, blasting the last of the worms. They exploded, clots of green acid splattering the sides of the MRI machine.

The lights came back on in the lab, ceiling fixtures swinging in the wind. A telephone pole jutted through the picture window, trailing torn cables like broken puppet strings. Dave was gone.

Will saw Lillian Robbins on the ground, near where the sled had hit the wall, staring at him. Power kicked back into the pole and electrified the loose black cables dangling around it. They arced and danced on the ground, thrashing in Robbins's direction, inches from striking her.

Will scrambled to his feet. Without thinking, he created a mind picture that reached out and grabbed the lines like an unseen hand gripping a cluster of venomous snakes. Manipulating the picture, he coiled the sizzling lines back around the downed pole, where they landed and sparked against a transformer box before shorting out and dying.

Robbins rose to her knees. Geist and Kujawa rushed into the lab and helped her to her feet. All three of them looked at Will. He was shivering in just his running shoes and shorts, thick snow swirling around him. Fried electrodes dropped off his torso like burned buttons.

"Are you . . . all right?" Robbins asked.

"I think so," said Will. "What happened?"

"The power went out and that pole came . . . through the window," said Geist.

"Freak gust of wind," said Kujawa.

"Had to be," said Geist, out of breath. "Macroburst, or a wind shear . . ."

"Some kind of electrical explosion," said Kujawa.

They looked at him, and Will thought, briefly, about telling them, *Well, when I'm about to die, apparently I can move things with my mind.* He turned and saw the rest of the lab, much of it ravaged and smoking from the acidic explosions, including big sections of the MRI machine's shell.

Then he remembered Dave's warning about their confidentiality agreement.

"Rotten luck with the machines today, Doc," said Will.

Kujawa nodded, speechless. No one spoke. Wind whipped around the room, and as his adrenaline subsided, the cold hit Will like an anvil. Kujawa hustled him into an empty ward and wrapped him in blankets while he checked his vitals. Will showed no serious ill effects and warmed quickly, although he felt weak and dizzy. But he knew the reason for that, and he wasn't about to tell them about it.

A crowd gathered outside when the fire department showed up. Will heard them calling for a construction crane to remove the pole from the third floor. Will had just finished dressing when Lillian Robbins came back into the ward.

"I've paged your roommates," said Robbins. "You can leave with them when they get here."

"Okay," said Will, tying his boots.

"Your parents are scheduled to arrive at four," said Robbins, "but the storm's diverted them north to Madison. Mr. McBride will drive them down in time for dinner. I've made a reservation in the faculty dining room. Mr. Rourke will join us as well."

"I'd like to bring Brooke," said Will. "If that's all right."

Robbins scrutinized him. "That would be fine."

Will saw a look on Robbins's face that he'd noticed before. Studying him, quizzical, deep in thought.

"Anything show up on the brain test?" asked Will. "I mean, before the whole lab blew up?"

"I'm not a neurologist. The doctors should go over this with you."

Will felt a cold rush up his spine. "So you did see something."

She studied him again. "Were you talking to yourself, Will?"

"Talking? Absolutely," said Will. "Could you hear me?"

"Not clearly enough to know what you were saying."

"You were right," said Will. "That tube put the zap on my head, so I just kept blabbing, 'You're fine; you're okay; don't think about where you are.'"

"Were any voices . . . talking back to you?" she asked.

Will waited a beat before responding. "Did *you* hear any?"

"I didn't *hear* anything." She frowned and held his eyes. "We *saw* profound levels of activity in an area of your brain often identified with visual, aural, and sometimes even olfactory hallucinations."

"So you heard me yakking nonstop," said Will, trying to defuse her inquiry with a joke, "and thought I was helping a leprechaun look for his Lucky Charms."

Robbins's patience frayed. "Will, we have real cause for concern because you've been under such extraordinary stress. I'm told you've also had conflicts with some other students—"

Hearing that, Will realized how he could tell part of the

story in a way she might be able to understand and respond to. "And I'm the new kid, so they think I'll keep my mouth shut. I should just be happy to be here, right? Well, I won't keep quiet about it any longer."

"About what?"

Careful how you frame this.

"There's a group of students here," said Will. "Seniors. They belong to a kind of club, or secret society, and they goof it up with rituals and masks that make the whole thing seem harmless. They're called the Knights of Charlemagne."

He thought by her reaction that she might have heard the name before.

"But it's *not* harmless," said Will. "It's a cover for abusing younger kids. New kids or weaker kids or ones who don't fit in, and this goes way beyond bullying. They single these kids out and terrorize them."

"If this is true," asked Robbins, "why haven't I heard about it before?"

"Because they're smart about who they target," said Will. "Because they shut them up with threats. The kids they go after are petrified. And I know for a fact one of them was Ronnie Murso. They might even have something to do with his disappearance."

That lit an angry fire in Robbins's eyes, but she worked to keep a handle on it. "I'll take this straight to the headmaster. Do you have any names of the people responsible?"

"Lyle Ogilvy," said Will.

"Anyone else?"

"Not that I'm sure about. But you can definitely start with him."

Robbins kept quiet, calculating. "Do your roommates know about this?"

#45: COOPERATE WITH THE AUTHORITIES. BUT DON'T NAME FRIENDS.

Will heard voices in the hallway. It sounded like it might be Ajay and Nick. "I don't want to get anybody else involved."

"Dude, check out the freakin' pole in the lab! That's awesome!"

Yep, Nick.

"I'll accept that answer on one condition," said Robbins coldly. "Your parents will be staying as Mr. Rourke's guests at Stone House. Take the rest of the day to collect your thoughts about what you've just told me. You're going to give me every last detail you know about this by tonight. A complete and thorough account—"

"But—"

"Or I'll have no choice but to immediately expel you from the Center. You'll leave tomorrow. With your parents. For good."

She stared straight at him, her violet eyes hard and unwavering. She wasn't bluffing.

INSTANT MESSAGE

Robbins left the ward and moments later Nick and Ajay trundled in, regarding Will with more than a little awe.

"So are the rumors true, Will?" asked Ajay. "They're saying you nearly got hit by that flying telephone pole!"

"Well, let's just say I was in the room at the time," said Will.

"Dude, no way, that had to be *ill*," said Nick, giving Will a fist bump.

"I'll tell you later," said Will quietly, leading them out the door. "I told Robbins we'd meet her in the lobby. I want to look for something first."

Will led them through the lab where the rescue crews were working and snuck out the door that led to the back stairs. They went down the empty, echoing stairwell to the second floor.

"What are we looking for?" asked Ajay.

"Evidence," said Will.

"Of what?" asked Nick.

Will opened a utility closet, flicked on a light, and started searching. There were brooms, mops, and cleaning supplies on shelves. Stashed in a recycling bin, Will found what he was looking for: a long black mesh metal box the size of a baguette.

"Lyle tried to kill me," said Will. He used a rag to lift out the box. "With what was in *this*."

"Dude, oh my God . . . Lyle sicced his *ferrets* on you?!"

"Not ferrets," said Will. "Worms, crossed with centipedes as long as this box, that bled acid. They crawled up my body when I was in the MRI machine."

"I may vomit," said Ajay, leaning against a wall.

"Did anybody else see 'em?" asked Nick.

"No. Not a word to anybody," said Will as he slipped the box into a plastic trash bag. Nick slung it over his shoulder as they hurried down to the lobby.

They found Robbins huddled near the front doors with Eloni and a woman who looked like his female twin. Eloni introduced her as his cousin Tika.

"Eloni will drive you back to Greenwood," said Robbins. "I want you in your quarters for the rest of the day, Will. I'll pick you up myself once your parents arrive. Call me immediately if anything else occurs to you." She gave Will one last stern look.

The boys followed Eloni and Tika out to a dark blue Ford Flex, parked and idling outside. Snow was still falling heavily. They climbed in and Eloni took the wheel. No one spoke on the ride to Greenwood Hall. They parked in front; Eloni and Tika walked them inside.

Eloni stopped and knocked on Lyle's door; Nick and Will exchanged an anxious look. When there was no answer, Eloni gave Tika an order in their native language. She went inside and opened the inner door. A moment later she came back and shook her head.

"Stay here," said Eloni to her, and then to the boys, in a no-messing-around voice, he said, "Upstairs. Now."

"You looking for Lyle, Eloni?" asked Nick.

"You could say that," he said.

Once on the third floor, he followed them into the pod and checked each bedroom. Brooke's and Elise's rooms were empty.

"I'll be just outside if you need me," said Eloni, heading for the door. He closed the door, and his heavy footsteps padded into the hall.

"So the school's put out an APB on Lyle?" asked Nick.

"I said just enough to get them interested," said Will.

Ajay put an eye to the peephole and saw Eloni outside, arms folded, standing guard. "He's planted," said Ajay. "Like a potted palm."

"We need to work fast," said Will. "Have you seen Brooke or Elise?"

"Not since this morning," said Nick.

"Robbins said she paged them when she called you guys, so they're probably on their way. Try them again, Nick, just to be sure."

Nick picked up the phone and asked the operator to page both girls.

"Ajay, is it safe to use our tablets?" asked Will.

"As safe as I can make them. I've got something else to show you as well."

"Meet in your room," said Will, heading for his. "Two minutes."

As Will entered, his tablet turned on. His syn-app stood on-screen, waiting. He looked more lifelike now, fleshed out with detail, and even more unsettling.

"Is everything all right, Will?" asked his syn-app.

He even sounds more like me. He must be recording and sampling my voice.

"Yes," said Will. "I want you to look for photographs of ANZAC Special Forces helicopter units that served in Vietnam. Look for a chopper with the call letters Alpha Tango Delta three nine Zebra."

"Are you looking for any person in particular?" asked "Will."

"I'm trying to find out what happened to an old friend," said Will. "His name was Dave Gunner."

"I'm on it," said the syn-app. "You have a video message from Nando."

The syn-app opened a video of Nando in his taxi, speaking into the lens of his camera phone. "Wills. Had a badass nightmare about bugs last night, but aside from that I'm okay. Listen, we ran this down on that National Scholastic Whatever Program." In his other hand, Nando held a BlackBerry. He read from it: "Corporate HQ in DC. Branch offices: LA, New York, Miami, Chi-Town, the ATL, and Denver. All in federal buildings, so it has some kind of relationship with government. But it's a nonprofit, privately owned by something called the Greenwood Foundation. Catch you later. Peace."

Will couldn't move for a moment. "The Greenwood Foundation," he repeated as it sank in.

"Yes, Will?" asked his syn-app.

"The Greenwood Foundation is the trust that runs the Center," said Will.

"That's correct," said his syn-app.

Will picked up his tablet and hurried to Ajay's room. Ajay was standing over something at his desk. Nick was on the phone.

"Brooke and Elise still haven't checked in," said Nick, hanging up. "Elise is on the equestrian team. She usually rides on Saturday afternoon."

"In this weather?" asked Will.

"There's an indoor ring near the stables," said Nick.

"She probably isn't wearing her pager," said Ajay. "I had time for a closer look at your bird, Will." The dismantled pieces were spread out on his desk. "Check out the eyes." Ajay picked up the eyes, twin buttons connected by strands of gold wire to a silver box. He held the intricate apparatus underneath a framed magnifier.

"Two sophisticated lenses," said Ajay, pointing with a stylus, "that, properly synchronized, deliver three-dimensional optics to here." Ajay pointed to the silver box. "A central processor equipped with advanced facial recognition software and a high-powered wireless transmitter. The real mystery is there's no power source. I can't figure out what was driving it, and I've never seen robotics this advanced."

"Aphotic technology," said Will softly.

"What's that?" asked Ajay.

"The name for this, and that gear we saw in Ronnie's video; the Carver and the glowing metal sheet," said Will. "You'd better sit down for a second, guys."

Looking apprehensive, Ajay and Nick sat down. Will took a deep breath.

Make it as simple as possible, and don't mention Dave or the Hierarchy. . . .

"The Black Caps and Knights work for a race of beings called the Other Team," Will said. "The Other Team is originally from here, but they've been trapped in the Never-Was since before humans were on the planet. And they want back in. They created all the monsters we've seen as part of their plan to break out."

Ajay and Nick looked at each other. "Uh, okay," said Nick.

"Speaking of which," said Will, "did you check out the bug from my computer?"

Ajay blinked, then picked up the Altoids tin from his desk and opened it, revealing a thin layer of black goo inside. "I'm afraid it's decomposed," Ajay said. "I've examined what's left and can't find anything that resembles biological DNA."

"That's because these creatures from the Never-Was have a different biology," said Will. "The Other Team needs help from people here, using technology that *they* gave them to bring them over."

"That's where the Caps and Knights come in," said Nick.

"Yes," said Will. "And the truth is, while we've uncovered a lot, in some ways we're only at the beginning of what we need to know."

Ajay's eyes were wide. "So this Other Team wants to break out of the Never-Was . . . in order to do what?"

"To, uh, take over the world," said Will, mumbling slightly. "And in so doing, capture, enslave, and destroy all of humanity."

Ajay and Nick looked at each other again. "How do you know this, Will?" asked Ajay cautiously.

"I have a source on the inside," said Will. "That I can't talk about."

"Although your end-of-the-world scenario strains credulity," said Ajay, swallowing hard, "our faith in you to date has not been misplaced. So I think I speak for both of us—"

"Dude," said Nick firmly, holding out his fist. "Whatever it takes."

Feeling greatly relieved, Will gave them both a fist bump.

Will's syn-app announced, "You have a message from Brooke, Will."

"There she is," said Will. "Ajay, put her on the big screen."

Ajay merged their tablets to his wall screen, and Will told his syn-app to play the message. Brooke appeared in the library, whispering to her tablet camera. "Will, I ran a global search through school histories, yearbooks, and newspapers for anything on the Knights of Charlemagne. I got several hits."

Brooke read from the articles as she browsed through them on her screen.

"The earliest mention of the Knights is in the 1928 yearbook. It was a newly formed social club limited to twelve members per year, all seniors. Their motto was 'Making Better Men for the Benefit of Man.' It doesn't seem that they were involved in anything more sinister than croquet tournaments and amateur productions of Gilbert and Sullivan. In 1937, the Knights appear in a photo with a distinguished visitor, Henry Wallace, then secretary of agriculture under President Franklin Roosevelt. Take a look."

A black-and-white photo came up on-screen, showing that year's twelve-man Knights of Charlemagne group and their guest of honor, Henry Wallace, around a long table in an ornately decorated dining room, raising glasses in a toast to the camera.

"Pause," said Will, and the image froze. Will pointed at one of the students. "I could swear I've seen that kid before."

"How is that possible?" asked Nick. "It's from over seventy years ago."

"I don't know," said Will. "Maybe I saw his picture somewhere. Where was this taken?"

"It looks like the formal dining room," said Ajay. "Strange. A big shot like the secretary of agriculture visits the Center, and no school officials, not even the headmaster, get invited to this dinner?"

"Continue," said Will.

Brooke's message resumed. "This event seems to have been the Knights' high-water mark. There are only a few more mentions of them; by 1941, they disappear completely. It seems that they were disbanded, some kind of disciplinary action, but I can't find any explanation."

"What happened in 1941?" asked Nick.

Ajay paused Brooke's message again. "America entered World War Two," he said. "It also happens to be the year that former secretary of agriculture Henry Wallace became vice president of the United States."

"The guy in the photo became the vice president?" said Nick, wide-eyed. "That's big. I have no idea what it means, but that's huge."

"It's not nothing," said Will.

"Search for Henry Wallace and the Knights *together*," said Ajay to his syn-app.

"That information is not available online," said Ajay's syn-app.

"Which means there *is* some," said Will. "Where do we find it?"

"Probably the Rare Book Archive," Ajay said. "You need a signed request from a teacher to get in." He continued Brooke's message.

"I also found this about the Crag," said Brooke; then she read from a book: "'The castle on the island was built by Ian Lemuel Cornish, a New England munitions manufacturer, who made his fortune during the Civil War . . . and it was later bought by Franklin Greenwood, the second headmaster of the Center, who used it as his personal residence.'"

"Franklin Greenwood," said Ajay. "Son of Thomas, the founder."

"And it's currently owned by Stan Haxley, an alum who's on the board of the Greenwood Foundation. That's all for now. Later," Brooke said, then winked at the camera. The message ended, the screen went blank, and their syn-apps reappeared.

"Get me what you can find on Lyle Ogilvy," Will said to his syn-app.

In seconds, Will's syn-app showed them a color yearbook photo of Lyle Ogilvy as a freshman. He was sallow, pimply, and unattractive but hardly the dark-visaged troll they knew. In his school blazer and tie he looked almost innocent. Vital statistics scrolled alongside the image.

"Ogilvy, Lyle," said Ajay. "Born in Boston, October fourteenth, 1992. The only child of a senior oil company exec and a prominent dermatologist."

"Which one of them went to the Center?" asked Will.

"Dad, class of seventy-four, then Princeton, class of seventy-eight," said Ajay.

Lyle's sophomore picture replaced the last one. He wore a

fake smile and the same outfit but looked older and heavier, a year deeper into a perilous adolescence. The dark circles under his eyes had started to blossom.

"Something's happened to him," said Will, studying the photo closely. "He looks frightened. Let's see his junior year photo."

Another photo appeared over the previous one. Lyle's transformation into the fearsome figure they knew appeared complete. His smile had warped into a sneer, and the fear in his eyes had been replaced by imperious contempt.

"Whatever happened to the bastard just hit critical mass," said Ajay.

"My guess is he's been recruited by the Knights by now," said Will. "And he's probably had a visit from the Bald Man."

A blinking icon of a black telephone mushroomed on-screen, accompanied by an ominous bass note.

"You have an instant message," said Will's syn-app. "Someone wants to speak with you. Would you like to open a conversation screen?"

"Maybe it's Brooke checking in," said Will. "Yes."

The phone icon expanded to a large frame. A signal connected; the image seemed to be from the point of view of an embedded tablet camera, but whatever it was pointed at was so dark no detail appeared. Then the image moved; they saw the surface of a gently shimmering fabric.

Will whispered to Ajay, "Record this."

The fabric swept to the side and a face swooped down to the camera. They saw dark eyes glinting through narrow slits in an armored mask. It was the Paladin who'd chased them through the tunnels.

"Will West," he said in a raspy growl, electronically filtered to disguise the voice. Will gestured for Nick and Ajay to move away from their camera.

"What do you want?" asked Will.

The Paladin tilted his head to the side, disdainful. "Your head. On a stick."

Will swallowed. "You're going to have to come and get it, then."

"I don't think so."

"I know who you are," said Will.

"You don't even know who *you* are," said the Paladin.

Will stared at the screen and listened hard. He heard faint sounds in the background of wherever this was—natural sounds that he subconsciously knew went together—and tried to identify them.

"At least I'm not hiding behind a mask," said Will.

"No. You're just hiding in your room."

"I'm not hiding anywhere. You know where I am."

"We are going to meet . . . and you're going to come to *me*," said the Paladin. "Right now. Alone."

The Paladin stepped to the side. Behind him, deeper back in the middle of the dark room, was Brooke. She was sitting on a plain wooden chair, her ankles tied to its legs with rope, her wrists secured behind her through the slats. She had a blindfold over her eyes and a gag in her mouth. Thick headphones covered her ears. Her whole body was tensed, coiled. She was clearly terrified.

"Son of a *bitch*," said Nick.

Nick stepped toward the screen. Will put both hands out to hold him back.

The Paladin's face swooped back in front of his camera,

obscuring Brooke. "You'll come to me, or there's going to be a lot of *this*."

The Paladin raised a gloved hand; he was holding a black device the size of a cell phone with buttons on it. He stepped aside so that Will could see Brooke again. Then he touched one of the buttons.

Brooke's entire body jerked taut and she cried out, muffled by the gag.

"Stop!" said Will. "Please, don't—"

The Paladin lifted his finger off the button. Brooke gasped for breath.

Will closed his eyes. To keep anger from overwhelming his mind, he focused on the background sounds again. This time it clicked: lapping water, the creak of ropes and wood.

I know where you are.

The Paladin's face filled the frame again. "Come alone, West," he said.

"Where?" asked Will. He felt sweat beading on his forehead.

"If you want to find me, look behind me."

"What's that supposed to mean?" asked Will.

"You have fifteen minutes to figure it out," said the figure. "If you're one second late, if I see that you've brought anyone with you or that you've alerted authorities—and trust me, I'll know—it's going to get a whole lot worse for her."

He pushed the button again; this time Brooke screamed through the gag. The Paladin reached toward the camera and cut off the feed.

"Oh my God, Will," said Ajay. "They must have grabbed her as she was leaving the library."

"I'll kill him. I'll freakin' kill him!" shouted Nick at the screen.

#75: WHEN YOU NEED TO MAKE A QUICK
DECISION, DON'T LET WHAT YOU CAN'T DO
INTERFERE WITH WHAT YOU CAN.

"Calm down," said Will firmly. "That's not going to help her." He set the stopwatch on his phone, counting down from fifteen minutes, and led the others into the great room.

"What can we do?" asked Ajay.

"It's not what we *can* do," said Will. "It's what we're *going* to do. Did you record that?"

"Yes," said Ajay.

"What about Elise? Do you think Lyle got her, too?" asked Nick.

"No," said Will. "He would have played that card. 'If you want to find me, look behind me.' What do you think that means?"

"I have no earthly idea," said Ajay.

"Dudes, it's the statue," said Nick. "Of the Paladin in front of the Barn. I mean, obviously."

"Another frighteningly reasonable conclusion," said Ajay.

"Maybe now you'll stop misunderestimating me," said Nick.

"So the Barn is where Lyle *wants* me to go," said Will. "But that's not where he *is*. Let's move. Nick, you in?"

"Does a duck have a waterproof butt?"

Will looked through the front door peephole at Eloni standing guard outside. "Which window is farthest from the front doors of the building?"

"Yours," said Nick.

#94: YOU CAN FIND MOST OF THE WEAPONS OR
EQUIPMENT YOU'LL EVER NEED AROUND
THE HOUSE.

Ajay and Nick trailed Will out to the kitchen, where he grabbed a couple of items before heading for his room.

"Will, you're not serious about doing as he says," said Ajay.

"What other choice do we have, Ajay?" Will said. "Nick, get some rope."

"I'm on it."

"I strongly advise against this. The situation's far too dangerous—"

"Would you please sack up, Ajay?" said Nick as he hurried to his room. "Or go clutch your pearls and faint someplace else."

"But maybe Eloni could help—"

"Not now he can't," said Will, checking the stopwatch. "There's no time."

Fourteen minutes.

"Will, be reasonable. Lyle's already tried to kill you once today," said Ajay. "We need the help of qualified professionals—"

#61: IF YOU WANT SOMETHING DONE THE RIGHT WAY, DO IT YOURSELF.

"If you want something done the right way, do it yourself," said Will.

He threw open his bedroom window. It was only two o'clock, but it looked like twilight. The temperature had fallen drastically. Will looked down at the three-story drop. Snow continued to fall, piling up around the base of the building.

"We can't help Brooke without you, Ajay," said Will. "What's it going to be?"

When he heard it phrased so bluntly, Ajay put some starch

into his full five feet. "You have my unqualified support. Even if it kills or severely injures me."

"Get your coat," Will said, and then asked him to bring along a few other pieces of equipment.

Will put on his winter gear and pocketed Dave's sunglasses. Nick ran in with two jump ropes, which he knotted together. Will and Nick secured one end of the rope to a leg of Will's bed and dropped the other out the window. Ajay ran back in, pulling on his coat and carrying a small knapsack.

"Here, we can use these," said Ajay, passing out his homemade walkie-talkies. He handed the blue electric brass knuckles to Nick. "These are for you. Push the button with your thumbs to activate the charge, which should be strong enough to take down a Cape buffalo."

"Awesome."

Nick slipped them into his pocket, took two steps back, then launched into a swan dive out the window. He tucked in midair and somersaulted twice. Will and Ajay rushed to the window and saw Nick land in the snowpack, roll, and hop to his feet.

"Why did he even bother getting rope?" asked Ajay.

"For us," said Will. "After you."

Will anchored their end. Ajay grabbed the rope and lowered himself down. When Ajay reached the end of the rope, Nick signaled him to let go. He splashed into a snowdrift. Will rappelled halfway down, untied the second rope from the first, pushed away from the building, and jumped toward Nick and Ajay. They sprawled into another deep drift, scrambled up, and brushed the snow off each other.

451

"Set your watches," said Will. "We need to be in perfect sync."

"Two-oh-eight," said Nick. "Central Standard Chuck Norris Time."

"Check," said Ajay.

"We have twelve minutes," said Will. "Here's how this is going to go."

He explained their assignments. Thirty seconds later, they took off running in three different directions.

THE PALADINS

Will had never run in snow before, and this was deep; in some nooks and hollows it piled up to his knees. Heavier and wetter than it had been earlier, it was the consistency of slick pebbled Styrofoam. His rubber-soled boots squeaked and struggled for stability with every step, costing him 30 percent of his speed. As he calculated time and distance, he realized that how he was running wasn't going to get him where he needed to be in time.

He had to run faster. In the last week, he'd twice reached into his reserves past where he'd thought possible; now he did it again. He ignored the uncertain footing. Stopped caring about his bulky coat and lousy visibility and the cold air searing his lungs. Will accelerated, and like a hydrofoil reaching cruising speed, he lifted above the snow, running on top.

He sped past the quad, across the fields where no tracks preceded him, toward the snow-covered woods. As the eye of the blizzard passed over the Center, the wind stilled, the temperature plummeted, and a cold mist rose from the cooling ground. The snow fell straight down, a blank white curtain dancing all around him. He scanned the tree line ahead, then shot the gap onto the path he was looking for.

The path through the snow-covered trees that Will had seen in his first dream about the Center.

No footprints led to the Barn. The broad plain in front of the building was a pristine field of white. The Barn wasn't visible through the snow and thickening fog until he was less than fifty yards away.

He checked his watch. Three minutes to spare, but he needed to give the others time to get in place. He slowed to a steady trudge. The statue near the front doors materialized through the mist, its head and limbs clumped with snow like icing on a cake. He pulled the hood of the new blue parka tight around his face until only his eyes showed.

Will had guessed there would be a hidden camera so they could verify he'd come by himself. He thought there would be a speaker as well so the Paladin could drop another clue that would lead him inside. Where'd they'd be waiting to spring their trap.

He walked up to the big bronze statue. The cold eyes stared past him. Between them he noticed a small button-sized lens just inside the mask. He waved at it. Then he waved at it again.

"You're alone," said the same warped and filtered voice from the instant message. With a speaker hidden inside the mask as well, it was almost like the statue was speaking.

Nice touch.

He nodded.

"And you're on time," said the Paladin.

He pointed to his watch and gave a thumbs-up. "What now?" he asked.

"Like I said, if you want to find me . . . look behind me."

Behind the statue, the front doors to the Barn swung open. Keeping his head down, he headed for the doors. He reached into the pocket of the blue parka and flicked the button on his walkie-talkie.

"Chuck Norris to Base," he said. "They bought it. I'm headed for a Barn dance. Going in. Over."

If he'd looked behind him, he would have noticed a black carbon-fiber canister, about the size of a thermos, attached to a hole on the heel of the statue's right boot. And he would have seen the head of the statue, with a fingernails-on-a-blackboard screech of wrenching metal, turn to watch him.

Ajay ran full tilt through the stable and into the riding ring, where he found Elise, alone, on her black stallion, working her way around the hunter-jumper course. Ajay waved her down, and when he'd explained—in less than one hyper-articulate minute—what had happened, where they needed to go, and how quickly they needed to get there, Elise held out her hand. Ajay took hold and she pulled him up behind her on the saddle.

"I'm not overly fond of horses," he said, alarmed.

"Too bad for you," said Elise. "Hold on."

Ajay wrapped his arms around Elise's waist—no complaints about that part of the arrangement—as she spurred the horse into a gallop. They soared over the top rail of the ring, back through the stable, then thundered out the open doors into the snow.

Ajay heard a voice crackle on the walkie-talkie in his pocket, but he was too petrified to reach for it.

A dim gray twilight filtered in from the casement windows in the Barn's roof. They'd left the ceiling spots turned off and opened the grandstands, enclosing the practice field on all four sides. He walked between two sections of stands, across the oval running track, and onto the turf infield. The Knights appeared before he reached the center, emerging from gaps all around the grandstands.

There were six of them, wearing black sweats and masks from the locker room trunk: Clown. Devil. Fox. Horse. The tusked Wild Boar. The grinning Jack-o'-Lantern.

He slowed to buy time as the masks tightened the circle around him. They carried black metal police batons made of hard composite steel, with rubberized grips.

He slipped his right hand into the parka's right front pocket, through the loops of Ajay's blue metallic knuckle-duster. In his left hand he gripped the handle of the jump rope, coiled in the other pocket next to the walkie-talkie.

When his six stalkers reached the inside edge of the running track, one of the overhead lights turned on, and the masked Paladin stepped into view behind the closing circle.

"You don't have your bodyguard this time, *West*," said the Paladin in his droning filtered voice.

The walkie-talkie in the parka's left front pocket crackled softly. It was Will. "Base to Chuck: In position. Two masks on the door. Go, dawg."

"Wrong, Chuckles," Nick said to the Paladin. "I'm right here."

Nick dropped the hood and shrugged off Will's blue parka. He raised his right hand, brandishing the knuckles, and assumed his guardian stance, alert and poised. He made eye contact with each of the masks as he turned slowly, whipping the end of the jump rope around in a tight, menacing circle.

"A little bummed at the turnout," said Nick. "Only six? Seriously? No Benjy Franks or George W? And where, oh, where are your funky-fresh lids? I wanted to catch you guys *stylin'*."

The Paladin stopped, then took a step back. The whole group slowed their advance, suddenly uncertain. Will's plan had caught them off guard: *So far, so good*.

The Paladin raised his hand and pointed a Taser at him.

"Let's party," said Nick.

With five minutes left, Will crested the last hill and Lake Waukoma came into view. Veering inland to avoid the shore, he ran under the cover of the tree line, and soon the boathouse appeared. He slowed and his legs sank into the snow as he closed to within fifty yards.

As Will had expected, there were sentries on either side of the shoreside front door. They patrolled a porch that ran along either side of the building to the waterline. Will took out the binoculars Ajay had given him and focused on them.

The one-eyed Pirate and the Pigtailed Girl were guarding the door. Too cold for their oddball hats, they wore black woolen watch caps pulled tight around the tops of their masks.

Will checked the time: less than two minutes. His walkie-talkie clicked on and he heard Nick: "Chuck Norris to Base. They bought it. I'm headed for a Barn dance. Going in. Over."

They'd all be focused on Nick now, for a short while anyway. Will scurried toward the boathouse, then crept down a slope that angled to the shore—the side where they wouldn't expect anyone to approach from: the water.

The snow hadn't yet collected under the eaves by the big lakeside doors. The doors were padlocked on the outside but ended just above the waterline. When he leaned down and looked under them, Will could see hulls of boats in their slips bobbing gently.

Will clicked on his walkie-talkie and spoke softly: "Base to Chuck: In position. Two masks on the door. Go, dawg."

Will peered around the corner and saw a side door.

"Get him!" shouted the Paladin.

All six masked figures ran toward Nick, shouting and raising their batons. The Paladin fired the Taser but Nick was ready for it. He leaned back, arching all the way down until his right hand found the floor, and felt the three darts pass just under his chin. The Paladin dropped the Taser and bolted for the door.

Nick pushed back up and twirled around. He snaked out the length of rope and whipped the handle around the knee of the nearest mask: the Wild Boar, charging at him, as enraged as its namesake. Nick yanked hard and pulled his leg out from under him. The Boar flipped a full 360 in the air, and crash-landed.

Nick dodged the first blow from a baton, turned, and smashed a hard straight right into the face of the Jack-o'-Lantern. His fat pumpkin head imploded; Nick felt the contact points of Ajay's knuckle-duster connect with his face and pushed the button on the bend of the knuckles with his thumb. A burst of forty thousand volts shot through the guy, with a sound like a vulture hitting a gigantic bug zapper.

Pumpkinhead went down and out.

Nick pivoted to narrowly avoid another blow, but a second

baton came in from an awkward angle and cracked him above the left hip. That whole side of his torso went numb. He ignored the pain, whipped the rope back out, and snaked it around the neck of the Horse. The Horse dropped his baton as his hands flew to his throat. Nick reeled him into a head-butt that flattened his long equine nose, then unspooled him toward the Boar, just getting back to his feet, knocking them both to the ground.

Nick heard a whoosh and dropped as a baton sailed past his ear. He rolled to avoid another that skipped off the ground, but a third baton smashed him square flush just below the right knee.

In a minute that is really going to hurt.

He sprang off the ground, landed on the balls of his feet, coiled, and hopped straight into the air as the Clown ran under him. As he came down, Nick twisted his legs around the Clown's neck. He gripped hard with his thighs and punched him five times on top of the head with the knuckle-duster. Fast, like a hammer pounding in a nail. On the final punch Nick pushed off, lifted straight above him, and pushed the button on the knuckles. The Clown crumpled as the current blasted him, out cold before he reached the ground.

Nick half twisted and landed on his feet. A painful throb shot through his knee, and he nearly collapsed. Out of the corner of his eye, he spotted the Boar rushing at him again, aiming low. Nick spun and delivered a roundhouse kick to the Boar's jaw that put him down and out.

The last two, the Devil and Fox, stood nearby, panting with exertion. They looked at their four friends, out cold on the ground, then at each other, and turned to run.

Nick flung the jump rope at them like a bolo. It snared them both around the ankles and sent them flying. Nick backflipped toward them and slammed them into the ground with a foot in each back, knocking out what was left of their wind. They turned, gasping for air, and saw twin fists descending toward their masks.

Nick stood up, looked around at the carnage, took a deep breath, and couldn't resist a little breathless commentary into an imaginary mic: "Hope you enjoyed our main event here at Laughton Field House today. Another impressive outing in the steel cage grudge match for this outstanding young talent. Nick McLeish six . . . masks nothing."

Nick tested his throbbing right knee; it was his only serious injury, but he could already feel it swelling. He'd have a doorknob there soon unless he got ice on it. He hobbled over to pick up his rope and parka. He took a handful of plastic garbage bag ties from the pocket, ready to hog-tie the six losers and rip their masks off.

When he heard heavy footsteps nearby, Nick looked up and was surprised to see the Paladin standing in the shadows of the aisle leading back to the front doors.

"Really, Lyle?" asked Nick. "You decided to stick around after watching your boys get schooled? Now I know you're crazy."

Nick started toward him. The Paladin stepped into the light and Nick realized it wasn't Lyle. Lyle was nowhere near seven feet tall, and Lyle didn't clank when he walked like he weighed two thousand pounds and was made of bronze.

"Farting rabbits," said Nick.

Nick stopped but the Paladin kept coming. It lowered its

head, raised its sword and hatchet, and stomped across the running track, caving in planks with every step.

"No way," said Nick. "No freakin' way."

Nick retreated to a rack of track-and-field equipment. He grabbed a javelin, turned, and hurled it at the Paladin. The spear flew straight and true but clanked harmlessly off the Paladin's chest. The Paladin kept coming. Nick whipped two discuses at him; they shattered on his shoulders like clay skeets. Nick picked up a hammer and chain, whipped it around in a tight circle, and let it fly.

The hammer arced down and caught the Paladin flush in the head with a hollow boom. The Paladin froze. "How'd that taste?" said Nick.

The Paladin shook its head once. Twice. Then continued toward him.

"Okay, dude, that's just not fair," said Nick.

Nick picked up a vaulting pole and ran in the other direction, his injured knee making him gimpier with every stride. As he neared the seats, he planted, pulled back on the pole, rose into the air, and cleared the grandstand. At the top of his arc, he let go of the pole and sailed toward the basketball court. He tried to tuck and roll but his injured leg buckled on impact. When Nick stood back up, his knee refused to take any weight. He hopped across the court, dragging his injured leg behind him.

He heard the Paladin crash into the grandstand he'd just cleared, hacking and slashing through a mass of wood and metal stanchions. Nick fumbled out the walkie-talkie:

"Yo, Chuck Norris to Base," said Nick. "Six masks down,

but the Paladin flew the coop. Could be headed your way. But, uh, there's another Paladin here? Only *this* time—and, dude, I know how freaky this sounds—it really *is* the statue."

No response. Sword and hatchet whirling like thresher blades, the Paladin broke through into Nick's side of the stands. The Paladin spotted Nick and headed toward him, steel boots leaving cracked footprints in the hardwood court.

"Uh, over," said Nick.

Nick shoved the walkie-talkie into his pocket, pushed through the nearest doors, and limped down the long corridor into the depths of the Barn.

Will heard a scuff of footsteps to his right. A third mask, the Ghost, stepped onto the far end of the walkway, heading for the waterline. Will ducked back around the corner.

The Ghost stopped and looked out toward the woods, checking the perimeter. Will focused on the back of his head and pushed a picture at him:

An image of the door near the water, standing open a few inches.

The Ghost turned and hurried to the end of the walkway. He stopped just outside the door. Will heard the Ghost try the knob. It was locked. Will closed his eyes, shuddering with effort, and pushed again:

An image of himself, hiding behind some crates inside the boathouse.

Will heard a key slide into the lock. The knob turned. The door opened and the Ghost stepped inside the boathouse. Will gave him a moment, then hurried around the corner and snuck in behind him.

The boathouse was a lot bigger than it looked from outside.

It consisted of three sprawling, rambling stories above a stone foundation at the waterline. The first two levels were all open flooring and exposed timbers. The only light trickled in from small windows along the sides. Dampness rising off the lake made the dead, still air feel even colder.

The Ghost was looking for him behind some racks packed with sculls and canoes. Will reached for a rowboat suspended just above him on ropes and pulleys. He grabbed the boat and shoved it as hard as he could. The Ghost heard the creak of rope and wood and turned to look, just as the boat swung in. It slammed into his mask. He shuffled his feet for a moment, twirled once, and then dropped to the ground.

Will dragged him behind the racks and stripped off the Ghost's jacket, watch cap, and mask: It was Wendell Duckworth, from the cross-country team. He secured Duckworth's hands behind his back with two plastic garbage bag ties, then put on Duckworth's coat, mask, and watch cap.

Will looked around. Wooden ladders on the walls led to the loft space above. There had to be some enclosed rooms on the top floor above that. From somewhere upstairs, one of the black campus phones rang. He heard footsteps as someone walked to the phone and answered.

Will's walkie-talkie crackled to life. He heard Nick's voice, faintly:

"Yo, Chuck Norris to Base. Six masks down, but the Paladin flew the coop. Could be headed your way. But, uh, there's another Paladin here? Only *this* time—and, dude, I know how freaky this sounds—it really *is* the statue."

Will heard a male voice shout from somewhere near the top of the building: "Everybody upstairs! Get up here now!"

#8: ALWAYS BE PREPARED TO IMPROVISE.

Will climbed one of the ladders to the second floor. Boats and gear filled most of the space. A windowed door led to a small office tucked against the right wall. Straight ahead, an interior staircase led up from the front doors to a landing, then turned and continued to the third floor. The Pigtailed Girl and Pirate who'd been stationed outside hurried in; they spotted Will as they headed up the stairs.

"You heard him," said the Pirate to Will. "Move your ass."

Will fell in behind them. His peripheral vision halved by the edges of the mask, he followed them up a flight of narrow unfinished stairs toward what looked like an attic. They passed through a narrow door at the top of the stairs into a cramped landing. Through an open door ahead, Will caught a glimpse of the dark room they'd seen in the video feed.

"What's going on?" he heard Brooke say from inside the room.

Behind him, Will heard the Paladin's voice, buzzed flat by the electronic filter. "Padraig?"

A moment ago he'd heard Nick say that the Paladin had just left the Barn. *But this was the Paladin's voice behind him.*

"Padraig!"

Then he realized Padraig must be the Ghost's Knights of Charlemagne name.

Will turned, trying to make it seem as if he was responding to the name.

The masked Paladin stood five feet behind him—Nick must have been wrong; he couldn't possibly have gotten here this fast—pointing something at Will.

Unless there was more than one of them—

Will heard a whirring sound as the Paladin fired a Taser. Three darts smacked into Will's chest, and a searing jolt shot through his body as he fell to the floor.

The last thing he saw was the Paladin lifting a black carbon-fiber container about the size of a thermos.

THE STATUE AND THE BEAR

Nick's first bright idea was to try the swimming pool. Two thousand pounds of metal couldn't float or swim, right? *No way.* So he took the first swinging door into the pool area. Motion-activated lights flicked on as he hobbled around to the middle of the far side of the Olympic-sized pool and hunkered down behind the lifeguard stand. A moment later, the overhead fluorescents flicked off.

The only light came through glass panels in a pair of swinging doors to the hallway across the pool. Nick heard the statue's clanking footsteps and saw the Paladin stomp by the first door. Moments later the second door slammed open, the Paladin stepped inside, and the lights flicked on again.

Nick waved to it from the far side of the pool.

The Paladin started around the deep end. Nick countered by moving to the shallow end. The Paladin stopped, Nick stopped. Nick waved again across the pool.

"Can't catch me," said Nick.

The Paladin started back the other way. Nick backtracked

to match him. When they were across the middle of the pool from each other, the Paladin stopped again. So did Nick, who had been trying not to let it see him limp. Nick tucked his hand under his chin and wiggled his fingers at it.

"Marco," said Nick. He stuck his thumbs in his ears, wiggled his fingers again, and said in a high falsetto, "Polo."

This time the Paladin walked straight at him and dropped into the pool. Nick stepped forward and looked down. He'd been right; the thing couldn't float or swim. But it was walking toward him along the bottom of the pool without any trouble.

"Okay, that sucks," said Nick.

He hurried toward the nearest door. The Paladin changed course, tracking Nick's movement, and seconds later stomped up the steps at the shallow end. This time it knocked the door off its hinges as it followed.

Nick limped down the long corridor and pushed through a door marked COACHING STAFF ONLY. He entered a modernized warren of offices and cubbies, videotape study suites, and conference rooms. The hallway lights were on but he didn't see anyone in any of the offices.

A desk light was on in one of the last rooms; Nick hurried to it. The plate on the door read COACH JERICHO. *Of course,* thought Nick. *One dude in the whole building and it has to be* him.

Nick pushed open the door. Lights burning, tablet open, stacks of statistical printouts on the desk. And nobody in the room.

"Crapalicious," said Nick.

Limping back down the hall, Nick failed to look to his right, where, in the kitchenette two glass walls away, Coach Jericho was leaning down into an open fridge.

Nick pushed through the door into the corridor and left

the coaches' complex. When Jericho stood up and closed the fridge, Nick was gone.

But Jericho heard thudding footsteps and turned in time to see the Paladin storming down the hallway outside his office. Without taking his eye off the metal figure, Jericho calmly set his mug down on the counter. With one hand, he reached for the necklace around his throat—a long, yellowed animal incisor attached to a string of rawhide—and with the other removed a stitched leather pouch from his pocket.

Ajay had heard the sporadic updates between Nick and Will from his walkie-talkie during their ride down toward the lake. But he'd never once removed his locked hands from around Elise's waist and had seen little more than a blurred and bouncy side-view landscape rushing past them at horrific speed. He'd wanted to plead with Elise to slow down, but whenever he opened his mouth, the words dribbled away before he could deliver them.

Elise never said a word, leaning into every jump and hurdle, steering them away from deeper drifts, attuned to every nerve and fiber of her mount in ways that made obvious dangers seem weightless. The cold didn't appear to bother her, although she wore only the riding habit she'd had on when Ajay had barged in on her.

She'd taken the shortest route from the stables, thundering straight down Suicide Hill without slowing. That prompted Ajay to shut his eyes and recite every prayer he knew until they reached level ground. As they rounded the lake and drew within sight of the boathouse, Elise finally reined in.

Ajay promptly fell off the back of the saddle into a snowdrift.

"I'm fine," he said. "I'm fine."

Elise tied the stallion's reins around a tree just off the path. She hugged her horse around the neck, whispered words of thanks, and began trudging toward the boathouse. Ajay hopped to his feet and, steering well clear of the horse, wrestled his walkie-talkie out of his pocket as he slogged after her.

"How much time do we have?" she asked him.

"Will should have gone in thirty seconds ago," said Ajay, consulting his watch.

"Then what?"

"He said you'd know what to do."

"Did he?" Elise seemed entertained by the idea. She stopped at the edge of the woods, held up a hand, and Ajay stopped alongside her.

On the porch near the front of the boathouse, they saw two Knights in masks—the Pigtailed Girl and Pirate—look up in response to a voice calling from somewhere above. Both hurried inside.

"What should we do?" Ajay asked.

"Give me one minute," said Elise, starting forward. "Then use your radio."

"And tell them what?" asked Ajay, stumbling after her.

"Tell them to cover their ears."

"Okay. So should I come with you?" he asked.

"Not until you hear something," she said. "Then come fast."

The door from the coaches' complex led to a flight of stairs. Nick followed them down to another door, which opened into a large, utterly dark space. Nick heard water dripping steadily nearby. When he finally found a light switch and fumbled it on, he realized he was in the locker room's showers. Still and echoing, the complex folded back and in and around, a maze of half-walls, off-white tile, and stainless-steel fixtures from another century.

Nick looked down and saw blood discoloring his right pant leg from the knee to his ankle. From the pain shooting up his leg with every step, he realized his injury was a lot worse than he'd realized. He caught the reflection of his face staring back at him from one of the mirrors above the sinks and realized something else:

I'm afraid. I'm actually afraid.

Nick held out his hands and stared at them; they were trembling. He couldn't remember the last time he'd felt this frightened. He had to go all the way back to the night when he was five. The night Pop had told him Mom wasn't ever coming home again.

Well, the hell with this. We're not playing that tune today.

"Damn, Junior," he whispered, getting close to his reflection. "You gonna let that oversized soda can take you out? You got any idea what the deposit's worth on that sucker? You could trade that tin man in for a freakin' *Kia*. Come on now, son, get crack-a-lacking—"

The door at the bottom of the stairs burst open. Nick hopped around the corner into the first row of showers and quietly worked his way back into the maze. He settled behind a freestanding tiled wall as he heard the Paladin stalk into the shower room.

Then it stopped. Nick strained his ears for any sound of movement. The leaky showerheads echoing in the empty space around him made it hard to track anything and prompted an even more frightening thought:

What if this steel juggernaut has a stealth mode?

Nick leaned back against the wall on one leg and shifted his gaze from side to side to keep an eye on both approaches.

Plink. Plink. Plink.

One of the Paladin's fists punched through the wall to the right of Nick's arm. Its other fist slammed through the wall and grabbed Nick's left arm, digging into his flesh like a vise. Then the Paladin reached across and wrapped its arms around him, squeezing Nick's chest. Nick tried to scream for help but issued only a feeble rasp with the last air from his lungs. After that, it was impossible to take another breath. As Nick struggled, his vision started to fade. . . .

He dimly heard something charge into the showers. It roared, a sound that would have been deafening if Nick hadn't been so close to passing out.

He felt a heavy shock wave as whatever it was smashed into the Paladin on the other side of the wall. The wall shuddered and cracked, tiles spitting out like broken teeth. Air hurtled back into Nick's lungs as the Paladin released him, and he dropped to the wet floor, his wounded knee screaming on contact. Nick shook his head, felt his brain coming back online—

And became aware of a titanic battle raging on the other side of the wall. Clanking, roars, chunking thuds: two monsters brawling in a back alley. The whole room shook from the sound and fury.

What the hell?

Nick crawled to the edge of the wall, dragging his bad leg, and stuck his head around the corner.

The Paladin had its right arm wrapped around the neck of an enormous brown bear. The bear reared back on its hind legs, every bit as tall as or taller than the statue. With its other hand, the Paladin whacked at the bear's back with the hatchet, clots of blood and fur flying with every stroke. The bear worked its vicious jaws around the Paladin's neck like it was chomping on a soup bone. Its gigantic paws ferociously raked the Paladin's back. Sparks flew off its curved yellow talons, each one of them as big as a man's hand.

What the freaking hell?

The Paladin bent its knees, lowered a shoulder, and drove the bear back into the wall. Nick scrambled out of the way as the wall shattered. Both figures crashed into the next stall in an explosion of plaster and tile. The bear rose first, with terrifying speed and agility, swiped at the Paladin, and sent it flying across the room. The Paladin crashed through another wall, obliterating it, landing unseen somewhere near the entrance to the showers.

Nick crawled out of its way as the bear blasted past him. For the briefest moment, he met its eye: black as night, rimmed red with primal fury, but sharp with intelligence behind its bestial rage. Then the bear was past him, galloping away. Nick limped after it toward the ruined entry.

He reached the smashed wall in time to see the Paladin stand from the wreckage. As the bear charged with a thundering roar, the Paladin extended its sword. The bear's momentum carried it straight into the blade, which thrust cleanly through the animal's left shoulder.

472

The bear gave a strangled howl. The Paladin yanked the sword out and the bear staggered back, blood gushing from the wound. The steel knight stepped after it and raised the sword overhead, about to land a killing blow.

Afterward, Nick couldn't explain why he did what he did next. It didn't involve conscious intent so much as blind instinct. He picked up an intact sink from the debris, screamed like an insane Viking berserker, and smashed it as hard as he could into the middle of the Paladin's back.

The porcelain shattered into a thousand pieces. The Paladin didn't react; the impact hadn't moved it more than a quarter of an inch.

But Nick had regained its attention. The statue turned and looked down at him, and its cold steel eyes seemed to recognize its original prey.

It swung the sword at him. Nick dodged back as the blade blasted tiles and furrowed into the concrete foundation. He took another step back, then another, and the Paladin followed him. Looking beyond it, Nick saw the bear limp around a corner and disappear into the darkness.

Nick didn't have a Plan B, but hey, if he bought it now, at least he'd go down fighting. No quit, no white flag. That had to count for something. And he'd saved the bear. That seemed important, in the moment.

Nick hobbled back a few more steps, out of the showers and into the locker room. The Paladin kept coming. Then Nick's back jammed into the metal countertop in front of the equipment cage.

Nick's last resolve collapsed, too spent and broken down to make another move.

"Okay," said Nick. "Okay." He tapped his heart twice and held up his right hand. "Love you, Pops."

The Paladin stopped right in front of him. Studied him. Sword in one hand, hatchet in the other. Then it raised them both. Nick closed his eyes.

Nothing happened. Except that Nick felt a weird little tickle around his back and arms.

He heard a sound and thought of the waves off Marblehead in the middle of a nor'easter that he'd seen once with his dad. He'd never forgotten that deep, rumbling ocean drumbeat. That same sound was coming from somewhere behind him now, rushing at him like one of those massive gray combers.

He opened his eyes.

The Paladin stood frozen in place, weapons raised above him just as Nick had last seen it. But it was struggling fiercely, almost imperceptibly, in the grip of what looked like thousands of tendrils shooting out from behind Nick.

Nick dropped to the floor and dragged himself off to the side, then turned to look.

Thin ropy strands of what looked like putty-colored string wriggled through the painted white cage, through every small diamond-shaped gap across the whole broad face of its middle section. Tendrils extending out and wrapping around every square inch of the statue. They moved in concert, like a nest of a thousand snakes. Nick watched in amazement as they wove themselves around the Paladin until it was completely covered and gradually, finally, helplessly unable to budge.

Nick looked past the tendrils into the darkness behind the cage. He got an impression of a huge, indistinct quivery mass pressed against the other side of the steel and he knew that ocean roar was issuing from this thing. Something in the middle of it glowed the color of blood.

Like an eye. Like the eye of some giant freakin' octopus.

The metal of the statue groaned as the tendrils squeezed relentlessly tighter. Then something yielded inside it with a sound that reminded Nick of a breaking bass guitar string. All at once, the tendrils released the statue and retreated through the air, waving gently like sea grass.

The sword and hatchet dropped to the ground. Something soft and black dropped out of the Paladin's right heel and melted to ooze on the floor. The statue cracked and shattered, crumpling to the ground in a dozen pieces.

Nick felt wooziness wash through him and knew he was about to black out. He watched, mesmerized, as the mass of wandering tendrils lifted something down to him, but he didn't feel afraid. He realized what it was and knew what it was for and struggled to stay awake long enough to use it.

The tendrils gently held the receiver of the equipment cage's black phone against his ear. As he watched, another cluster of tendrils flowed around the base of the phone and pressed the C in the center of the enamel button.

Nick heard the operator answer.

"Dr. Robbins, please," he said, shocked at how calm he sounded.

While he waited for the operator to find her, Nick's eyes drifted to the gate in the steel cage just to the side of the counter.

Bizarre. I never noticed that before.

The lock is on the outside.

THE BOATHOUSE

The foul smell brought him around, then voices getting gradually louder, as if he were emerging from a tunnel.

"What should we do with him?" someone asked.

"Wait," said the filtered voice of the Paladin. "Wait for it to imprint on him. It works better that way."

Will was careful not to move so they wouldn't know he'd come around. He was lying on his side on the wood plank floor of the boathouse attic. They'd secured his wrists behind his back with one of his own plastic ties and connected them to his ankles; his legs were bent back uncomfortably. His whole body ached from the Taser charge. His mask had slipped, covering his eyes so he couldn't see a thing.

He summoned his sensory grid. Two Knights stood over him along with the tall, stooped figure of the Paladin. Brooke was in the next room, still bound to a chair. The horrible smell was coming from a thermos-sized black container resting on the floor less than a foot from Will's face.

Will felt energy flowing from the vile thing moving inside

the container and knew it was a Ride Along, somehow "tuning" into him, getting ready to merge. He moved his hand down a few inches to the Swiss Army knife he'd tucked into the back of his boot.

"What about her?" asked one of the masks.

"She's going to watch," said the Paladin. "One last chance to come to her senses, or she'll get one, too. Bring her in before I open it."

Will heard boots scuffle into the next room. He flipped the knife into position between both hands, flicked open a blade, and with as little motion as possible started sawing at the ties. The plastic started giving way; he needed ten more seconds—

Then a voice slid into his thoughts: "Are you upstairs?"

Elise. At first it made no sense. Then it made all the sense in the world.

Will tossed out the net of his senses and let it filter down through the building until he found her one floor below, just inside the front door.

"Yes," he answered.

Will heard the Knights head back his way, dragging Brooke with them.

The first tie snapped under the blade. He moved to the second—

"Stand back while I break the seal," said the Paladin. He reached down to open the black canister. The creature inside rustled in anticipation.

Will heard footsteps running up the stairs: Elise charging hard. He could see her shape flowing through space, growing brighter and stronger, filling with some kind of vibrant power.

The walkie-talkie in Will's pocket crackled, and he heard Ajay's voice, low and urgent: "Will. Cover your ears."

Two of the Knights rushed to the stairs: "Who's there?" Another reacted to the walkie-talkie: "What was that?"

Will cut the final tie, clamped his hands to his ears, and called out, "Brooke, cover your ears!"

A wave of energy burst through the doorway. Will's first impression: a single note encompassing every known frequency, above and below the range of human hearing. Then the note exploded throughout the enclosed attic space like a sonic boom. Even with his hands pressed tightly against his ears, Will felt as if a howitzer had gone off beside his head.

The windows blew out, the planks beneath him rippled, and at the center of this gash in the surface of things he saw Elise standing at the top of the stairs, jaws wide open, arms spread, palms up, her body a field of wild energy, the epicenter of this concussive shock wave.

And it *all* made sense to him: Elise had talents, too. And she was *Awake*.

Crouching near the porch, Ajay had waited exactly a minute, like Elise had told him to, his eyes glued to his watch. "Will. Cover your ears," he said into his walkie-talkie.

He'd taken two steps forward before it occurred to him: *Oh, dear, I should probably cover mine as well.*

He raised his hands to his ears just as all the windows in the boathouse exploded and the whole building shuddered. The blast wave knocked Ajay backward into another snowdrift.

"Mother of mercy," said Ajay.

He wobbled to his feet and staggered onto the porch. He

opened the front door and walked straight into the sill before he course-corrected and made it inside.

"Elise? Will?!"

"Up here!"

It was Will's voice. He sounded miles away. Ajay's ears were ringing louder than at a rock concert. Ajay launched himself at the stairs, weaving from one wall to the other.

"Good grief," said Ajay. "A direct hit to the gyroscope."

As he passed a window in the stairwell, Ajay looked down and saw a snowmobile pull out of a garage and head for the woods. The Paladin was driving. Ajay stumbled through a door at the top of the stairs, where he found Will crouched over Elise, who was unconscious and pale on the floor.

"Is she all right?" asked Ajay, but couldn't hear himself, so he repeated the question, much louder than before.

Will didn't seem to hear him either time. He said something and Ajay saw his lips moving but couldn't hear a word.

"What?!" yelled Ajay, moving closer.

"Use the phone! Call for help!"

"Okay! Where's Brooke?!"

"In here!"

Will led him to a doorway, where Brooke lay on the floor just inside. Two Knights—Pigtail and Pirate—were slumped crookedly against a wall, out cold. They looked like they'd been hit by a bus. Their masks had been knocked off. They were Hodak's attack dogs from the cross-country team: Durgnatt and Steifel.

A trapdoor in the middle of the room stood open, and a rope descended to the floor below. Will pointed to the rope and said something.

"What?!" shouted Ajay.

Will yelled into Ajay's ear, "There's a phone! In the office downstairs! Kidnapping! Attempted murder!"

Ajay gave the "okay" sign and said, "One of them got away! Snowmobile!"

"I know!" shouted Will. "Lyle!"

Ajay grabbed the rope in the trapdoor and tried a heroic slide to the floor below. He lost his grip halfway down and crash-landed on his rump. After making sure Will hadn't seen him, Ajay lifted the receiver of the black phone in the office. He had to assume an operator answered because he couldn't hear a thing.

"I'm afraid I'm going to have to ask you to yell!" shouted Ajay.

Upstairs, Will gathered Brooke in his arms, carried her into the other room, and laid her gently beside Elise. He covered Elise with his jacket. Will stripped the winter coat off one of the downed Knights and was about to cover Brooke when she opened her big blue eyes.

"Who wins the Drama Club Award now?" he asked.

"You came for me," she said.

"What?!" he said.

She threw her arms around him and closed her eyes and said into his ear, "You came for me."

He heard her that time.

Downstairs, Ajay had to shout to make sure he got the message across. He was pretty sure the operator told him help would be there in fifteen minutes.

"I'm sorry!" he shouted to her. "I feel like I'm inside a

large bell! Actually right inside it! In a bell tower! And it's ringing incessantly!"

Ajay hung up the phone and left the office as Will leaped down through the trapdoor, grabbed the rope, and landed—without falling—right beside him.

"You stay here," said Will. "Take care of the girls, wait for help." Will headed for the door.

"Where are you going?" shouted Ajay, following him.

"I'm going after Lyle."

"On foot? Wait, Elise brought her horse. You could take him."

"I won't need a horse," said Will.

THE CAVES

The snow had slowed to flurries when Will left the boathouse and started after Lyle. The tracks and furrows of the snow-mobile led Will deep into the woods. He dodged and lunged over the unfamiliar ground, training all his senses ahead, call-ing on his speed to keep pace or narrow Lyle's lead.

Will pulled up his sensory grid, throwing it out ahead to track Lyle, but it felt muddy, imprecise, and he realized that his hearing, stunned by the sonic explosion, played a major role in this ability to "see." He couldn't find Lyle anywhere, and as the ground grew steeper and rockier, he needed more time to pick his path. He left the trees and crossed onto a clear plateau that sloped gradually up toward the ridgeline, where, high above, were the caves he'd noticed the other day.

As he crested the next rise, Will caught a glimpse of Lyle on the snowmobile, moving straight for the ridge. As his hear-ing returned, Will heard a sound like the distant buzzing of a swarm of angry hornets. He thought it must be Lyle's engine, but then he realized it was coming from behind him.

Three more snowmobiles were cutting and plunging through the drifts, approaching from behind him to the east. Three more Knights: Ben Franklin, George Washington, and the Wolf. All three masks had rifles strapped across their backs. They were less than a hundred yards away.

Will would reach the base of the ridge in another minute. The snowmobiles weren't gaining on him, but it occurred to Will that catching him might not be their plan. Maybe they wanted to herd him this way and flush him into the open where they could stop, sit back at range, and pick him off with their rifles.

But if the situation escalated to life-threatening, Will knew his insurance policy would kick in. Dave hadn't let him down yet, four times without fail. He could count on his angel riding to the rescue. Couldn't he?

Will hopped over a line of boulders and glanced at his watch: seven minutes since he'd left the boathouse. Help should reach his friends within fifteen minutes of Ajay's alert. He just had to keep the Knights occupied until then.

As he neared the escarpment, Will saw Lyle scrambling up a rough path in the face of the rock. Piles of rubble ran along the edge of the path, offering some cover. Will passed Lyle's abandoned snowmobile, struggled through a field of loose, crumbled shale, and reached the bottom of the path. He looked up; he had forty yards to climb, with two switchbacks, to reach the ridge. Will ducked behind a rock and looked back.

The other snowmobiles had stopped in a cluster, fifty yards back. The drivers, already dismounted, rifles cradled in their arms, were walking toward the bottom of the ridge.

If they plan to shoot me, this would be the place. And if I want

my friends to figure out where the hell I am, a few gunshots ring-
ing out in this cold clear air should do the trick.

Will took a deep breath and sprinted straight up the gradi-ent. Something kicked off a rock three feet to his right before he heard the report of the rifle. Another shot ricocheted to his left, and a third hit just behind him. Will dropped behind a low cluster of rocks, about halfway up the path.

"Any time, Dave," he grunted. "Now would be really good."

Will looked up and saw Lyle pulling himself over the top onto the ridge. As Will looked back, a fourth shot kicked off the rocks just in front of him. Will launched himself up the path, pulling with his hands, driving hard with his legs, bursting out of hiding so quickly that the next few shots landed well behind him. As he turned the final switchback, the last ten feet to the top left him completely exposed, so he kept pushing and grab-bing and pulling until—

He leaped for the top of the ridge, scrabbled over, and rolled away from it as three shots in a tight pattern zipped just above him. One clipped the shoulder of his down vest and feathers flew into the air.

Will lay still, gasping for breath, cradled in snow as the rifles' sharp reports echoed off the rocks. He raised his head just enough to look around for Lyle. The ridge, snow laden and only thirty feet across at its widest, ran off in both direc-tions until it curved and disappeared. Another sheer rock wall, unscalable, rose straight ahead of him.

Lyle was nowhere to be seen. The mouth of the largest cave, taller than he was, opened in the wall straight ahead. Two slightly smaller caves cut in on either side of it.

Which cave is he in?

Will peered back over the ridge. The three riflemen had made no move to follow him. Will looked at his watch: fifteen minutes. *Good.* The cavalry should have reached the boathouse and connected with Ajay, and if they'd heard the shots, they might already be on their way.

But how quickly would they be able to find him?

Will crept toward the caves. The Paladin mask lay in the snow outside the central cave. Will took out his Swiss Army knife and unfolded the biggest blade. He peered into the darkness of the central cave. A slight breeze blew from inside, and he smelled something foul in the air. Something old and sour and forbidding.

Then he heard Lyle's voice call out from somewhere deep inside. "I guess you don't know what an *oik* is, West."

Will froze. Lyle's voice echoed and rolled. The caves sounded very deep.

"An *oik* is a clot. A commoner. A lesser being of the lower classes, the kind who *used* to know their place. Visit a mall. Ride a bus. Walk into any public school. They're *infested* with them."

Will stepped into the smaller cave on the left and crouched in the shadows just inside, waiting for his eyes to adjust. He collected two round rocks the size of baseballs and stuck them into the pockets of his vest. He couldn't see Lyle yet, so he closed his eyes, pulled up the grid, and found him:

Thirty yards to the right, in the next chamber. He saw that all the caves were interconnected, a vast warren of chambers and passages honeycombing the entire ridge.

"The problem is you *oiks* don't know your place anymore. Oh, you still want your bread and circuses, your junk food and blood sports. But a steady diet of garbage isn't enough to pacify

485

you now. You think because our culture panders to all your infantile impulses that now you're supposed to have a *voice*. That we should have to *listen* to you."

Will inched forward to the nearest opening in the sandstone. A white-hot glow issued from the chamber to his right.

"You believe you're all so *special*! You couldn't possibly be responsible for your own dead-end lives—you've got too much self-*esteem*. You're all *stars* just waiting to be discovered. Forget self-*discipline* or education or knowing the right people. The world's one big talent show and all you have to do is show up."

Will reached the edge of the passage and peeked around; the ceiling of the adjacent chamber arched up more than thirty feet. It was illuminated by the unnatural light issuing from the hooked steel rod—the Carver—that Lyle held in his hand. He was using the rod to trace a huge circle in the air, nearly complete, over six feet in diameter. Its rough outline burned with blinding intensity.

"We stand for something different here. Eternal verities: honor, values, leadership. Now more than ever. A new breed ready to maintain our traditions. It was all going according to plan until *you* walked in. An *oik* crashing the cocktail party. Well, let me make one thing perfectly clear: *Over my dead body.*"

Lyle finished tracing the circle. An energy field crackled to life around the edges, the air blurred and glimmered, and a portal slowly opened inside the circle. Lyle held up the rod, the glyphs engraved in its handle glowing brightly.

Dave's got my back. With that thought fortifying him, Will gripped one of the rocks in his pocket and stepped forward. "If that's the way you want it, Lyle."

Lyle whipped around, and his wild eyes found Will. "You know what happened to the *last* people who stood in our way? They call themselves *Native* Americans, as if they were here *first*."

"They *were* here first."

"Those pathetic primitives believed these caves led to the underworld," said Lyle. "That their gods used them to pass between here and the spirit realm. They had it all wrong." Lyle held up his hands to the hole, proudly displaying his handiwork. "The only passage here now is to the Old Ones . . . in the Never-Was."

Lyle pointed the rod at Will and a beam of burning white light shot out at him. Will pushed out a thought shield just in time and deflected the beam into a wall, but it nearly knocked him over. Lyle was still stronger, and with that weapon in hand, he was a *lot* stronger. Will ducked back into cover. Two more bursts followed, cracking the rock, blasting holes in the walls.

What if Dave isn't coming this time? What was it he said? "Learn. Learn fast."

Will rose up and threw the first stone three feet to Lyle's right. Lyle smiled confidently and raised the rod to fire again. Will closed his eyes, stretched out his grid, and found the rock flying into the darkness. He grabbed hold and found a way to invest its mass with some part of himself. Then all he had to do was *think* about it: The rock swung around and boomeranged back toward Lyle.

I'm learning.

#48: NEVER START A FIGHT UNLESS YOU CAN FINISH IT. FAST.

The rock cracked into Lyle's arm just above the elbow, knocking the rod out of his hand. Lyle screamed in pain and fell to his knees. Will threw the second rock at the rod and knocked it back into the cave, out of sight.

Lyle went down hard, turning to protect his wounded arm. Will jumped on top of him, straddled his chest, and pinned him to the ground. He held the blade of his knife under Lyle's chin. Lyle looked up at him once, gulped in a deep breath, and started to bawl in great chuffing sobs, like a heartbroken toddler. The creep's anguish was so authentic it almost made Will feel sorry for him.

Then he saw a knot of raised flesh on the left side of Lyle's neck, twitching around like a joystick.

Damn. A Ride Along.

Will watched in horror as the thing extruded out of the knot on Lyle's neck. A mottled six-inch black stalk with short barbed arms and eight blinking angry eyes in a furious, contorted half-human face spit and hissed at Will.

Without even thinking, Will flicked his knife and sliced the creature off at the stem. The severed stalk flopped to the ground, uttered a hideous mewling screech, and scuttled into the dark, dragging its leaking, carved-up carcass.

The knot on Lyle's neck collapsed like a deflating balloon, lost its color, and lay flat. Lyle heaved a blubbering sigh.

"I hurt," said Lyle, looking at Will with wounded eyes. "Really bad. All over."

"What do you expect from me?" asked Will. "First aid? You tried to kill me!"

Lyle cried some more, softly, inconsolable. "I didn't want to," Lyle whimpered. "They made me do it."

"Why?"

"Because they're *afraid* of you," said Lyle.

"Who made you do this? *How?*"

Lyle showed Will his neck. "He ordered me to put that thing on *myself*," he said, his voice thick and trembling. "Two days ago. Because I *wouldn't* kill you."

"The Bald Man?"

Lyle nodded, looking for sympathy.

"Who is he, Lyle?"

"We call him Mr. Hobbes," said Lyle in a small voice. "He showed up last year when I joined the Knights. He tested me. My abilities."

"You mean, what you can do to people," said Will.

Lyle nodded, tears leaking from his eyes. "And he said I was going to be very important . . . because I was the *first* one to Awaken."

"What does that mean? The first of *what?*"

"Of the *Prophecy*," said Lyle intensely. "He said I was the first, and because of that *big plans* were in the works for me to help them—"

"What's the Prophecy, Lyle?"

"—and then *you* came along," said Lyle, turning petulant. "It's all your fault. You ruined my *life*."

"What is the Prophecy?"

"We *all* are!" Lyle's face twisted into a knot and his voice fell to a whisper. "A-T-C-G. A-T-C-G—"

Will shook him with both hands. "Goddamn it, Lyle, tell me what I need to know! Is the school behind this?"

"The *school?*" Lyle looked perversely pleased, almost giddy.

"Do they know about it?" demanded Will.

"Some. I don't know how many," said Lyle, then lowered his voice again. "You need to start at the beginning. At the clinics."

"What clinics?"

"See how *you* like the news. Then ask yourself, Who am I . . . *really*? And the best of luck to you," said Lyle as all his brute nastiness returned. "*Oik*."

A deep rumbling burst out of the portal behind them and grew louder until the ground shuddered around them, shaking rocks loose from the walls. An eerie moan pierced the air. The hair on Will's neck stood up. He turned to look.

A shadowy swirling mass loomed up inside the portal Lyle had opened.

"What did you bring over, Lyle?"

Lyle stared at the portal, terrified. "Wendigo," he mumbled.

Will slipped Dave's glasses out of his vest and put them on. An immense semihuman frame appeared on the far side of the portal.

"Please, help me," pleaded Lyle.

Will yanked Lyle to his feet and pulled him toward the mouth of the cave, but Lyle broke free, pushed Will away, and ran toward the portal. Will looked back and saw the thing step out of the hole.

It was a gaunt giant with a sickening loose hide, mottled and gray, covered with long dank hair. Its long leathery arms and legs ended in talons. Clumps of eyes and knots of gnawed limbs poked out of its exposed rib cage. A grotesque grin of razor-sharp teeth split its face below poisonous deep-set yellow eyes gleaming with hunger and spite. A jet-black darkness moved with it, flowing around it like a cloud.

Lyle walked right up to it, raising his hands in supplication. The creature regarded him curiously.

"I called you over," said Lyle, smiling darkly; then he turned and pointed at Will. "*He's* the one you want."

When Lyle turned back to it, the thing opened its maw and a long tentacle of flesh shot out and attached itself to Lyle's face with a wet slap. Lyle's body stiffened. His limbs thrust out and his whole body pitched and thrashed violently. He let loose an unearthly muffled howl, as if his soul were being run through a log splitter. Moments later, Will thought he saw Lyle's face appear inside the cage of the thing's ribs, screaming in agony.

Will backed away, numb with terror, as the wendigo released Lyle and he flopped to the floor of the cave. As Will fled the cave, he heard the wendigo stomping after him. He expected its vile touch to fell him at any moment.

Then he heard . . . what, an engine? Some kind of motor? Will looked up but the sky seemed unbelievably bright.

"Get down, mate."

Dave's Prowler ripped up and over the ridgeline. It soared into the air, arcing over Will, gunned full throttle. Dave leaned out the window, his sidearm blazing as he slammed the Prowler straight into the wendigo at the mouth of the cave.

The collision drove the creature back inside. It planted its feet and grabbed the car in its massive hands. Metal pinched and notched as the wendigo crushed the car like a child's toy. Dave leaped out of the wreckage and with a burst of light powered up into the full angelic form Will had seen briefly in his room: eight feet tall, platinum armor, wielding a gleaming silver-blue sword.

Dave and the creature savaged each other, trading staggering

491

blows. Dave absorbed fearsome damage in order to drive the thing back. It yielded ground, Dave spinning his sword like a scythe. The air sparked around them like the Fourth of July until, with a devastating combination, Dave smashed the wendigo's shadowy mass back into the portal.

Will watched from his knees just outside the cave as the portal began to contract. Dave shrank back to human size, bleeding from a dozen wounds. Will saw a fearful look in Dave's eyes he'd never seen before.

"You all right?" asked Dave, his chest heaving.

Will nodded. "What about you?"

"Been better. That was a nasty one. One of the big boys—"

He took one step toward Will. Suddenly the long desiccated limbs of the wendigo shot out of the contracting portal behind Dave and snared him around the waist.

"Buzzard's luck, mate," said Dave. He reached into his pocket and threw something. It plugged down into the snow just outside the cave.

"No!" shouted Will.

Then the thing yanked Dave back into the Never-Was just as the portal winked shut and vanished.

The cave went silent. Will pulled off his glasses and fumbled them into his pocket. Heart thumping, he staggered outside, dropped to his knees, reached a hand down into the puncture in the snow, and found something solid.

Dave's glass cube, with the two black dice spinning inside.

Will heard an engine sound again, loud and getting louder. He looked up at the sky.

Hovering above him, a helicopter angled sideways as it

slowed and lowered toward the ridge. He saw a door slide open on its side, and a rope ladder tumbled out, someone tossing it down to him, and he thought—

I know him. Who is he? Wait, it'll come to me. . . .

Yes, that's Headmaster Rourke.

MOM AND DAD

Are you Awake? He's an only child . . . 1990 . . . the Paladin Prophecy . . . Roman numerals . . . clinics . . . test scores . . . the Greenwood Foundation.

Open all doors, and Awaken.

Fragments swirled in Will's mind. He slowly became aware that he was lying on his back, on a bed with crisp linen sheets. No idea how long he'd been out. And he felt someone was there with him. He opened his eyes. He was in a room in the medical center. When he looked around, there they were, both of them, sitting by his bed in the pale moonlight.

Mom and Dad. Jordan and Belinda. *Really* them. When they saw him come around, they hurried to his side and held him in their arms, took turns hugging him.

"We were so afraid we'd lost you," said his mom. "Thank God, Will."

"I knew you were all right," said Will. "The whole time. I just *knew* it."

"We're so proud of you, son," said his dad. "They've filled us in on everything. We knew you could do it."

"I don't know how. I really don't. I had a lot of help from my friends. I couldn't have done it alone."

"We never doubted you," said his mom.

"You came through for us, Will," said his dad. "Exactly the way we trained you. The way we always expected you to."

"Where have you been?" asked Will. "What happened to you?"

Jordan and Belinda looked at each other and smiled a secret smile. As his mom turned her head, Will saw her neck: *no scar*.

"Should we tell him?" asked Jordan, cleaning his glasses.

Belinda smiled gently, reached over, and absentmindedly brushed the hair off Will's forehead. "There's so much to tell," she said.

Will heard soft music. His dad had brought along a record player. A black disk was spinning on the turntable on the other side of the room, the needle riding on the vinyl, a hiss and a pop during the chorus: *All you need is love . . . All you need is love . . . All you need is love, love . . . Love is all you need . . .*

"You're so close to cracking it, Will," said Jordan.

Feeling suddenly uneasy, Will's eyes darted around the room. A vase of fresh flowers—white chrysanthemums—sat on a table under the window, in a shaft of moonlight. A compass and a steel ruler sat next to the vase. There was a chessboard nearby: two black knights confronting a squad of white pawns. He heard a ball bouncing on the floor, looked to his left, and saw two old wooden tennis rackets resting in the corner. Strangest of all, a falcon perched on the top of a chair beside them. Staring right at Will, fierce and regal.

In the doorway, half in the shadows, stood Coach Jericho. What looked like blood dripped steadily from his left arm, hanging limp at his side.

"You saw one of them," said Jericho. "One of the Old Race. Wi-indi-ko."

The needle got stuck in a groove, skipping the lyrics: . . . *love . . . love. . . . love . . .*

"I'm sorry?" asked Will, confused.

"The Prophecy," said his dad. "We should have told you. A long time ago."

"But there were things we didn't want you to know," said his mom, leaning in. "We love you so much, but you never really knew us. We couldn't let you. For your own safety. Even before you were born."

Will opened his eyes.

He was in a hospital bed, in a room in the infirmary or medical center. Lights dimmed, darkness outside the window. He winced; everything ached. An IV was plugged into his left arm.

Coach Jericho sat by the side of the bed. His left arm was in a sling, under a long black leather coat hanging over his shoulders. His bronze face looked as hard and unyielding as flint.

"Am I still dreaming?" said Will.

"No," said Jericho. "You're awake."

Awake. Will tried to read him but couldn't. "How much do you know?"

"Enough."

"Did you know some of your guys were involved?"

"I do now," said Jericho.

"You won't have much of a team left."

"Don't need a team," said Jericho. "I have you."

Will closed his eyes, remembering parts of the dream. "What's a wendigo?"

"Apex predator," said Jericho. "Strong expression of weasel medicine."

"What, they kill more than they eat?" asked Will.

"Except the Wi-indi-ko feeds on souls," said Jericho. "And it's never satisfied."

Will thought about Lyle's body, twitching on the ground, and shivered. "I saw an animal in my dream," he said. "A falcon."

Jericho thought about that and gave the slightest smile.

"Is that good?" asked Will.

"You tell me, when you get to know it better," said Jericho. Then he leaned in and whispered, "It's a crucial time now. Be careful what you say, and who you say it to."

Will nodded, took a breath, and closed his eyes for a moment. "Hey, Coach, is it true what they say? Are you really related to Crazy Horse?"

Ajay appeared at the door. "Thank God. I didn't want to wake you, but it sounded like you were mumbling in your sleep."

"Coach Jericho was just—" Will turned back to Jericho. He was gone.

"What's the matter, Will?" asked Ajay. "What about Jericho?"

Will felt a sudden chill and pulled the covers up. "How long have I been here?" he asked.

"They brought you in two hours ago," said Ajay. "We're all here. Nick has a broken leg. They found him in the locker room, pretty badly banged up."

"Elise? Brooke?"

"Elise is here, stable but still unconscious. Brooke has no serious injuries, but she's severely shaken. Her parents are flying in tonight."

Will focused on him. Ajay looked worn to a nub. "And how are you, Ajay?"

"I'm all right," said Ajay, but he sniffed and fought to hold back tears. "Mild hypothermia. Nothing a few cups of cocoa couldn't take care of. But I've been worried sick about the rest of you."

Will reached out and took his hand and waited until Ajay could talk again.

"I feel so completely ineffectual, Will," said Ajay. "You guys did all the important stuff and what did I do? I went for a bumpy ride on the back of a horse."

"No, Ajay, no. You were great. We couldn't have done it without you."

"You're just saying that to make me feel better."

"But it's also true," said Will. "And we need you even more now. Because you're the best witness to all this they could ever hope to find. You see everything, and it's not like you're going to forget any details, are you?"

"Never," said Ajay, smiling, and then proved it. "Help arrived at the boathouse exactly fourteen minutes after you left. Mention kidnapping and attempted murder and an entire regiment shows up: cars, trucks, boats, police, ambulances, troopers."

"What did you tell them, Ajay?"

"That someone dressed as the Paladin kidnapped Brooke and threatened to harm her if we didn't do as he said," said Ajay. "So we felt we had to rescue her without informing authorities. And I was able to show them your conversation with the Paladin on my tablet to prove it."

"Perfect," said Will, patting his arm. "And that's *all* we should tell them."

"I read you loud and clear, Will," said Ajay. "I saw police taking away Durgnatt, Steifel, and Duckworth at the boathouse. In handcuffs."

"What about Lyle?"

"They brought him in on the chopper with you, but I haven't heard anything."

"And Todd Hodak?"

"Apparently police picked up six more kids at the Barn," said Ajay, "but no one's mentioned Todd."

Will thought for a moment. "There were *two* Paladins, Ajay. It was Lyle at the boathouse. The one at the Barn had to be Todd. When he figured out it was Nick and not me, he ran off."

"So Lyle's the one we saw on camera, then?" asked Ajay.

"Had to be," said Will. "Lyle was in charge. Will they let you out of here?"

"They haven't said they wouldn't. Why?"

"I need my iPhone. It's on a shelf in Lyle's office, in a plastic box with my name on it. If they haven't clamped down Greenwood Hall, you might be able to sneak in and grab it."

"Not to argue, but don't you think we're in enough trouble already?"

"All the trouble's pointing at the Knights," said Will. "It's not like *we* kidnapped anybody, right?"

"If you say so," said Ajay, still uncertain.

"We've got more work ahead of us," said Will. "We need that phone."

"I'll get right on it." Ajay started out but stopped at the door. "Will, I know we can piece together a lot of the *facts* . . . but do you have any idea of the big picture?"

"I've got some ideas," said Will. "I don't want to say anything until we're all together again. Do you play tennis?"

"What a thoroughly bizarre non sequitur."

"I'm trying to figure something out from a dream. So do you?"

Ajay shrugged. "I'm more of a Ping-Pong man myself."

"What's the meaning of love?"

"Dear me, from the absurd to the profound—"

"I mean in *tennis*," said Will.

"In tennis? In the scoring of tennis, *love* means zero. Its origin is somewhat in dispute, but since the game evolved in France, one theory has *love* deriving from the French word *l'œuf*. French for 'egg.' Because an egg looks like a zero."

"An *egg*."

Will felt the click of cold hard logic fit together, as if he'd set the keystone and all the other pieces had fallen into place.

"That's the most popular theory, but no one seems to know for sure. Will, if you're dreaming about eggs, are you sure you're not just . . . hungry?"

"Actually, I'm starving."

"Should I tell the doctors you're awake?"

"In two minutes," said Will. "Make a big deal out of it. That should give you enough cover to slip out unnoticed."

Ajay stepped into the hall. Will eased the IV needle from his arm, got unsteadily out of bed, and pulled on a robe. He moved through the door connecting to the next room.

Nick lay on a rolling hospital bed, his right leg elevated by a pulley device, wearing a cast up to the knee. Will moved to Nick's side. His eyes were closed; the right was badly swollen and blackened. He'd gotten stitches in his lower lip and left cheekbone and had scratches and scrapes everywhere. He looked like he'd survived a train wreck.

"Hey, slacker," Will whispered. "Nice sympathy play. Chicks'll dig the cast."

"You should see the other guys," croaked Nick. He cracked open his good eye and clasped Will's hand. "By the way, I'm telling everybody these are UPIs: Unidentified Party Injuries."

"Some party."

"Brooke okay, bro?" asked Nick.

"That's the word."

"So we nailed the bastards."

"To the wall," said Will.

"For reals," said Nick, then leaned in and whispered, "And, dude, I've got great news: Whatever drugs I'm on right now? They're *awesome*."

"Nick, this is really important. Between the drugs and your concussion, it's even *more* important: Don't say *anything* they don't need to know."

Nick gave Will a fist bump. "I'm all over that. I got a concussion, too?"

"Dude. You were born with one." Will started for the door.

"Hey, chill a sec. I was going to tell you something . . . real important about Nepsted," said Nick sleepily. "But, damn, I can't remember what it was. . . ."

Nick nodded off. Will moved through the next door to an identical room. Lying on her back, eyes closed, with an IV in her arm and hooked up to a battery of monitors, was Elise.

Will took her hand, leaned in, and whispered, "Elise, can you hear me?"

"No," she said. "I died. Tragically." She opened one eye.

"Ajay said you hadn't woken up yet," said Will.

Elise arched an eyebrow. "You think I'd let them know that before we had a chance to talk? Is that how little you think of me?"

"I should know better."

"Yes, you should," she said. He tried to disengage his hand, but she held on. "I didn't give you permission to let go."

"Maybe I don't want to, then," said Will.

They stared at each other for a moment. "Great," said Elise. "Now I'm completely self-conscious about the whole *hand* thing."

But neither of them let go.

"Did you know you could . . . do . . . whatever it was you did at the boathouse?" asked Will.

"Let me ask you this first," she said. "It's a strange question, but since you sent Ajay to bring me there, I'm asking it anyway: Did *you*?"

"Not exactly. I had a feeling you'd be able to do *something*."

"Why? How?"

"Because of a question you asked me once," said Will. "In a dream. You asked me if I was 'Awake.' That was you, wasn't it?"

"*Awake* was just the word I used. To describe this feeling to myself." She held his eyes steadily. "I was dreaming, too. I saw you, twice, before you got here, before I had any idea who you were, or if you were even real. I saw the trouble you were in. And then when you showed up, it scared the pants off me."

She gripped his hand, hard. "I've always been weird, okay? And I don't mean geeky-weird. I mean the Old English definition: the power to see fate or the future, or to know what people are thinking. Then you got here and woke it up *for real*."

"You mean, what you did at the boathouse?"

"I had no idea I could do anything like that," she said. "Hitting a high C that shatters a wineglass is one thing. Blowing the doors off a building and knocking a roomful of people senseless? That's a whole different level of 'Awake.'"

"I felt something else, too," said Will, studying her. "A couple of times with you." He held her eyes and thought:

Do you know what I'm thinking right now?

She held his eyes steadily: *Of course I do, dummy.*

Will gasped. "Damn. What is up with that?"

"Don't know, but it sure beats the hell out of texting," she said, grinning slyly.

They both heard voices in Nick's room next door and saw lights under the door.

"Don't worry, I know the drill," said Elise, whispering. "Mum's the word. An explosion knocked everybody out and we don't know what caused it. Maybe the bad guys set it up ahead of time—"

"You are good," said Will.

"You're dismissed," said Elise, settling into the bed. "I'm going back to my Sleeping Beauty act. I'm pretty worn out from the effects of my, uh, 'explosion.'"

I know what that's like, too, thought Will.

I know you do, she thought. Then she said, "And that's *deeply* weird, isn't it?"

"Nothing's weirder than the truth," said Will.

"Hmm. Okay. I'll ponder upon *that*," she said. Elise squeezed his hand one more time, closed her eyes, and let him go.

Will went back to the door, gathered himself, and then walked through it. Dr. Robbins, Dr. Geist, Dr. Kujawa, and Head-master Rourke stood over Nick's bed. Eloni and another security guard stood by the door to the hallway. Rourke wore his shearling coat and held his black cowboy hat in his hand.

"There you are," said Dr. Robbins. "Will, what are you doing out of bed?"

"I wanted to make sure everyone was okay," he said.

"Come sit over here, please, Will," said Rourke, calmly patting the empty bed next to Nick's. "Don't get ahead of yourself. Making sure that *all* of you are okay is *my* first order of business, not yours. Are we clear on that?"

"Yes, sir."

Will sat on the bed. Dr. Kujawa checked his pulse and gave him a quick once-over. As Kujawa worked, Will exchanged a look with Nick over his shoulder. Nick nodded subtly: *We got this.*

Kujawa looked back at Rourke: *He's okay.*

Rourke pulled up a chair, turned it backward, and sat astride it, between the beds, so he could see them both.

"Dr. Robbins and Mr. McBride have brought me up to date about some earlier conversations," said Rourke, "in which you raised concerns about this secret club called the Knights of Charlemagne. Let's hear your side, Will."

Will told them about the Paladin's threats against Brooke. He apologized to Robbins for leaving against her orders, but he'd felt they had no choice. What he'd seen in the message told him they'd find Brooke at the boathouse and that it was his decision, alone, to try and free her. An explosion had gone off when they got there. A trap set, they assumed, by the kidnappers. He explained how he chased the Paladin—who turned out to be Lyle—up to the ridge and that shots had been fired at him. He'd cornered Lyle near the caves where they'd found him with the helicopter.

And that was all that he remembered.

Rourke looked at him, then took something from his coat. "I found these in your pockets, Will."

His Swiss Army knife, dark glasses, and a pair of black dice. Normal, six-sided black dice, like you'd find in a Monopoly game. Will tried to mask his alarm: *Regular dice? Are these the same ones from Dave's glass cube?*

Then Rourke turned to Nick and asked for his account.

Nick echoed Will's version, adding that they changed coats so the Knights would mistake him for Will. He'd gone to the Barn to create a distraction while Will and the others went for Brooke.

We're home free, thought Will with relief. Then Nick kept going.

"And when I got there, a bunch of masked dudes, like six of 'em, were trying to steal the statue of the school mascot. They'd already knocked it off its pedestal and dragged it to the locker room, and I didn't know if they were gonna deface it or something, right, so I made some citizen arrests. All of a sudden, this ginormous *animal* charges in—I guess 'cause they'd left the doors open and it was trying to get out of the storm? And I know this sounds totally shwhacked, but I think that maybe it was . . . a bear?"

Dead silence.

"So, next thing I know, my leg's busted up real bad and I somehow call the operator and I have this voodoo nightmare that there's a giant squid talking to me. . . . Then I woke up here. You know, pretty confused and all."

Will tried not to wince.

"There *was* an animal down there," someone said from behind Will.

Everyone turned. Coach Jericho had come into the room while Nick was speaking.

"I was in my office when I heard it," said Jericho evenly. "Luckily, I was able to open a few doors and keep away from it until it chased me outside."

"A bear?" asked Rourke.

"Judging by the tracks, it might have been a bear," said Jericho. "But to be honest, Stephen, it was dark and I didn't turn around to take a look."

"What happened to your arm?" asked Robbins.

"I slipped on the ice outside, after I made it out of the building. Nothing serious."

"A bear," said Rourke, looking at Nick again.

"Unlikely as it sounds," said Jericho, "I've seen Mr. McLeish part company with the facts before, but I think he's telling the truth. Those kids did drag the statue to the locker room and vandalize it. That's where we found what was left."

"Thank you, Coach," said Rourke.

Jericho met Will's eye, then stepped out of the room. Nick exhaled slowly and glanced at Will. Will silently mouthed, *A giant squid?*

Nick shrugged and nodded. Rourke stood up and ran a hand through his thick hair.

"We found three rifles, abandoned at the base of the ridge," said Rourke. "Target guns used by the biathlon team and stolen from a locked cabinet in the field house. We also found spent shells and four snowmobiles from the motor pool.

"Obviously, Will, your concerns were well founded: A small group of students appears to have revived the Knights of Charlemagne, an organization that was banned here seventy years ago. These are deadly serious crimes, and ten students are in custody. Their families have been notified, and arrests are forthcoming. The safety of our students is a sacred trust, and we're going to conduct a full investigation to get to the bottom of how and why this happened."

Rourke paused as another of Will's teachers entered the room: It was Sangren, the little civics professor. He took Rourke aside and whispered urgently.

"Excuse me," said Rourke. He gestured for Dr. Geist to follow him. Both hurried outside.

Sangren turned to Will. "Will, come with me, please. In here."

Will followed Sangren into his own room. Sangren pointed to the bed. "Sit down, please, Will."

Will did as he asked. Sangren went back to the adjoining door and spoke quietly to Dr. Robbins and Dr. Kujawa. Something he said caused Robbins to involuntarily raise a hand to her mouth and gasp, then glance at Will. Kujawa looked at Will and immediately left the room. Sangren braced Robbins's arms with his for a moment as she composed herself; then both walked over to Will.

"What is it?" asked Will, his heart sinking before he heard a word.

Dr. Robbins knelt and took Will's hand. "Will, Dan McBride just called," she said.

"What happened?"

"There's been an accident."

THE ACCIDENT

He insisted they take him there. When they resisted, he raised his voice, just once, to let them know it was nonnegotiable. They left an hour before dawn, in the school's helicopter, lifting off from the roof of the medical center. Will sat in back between Dr. Robbins and Coach Jericho. Headmaster Rourke, they'd told him, had gone up ahead to meet with authorities.

They touched down on the tarmac in Madison a few minutes after six, as the sky turned light gray in the east. Headmaster Rourke and Dan McBride were waiting beside a large black SUV driven by Eloni. They climbed in and followed two Wisconsin state patrol cars, flashing their light bars, for a mile to the west. When they parked near the site and climbed out, Headmaster Rourke put his arm gently but firmly around Will's shoulder and quietly talked him through it.

The pilot had radioed air traffic control that they'd lost power just after beginning their descent. The storm severely limited visibility. There had been hope they could coast to a landing but the landing gear clipped some treetops well short of the runway. The plane tumbled and crashed and then caught fire.

There had been four people on board, including the two-man crew. No survivors.

As they walked toward the woods, Will saw firefighters and rescue teams wrapping up. Investigators were setting up lights focused on a charred twisted mass among burned evergreens at the end of a long debris field.

One section of the fuselage and tail remained intact. On its side was the writing Will had come here expecting to find: N497TF. A Bombardier Challenger 600. The same private twin-engine passenger jet his parents had rented in Oxnard three days earlier.

Will had gone cold inside when Dr. Robbins told him the news. He'd felt that way all night, and seeing this for himself didn't change it; Will still felt nothing, numb.

Rourke explained there were some officials in the terminal who had asked to speak with him, but that if he didn't feel up to it, he could postpone it to another day.

"Let's get it over with," said Will.

They met in a conference room at Dane County Regional Airport, in the general aviation offices. Headmaster Rourke insisted on staying with Will. Two troopers manned the door outside. Two suits waited inside, local detectives.

They made polite attempts at expressing sympathy. They reported that efforts to identify the passengers were under way and they were hoping he could help. They showed Will the blackened remnant of a wallet and a partially destroyed

California driver's license in a plastic bag and asked him if he recognized the photo.

"My father," said Will. "Jordan West."

They showed him a scorched woman's leather handbag. Will recognized it as one that belonged to his mother, Belinda West. They asked if it was true, as had been reported to them, that his parents had been flying in to visit him at his new school.

"Yes," he said.

They asked Will if he knew the name of his family's dentist back in California. He said they hadn't yet found one in Ojai to his knowledge. He realized they were looking for dental X-rays to identify the bodies.

Their interview was winding down when a man in a black suit entered. Will felt his blood run cold when he took off his hat.

It was the Bald Man. Lyle's Mr. Hobbes.

He showed a badge, identifying him as Inspector Dan O'Brian from the Federal Aviation Administration, then addressed Will. "I've been tracking your parents for the last three days," he said. His voice was cold, almost robotic. "When was the last time you spoke to them?"

Will stared him right in the eye. "Two or three days ago."

"Did they tell you they planned to rent a private jet for this trip?"

"No."

"Had they *ever* rented a private jet before?" asked Mr. Hobbes.

"Not that I'm aware of."

Hobbes stepped closer; he was big and wiry, much bigger than he'd looked from a distance. He had dark, dead eyes and gleaming white teeth. Will couldn't read him, but he remembered this and it helped him:

He doesn't know that I know who he is.

"Can you explain why they went looking for you in Phoenix if they knew you were here in Wisconsin?" asked Hobbes.

Will glanced at Rourke, who stepped to his defense. "Sir, you may have a job to do, but this young man just lost his parents."

Hobbes never took his lifeless black eyes off Will. "The Wests chartered that jet last Wednesday in Oxnard. They flew to Phoenix and spent the night searching YMCAs and youth centers. Instead of returning to Oxnard the next day, they took off without filing a flight plan or notifying the owner. The plane disappeared from the FAA's grid for the next two and a half days."

Rourke looked at Will, who shook his head, mystified.

"The day before they chartered the jet, Mr. West set off an explosive device that destroyed a hotel room registered to him in San Francisco. He fled the scene before he could be questioned. That night, Mr. West's offices at the University of California at Santa Barbara were broken into; files and valuable equipment, including two computers, were stolen. Mr. West remains the prime suspect—"

"Why would he steal his own computers?" asked Will.

"Two days ago," the man said, talking over him, "a house rented by the Wests in Ojai, California, for the last four months burned to the ground under circumstances that triggered an arson investigation—"

"Will, did you know about this?" asked Rourke.

"No, sir."

Hobbes took out a pair of handcuffs. "An impressive crime

spree. The theft of a private airplane is no ordinary Class One felony; it's the kind that attracts the interest of Homeland Security." Hobbes smiled for the first time, but not with his eyes. "I'm taking Mr. West into custody for questioning. Social Services is waiting outside. Come with me."

The sun crested the horizon, flooding the room with bright morning light. Through the window, Will saw a black SUV parked outside with four men in black caps waiting beside it. Hobbes pulled Will to his feet and prepared to cuff him.

Rourke grabbed the man's wrist. "Take your hands off him," he said.

Hobbes scowled. "I'm a federal officer—"

"And I'm his legal guardian," said Rourke, raising his voice. "He's not going anywhere."

Eloni and Coach Jericho burst into the room, flanked by two Wisconsin state troopers, who made it clear they were ready to back Rourke's play. The other detectives showed no interest in interfering.

"Do we have a problem?" asked Rourke.

Rourke put on his cowboy hat. Eloni and Jericho stepped closer to Hobbes. The man's eyes burned hot. For a moment Will thought he might yell to the Black Caps and try to take him by force. But he didn't.

Will shook Hobbes off and stepped next to Rourke, who put a hand on Will's shoulder and guided him toward the door. Will followed but stopped at the door, turned, and slipped on Dave's sunglasses.

A nimbus of light flared around Hobbes the Bald Man . . . and beneath his flesh Will saw a freakish armature of solid bone covering his entire head and neck, with overlapping scales as thick as armor plating.

Will's numbed indifference fell away, and a blind fury for everything he'd been through, everything his parents had endured, ripped through him. Without Will's even directing it, his anger coalesced into the shape of a war hammer and Will sent it scudding toward the man's alabaster skull.

And if you can hear me, thought Will, *that's for my parents, you ugly son of a bitch!*

Hobbes gasped as his head snapped back, hit by the invisible blow. Blood trickled from his nose and ear.

Will turned and followed Rourke out of the room. Eloni, Jericho, and the troopers fell into step around them, a protective phalanx that cleared the hall as they exited the building.

Will spoke quietly to Eloni when they stepped outside. "Sorry I ditched out on you, man."

"S'okay, Will," said Eloni softly. "For Miss Springer, I'd've done the same."

"Mr. Rourke?" asked Will as they crossed the parking lot. "Are you really my legal guardian?"

"We'll look into that, Will," said Rourke, then winked. "But it didn't hurt to let him think so."

Within minutes, they were back in the Center's helicopter, soaring above snow-covered forests and hills, a bright sun rising in a clear blue morning sky. Cerulean blue. Will noticed that the pilot was another Samoan from the Center. Rourke rode next to him. Will sat in back with Dr. Robbins, Mr. McBride, and Coach Jericho.

"What day is it?" asked Will, feeling shell-shocked.

"Sunday," said McBride.

Coach Jericho laid his good hand on Will's shoulder. Dr. Robbins took Will's right hand between hers. Will caught a glimpse of the crash site—a vivid black scar in the white fields below—as they banked up and away.

If they were on that plane, I've lost my parents. I've probably lost Dave, too. He put his hand in his pocket and found the black dice. He had nothing else to hold on to.

Always and forever, Will. Always and more than anything.

"What should I do?" asked Will, to no one in particular. "I don't know . . . what am I supposed to do?"

Will's grief rose up with tidal force, all his anger and terror and grief washing out of him in racking, gut-wrenching sobs.

"It's all right, Will," said Robbins. "It's all right."

But it wasn't all right. No one said another word until they touched down forty-five minutes later on a parking lot, near a flat, busy stretch of interstate. A cadre of state troopers had cleared out their landing area. Will was confused as they climbed out, until he looked over and saw the red neon sign. Rourke put on his hat, nodded at Dan McBride, and put an arm around Will's shoulder.

"You need a good meal, Will," said Rourke kindly. "As strange as it sounds, you have to eat at a time like this."

They were at Popski's.

IT'S ABOUT US

It was almost noon when they returned to the Center. Rourke drove them to Greenwood Hall and walked him to the door.

"Stay close to people who care about you," said Rourke. "Tell them how you feel. They can't help you if you don't. That's where you have to start."

Dr. Robbins walked Will inside to the elevator. A line of yellow tape sealed the open doorway to Lyle's rooms. Lots of uniformed officers were working inside.

"Are there any friends or relatives we should notify, Will?" asked Robbins. "We could have them flown in. I'm sure they'd like to be here for you as well."

"Thanks," said Will. "May I think about that and let you know?"

"Of course."

He didn't want to tell her the truth then and there: He had no living relatives that he knew about on either side of the family. Nor did his parents have any friends that he was aware of. In fact, the only friends *he'd* known in his own life were the ones who lived upstairs in pod G4-3.

They got off the elevator. Knots of students were grouped in the atrium whispering to each other, with a partial attempt at discretion, as Will passed.

The story had made the rounds already. He wasn't just the "new kid" anymore.

A security guard waited outside the door to their suite—Tika, Eloni's other cousin. She opened the door as they approached.

"She's not here to keep you locked up, Will," Robbins whispered. "Just to make sure you're okay. Call me, immediately, if you need anything."

"I will."

Will walked into the great room. Brooke sat at the dining table next to Nick, who was in a wheelchair with his right leg elevated. She jumped to her feet when Will came in. Elise rose from the sofa, and Ajay popped out of his room.

Brooke got to him first and hugged him as hard as she could. She tried to keep from crying and failed miserably, while everyone else bunched around him. Even Elise brushed away a tear when she got her chance to hug him.

"Damn it, bro," said Nick. "Damn, I'm so damn sorry. I don't know what to say."

Will had to squat on an arm of the wheelchair to hug Nick, and Nick nearly broke Will's ribs. The girls made hot chocolate. Ajay got a fire going and they gathered around it, even Nick, who climbed out of his chair and limped down onto the sofa.

Brooke started to explain that she'd been walking back

from the library when two masked figures had come out of the woods. Will saw the trauma carving lines on her face and took her hand.

"We know the rest," he said. "Don't go back there."

Brooke seemed grateful. "Were your parents really on that plane?" she asked.

"I don't know," said Will. "They were a few days ago. We'll have to wait and see. Did they ever find Todd?"

"Not yet," said Ajay.

"They nabbed six Knights at the Barn, three at the boathouse," said Elise. "And Lyle."

"That leaves three of the thirteen Knights still unaccounted for," said Ajay. "Including Todd. Nick thinks you're right. Todd must've been the Paladin at the Barn."

"Any word on Lyle?" Will asked Ajay.

"I talked to a friend at the med center," said Ajay. "He says Lyle is one hundred percent *non compos*."

"Whoa, he's not even on *campus* anymore?" asked Nick.

"Non compos mentis," said Elise. "Look it up."

"It means he's fried his motherboard," said Ajay. "Blown his circuit breakers. Catatonic and nonresponsive. A condition most often associated with a devastating and perhaps irreversible nervous breakdown."

Will thought back to the cave, when he'd seen Lyle's face inside the wendigo's rib cage. What had that thing taken from him? How much of Lyle was left?

"Well, pardon me while I break out the world's smallest violin and play a really sad song," said Nick.

"He's still a *person*, Nick," said Elise.

"Or was," said Ajay. "At least sort of."

518

"He was a little kid once, like us," said Brooke. "With people who cared about him."

"I was told Lyle's parents are flying in as well," said Ajay.

"There, see?" said Elise. "He has *parents*."

The word appeared to bring Nick back to the weight of Will's loss. "Sorry," he mumbled.

#79: DON'T MAKE ANOTHER'S PAIN THE SOURCE OF YOUR OWN HAPPINESS.

"Lyle got messed up by a nasty from the Never-Was that he brought over in the caves," said Will, filling them in about the wendigo. "Lyle told me the Caps made him put a Ride Along in his own neck. I cut it off him. He hated me, he hated all of us, but I don't think he would have tried to kill me if they hadn't made him do it."

No one said anything for a moment.

"Lyle also told me that the Bald Man is in charge," Will said. "His name is Mr. Hobbes. Hobbes and the Caps tried to grab me at the airport in Madison."

"What?!" said Nick.

"Good God, Will," said Ajay.

"Another thing: He's not exactly human," said Will. "He's not completely from the Never-Was, either. He seems like he's . . . some kind of hybrid."

"How do you know?" asked Elise.

Will held up his dark glasses.

"That's it," said Nick. "I'm getting a pair of those."

"Did you tell the cops what he's done to you and your family?" asked Brooke.

"No. He's got heavyweight connections and I don't know who we can trust yet. But Rourke definitely did not know this guy. That's a good sign. Now I need to catch up on something. Nick: What the hell happened at the Barn?"

"Dude, the Big Paladin *Statue* Dude started chasing me," said Nick. "I think they must've slapped one of those Ride Alongs on it."

"And this was just before you were attacked by the grizzly bear and the giant squid," said Ajay dryly.

"Dude, I told you—I wasn't *attacked* by them. They were *defending* me. *Against* the statue."

Will put his hand on Nick to calm him. "I have no idea why, Nick," he said, "but I believe you."

"Thanks, man."

Everyone fell into a sober moment of silence. Brooke took Will's hand.

"So, is it over, Will?" she asked. "Are you safe now?"

"I'm not sure," said Will. "We know that Lyle ran the Knights, and Mr. Hobbes was running Lyle."

"And Hobbes gave the order to kill you," said Elise. "That's why they staged this whole thing."

"*Except*," said Will. "Except that Lyle had a Ride Along at the boathouse that he was going to hit me with. So maybe the order changed and they decided they'd rather control me than kill me."

"Why would it change?" asked Brooke.

"Lyle said they were afraid of me."

"Afraid of you?" asked Ajay. "Why?"

"I don't know," said Will, stirring the fire. "But I expect the school's going to tell us the Knights of Charlemagne are finished now. A sickness, like an outbreak of measles they've stamped out. And they have two perfect fall guys: Lyle and Todd."

"But they *are* guilty," said Ajay.

"Up to a point," said Will. "I think Lyle realized he'd become a scapegoat, expendable in some way, and that lets the Center nail a lid on this whole rotten barrel. The other Knights will be expelled and face criminal charges. Todd's still missing, and I don't think they'll find him. And Lyle probably spends the rest of his life drooling into a tube."

"You almost sound like you feel sorry for him," said Ajay.

"I do," said Will. "He's as much a victim as anybody, maybe even more so. The point is, all of this lets the school send a message to their students' families that they've weeded out the bad apples and everything's under control."

Elise, watching Will closely, asked, "Is that what the school really thinks?"

"I hope so," said Will. "That's exactly what we should *want* them to think. And for our sake, we'd better hope it's true."

"Why?" asked Ajay.

"Because if it isn't, it means the Knights of Charlemagne have been in business all along, ever since they were supposedly disbanded back in 1941. It means they still are, and that powerful alumni, possibly some parents and even teachers, have been mixed up in this all along—"

"Dude, you're scaring the crap out of me," said Nick. "I'm serious. I literally have no crap right now."

"—working on a secret plan they call the Paladin Prophecy," said Will, looking at each of them. "I figured out how it all fits together after Lyle said some things to me today. None of you are going to like it."

Ajay's eyes grew bigger and rounder than a bush baby's. "I have a feeling this may require a beverage more fortifying than cocoa."

Will stood up and walked around. "Why did they put us all together in this pod? Think about it for a second. What do we have in common?"

The others looked at each other, all thinking.

"We're scholarship students," said Ajay. "Our families aren't wealthy."

"That describes four of us," said Elise. "But not Brooke."

"We're all incredibly good-looking," said Nick. "Except Ajay."

"Don't get me started, birdbrain," said Ajay.

"Something else," said Will.

"We're the same age," said Brooke. "We're all fifteen."

"Correct," said Will. "Good. Keep going."

"We all appear to have rather . . . unusual abilities," said Ajay.

"Really?" asked Nick. "What can you do?"

Ajay glanced at Will, who encouraged him to answer. "Perhaps you haven't noticed, but I possess extraordinary eyesight and a photographic memory."

"That's awesome. Dude, you are so helping me with my homework."

"What about you, Brooke? Any unusual abilities?" asked Ajay.

"Like what?"

Ajay pointed at Will, Nick, himself, and then Elise. "Stamina, agility, memory, sonic booms, that sort of thing."

"None that I'm aware of," said Brooke, disappointed. "I'm feeling completely left out."

"Don't worry," said Will. "They can activate at different

times. We know that Lyle had powers, too, but we don't know when they started. For us they came on gradually over time."

"Except my sonic thing hit just yesterday," said Elise. "Boom."

"Yeah, don't bum about it, Brooke," said Nick, sincerely trying to help. "Tomorrow you could wake up and be able to eat a hundred hot dogs or something."

"The woman of your dreams," said Elise.

Will brought them back on task. "Something else we have in common: None of us have brothers or sisters. Including Ronnie and Lyle. All of us are only children."

"Is that really so unusual?" asked Ajay. "American families have been trending smaller in recent decades. In fact, demographics from all of the industrialized Western societies suggest that the rate of birth—"

Elise rapped his knuckles. "Ajay: It's *unusual*. Keep going, Will."

"How did we get to the Center?" asked Will, still pacing. "What brought us here?"

"Test scores," said Ajay. "At our old schools."

"Tests given to us and every other kid in the country," said Will. "By an organization called the National Scholastic Evaluation Agency. Sounds harmless and neutral, right? Vaguely governmental."

"So why is that a concern?" asked Brooke.

"It's not a government agency, although it has some kind of federal affiliation," said Will. "The NSEA is a private company, owned by the Greenwood Foundation. The same Greenwood Foundation that owns and operates the Center."

The others exchanged worried looks.

"That's more than a little unsettling," said Ajay.

"So the NSEA conducts evaluation tests," said Elise, thinking it through. "Trying to identify the best and brightest students in the country. And the Center invites them to come here. I don't *necessarily* see anything sinister."

"And my friend Nando saw Black Caps at their LA office," said Will.

"Oh, dear," said Brooke.

"Where were you born, Nick?" asked Will.

"Boston."

"Elise?"

"Seattle."

"Ajay?"

"In Atlanta, although my parents lived in Raleigh at the time. Something to do with where our obstetrician worked, I believe."

"Dallas," said Brooke.

"Lyle was born in Boston," said Will. "What about Ronnie?"

"Chicago," said Elise.

"The NSEA has six offices," said Will. "All in federal buildings around the country: Boston, Seattle, Atlanta, Dallas, Los Angeles, and Chicago."

"All big cities," said Ajay. "That could easily be a coincidence."

"Where were you born, Will?" asked Elise.

"Albuquerque, New Mexico," said Will. "That's what my parents told me."

"Albuquerque's not on the list," said Nick.

"Just because they told me that doesn't mean it's true," said Will. "Ajay, would you mind pulling up Ronnie's video? I want your isolated image of that silver box. This part came to me in a dream I had this morning. A dream about an egg."

On his tablet, Ajay quickly retrieved an image of the metallic case with THE PALADIN PROPHECY engraved on its cover above the Roman numerals.

"Look at the Roman numerals," said Will. "I think this means that the Prophecy started in 1990. Lyle told me that if I wanted to know about the Prophecy, I needed to start with the clinics."

"What kind of clinics?" asked Elise.

"Look at the *second* number," said Will, pointing to the *IV* after the numbers for 1990.

"Roman numeral four," said Nick.

"But we were wrong about that," said Will. "There's no line across the top or bottom like the other figures. It's not the *number* 4 because this isn't a numeral. These are the letters *IV*."

"Okay, so what?" asked Nick.

"It's a common abbreviation," said Will. "Used in medicine."

"Intravenous?" asked Brooke.

"*In vitro*," said Will.

"Which means 'in the glass,' or test tube," said Ajay, accessing his prodigious memory. "A medical procedure often conducted in fertility clinics to help couples who can't get pregnant. Couples who often end up with only one child. A procedure that entered the medical mainstream about 1990."

No one spoke. A log popped loudly in the fire and everyone jumped.

"Dude . . . what does this have to do with an egg?" asked Nick.

525

"You're not seriously suggesting we might all have been . . . ," said Brooke.

"I am so way beyond grossed out," said Elise, frozen.

"Lyle said we were *all* the Prophecy," said Will.

"Okay, I have no idea what we're talking about," said Nick.

"In vitro fertilization," said Ajay impatiently. "Wherein an egg is extracted from a woman's ovaries and fertilized by sperm from her spouse or a donor. Two or three days later, after replicating into a zygote of six to eight cells, the growing embryo is reintroduced to the woman's womb. Leading, in approximately thirty-five percent of cases, to successful pregnancy. In vitro fertilization."

"If Will's right," said Elise, explaining softly to Nick, "it means we're test-tube babies."

Nick's face scrunched up. "Eww," he said.

"And maybe more than that," said Will. "Lyle said one other thing. Four letters: ATCG. Do any of you know what that means?"

"Adenine. Cytosine. Guanine. Thymine," said Ajay. "The four basic nucleotides, the building blocks of DNA."

"Genetic—in vitro—manipulation," said Elise, turning pale.

Ajay fell back into the cushions. Nick fanned himself with a pillow.

"Special abilities," said Brooke.

"I think it happened secretly," said Will. "Your parents probably weren't aware of it, although I think mine may have been. Whoever was in charge tracked us over time, then used these 'random' tests to see if whatever changes they'd manipulated were . . . awake. Then they brought us here."

"We're the Paladins," whispered Ajay, looking stunned.

"I know how crazy this sounds," said Will, pacing again. "I'm not claiming it's true; I'm just laying it out there. A theory, that's all. A theory I'm more than happy to see disproved. And if it isn't true—if it's completely, totally insane—it won't take long to find out."

"So where did this all start?" asked Brooke. "Who's responsible for the Prophecy?"

"I don't know where it started," said Will. "The Caps, the Knights, and the Never-Was are involved somehow . . . but it sure seems to be ending up here."

"But if they wanted you at the Center, why were the Caps trying to kill you?" asked Elise.

"I don't know that either," said Will. *Unless it's because, like Dave said, I'm an Initiate.*

"So it seems the crucial question facing us now," said Ajay, "is what, if anything, does the Center have to do with the Paladin Prophecy?"

"That sounds right," said Will.

"But if it *is* true, what is it all for?" asked Brooke emotionally. "Why would they do something this twisted to anybody?"

Will took her hand. "We're going to find that out," he said simply. "All of us."

"How many of . . . 'us' are we?" asked Elise.

"For now, the five of us in this room," said Will.

"How can we verify that this genetic theory is true?" asked Ajay.

"There's one obvious place to start," said Will. "Drop the idea into a conversation with your parents. See what they say, decide what you think."

"Okay," said Ajay, a little shaky, looking at the others.

"You can also, really quietly, ask Dr. Kujawa to run tests on you," said Will. "He was amazed by what he found with me and told me the truth about it. Maybe he finds something that helps us rule this out. Either way, it can't hurt to check."

"Word," said Nick.

"Ajay, there's something else you can do," said Will. "First thing tomorrow, grab a note from a teacher for the Rare Book Archive. Read everything you can find about the Knights of Charlemagne, the Crag, and how they picked the school mascot before anyone has a chance to get rid of it."

"Dude, build a spy camera," said Nick.

"He won't need a camera," said Will. "Any more than I needed a horse."

"Correct," said Ajay, a smile dawning.

Tika knocked on the door, then stuck her head in and said to Brooke, "Car's here for you, Miss Springer. Your parents are downstairs."

Brooke explained that her parents had flown in from Washington. They'd decided it was best for her to spend a few days at home in Virginia before returning to class. She collected her bag, then gave everyone a hug. Will walked her out the door and into the corridor. Brooke dropped her bag, grabbed Will, and kissed him.

"Call me," she said breathlessly. "Text me or email me or—"

"Okay," he said between kisses.

"Don't let an hour go by without letting me know what's going on, what you know, and how you are." Then with a sweet whispered goodbye and a heady rush of freshly washed hair, she was gone.

Will walked back inside and closed the door. The rest of

them stared at the grin on his face, then pretended to find something else to look at. Elise, who knew *exactly* what he was thinking, turned away and crossed her arms.

"Dudes, we need a name for . . . whatever we are," said Nick, climbing back into his wheelchair. "The Resistance or . . . wait for it"—Nick lowered his voice dramatically—"the *Awesome* Resistance."

"Thanks for playing, Nick," said Elise.

"The Alliance," said Ajay.

"The Alliance," said Elise, trying it out.

"What do you think, Will?" asked Nick.

"I'm sorry, what?" asked Will, looking up as if just realizing they were there.

"Never mind." Elise scowled.

Will yawned. "I need to sleep now," he said.

Nick gave him a fist bump, and Elise held his hand for a thoughtful moment; then Will headed for his room. Ajay followed him to his door.

"I didn't have a chance to tell you," said Ajay. "I found your iPhone where you said it would be in Lyle's office. The police were driving up as I came out. It's under your mattress. As a precaution, I removed its GPS transmitter."

"Great job, Ajay," said Will. "You're the man."

"No," said Ajay. "I believe it's safe to say that would be *you*, my friend. And I remain, sir, entirely at your service."

Will smiled, took the dark glasses out of his pocket, and handed them to Ajay. "When you get a chance, take a look at these. We're all going to need a pair."

DECISION

Will found his iPhone where Ajay had stashed it, under the mattress. It felt good to feel its familiar contours in his hands again, but also sobering and sad, this artifact from his former life. Will sat on the edge of his bed. He looked at his parents' photograph in its cracked frame. He picked up from the table Dad's tattered book of rules and opened to the first page:

The Importance of an Orderly Mind.

Sticking with the rules had kept him alive this far. Had he been a little lucky? No doubt. And he knew enough to know he couldn't count on that from here on out.

#7: DON'T CONFUSE GOOD LUCK WITH A
GOOD PLAN.

He flipped the book to the final page, and the last rule Dad had written: OPEN ALL DOORS, AND AWAKEN.

The biggest question Will had been unable to answer: How did his dad know about the Prophecy? Because it was clear that his parents had known, or they wouldn't have spent his whole life watching so closely for signs of his Awakening, then training and preparing him the way they did. But why that meant they had to keep him hidden while living like fugitives was another mystery.

He had to face the possibility that he'd never be able to ask Dad about it. He might never see either of them again. Who was going to take care of him now if they had been on that plane, or even if they hadn't been? In the clear, cold, practical part of his mind, he knew that he'd have to do it, for the most part, by himself now.

Didn't everybody, sooner or later, once you stared down the barrel of whatever form the truth is hiding in? We're born; we die. In between you make the best of what's handed to you, and you love the people closest to you.

What else is there?

At least he *had* friends now. But who could he turn to for answers to these big questions, the ones his parents had always guided him through before? Dave had been that guy, but he might be gone now, too. Could anybody, even a kick-ass Special Forces Wayfarer, come back from the Never-Was?

Will took out the dice from his pocket and looked at them. Black, with white dots. He *wanted* to believe these were the same unearthly devices Dave had shown him, but they looked and felt like regular dice. A little heavier and denser, maybe.

Without his realizing he'd moved, Will's head eased down to the pillow. His orderly mind winked off as quickly as if he'd tugged a string to turn off a light.

Moments or hours later, Will heard a soft *bing*. He opened his eyes and saw his tablet on the desk, the screen turned toward him. The Center's screen saver crest was bouncing gently from one side to the other.

He had no sense of how long he'd been out, but it was dark outside. Will glanced at his phone, still cupped in his hand: almost seven in the evening. Sunday. Still Sunday. The tablet sounded that gentle tone again. Will rubbed his eyes, walked over, sat at his desk, and touched the screen.

His syn-app appeared in his "room" and waved to him, smiling. "You're not alone, Will," said his syn-app. "And you never will be. Not while I'm around."

"Thanks," said Will dryly. "You're a real pal."

"You've been gone quite a while."

"What, I'm supposed to keep you informed of my whereabouts now?"

"Not at all," said the syn-app. "I was just worried about you."

Will looked at his little double closely. "You sound like you mean it," he said.

"I do."

"Why should I believe you?" asked Will.

"If you can't trust yourself, Will," said his syn-app with a smile, "who can you trust? Would you like to see the photograph I found for you?"

"I'm sorry, which photograph?" asked Will sleepily.

"Of the helicopter."

The screen filled with the hazy washed-out colors of ancient Kodachrome. A dynamic captured moment: An airfield, full of movement, a couple of helicopters lifting off and another in the air, closer to the camera, tilting in for a landing. A tropical jungle in the background framed the asphalt landing strip. An explosion bloomed above the palm trees.

A credit line along the bottom margin of the photo read *The Battle for Pleiku, Vietnam/New York Times, September 14, 1969.*

In the foreground, a soldier ran toward the landing chopper, his back to the camera. A tall man with big, broad shoulders, wearing fatigues and a worn leather flight jacket. Three round patches were sewn onto the back.

The first had a red kangaroo with the words SPECIAL FORCES below it. Beside that was the helmeted head of a knight and the words LONG-RANGE RECONNAISSANCE. In the third patch were the silhouette of a helicopter and the words ANZAC/VIETNAM. Below that were the same call letters that Will had seen on Dave's flight jacket: ATD39Z.

The man's right arm was raised high in the air. It looked like he was hailing or signaling urgently to the pilot of the chopper just above him.

Holding up all five fingers.

That's five.

In the caves, Dave never had a chance to say that before the wendigo took him. Was he saying it here, after the fact? Will's heart leaped at the idea.

His eyes shot to the two dice sitting on his desk. The dots were glowing. As Will watched, the dice lifted off the surface and spun slowly . . . until a three and a two were facing him.

"That's five," whispered Will. "And it's good to be alive."

For the first time since leaving home, he *believed* it.

Will looked back at the photo. "In case I don't see you again," he said, "thanks for everything, mate."

Will's syn-app asked, "Did you know this person in the photo, Will?"

"I sure did."

"Would you like me to find out anything else about him for you?"

Will thought about it. "Yes," he said. "See if you can find a woman named Nancy Hughes. She's from Santa Monica. If she's still alive, she'd be in her early sixties. All I know is that she served as an ensign in the Navy Nurse Corps during Vietnam in 1969."

"I'll get right on it," said his syn-app.

Will caught movement out of the corner of his eye and turned to look at his book of rules, lying open on the bed. Had he imagined it or had a page just turned by itself? Will walked over and his eye went to the middle of the page:

#25: WHAT YOU'RE TOLD TO BELIEVE ISN'T
IMPORTANT: IT'S WHAT YOU *CHOOSE* TO
BELIEVE. IT'S NOT THE INK AND PAPER
THAT MATTER, BUT THE HAND THAT HOLDS
THE PEN.

And here's what I choose to believe, thought Will. *The one answer I couldn't tell my roommates about: Dave said the Never-Was wanted me dead because I'm an Initiate. And they somehow realized it even before the Hierarchy did.*

"I'm an Initiate now," Will whispered. "Deal with it."

If that's why the Caps are afraid of me, I'm going to give them damn good reason to be. If the shag-nasties from the Never-Was think they can bust in here and take our planet from us, they're going to have to go through me. I'm going to stop them, for my parents, Dave, and my friends. And if anyone else feels like helping me, like Coach Jericho, well, who knows, maybe I'm not even the only Initiate around here.

A soft bell sounded from his tablet. His syn-app appeared inside the photo on the screen, standing next to the still figure of Dave.

"An email just arrived from Nando," the double said. "It's a video file."

"Open it, please," said Will.

The photo dissolved into a video file. A moment later he *saw* Nando, speaking into his cell phone camera in an intense whisper. "Wills, I found something you gotta see."

Nando moved the camera to an object sitting on a table: the black doctor's bag he'd retrieved from Will's house in Ojai. He moved in on the pair of worn initials embossed in gold below the handle: H. G.

"The bag was empty but I found something in the lining. Take a look."

Nando opened the bag and moved the camera inside to a small label, sewn into the interior fabric of the bag. The label read THIS BAG BELONGS TO _____.

A name was on the blank line, block-printed in old, faded ink: *DR. HUGH GREENWOOD*.

Will froze the image and stared at it, his mind racing in a dozen different directions. The black phone on the desk rang, jolting him. He picked up on the second ring. "Hello."

"Will, the headmaster would like to see you," said an operator. "In his office, at Stone House."

* * *

Rourke shook Will's hand and asked him to take a seat on one of the heavy leather sofas in his inner office. Coach Jericho, already there when Will arrived, sat across from him. Rourke stayed on his feet in front of the roaring fireplace and talked him through it, calm and clear.

The ten captured members of the Knights of Charlemagne had all been expelled and were being held by state police on charges of kidnapping, accessory to and conspiracy to commit kidnapping, and attempted murder. The same fate awaited any other Knights they subsequently found, like Todd Hodak. Rourke said he had already called for a special assembly of the entire school to explain all this and to halt the spread of the rumors that would inevitably follow.

"Will, it seems clear to me," said Rourke, "that in your haste to respond to these outrages, you gave no thought to the consequences of your actions. Most of which were shockingly reckless."

Will glanced at Jericho, who gave nothing away. Will's eyes went to the portrait on the wall of the school's founder and first headmaster, Thomas Greenwood, staring down at him, solemn, stern, and wise.

Rourke sat on the edge of the table in front of Will. "They were also selfless, valiant, and almost unimaginably brave," he said. "You've suffered a loss that by any civilized measure is impossible to calculate. How you respond now, and in the months to come, may set the course for the rest of your life." Rourke gestured at the portrait on the wall. "Dr. Greenwood always used to say that it's not the ink and paper that matter, but the hand that holds the pen."

Will's eyes opened wide. Rule #25. *Word for word*.

Rourke lowered his voice almost to a whisper. "Will, I

checked on that officer who questioned you at the airport in Madison. The FAA has no record of 'Agent O'Brian.' Tell me, had you ever see that man before?"

"He's one of the men who chased me in California," said Will.

"I thought so," said Rourke, and glanced at Jericho. "Until we know the exact nature of what's going on, I want you to observe a strict curfew: in your quarters by nine, without exception, every night. I'm putting Coach Jericho in charge of your security. You'll be safe here. I make you this promise: No harm will come to you."

Rourke's eyes held him with such kindness, Will had to look away.

"Thank you," he said hoarsely.

Rourke put a hand on Will's shoulder. "There are things in this world more dreadful than you know. Things a young man your age should never have to face—certainly not alone. But we have two families in life. The one we're born with that shares our blood. Another we meet along the way that's willing to give its blood for us."

Will looked up at both of them.

"You have found those people here," said Rourke.

Coach Jericho held out a small leather pouch. Will took it from him and opened it. A small figure of a falcon, carved from dark rock, fell into his hand.

"You let me know if you have any more dreams," said Jericho.

Will met his eye and nodded his thanks.

Rourke stood. "Will, do you have any questions for me?"

Will stood as well, clasping the falcon figurine tight in his hand. He looked at the portraits of the previous headmasters on the walls, Thomas and Franklin Greenwood, and thought back to his father's medical bag.

"Do you know a man named Hugh Greenwood?" he asked.

Rourke and Jericho glanced at each other before Rourke answered. "Hugh was Franklin's son." Rourke nodded to his portrait. "Our second headmaster."

"So he was Thomas Greenwood's grandson," said Will.

"That's right. He used to teach here," said Rourke. "Before I came on board. What was his subject, Coach?"

"Science. Biology, I think," said Jericho.

Will tried to keep what he was thinking from his eyes. "Where is he now?"

"He and his wife left the school," said Coach Jericho. "Resigned about sixteen years ago. I had just started here then, but I knew them both."

"Was he a doctor?" asked Will.

"Yes," said Jericho.

"Why do you ask, Will?"

"His name came up in a conversation," said Will. "I was just curious. Would you mind if I had another look at the Infinity Room, sir?"

"Of course," said Rourke. "May I ask you why?"

"Because I was afraid before. And I'd like to see how I feel about it now."

Headmaster Rourke walked Will to the door leading to the long strange hallway and opened it for him. "Shall we wait here for you?" asked Rourke.

"If you don't mind, sir," said Will.

"I don't mind at all," he said. "It's a beautiful night. Believe it or not, after that storm, they say we're about to have Indian summer."

Will walked out along the narrow suspended corridor, lit by silver moonlight reflecting off the new-fallen snow. He looked straight down through the clear panels to the ground far below his feet and out the windows lining either side. The whole room felt different in the dark, when you couldn't see as much—far different.

And so, as he'd hoped he would discover, was he. His heart beat a little faster as he moved along, and maybe he took in a few extra breaths. But he wasn't afraid.

He reached the far end of the corridor and stepped into the peculiar glass observatory bubble, where the night sky opened up around him. The lights of the campus off to his left cast a warm, reassuring glow—evidence of civilized life, solid grounded lives, safe and secure. Stars scattered, an immensity, an almost indulgent surplus of them, overhead.

No, Will wasn't afraid. Even with the hardest truth he'd had to face in front of him. He didn't feel afraid of that, either. Because he knew now, after coming this far, that he would find a way to reckon with it.

Something in his pocket buzzed. *Oh my God, did I leave it there? Really, Will?* The iPhone had been in his front pocket the *entire time* he was in Rourke's office. *What a knucklehead.*

He flicked it on, saw he'd received a text. It came up onscreen, all in caps, and time stood still:

THEY HAVE ME, WILL. I DON'T KNOW WHERE. ONLY YOU CAN FIND ME. 51. 51. 51.

Through a heart-pounding haze, Will fumbled through the rules in his mind, until he remembered #51: THE ONLY THING YOU CAN'T AFFORD TO LOSE IS HOPE.

Will's father was Dr. Hugh Greenwood. And he was still alive.

TO BE CONTINUED IN

THE PALADIN PROPHECY
BOOK 2: ALLIANCE

#4: IF YOU THINK YOU'RE DONE,
YOU'VE JUST BEGUN.

Ajay laid the glossy black-and-white photograph on the table.

"There's a lot more detail in the original," he said.

It was the same photograph from 1937 that they'd seen online: the Knights of Charlemagne hosting a gala dinner for Henry Wallace, the country's soon-to-be vice president. Will's eye immediately went to one of the twelve young men at the table—a student, one of the Knights. The one, when he'd first seen the photo, whom he'd thought he recognized but couldn't place. He could now.

It was the Bald Man, Mr. Hobbes.

He didn't know how this was possible—the picture was taken over seventy years ago—but then something even stranger happened.

He recognized a *second* student, across the table from Hobbes. Looking straight into the camera, smiling. The closer Will looked, the more certain he became. The photo had been taken before he'd been changed or altered into the twisted miserable wretch they knew now.

The second student was Happy Nepsted.

Dad's List of Rules to Live By

#1: THE IMPORTANCE OF AN ORDERLY MIND.

#2: STAY FOCUSED ON THE TASK AT HAND.

#3: DON'T DRAW ATTENTION TO YOURSELF.

#4: IF YOU THINK YOU'RE DONE, YOU'VE JUST BEGUN.

#5: TRUST NO ONE.

#6: REMAIN ALERT AT ALL TIMES TO THE REALITY OF THE PRESENT. BECAUSE ALL WE HAVE IS RIGHT NOW.

#7: DON'T CONFUSE GOOD LUCK WITH A GOOD PLAN.

#8: ALWAYS BE PREPARED TO IMPROVISE.

#9: WATCH, LOOK, AND LISTEN, OR YOU WON'T KNOW WHAT YOU'RE MISSING.

#10: DON'T JUST REACT TO A SITUATION THAT TAKES YOU BY SURPRISE. *RESPOND.*

#11: TRUST YOUR INSTINCTS.

#13: YOU ONLY GET ONE CHANCE TO MAKE A FIRST IMPRESSION.

#14: ASK ALL QUESTIONS IN THE ORDER OF THEIR IMPORTANCE.

#15: BE QUICK, BUT DON'T HURRY.

#16: ALWAYS LOOK PEOPLE IN THE EYE. GIVE THEM A HANDSHAKE THEY'LL REMEMBER.

#17: START EACH DAY BY SAYING IT'S GOOD TO BE ALIVE. EVEN IF YOU DON'T FEEL IT, *SAYING* IT— OUT LOUD—MAKES IT MORE LIKELY THAT YOU WILL.

#18: IF #17 DOESN'T WORK, COUNT YOUR BLESSINGS.

#19: WHEN EVERYTHING GOES WRONG, TREAT DISASTER AS A WAY TO WAKE UP.

#20: THERE MUST ALWAYS BE A RELATIONSHIP BETWEEN EVIDENCE AND CONCLUSION.

#23: WHEN THERE'S TROUBLE, THINK FAST AND ACT DECISIVELY.

#25: WHAT YOU'RE TOLD TO BELIEVE ISN'T IMPORTANT: IT'S WHAT YOU *CHOOSE* TO BELIEVE. IT'S NOT THE INK AND PAPER THAT MATTER, BUT THE HAND THAT HOLDS THE PEN.

#26: ONCE IS AN ANOMALY. TWICE IS A COINCIDENCE. THREE TIMES IS A PATTERN. AND AS WE KNOW . . .

#27: THERE IS NO SUCH THING AS A COINCIDENCE.

#28: LET PEOPLE UNDERESTIMATE YOU. THAT WAY THEY'LL NEVER KNOW FOR SURE WHAT YOU'RE CAPABLE OF.

#30: SOMETIMES THE ONLY WAY TO DEAL WITH A BULLY IS TO HIT FIRST. HARD.

#31: IT'S NOT A BAD THING, SOMETIMES, IF THEY THINK YOU'RE CRAZY.

#34: ACT AS IF YOU'RE IN CHARGE, AND PEOPLE WILL BELIEVE YOU.

#40: NEVER MAKE EXCUSES.

#41: SLEEP WHEN YOU'RE SLEEPY. CATS TAKE NAPS SO THEY'RE ALWAYS READY FOR ANYTHING.

#45: COOPERATE WITH THE AUTHORITIES. BUT DON'T NAME FRIENDS.

#46: IF STRANGERS KNOW WHAT YOU'RE FEELING, YOU GIVE THEM THE ADVANTAGE.

#48: NEVER START A FIGHT UNLESS YOU CAN FINISH IT. FAST.

#49: WHEN ALL ELSE FAILS, JUST BREATHE.

#50: IN TIMES OF CHAOS, STICK TO ROUTINE. BUILD ORDER ONE STEP AT A TIME.

#51: THE ONLY THING YOU CAN'T AFFORD TO LOSE IS HOPE.

#54: IF YOU CAN'T BE ON TIME, BE EARLY.

#55: IF YOU FAIL TO PREPARE, YOU PREPARE TO FAIL.

#59: SOMETIMES YOU FIND OUT MORE WHEN YOU ASK QUESTIONS TO WHICH YOU ALREADY KNOW THE ANSWER.

#60: IF YOU DON'T LIKE THE ANSWER YOU GET, YOU SHOULDN'T HAVE ASKED THE QUESTION.

#61: IF YOU WANT SOMETHING DONE THE RIGHT WAY, DO IT YOURSELF.

#63: THE BEST WAY TO LIE IS TO INCLUDE PART OF THE TRUTH.

#65: THE DUMBEST GUY IN A ROOM IS THE FIRST ONE WHO TELLS YOU HOW SMART HE IS.

#68: NEVER SIGN A LEGAL DOCUMENT THAT HASN'T BEEN APPROVED BY A LAWYER WHO WORKS FOR YOU.

#72: WHEN IN A NEW PLACE, ACT LIKE YOU'VE BEEN THERE BEFORE.

#73: LEARN THE DIFFERENCE BETWEEN TACTICS AND STRATEGY.

#75: WHEN YOU NEED TO MAKE A QUICK DECISION, DON'T LET WHAT YOU CAN'T DO INTERFERE WITH WHAT YOU CAN.

#76: WHEN YOU GAIN THE ADVANTAGE, PRESS IT TO THE LIMIT.

#77: THE SWISS ARMY DOESN'T AMOUNT TO MUCH, BUT NEVER LEAVE HOME WITHOUT THEIR KNIFE.

#78: THERE'S A REASON THE CLASSICS ARE CLASSICS: THEY'RE *CLASSIC*.

#79: DON'T MAKE ANOTHER'S PAIN THE SOURCE OF YOUR OWN HAPPINESS.

#81: NEVER TAKE MORE THAN YOU NEED.

#82: WITHOUT A LIFE OF THE MIND, YOU'LL LIVE A MINDLESS LIFE.

#83: JUST BECAUSE YOU'RE PARANOID DOESN'T MEAN THAT SORRY IS BETTER THAN SAFE.

#84: WHEN NOTHING ELSE WORKS, TRY CHOCOLATE.

#86: NEVER BE NERVOUS WHEN TALKING TO A BEAUTIFUL GIRL. JUST PRETEND SHE'S A PERSON, TOO.

#87: MEN WANT COMPANY. WOMEN WANT EMPATHY.

#88: ALWAYS LISTEN TO THE PERSON WITH
THE WHISTLE.

#91: THERE IS NOT—NOR SHOULD THERE BE—ANY
LIMIT TO WHAT A GUY WILL GO THROUGH TO
IMPRESS THE RIGHT GIRL.

#92: IF YOU WANT PEOPLE TO TELL YOU MORE, SAY
LESS. OPEN YOUR EYES AND EARS, AND CLOSE
YOUR MOUTH.

#94: YOU CAN FIND MOST OF THE WEAPONS OR
EQUIPMENT YOU'LL EVER NEED AROUND THE
HOUSE.

#96: MEMORIZE THE BILL OF RIGHTS.

#97: REGARDING EYEWEAR AND UNDERWEAR:
ALWAYS TRAVEL WITH BACKUPS.

#98: DON'T WATCH YOUR LIFE LIKE IT'S A MOVIE
THAT'S HAPPENING TO SOMEONE ELSE.
IT'S HAPPENING TO *YOU*. IT'S HAPPENING
RIGHT NOW.

OPEN ALL DOORS, AND AWAKEN.

Acknowledgments

Many thanks are in order: to my great friend and comrade Ed Victor, the estimable Sophie Hicks, and all the stalwarts in the London office of Ed Victor, Limited; to Chip Gibson, Annie Eaton, Ellice Lee, and my sagacious and resolute editor, Jim Thomas, at Random House; to Dr. Hal Danzer, Dr. Sheri Fried, Dr. Bob Garrett, Alan Kerner, Dr. David Miller, Dr. Carolyn Roberts, and Dr. Benjamin Shield for their expertise on matters medical and metaphysical; to friends and colleagues Frank Bredice, Derek Cardoza, Dennis Colonello, Keiko Cronin, Jodi Fodor, Jeff Freilich, Alicia Gordon, Stephen Kulczycki, Susie Putnam, Jason Spitz, Alan Wertheimer, and Steve Yoon for their encouragement and support; and most of all to my sister, Lindsay, my wife, Lynn, and my son, Travis, who make traveling this path worthwhile.

ABOUT THE AUTHOR

MARK FROST studied directing and playwriting at Carnegie Mellon University. He partnered with David Lynch to create and executive produce the groundbreaking television series *Twin Peaks*. Frost cowrote the screenplays for the films *Fantastic Four* and *Fantastic Four: Rise of the Silver Surfer*. He is also the *New York Times* bestselling author of eight previous books, including *The List of Seven*, *The Second Objective*, *The Greatest Game Ever Played*, and *The Match*. To learn more, visit ByMarkFrost.com.